Unexpected Surprises

A Contemporary Romance Collection

Mia Faye

Mia Faye

ISBN: 978-1-63821-642-1

Author's note: This is a work of fiction. Some of the names and
geographical locations in this book are products of the author's
imagination, and do not necessarily correspond with reality.

For my readers

TABLE OF CONTENTS

Chapter One – Marjorie

I stood there, surrounded by the boxed-up remnants of my old life, and wondered what the hell had *happened* to bring me to this point.

I mean, yes, I could count back the days and the weeks and the months and the years that had brought me here. I could remember when Robert and I had just met, fresh out of college, and how I had told everyone I knew he was the one even though we had only been on two dates together. And I could remember when he proposed to me, and when we got married just six weeks later, so eager to start our lives together that there was no room to wait or hold back.

And I could remember if I wanted to, all that time we spent promising each other that we would get started on a family soon enough. I had wanted kids for as long as I could remember, but it just never quite seemed like the right time or place or ... well, there was always a reason. Even when we stopped using birth control for a while, nothing happened. I hoped that I was going to wake up one day with a baby in my belly, something that could force me to stop for a second and take stock of the life that I was in, but it didn't happen. We started using condoms again when he got another promotion. He couldn't risk having a kid given the circumstances, he told me. And as time went on, it seemed like he just didn't want to have a kid at all. At least, not with me.

And, as the distance drifted between us, I supposed it was only obvious that he was going to get involved with someone else. Someone younger. Someone who was the same age that I had been when we met, actually. She even looked a little like me, this girl – I knew because he had introduced me to her in the process of telling me the marriage was over. Salting the wound. I still remember the ring of panic in my ears, the sureness that this had to be some kind of sick, twisted joke at my expense.

But it wasn't. He was leaving me. He had left me; the papers had been signed, and he had moved his new girl into an apartment that he was paying for on the other side of the city. It wasn't much, he had told me excitedly, but he was looking forward to getting a new start. I couldn't believe that he really thought I wanted to hear a word of this. Every time he spoke to me about her, I felt like he was scraping out the hollow in my chest to make sure that nothing was left.

1

And now, here I was, cleaning out the last of our lives together. The apartment we had shared that had been my home for so long, it was empty – everything I had was boxed up and ready to go. He'd already taken his stuff to his new apartment a long time ago, eager to get started on the next phase of his life. But then, he had a lot to look forward to. I didn't know what I was facing now that I was alone again.

Alone.

The word stung as it passed through my head. I had never imagined getting to thirty and finding myself alone again. It is easier for men because they just get more distinguished as they get older, but for women, it's just this rolling countdown until everything implodes and they become hopeless cat ladies hanging out in their apartments with nobody to speak to but their fellow spinsters.

I knew that I should have planned better for something like this to happen. I mean, shit goes down every day, doesn't it? People break up, people leave each other, and people move on. I shouldn't have been surprised that it happened to me. Yes, of course, everyone likes to think that their marriage is totally and utterly stable and that nothing could pull it apart, but that's just not the reality of it. After what happened with the first boy I fell in love with, I should have realized that for sure...

No. The last thing I wanted to do was torture myself with his memory, too. I had already been burned enough by the men in my life. I needed distance. I needed space. I needed ... well, anything but to be in this apartment a moment longer, to be honest.

I texted Terri and Stephanie to let them know that I was ready for them to pick me up. They had both offered to help me pack, but I knew that I had to do this by myself. There was something ceremonial about it, putting away the pieces of this old life to step into a new one.

It felt like mourning – mourning the life I thought I'd had, mourning the life I had committed myself to such a long time ago with the real belief that it would work for me. How could I have gotten it so wrong? When I thought about the version of Robert I had met when we first started dating, I could hardly believe that they were actually the same person. That Robert would have rolled his eyes at the cliché of a man leaving his wife for a younger woman as soon as he hit thirty-five. He would have laughed at him and called him pathetic and put his arm around me and made me feel safe that something like that could never happen to us; of course, it couldn't, because he just loved me too much, and I needed to trust him on that, okay?

I had been so stupid. I wasn't going to trust another man again as long as I lived. I mean, Robert had done this to me – and my father had abandoned my mother not long before he died to go off and sleep with some random strangers. And then, amongst it all, buried way down deep in the back of my brain, there was Blake, too.

Blake. That was a name I tried to keep out of my head as much as I could. I felt like he was the reason I had dived into marriage with Robert so quickly. I had been so fearful that Robert was going to leave just the same way Blake had, and I didn't want to be left heartbroken ever again.

There was a buzz at the door, and I jumped out of my skin, lost in my memories as I tried to gather myself. Terri and Stephanie were here. They had just parked the van a couple of streets away so they could be here for me as soon as I needed them. They were sweet like that. It was the reason that the three of us had remained best friends through all the ups and downs of the business, through the stress of the city, through our chaotic dating lives to boot.

"We're here to pick up a newly single lady!" Terri's voice came through the intercom, full of verve. She was the one out of the three of us who could probably have dealt with an earthquake by just looking it in the face and asking it nicely to go away. She had always had so much energy, so much life to her, and I was grateful to have her around for this, probably one of the worst days of my life.

"Don't remind her of it!" Stephanie cut in, hissing to Terri in a way that made me laugh. I had no idea how two women who were so totally different managed to get along as well as they did, but they always stuck it out together. Maybe they needed each other's perspectives on their lives – I knew that the outside world could get shut out when things were going badly and that I wouldn't have gotten anywhere without them there to help me.

"Oh, come on, it's not like she doesn't know–"

"Guys, you know I can still hear you, right?" I called through the intercom. I couldn't help smiling. They were such dorks. They made me feel better about my own dorkiness.

"Shit," Terri muttered, and the intercom went dead again. I buzzed them into the building, and they came upstairs to grab my stuff from the apartment. We had closed the store down for the day and were using the van that was usually put aside for big orders to help move my stuff into the little studio apartment that I had started renting across the city. It was small, and it was slightly pathetic, but it was what I could afford, and as long as it was far from this place, I didn't care. Robert had offered to keep paying his half of the rent here so I could stay for a while longer, but I couldn't think of much worse in the world than living in this graveyard for my marriage.

I opened the door as I heard their footsteps coming up the stairs and saw them making their way toward me like they were moving in on some toxic wasteland. That was what it felt like these days if I were being honest. I hated being here. It felt like I had been infected by the creeping, grasping hold of what had been, of the promise that had come before hanging over my head ...

"Alright, you're not allowed to look sad," Terri told me firmly. "Because if you look sad, then I look sad, and then I feel like I'm trying to steal your thunder ..."

"You can look as sad as you want," Stephanie assured me, drawing me into a tight hug as soon as she stepped into the apartment. "Feel anything you need to feel."

"Hey, I thought that was what drinking was for," Terri joked. "You just bottle everything up until you get drunk enough to blurt it all out, don't you?"

"You might, but some of us are actually capable of talking about our emotions," Stephanie teased her. She pulled back from me, clasped my shoulders, and flicked her gaze from eye to eye as though she was trying to get a look inside of me. "Now, tell me, how's it going?" she asked, reaching up to brush a strand of my messy blonde hair back from my face. Stephanie was the very first staff member I hired at my store, Threads, when it first opened – she had been a fashion design student but dropped out of that when her family needed her to earn more money to support them again. She was tall, elegant, and maternal, with long brown hair that she usually wore up in a tight bun on top of her head. Her dress sense was ethereal and yet somehow practical, and she always seemed to be able to match these odd pieces together in a way that just looked gorgeous. That said, on her tall, willowy frame, it was hard to imagine anything looking bad.

"I'm okay," I told her. I wasn't, of course, but I didn't want to worry her more than I already had. The two of them had come out here to help me when I needed them most, and I was beyond touched that they had gone to all this effort. They always worked their asses off in the store, and sometimes I worried that I was putting too much pressure on them when it came to asking for off the clock stuff like this.

"You know, you don't have to be all brave and noble because you're worried about putting too much on us," Terri remarked, reading my mind as she went to grab the first of the boxes she could see. I sighed. They knew me too damn well, that was for sure. It was hard for me to accept that they were both my friends before they were my employees. I guess I was just having a hard time trusting people to do what they had promised to at that point in my life.

Terri, who put on this big blustery front and liked to pretend that she was a badass, was actually one of the sweetest girls I'd ever had the pleasure of meeting. She was the youngest of the three of us at twenty-six, and she had applied to work as an assistant at the store just out of college. All her friends had been off traveling the world and taking on their fancy jobs, she explained to us, but she loved New York, and she didn't want to leave so soon. Well, of course, I would later find out that it was a boy she had stayed here for, but that didn't matter to me. With her cropped red hair, olive skin, and bright green eyes, she was a striking woman, and she always seemed to be able to back that up with her personality. Her outgoing nature was enough to get people coming back to the store over and over again just for a chance to run into her once more, and I sure as hell wasn't going to pass up the chance to have someone like her working for me.

But more than that, over the time that we had all worked together, they had become intrinsic parts of my life. Threads was a small place, and it was just the three of us who worked it together, and that formed a kind of camaraderie that couldn't have been built any other way. We had formed a deep bond that I was so grateful for. There was so much I couldn't have survived had it not been for the two women in front of me right now. Hell, if I'd had to make it through this divorce without them, I'd have had no idea what I would do with myself. They had both offered to help me put down the deposit on my new apartment, agreeing that they would take pay cuts for a little while if they had to, but I refused. I never wanted them to be put out because of me, even when I could have used a little more extra cash.

We carried the boxes down to the van, and the two of them kept up a bright conversation with me the whole time to keep me from dipping too far into my sadness. It was there, barely held back, threatening to swell forward and take control of me if I didn't watch out. I hated the way I was feeling right now, so self-involved. I didn't want to be this person. In fact, I wanted to be the person who gave everything to someone else – specifically, to my kid.

"You want to go up and check that we got everything?" Terri suggested, and I nodded and gave them both a quick hug as they finished loading the back of the van.

"You have no idea how much you've helped me," I confessed. "I couldn't have done this without you."

"And this goes on our overtime hours, right?" Terri joked. Stephanie nudged her, and I laughed.

"Hey, Stef, it's alright, I can take a joke," I assured her. She had been so careful with me since the divorce like she was worried I might break. Maybe that was the vibe I was giving off. I hoped not.

I headed up to the apartment one more time, and I was surprised that I was able to hold myself together as I took it in. This was the place my future was supposed to be built. This was the place I was going to raise my family. Well, not any longer. I had to come to terms with that one way or another, no matter how much it hurt to think about all I had to leave behind now that this was over.

Maybe it was for the best. Maybe this was the way it just had to be for me. Yes, it would have been wonderful to have the life that he'd promised me. With kids, a family. And yes, I might have been more than a little freaked out at the thought of finding someone new to do all of that with. But it happened to be my future, and I planned to dive into it any way that I could, no matter what. I was tired of waiting around, and moving out of this apartment was the best choice I could make to get started with my new life.

I headed back downstairs to where they were waiting for me in the car. Terri had her head laid back on the plush leather of her seat, her feet propped up on the dashboard. Stephanie was at the wheel – she didn't trust either of us to drive, and frankly, I couldn't say that I really blamed her.

"You ready to get out of here?" she asked as I approached the van. I hesitated for a moment – and then nodded. I might not have felt totally ready, but I was as ready as I was ever going to be. I had a new life to get to, and that meant no more standing around and feeling sorry for myself. So, things hadn't gone the way I wanted? I would just have to find a path that would take me there, anyway.

Chapter Two – Blake

I leaned back in my seat and closed my eyes. Man, it had just been a hell of a long day. I could use some time to myself, some time to kck back and relax. My mind was already mapping out the bars that were closest to the office when my phone rang. I considered ignoring the call, letting it go to voicemail, but I was a workaholic before I was anything else in this world. I picked up the receiver and took the call.

"Hello?"

"Hello, Blake?" An excited voice came tripping down the phone and into my ear. "It's Annie here, Annie Atwood?"

It took me a moment to place her – I saw so many women through my line of work that it was easy for them to start running into one another. But I recalled her now. She had been coming by here for a few months about a year ago with her husband, trying to get pregnant with the help of the facilities at the clinic. I had taken on their case because I liked them – they seemed like a sweet, well-meaning couple, and if there was anyone out there that deserved to have children, it had to be them. I had seen so many useless parents come in and out of here over the years, people who didn't have kids because they clearly didn't actually want them, but they were buzzing with excitement the moment they got their appointment.

"Hello, Annie," I greeted her. "Is everything alright?"

"Everything's amazing," she replied happily. "We just wanted to call you and let you know ... well, we're in the hospital right now, and our daughter is finally here with us."

I grinned. Alright, so maybe I happened to be a little of a soft touch when it came to stories like this one, but I couldn't help feeling happy when I came across a family that I knew would never have existed before me. I was touched that they'd even thought to reach out to me again – they weren't the first, but people tended to forget everything that had brought them to where they were by the time their babies actually arrived.

"And we know that we could never have done this if it hadn't been for you and the clinic," Annie told me excitedly. "I mean, we never thought ... not really. We always felt like having a baby was just something that was never going to happen for us. But you ... you made it come true."

She laughed. "I'm sorry; I must sound totally crazy to you right now," she admitted. "I just wanted to let you know that you're the reason I'm holding my daughter right now, and I couldn't be more grateful if I tried."

"Well, I'm glad to hear it," I told her. "Now, you get back to that baby, you hear? And get some rest for yourself."

"Will do," she agreed, and she bid her farewell and hung up the phone.

I grinned to myself for a moment. These small victories that changed the lives of the people they happened to, they were what made this job worth doing. They were the reason that I had stuck it out in this demanding career as long as I had.

It was about six years since we got the clinic off the ground. Jason and I had always known this was where we were headed, all the way back to when we first met at college. Both of us were majoring in medicine, and I had always known that I wanted to work in the fertility sector. When I was growing up, my aunt had struggled so hard to find someone willing to treat her issues when she was trying to get pregnant with my cousin Toby, and a lot of that came down to just not being able to afford what she needed. Jason was passionate about the same thing, determined to make this kind of healthcare accessible to anyone who needed it. I had seen the impact this could have on a woman, on a couple, on a family, and I didn't want anyone else out there having to count their pennies to make sure they could afford it.

I was at the New York office when I took that call – we had one in LA, and another in Chicago, but I usually worked out of this one since it was so close to where I lived anyway. I had moved from a small town upstate to New York City the first chance I'd got – this was the place where dreams came true, as far as I was concerned. And yeah, sure, okay, I would have been lying if I said that the nightlife hadn't been a little intriguing to the asshole twenty-something version of me. Maybe I shouldn't be so dismissive of that guy. I was him up until a few months ago. I had just turned thirty, so looking back on my twenties with rose-tinted glasses was a little soon.

I stared at the phone for a long moment, the words still fresh in my ears. She had sounded so happy. I couldn't imagine feeling like that – that complete absence of anything that weighed down, the lack of fear for the future or panic at what was to come. She was just ... she was just happy.

9

And maybe I was starting to get a little jealous of that.

It wasn't like I had gone out of my way to find someone to settle down with since I arrived in the city. In fact, one of the things I always loved the most about it was that you could move around with relative anonymity if you wanted to – nobody had to know who you were, where you were from, what you were doing here. All they cared about was the person right in front of them. Back in the small town I'd grown up in, everyone had known everyone, and it was hard to keep track of who was thinking what about you, who you had pissed off enough to keep them from dating your daughter ...

Not to mention the fact that dating here was so ridiculously easy. There was a certain handful of clubs in the city, clubs that if you had a pass to, you would be drowning in women for the rest of the night. Jason and I used to head out and hit them up all the time before he had to go and get married to his wife, Julianne. Sure, she was smart and funny and would make a great mother when the time came, but that didn't mean that I wasn't a little miffed that she had taken my wingman off the market.

Ever since Jason had settled down with someone, I found myself wondering if I should be doing the same thing. Our lives traced along similar lines, and I had assumed that we would both find our people at the same time. Jason was a couple of years older than me, sure, but he had just taken a huge step out in front and left me behind.

I couldn't think of anyone I wanted to settle down with. Of all the women I had met in this city, I couldn't think of one who stuck in my mind as someone who mattered. They were fun, sure, good for a night or two, but nothing more than that. Nothing that went any deeper. I hadn't met anyone who made me feel that way since–

No. I couldn't let her into my head. Because if I were going to do that, then I would have to accept everything I had done that had led me here, and I was already feeling down enough on myself as it was.

The voice of the woman on the phone rolled around my head a few more times. She was happy. Maybe what she had would have made me happy, too. Maybe I approached the situation with a little too much simplicity, but I had always been logical above all else. I hadn't tried having a family. In fact, that had to be one of the only things left on this Earth that I hadn't taken for a test-drive yet.

Before I could let my thoughts stray any further down that dangerous path, the door to my office opened, and Jason stood there before me. My best friend and business partner, I knew that nobody understood me better than him. And yet, the thought of telling him about the notions that were running through my mind at that moment just seemed ... callous, somehow. As though I was trying to devalue what he and his wife had.

"Evening," he greeted me. "How's it going?"

"Pretty good," I replied with a nod. "Got a call from the Atwoods. They've finally had their daughter, said it was all down to us."

"That's what I like to hear," Jason replied with a grin. "So, what you up to tonight?"

I opened my mouth, and I had really planned on telling him that I was going to go out and get drunk and that I wanted him to come with me, but that wasn't where he was at any longer. He would have just felt guilty that he couldn't come out and party with me the way he used to.

"Just heading home," I told him, and I stretched and got out of my seat. "You?"

"Julie and I have dinner tonight," he replied, a big grin on his face. I couldn't imagine being with someone for as long as he had been with his wife and still getting just as excited about the thought of spending an evening with them. That was the whole point of marriage, I supposed, but it still didn't make a lot of sense to me.

"You guys have a good night," I told him, and I went to gather my stuff. Jason leaned in the door for a moment longer, eyeing me.

"What is it?" I demanded a little defensively.

"Something up with you?" he asked. "You don't seem yourself."

"I'm fine," I replied at once, hoping that I didn't come off as too eager to prove him wrong. "I'm fine, really. Just been a long day. I need to blow off some steam."

"Well, make sure you use a condom when you do, alright?" he teased, seeing straight through me as he always did. "The last thing we need is more of you out in the world."

"Agreed." I nodded. "Can't imagine you want that competition."

"Alright, get out of here." He laughed, and I got to my feet, bid him farewell, and headed out of the door. I was done with this place for today. I was proud of everything we had worked so hard to make here, of course, but sometimes a guy just needed to forget that work even existed, and see what New York had to offer.

I knew exactly the club that I wanted to hit up for the night – it might have been a go-to, but it was a go-to for a reason. Club Connelly. It wasn't far from the office, the drinks were always strong, and the music was always loud enough to drown out the thoughts in my head. I might have just been running from my problems, but hey, better than running toward them, right?

The clubs were full that night – everyone trying to forget everything that they were leaving behind in their day-to-day. The city buzzed with activity and life and excitement, and I wondered if anyone was looking at me and wondering what the thirty-something dude was doing out with all the beautiful young people.

But as soon as I got to Connelly, all of that fell away. When the clinic had first taken off, this was the bar I'd come to. I had eyed it for months, promising myself that as soon as I got the chance and the money and the prestige, I would buy a membership there. Jason had never been as bothered about that stuff as I had, but then he had grown up with money – he didn't know what it was like to be left out of everything because you didn't have the cash to tap in.

The place was buzzing, as it always was, with people who could afford the fees and were willing to pay to get in. I suspected there were a lot of people like me here, people who had grown up on the outside of all of this and weren't going to pass up the chance to take a bite of the apple now it had been offered to them.

The rest of the night rolled by in something of a blur. I had a little too much to drink, and I could remember the deep chestnut locks of some pretty woman as she tossed them over her shoulder to laugh at one of my jokes. Outside of work, this was what I had always been good at – women. Women made sense to me. Not just their bodies, but their minds, too – the way they thought, the way they spoke. And when I was having a hard day, a day that was making me second-guess some of my life choices, well, I was always happy to find a woman to slide into bed with to make it all go away for a little while.

And that's just what I did. I waited until the inhibition wore off and kissed her outside the club, and she moaned and hung on to me tightly, but it was all a performance. Both of us were hiding in one another for tonight. I didn't know why she felt the need to do it, and I didn't want to know, either. Tonight, for as long as we were around one another, we could pretend that this was all there was to the world. That we were happy. And that there was nothing more we were looking for. Even though I knew, in the back of my mind, that something had to change. What, though? That, I wasn't sure how to answer.

Chapter Three – Marjorie

"Ugh," I groaned, slumping down over the desk in front of me as soon as the customer I had been serving was out of my store.

"Long day?" Terri asked.

"Stupid-long," I replied, and I closed my eyes and leaned my head into my crossed arms. I felt like I had been dragged through a hedge, backward, several times over. I felt like I needed to crawl back into bed before I so much as thought about looking another person in the eye.

"You know it's only ten in the morning, don't you?" Terri pointed out, with a small chuckle.

I groaned again. "Okay, the least you could do is lie to me about that," I replied.

"Lying to my boss? I don't think that would go down so well with management," she joked.

"You know I'm not really management," I pointed out. "We're friends now."

"Yeah, and so that means I get to take my lunch break two hours early, right?" she kidded. "And maybe I could make it last for the rest of the day."

"Okay, okay, point taken," I conceded. "I could do with something to perk me up, though."

"I was going to make a coffee run; you want something?"

I clapped my hands together in a prayer position as though she had just answered a call from the Lord above. "That would be amazing," I agreed. "Can you get me a pastry or something, too? I could use some sugar to take the edge off this day."

"Coming right up," Terri replied, grabbing her jacket and heading for the door.

As soon as it fell shut behind her, I let out a little breath of relief. It wasn't that I was not glad to have her around right now – far from it, actually, given that this was my first day at the store after I'd moved out of my old apartment for good – but I figured that I must be a total drag to be around. Sure, they were giving me the space and time to recover as best they could, but I didn't want my friends to find me boring.

I had barely slept the night before, tossing and turning in my stiff new bed as I tried to figure out what the fuck I was meant to do from here on out. Yes, I had been feeling optimistic when I had left the apartment, but now it was all bearing down on me so heavy that I could hardly see a way around it. What was I supposed to do? How was I supposed to survive? What did my life look like now this was over? Not just my marriage, but the promise of my future, too.

I had this store, at least. That was something, a start. I could cling to this and tell myself that my life was worth living and that there was still a future out there for me. I had been running this place for about eight years now, and I had developed a pretty small niche in the market, which was really saying something considering this was New York. An affordable hipster aesthetic, something delicate but not too feminine. Most of the people who came here were recent grads looking to get their lives together, and with that, their fashion choices, too.

Stephanie and Terri had been my first hires at this place way back when I was just beginning to accept that I couldn't do it all by myself. And, luckily for me, they had proved that I didn't actually need a single other person to join us. We ran this place together – Stephanie had even purchased some of the holdings – and I knew that I was never going to need to look further for people who would support my store.

But what about me? That was the question I still had to answer. What did I want? I knew that a family was in the cards for me at some point, but the truth was that I couldn't see myself stumbling over too many eligible men of my age who were looking to settle down. Most of the ones who wanted that had already done it. I had been sure that I had found a man who wanted that, too, but it turned out ...

I shoved him to the back of my mind and started restocking the blocky shelves next to the window that looked out onto the street. He wasn't thinking about me, and I saw no reason why I should allow him into my brain after what he had done to me. He was out; I was in. Now I just needed to figure out what I actually wanted, and then I would be off to a great start.

Terri arrived back with our coffees a few moments later and handed me the paper cup. "Here's your rocket fuel," she told me with a grin. She knew just how I liked it – fiercely black, with enough caffeine to strip the roof of your mouth raw. I took a sip and closed my eyes. Okay, now I was feeling a little more human.

"What were you thinking about?" Terri asked with interest as she went to wipe down the counter. "You seemed pretty lost in thought."

"I'm just trying to figure out what I'm going to do next," I admitted. "You know, now that things with Robert are over."

"Never getting involved with someone like that again is a good place to start," she suggested, and I gave her a smile.

"Yeah, I know, but they don't exactly announce themselves on arrival, do they?" I pointed out. "It would be a hell of a lot easier if they did, but no such luck."

"I guess you're right," she conceded. "But you don't have to worry about getting back into dating so soon, do you?"

"I guess it could be fun given that we're all single together now," I admitted. It was the first time that had happened since I'd met them both – I had always been with Robert, after all.

"Yeah, we'll go and do all the stereotypical girly things," she agreed. "Manicures and pedicures and pink cocktails ..."

"And sex toys," I joked.

"And sex toys," she agreed. "Especially if you want to keep your life man-free for a little longer."

"That's the thing, though. I don't think I do," I admitted. "I mean, I don't want to end up with someone like Robert again, that's for sure. But I'm not ready to just give up on all of that because it didn't work out one time. I still want to have a family; I want to be someone's wife and someone's mother ..."

"Well, there's really no need to rush the wife thing," she remarked. "You can do something about the motherhood issue yourself, can't you?"

"What are you talking about?"

"You could go to a sperm bank," she pointed out. "They're pretty common now. And once you have your savings back together, you could move into a bigger place so you could raise your kid ..."

"I don't think I could commit to something like that by myself," I admitted. "That scares the shit out of me."

"But why?" she asked. "You're a total badass. You got this business off the ground all by yourself, and in New York, no less! You know how many people have tried and failed to do what you do?"

"Yeah, yeah, I get it." I sighed. "But a baby? That's something else entirely."

"I don't see it as that big a difference," she argued. "You can hire people to take care of it just like you do with the store, right?"

"I mean, yeah, I could," I agreed, chuckling. "But that's not really what I had in mind when I thought about having a baby, you know?"

"Then you need to expand your mind a little," she suggested. "Come on, you have to give it some thought. You can't let some asshole like Robert trip up all the plans you had in place; you're better than that."

"Well, if I ever start believing that, I'll let you know," I promised her. This conversation was making me uncomfortable, mainly because I knew that I didn't have the defenses to deflect what was, on the surface, actually a pretty solid idea.

I took another sip of my coffee, and we went about the rest of the day. Even though she didn't bring it up again, I found Terri's suggestion was bouncing around the back of my head. I tried not to think about it. I had enough going on in my life for the time being without throwing the notion of a baby on top of it all.

I closed the store at the end of the day and was halfway to walking to my and Robert's apartment when I remembered that I didn't live there anymore. I tried to ignore the gut punch that reality gave me as I turned on my heel and headed back to the place that was my home now.

I got to the small apartment that didn't really feel as though it could be the place I was actually living, closed the door behind me, and looked around. How could this have happened to me? Only a few months before, I had been living the dream, with a husband who loved me and a business I was proud of and friends I adored. It couldn't just go from that to this so quickly, could it?

I poured myself a generous measure of rum and flopped down on the couch. I would normally have been putting away a little wine, but wine tasting was something that Robert and I had done together, and it was too painful right now. Besides, drinking rum reminded me of being in my early twenties, before I met him, and goodness only knew how much I could use a reminder of those heady days right about now.

I found my mind drifting back to what Terri had said to me earlier about raising a baby by myself. No men involved. I had to admit, at the point of my life that I was at right now, it was an appealing proposal. I didn't want to have to think about anyone new, not after everything that had happened ...

It was more than just Robert, of course. My father had run off with a younger woman a few years before he died – and then another young woman, and then another, then another. I could remember comforting my mother like it was yesterday and seeing the hurt written all over her face as she tried to understand why this man she had loved so much for so long had walked out on her when she needed him the most. She put her life on hold while he was away, sure that he would come back, walk through the door and arrive in her life again like nothing had changed. I couldn't bear that for her.

And I wasn't going to bear it for myself, either. I had everything I needed here. It might not be everything that I wanted, but you worked with what you had, right? I sipped my rum and thought, and thought, and thought, letting everything flow through my head for a change instead of trying to shut it all off before it got anywhere. I had been pushing down my emotions long enough, and I needed to do something about that. I needed to try something big and bold and different. Something that I would never have allowed myself to think about before.

Maybe having a baby by myself, was it. I had tried with Robert, after all, and nothing had happened. Perhaps that was my mystical woman's intuition telling me that he couldn't have been a good father even if he wanted to because he'd always have one foot out the door and his eye on the youngest, prettiest thing who would give him attention.

I was alone now, and I had to come to terms with that, but that didn't mean I had to stop everything that I had planned for myself. Terri was right – I had money, and I had time and flexibility too, given that I ran my own store. This wasn't exactly how I had planned my future to go, but maybe this was what had meant to happen all along.

Once the booze had hit my system, I pulled out my laptop and started looking up clinics in the area. All I had to do was go in for a consultation, right? I didn't have to go out of my way and prove a point to anyone. Nobody else even had to know that I was going to this place. I certainly wasn't going to tell Terri or Stephanie – they would both start planning my baby shower before I'd had a chance to book my first appointment.

I felt a swell of excitement take over for a second, and I had to catch myself before I allowed it to take control. It just felt so good, after all this time, to have something to look forward to. Even if nothing came of this, I could still be happy that I had done something for myself.

I leaned back in the soft pillows of my new couch. Okay. Okay. Okay. I could actually do this. I was a strong independent woman and, as the old saying went, I didn't need no man. Apart from the fertility doctor I was hoping would get me checked out and on the road to a family of my own once more.

Chapter Four – Blake

I stirred slowly. I would rather have just stayed here in bed all day, but I knew I had to get to the office and speak to Jason and ...

I peeled my eyes open and tried to remember where I was. Because I sure as hell wasn't in my apartment.

What had happened last night? I did my best to piece everything back together inside my head. I'd had that phone call at the office from the new parents thanking me for my involvement in their baby coming into the world. That had thrown me. I had gone out drinking after that, trying to take the edge off, and while I was at the bar, I had met someone...

I groaned and flopped back onto the bed. I was at her house. The last place on Earth I wanted to be. I must have been too exhausted to think about getting myself home, but I always made a point to hit the bricks before the daylight came. Otherwise, some women had a habit of getting a little too invested in what they thought we had ...

I heard singing coming from a room or two away, and I lifted my head and narrowed my eyes and wondered how feasible just running out of here would be. Would she notice? Probably. Maybe she was hoping that I was going to be gone by the time she came through. Yeah, she probably didn't want me sticking around any further than I already ...

"Oh, hey, baby. You're awake!" a perky voice exclaimed from the corridor outside the bedroom, and I had to bite back a groan. *Baby?* That wasn't a good sign. Had I said something to her last night? Something that might have given her the false notion that I was looking for something serious?

"Oh, hello," I greeted her, hoping that my voice didn't sound as odd as I felt it did. "Good to see you again."

"Why are you talking like we're at the office?" She laughed. She had a high-pitched laugh, the kind that seemed to slice straight through my brain and into my head.

"I think I need to get to the office, speaking of," I told her. I made a face, trying to look as though I was disappointed about the revelation. Her face didn't move a muscle. She was set into a rictus grin that would have almost been funny if it wasn't freaking me the hell out.

"I'm making breakfast," she told me, as though she hadn't heard what I just said to her. I raised my eyebrows and watched as she headed through to what I assumed was the kitchen. Did she expect me to follow her? I scrabbled for my phone in my pants where I had tossed them on the ground the night before and checked the time. Shit. I didn't even know where I was exactly, or how long it was going to take to get to the office from here. I really didn't have time to be indulging her.

I got dressed as quickly as I could. Maybe I would even have time to go back to my apartment and change so that nobody would know that I had spent the night out on the town. I mean, Jason would see right through me because he always did, but I could live with that. As long as the rest of the staff didn't catch on ...

I headed for the door, figuring the politest thing would be to just get out of there before she caught on, but before I could even get my fingers on the handle, I heard her calling for me again.

"Baby!" she cried out, as though she had been profoundly injured by my actions. "Where are you going? What are you doing?"

"I'm sorry; I really have to get to work," I told her again, a little more forcefully. I didn't want to have to be an ass, but if that's what it took to get her out of here, then I would do it. I didn't want to stay here a moment longer, and she was out to make that as difficult for me as humanly possible. It wasn't my fault that she had gotten attached. And yet, as she pouted at me, I let my guilt get the better of me.

She seemed to sense the slight shift inside of me, and she clapped her hands together and gestured for me to follow her into the kitchen.

"I made some sausages and eggs," she told me happily, and I winced. That was going to be way too heavy on my stomach this early in the morning. I should have been out for my run right about now, not standing here trying to figure out how long I was going to have to wait before I could split and get the hell out of here.

"And I was thinking," she continued, and I realized with a surge of panic that I had no idea what this woman's name was. Natalie? I had a feeling it started with an N, though I could be getting her mixed up with the last woman I hooked up with. I knew she wouldn't appreciate the confusion. I tried to keep my face neutral as I racked my brain to figure out what her name was.

"If you want to take the rest of the day off work, there's this musical on over the other side of the city that I've been meaning to check out," she continued. "We could go for dinner afterward, too? And maybe we could come back here and ..."

She trailed off as it clicked with her that I wasn't reacting to a word coming out of her mouth. Her face dropped. She suddenly looked borderline demonic.

"What's wrong?" she asked.

"Look, I'm sorry if I gave you the wrong idea, but I'm not looking for a relationship," I told her. Her eyes widened.

"But you ..."

"Did I tell you something different last night?" I asked. I might have been drunk, but I didn't think I had been drunk enough to come out with anything that might have led her to believe I wanted anything more than sex.

"No, but you ... you slept over," she shot back. "I thought you had changed your mind. And now you get up, and you just ..."

"Tell you the same thing that I told you last night?" I finished for her. As soon as I said it, I knew it had been the wrong thing. Her face darkened like a cloud had passed over it.

"You're really just going to walk out of here?" she demanded. "After what we ... after what we did last night?"

"I appreciate you giving me a place to sleep off the hangover, but yeah, I need to go to work," I told her.

She took a deep breath. And then, without warning, she snatched one of the eggs from the cooling pan and whipped it right at me.

"What the fuck!" I exclaimed, jumping away from her in shock as it hit me square in the chest. I had been called many things over the course of my life, but having eggs thrown at me was a new low.

"All you guys are the same!" she shrieked. "You tell me that you're not looking for something, and when I try to actually offer you something nice for a change, you won't even think about it!"

She chucked another egg at me. This one I managed to dodge, sending the yolk splattering across the wall behind me. The yellow had begun to seep into my shirt – I was going to have to go home now and change, no choice in the matter. As though I needed to be any later to work ...

"Natalie, calm down," I ordered her, and her jaw dropped.

"Natalie!" She yelled. "Who the fuck is Natalie?"

"I don't—"

"I'm Nina, you asshole!" she shrieked. "Get out of my apartment! Go on! Get out! I never want to see you again ..."

The feeling was firmly mutual, and I figured my best course of action was to get out of there before I could find myself at the business end of any more flying breakfast food.

I managed to make it out of the apartment before anything else happened, and I couldn't help chuckling to myself as I headed out into the corridor. Okay, that had to rank up there with some of the most ridiculous situations that I had ever managed to get myself into in my life. How did I manage to pull this off? I was sure everyone else just got their kicks and got out, and somehow, I managed to find the one woman to whom the concept of casual sex was more a theory than anything else.

I headed back home and hopped into the shower, getting myself cleaned up well enough that I felt like I could actually pass for decent when I got to the office. The last thing I needed right now was for Jason to come in and bust my chops for staying out too late last night.

I looked at myself in the mirror, and I couldn't help wondering if this was a normal way to be spending my thirties. I mean sure, I seldom did anything just because I thought it was normal, but that wasn't the point. Everyone else seemed to be settling down, getting involved with long-term partners, even getting married and having kids. I could count on one hand the number of my graduating class that I knew to be unmarried and without any kids at all. I was starting to be the odd one out, and I wasn't sure I liked it.

I turned my head from side to side to get a look at myself. No grey hair yet, thank fuck. A few wrinkles here and there, but nothing that couldn't be passed off as laugh lines if anyone asked. I looked like a grown adult, for sure, and yet I couldn't even stomach the thought of a woman making me breakfast without freaking out of the situation. Sure, she had been looking for more than that, but even the thought of eating with her had been enough to set my hackles rising.

Why did it scare the shit out of me so badly? It was just dating.

Something that I had even been good at one point in my life, at least. I had known how to make them laugh, keep them entertained, how to seduce them without letting them get too attached to the thought of me. And now, it seemed like I had just managed to lose that entirely.

Mainly because it seemed like every woman around my age was looking for commitment, and they weren't willing to wait around much longer to be assured that they were going to get it. And I understood that, I did, given that the world I grew up in defined success as marriage and kids and a happy face plastered over the top of it. But surely, they would have rather waited to find someone who actually wanted that as well, instead of trying to mold people like me into the versions of men that they wanted ...

Apparently not. Pickings were that thin, it seemed. I looked away from my reflection and continued getting ready. It was best not to dive too deep into this because then I could dig up what I knew was the real truth behind my fear of letting anyone get too close. And I didn't have long until I had to get to work – an existential crisis over a decision I'd made more than ten years before wasn't something I had time for.

I dressed and headed to the office, deciding to walk to get a little fresh air and get rid of the final few remaining sniffs of egg that were hanging onto me. Had it scrambled in the shower or something? I felt like it was still sticking to me. I would find out when I got to work, I guessed, depending on how everyone reacted to the way that I was smelling.

When I got there, I saw Jason's car sitting in the lot already – he had probably got in early to take care of the paperwork and make sure everything was ready to roll for the day. Even before all of this, he had been the more sensible out of the two of us.

All of this, of course, referring to the fact that he had committed the ultimate bachelor betrayal and gone and got married. Before, I would have been regaling him with the story of the last night over hangover coffee.

Jason would have told me now, of course, that I needed to grow the hell up and stop hooking up with random women that I met at fancy clubs, hoping that their membership there was proof enough that they were decent people. I had to actually start focusing on finding someone who mattered to me, someone who I wouldn't freak out over if they cooked some eggs for me in the morning. Honestly, the sight of that chick hanging over the stove had been enough to make my blood run cold. Other people would have had the same reaction to getting a phone call about a loved one. I just didn't want to have to deal with any of that, not right now, hopefully, not ever.

Hopefully? Was that really how I was thinking about it these days? Was I that averse to the very thought of getting involved with anyone at all? Honestly, the answer was probably yes. I had seen what happened when you let yourself get too close to someone; I had seen what happened when it didn't work out. When you opened up your whole life to another person, let them into your heart, then the pain after they didn't stay ... yeah, it wasn't something I ever wanted to have to deal with again. Not in my whole life. Not if I could avoid it.

I didn't let myself think about her so much, not these days. It had been twelve years, so you would have thought that it was firmly in my past by now. And you'd have been dead wrong because I still found myself thinking about her way more than any single man should.

Marjorie Kline. Even letting her name pass through my head was enough to set something on fire within me. I always thought that her name made her sound like the lead character from some children's fantasy novel – a brave princess, something like that. I told her that once, and she'd laughed at me, and then snuggled up against me in the car and tipped her head back to look at the stars above us ...

I tried not to let that image get hooked in my head. It was strange, even after almost a decade apart, that the memory of that still burned as brightly as it did. I would have thought that with all the other women I had been with and all the time that had passed, that it would have laid off a little. Instead, whenever I went back to any of the time I had shared with her, it seemed to pulse brightly inside my brain, letting me know that it was still there, still ready for me to come back to any time I wanted.

I hadn't wanted to marry anyone else since her. Of course, I had been a kid, I had been in love, and I had been arrogant and stupid enough to think that I had found the woman that I was destined to be with forever when I was seventeen years old. But still, I could remember the sharpness of my passion for her, how badly I wanted her, and how sure I was about it. If she had cooked me eggs the morning after, in her parents' kitchen while they were out of town, it wouldn't have scared me at all. In fact, it would have just been a reflection of what I already knew that I wanted with her, from her, beside her.

But that was behind me now, had been for twelve whole years. And yeah, sometimes I looked back on the choices that I made back then and wondered if I should have acted a little differently. Now, if I had the choice, I would have found some way to keep both – to keep her, and my family above water. But the way everything had conspired when I turned eighteen drove me away from her, and I just had to accept that. We all have to live with the choices we make, right? Whether that is getting eggs chucked at me first thing in the morning by some crazy woman who had decided that we were meant to be, or leaving the girl who could well have been the love of my life behind.

I headed into work that morning and tried to keep a straight face as I ran into Jason first thing – he cocked an eyebrow at me and looked me up and down, clearly able to tell that there was something going on.

"You have a busy night last night?"

I shrugged. "Might have. Busier morning this morning, though."

"Sounds exciting," he remarked and glanced at his watch. "I have a few minutes before my first appointment. You want to grab a coffee and you can tell me all about it?"

"If you can deal with spilling hot coffee all over your lap in shock when you hear this," I warned him, and he laughed.

"Okay, so now you've convinced me that this has got to be good," he replied. "Come on; I want to hear what happened last night ..."

And with that, I slipped back into my bachelor mode, the mode that I had always felt safest in. I knew how to function like this, knew how to move through the world. This was how people understood me the best. I could put on this game face, and I could hide behind it, and I could make sure that nobody got to see the painful memories that lay underneath all of this. The memories of a woman named Marjorie Kline and everything that I left behind when I walked away from her.

Chapter Five – Marjorie

I sat there in the waiting room, fidgeting back and forth, wondering if I had made the right choice by coming here or if there was still time for me to get the hell out and leave before I had to go through with this.

I had booked an appointment with the best fertility clinic in the city. I just wanted to make sure that there wasn't something totally wrong with me given that I hadn't been able to get pregnant before. And yeah, I knew thirty was hardly too old to be having a kid, but there was nothing wrong with making sure that everything was in full working order, right?

Ever since I booked the appointment, I had been going over all the reasons I should cancel it before I so much as walked through the door. I wasn't going to actually go ahead and have a baby, was I? I was all by myself, and that was hardly how I had imagined I was going to raise a kid. I had pictured a husband, a nice home, maybe somewhere just outside the city – not in the middle of New York. All those fantasies that I had allowed myself about how I wanted this to go were falling apart, and it was freaking me out that I was pushing forward regardless.

And now I was sitting here in the waiting room, basically trying to talk myself out of going through with this at all. I hated this. I hated the way it made me feel. I hated that I didn't have someone by my side to comfort me right now – Stephanie had offered to come with me, but I turned her down. There was something too intimate about this, so intimate that I didn't want even my best friends being a part of it if I could avoid it.

Okay, no, I couldn't do this. I couldn't. I was wasting my time, and everyone else's. I would just tell the receptionist that I had forgotten about another obligation and had to go. No, don't worry about rescheduling. I would just walk away and get out before I could get committed to anything that I didn't want to. I got to my feet and hooked my bag over my shoulder, my blood pulsing in my ears. I knew I was being a coward, and I didn't care. This was my body, my choice, my theoretical future baby, and I wasn't going to let anyone else in on this decision, let alone some fertility doctor I had never even met who didn't even really know who I—

And that was when I saw him.

He emerged from the office opposite the seat I was in, and it took me a split-second to place him. Well, no, I realized who he was at once, but I think my brain was just racing to try to make sense of the fact that he was actually there in front of me because there was no way... Not after all this time, not after all this distance, not after all this space between us. It just couldn't be him.

But when he locked his eyes onto mine, I knew it was Blake. The man who had broken my heart when I was a teenager. He was standing there looking at me, an impenetrable expression on his face, and I knew who he was and he knew who I was, and all the history we had together seemed to come surging back to the forefront of my brain, forcing me to take notice, forcing me to relive every single moment.

He was as handsome as ever – in fact, he had grown into his looks over the last decade, his jaw sharper and his hair darker and his eyes a little brighter, like he was spending less time drinking beers under the bleachers and more time hitting the gym. He was wearing an expensive suit, which seemed out of place on him, somehow – at least, the version of Blake that I used to know. He had been the kid who squirmed away from his parents trying to put him in something formal, but now, he was wearing that thing like it had been made for him. His eyes were locked on mine as he stepped toward me; the waiting room was all but empty apart from me, so it wasn't like he could get me mixed up with anyone else.

"Ms. Kline?" he asked me, and I nodded. I felt like the world had slowed down to a crawl around me. Outside, New York City carried on, alive with energy and people and activity, but in here, everything had fallen to a halt as I tried to make sense of what the hell was going on.

"Yeah, that's me," I replied. I had never taken my husband's name, and at that moment, I was glad I had made that choice, because the sound of him saying my name out loud like that took me back to being a teenager again, in the best way possible.

"Marjorie?"

I nodded and laughed and clapped a hand over my mouth. "Yeah, Marjorie," I replied, and he stepped toward me at once and swept me up in a huge hug. Even though I knew that I still had every reason in the world to be mad at him, I couldn't help hugging him back. I had waited so long for this moment – waited so long to find myself in his arms again, to be close to him and to forget everything that had torn us apart. I didn't care that he had abandoned me with no explanation. All I cared about was that I finally had him back, just where I wanted him. All this time had passed, and he still felt the same when he held me. I closed my eyes and let myself remember it, if just for a moment – to remember the sweetness of being close to him like this, how much I had missed it, how much I had craved it all this time.

When he pulled back, I looked up into his eyes and had to fight the urge to kiss him. It was a learned response more than anything else – just that when we were this close, I always planted one on him. I quickly stepped back before my muscle memory took over. I could feel the heat rising in my cheeks, and I wondered if he could see what was going on in my head. I hoped not. I hoped to *God* not.

"I saw the name on the books this morning, and I thought it had to be a coincidence," he told me, as he led me through to his office. "I didn't think ... well, I never thought that you would come all the way out here, that's all."

"I have a store now," I explained. "Threads. The kind of clothes that wouldn't have sold too well with the people that we grew up with, you know?"

"Right, right," he agreed with a chuckle. "So, a little too modern for them?"

"Exactly," I replied. I felt giddy. How could I be standing here and having anything close to a normal conversation with this man? All the questions that I'd had for him for the last twelve years were swelling up inside of me and demanding attention.

He had just left me. Was this what he had left me for? He'd never told me why he left, despite my frequent attempts to get in contact with him. I had tried to reach his family, but they had been quick to cut me off as well – whatever had happened, he had made sure to pass it on to them so that they didn't get caught up in me as well. He had just walked away from me, even though we had been in love, even though we had been talking about a future together. All this time, I had nurtured so much rage and anger for everything he had done to me, but now that I was there in front of him, all I could think about was how *grateful* I was that the universe had gifted me with another chance to see him.

He closed the office door behind me and gestured for me to take a seat in the chair opposite him. I did as I was told. I felt like I was walking on air like some bizarre glitch had brought this person from my past back into reality once again. Maybe it was just that I was hallucinating with all the stress of the divorce and everything ... but I knew that I couldn't have come up with someone that real even if I had been trying.

"I can't believe it's really ... *you*," I blurted out finally. I had no idea what else to say to him. The same thoughts had to be running through his head as well, didn't they? This was just too fucking weird. I wanted to grab him by the shoulders and demand to know why he had left me all those years ago, and I wanted to lunge across the table and kiss him in exactly equal measure. I wrapped my arms around myself, trying to contain the rush of emotions that were coursing through me, and hoped that he couldn't see the flush of red rising in my cheeks.

"Yeah," he replied, spreading his hands wide like he was introducing some incredible stage performance. "In the flesh."

"This is what you do now?" I asked, feeling stupid. "I mean, the clinic?"

"Yeah, a friend and I have run this place for a good few years now," he explained.

"You must have done an amazing job," I remarked.

"Or maybe we're just really good at creating fake reviews," he replied, still with that goofy sense of humor.

"Okay, maybe you wait until after I've put some money down before you start telling me that," I advised him.

"Good note," he agreed. "Might explain why people have been walking out of these meetings when I bring that bit up."

I laughed, already feeling a little looser and lighter. To think, I had come so close to just walking out of here ... We would have spent the rest of our lives in this city, unaware that we were so near.

"So, I'm assuming you didn't come in here to catch up?" he remarked and pulled some papers from his desk and laid them out in front of him, frowning down at them. He still got that little furrow in his brow when he was concentrating on something. Before, when we had been together, I had liked to reach out and stroke my finger down the center of it to try and distract him. It usually worked. But that was back when my touch had the power to do anything I wanted it to do.

It hurt to think about that, to be honest. To think about the woman I had been when I was with him. He had been my first love, my first real love, the first man I ever felt truly connected to in that way. And how had it ended? It had crushed me, eaten me alive, turned me from someone who could actually trust men into someone who wanted nothing to do with them if she could avoid it. It had taken me years to get over what he did to me. It hadn't been until Robert that ...

And now Robert was gone, and Blake was back, and it felt more than a little like fate that I was sitting here before him right now.

"No, I'm not," I replied, shaking my head. "I want ... well, I just wanted to see what kind of things you guys offered here."

"You're trying to get pregnant?" he asked, and I shook my head, then nodded, then shook it again.

"I was trying with my husb – uh, with my ex-husband," I corrected myself. It was still strange to think of him in that way, though this was the first time that the revelation had crossed my mind and hadn't come with the sharp sting of reality. Maybe it was because Blake was sitting there, looking at me, his eyes pinned to mine like I was the most fascinating thing he had ever seen in his life.

"But we didn't have any luck," I explained. "And after the divorce, I decided I wanted to explore my options a little, you know? Maybe look into using a sperm donor or something. But I need to make sure that I can actually have kids of my own to start with if I'm going to pull that off ..."

I felt like I was rambling. I didn't know what I was supposed to say to him. How did I capture all the sadness and heartbreak that had come with letting go of the family I'd been sure I was going to have? I didn't even want to think about that, not here, not now, not right in front of him ...

"We do have a connection with a sperm bank if that's the route you decide to take," he replied. "But I think you're right – checking out the state of your fertility is the first and foremost option right now. I can get you hooked up with one of our nurses for an appointment later this week if you'd like. Get things moving ..."

I could hear the words coming out of his mouth, but all I could think about was the shape of his lips. I could remember, with an almost shocking vividness, how it felt to have them against mine. He had been my very first kiss, outside the fire exit at a school dance. The heat of his body against mine and the taste of the cheap liquor on his tongue was burned into my memory.

"Marjorie?"

When he spoke my name again, I came snapping back to reality, silently cursing myself for letting myself get so caught up in the thoughts that were running through my mind. He was here to do a job, not to have some old flame sit opposite him and make bug-eyes in his direction. Was he thinking anything along the lines of what I was? I couldn't just come out and ask him, but the way his eyes were flickering down my face to land on my lips, I got the feeling he might have been ...

"Uh, yes, that sounds good," I agreed swiftly before I could get too caught up in where my brain was trying to take me. "What do I do next? Will someone get in touch with me, or do I reach out to them, or ...?"

"Here's my number," he told me and handed me a business card. I could hardly believe that he actually had a business card. It still seemed a little crazy that he would be sitting on the other side of that huge desk in this expensive-ass office when the last time I saw him he had been drinking beer in the back of his friend's car. But I supposed that was what happened when adulthood came to pass. Everything changed. The person that you had been before took a back seat and the person that you were meant to be stepped forward to take their place. I wondered what he was thinking, sitting there looking at me – how he thought I had changed from the girl he had been with in high school. I was tempted to ask him, but I figured that broaching that subject would be accepting that there was a past here between us. And both of us seemed to be avoiding that as best we could for the time being.

"You can call me to let me know how you want to move forward, that'll put you through to me directly," he explained. "It's a slow process, just to warn you, but we've had great success with almost everyone who's come through here, one way or another."

"So I hear," I agreed, and he smiled at me. Fuck, that *smile*. That smile still did things to me that felt as though they should have been illegal. He had this flash of playfulness in his eyes when he smiled at me like he was trying to share a secret without coming out and saying what it was.

"I can't believe you've been in New York all this time and we didn't come across each other till now," he murmured. He seemed like he was almost saying it to himself more than anything, and his professional visage dropped for just an instant as he looked at me. I could feel my breath coming a little faster in my throat, faster than it had before. This was dangerous. Seriously dangerous.

"But these are the details you'll need to take a look over," he explained, drawing his gaze from me and reaching down under the desk to grab what he needed. "Just your age, your profession, your current financial situation ... the standard-issue stuff. Plus, you'll need to read through all the documents that we'll be sending out to you. I know it's a lot of homework, but we always find it's better to have this stuff clear upfront than it is to leave questions unanswered."

He talked quickly, as though he was worried that if he left the silence hanging there between us, he might say something that he didn't intend to. I knew just how he felt. Sitting there opposite him, I just wanted to reach across the desk and ... and, well, I wasn't even sure what I wanted. To touch him? Yes, that would have been a good start – I wanted to touch him, caress him, tell him in any way that I could that I missed him. That he had never left my mind in all the time we had been apart. That if he had walked into my wedding, the very day I was meant to be getting married to another man, I would have tossed my ring and run off to be with him at once.

"If you have any questions for us, you can always just reach out to me," he told me. "Or if there's ... if there's anything else that you'd like to talk about."

Even though he didn't come out and say it, I knew just what was running through his head. I smiled. Tempting. I could just go home and call him up whenever I wanted, just to hear his voice again.

"I will," I replied and paused for a moment – there was so much that I wanted to ask him already, so much I wanted to say, so much I wanted to do. But I wasn't even sure that I had a clue where to begin with any of it. I felt like my skin was aching for his touch, but at the same time, I was fearful as to what giving in to it would do to me.

"It's been really nice to see you, Marjorie," he told me, and he leaned slightly toward me across the desk, as though he was trying to make certain that I knew he was telling the truth. I could smell his aftershave – it was different than the one he had worn in high school, but still just as tempting.

"You too," I replied. "Maybe we could ...?" I trailed off before I could let myself stray any further. That was dangerous talk. I needed to be careful how I spoke because I could land myself in exactly the same kind of trouble that I had just walked away from. I silently urged him to finish off the sentence for me, but he didn't. I shifted in my seat. His eyes flickered up and down to my lips again like he couldn't stop himself.

"I should get going," I finished up for myself, and I got to my feet and tucked his card in my bag. He pushed a few documents toward me, which I grabbed quickly.

"Bring these back as soon as you have the time," he told me getting to his feet, and the moment that had existed between us was gone, all at once. Maybe that was for the best. Even though I couldn't seem to convince myself of that, no matter how much I might have liked to.

"Will do," I agreed, and he extended his hand to me. I took it. He was as strong as he had ever been, and I could feel something quiver dangerously within me as soon as our skin touched.

"It was great to see you, Marjorie," he told me. It had been so long since I had heard him speak by name I felt like I was going to swoon on the spot. He had never used a nickname for me —he told me he liked the sound of my full name, like something out of a fairy story. When he said it, I could almost believe that he was right.

"You too," I agreed, and I realized I was still holding on to his hand. I let go at once, and the skin felt overheated like something had shocked sharply through my whole system.

And with that, I had no excuse to stay any longer, so I left. I knew that I had to get out of there quickly before I said or did anything that I couldn't take back. As I stepped out onto the street again, it felt like a bucket of cold water was being dumped over me – back to reality, to the reality of a life that I would rather have been navigating with him at my side.

Was it odd that I missed him already? I had spent so long missing him that it was almost a natural state of being for me. I hooked my bag over my shoulder and headed back to my apartment, wondering why this man had already made such a dent on the inside of my head.

I should have looked over the papers that he gave me, but my mind was somewhere else entirely by the time I arrived home. Suddenly, this new apartment didn't seem like it was as much of an empty void as it had been before. I smiled as I entered it, glad that I had all this lovely space to myself – after all this time. God knows I could use it.

I headed to the bathroom and had a quick shower – or at least, it was meant to be a quick shower.

As soon as I stripped down, and as soon as the cool water started running over my body, I found my mind drifting back to the man I had just been with. He had been my first. My first everything. I could still remember how it felt to be with him for the very first time, actually – a little scary, but thrilling and hot and delicious all at the same time. He was so careful with me, taking his time, going slow, letting me get used to him. I couldn't have asked for a kinder, more respectful person to lose it to.

But now, now that I had a little more experience – there was something else entirely that I found myself craving from him. I could imagine, vividly, how strong he would be under that expensive suit – he took care of himself, that was for sure, and his muscles practically bulged through the fabric of the shirt he had been wearing. He would take me hard, stripping me down like he had been waiting as long as I had for this moment. And I would let him touch me, and kiss me, and hold me the way he used to. I would let him do anything he wanted to me ...

As the water coursed over my body, I closed my eyes and let myself believe that his fingers were caressing me, instead. I slipped my hand between my legs and started to stroke myself, going slow at first, and then finding the pleasure spreading swiftly out from between my legs. I couldn't stop thinking about the way that he had looked at me like he wanted to take a bite of me. He had felt it, too. Whether or not he wanted to admit it, he had felt that burning tension between us, the way it had always been – fiery and furious and needy.

I could imagine how it would feel to have him fuck me deep and hard – maybe right over the desk at that fancy office of his, the whole world carrying on outside while we stole those few frantic moments together – all the time we needed to get where we were going. I could remember the way he breathed when he was close, the way his breath caught at the back of his throat. I wanted to hear that again. I wanted to hear him getting closer and closer; I wanted to be the one to tip him over the edge into that release that he couldn't hold back from. I conjured up the scent of that new aftershave, imagined his bare skin, scented that way, pressed against my own, and I came.

It was the kind of orgasm that nearly knocked me off my feet in surprise. I had to plant my hand on the wall of the shower to keep from tumbling over on the spot. The water was still rushing over me, soothing me, and my muscles were beginning to unclench. I felt like I had given myself something that I had needed for a hell of a long time, even if I hadn't been able to accept it. I had pushed down the powerful need that had consumed me for so long because of the sadness of my divorce – but there, in that shower, with the water coursing over me, I couldn't even remember what my ex-husband's face looked like. All I could think about was Blake, Blake, Blake – and when exactly I was going to be able to steal the chance to see him again.

Chapter Six – Blake

What. The. *Fuck*.

I couldn't believe that had just happened. I sat back in my office chair and stared at the door she had just walked out of. Marjorie Kline. Marjorie fucking Kline. She had just been in my office, sitting opposite me, talking to me like nothing at all had ever changed between us.

What were the chances that she picked this clinic to visit? And what were the chances that she ended up in my office instead of Jason's? He could have dealt with her entire intake, and I would never even have known that she was in the building.

Though I was sure that I would have sensed her in some way. I couldn't believe that she would be so close to me and some radar wouldn't ping to let me know she was near. Sure, it might sound crazy, but I still felt like we had that connection, the one we had built when we were kids. They said you never forgot your first love, and Marjorie had been burned into my brain from the very first moment I saw her, freshman year of high school.

Even back then, I could still remember thinking that she had to be one of the hottest girls I had ever seen. It wasn't just the way she looked, though that was a part of it, too – it was the way she moved, the confidence with which she carried herself. Like she knew that she owned the place and everyone in it. She had been laughing with a friend the first time I saw her, and that was how I had always pictured her in my head since. Joyful, bright, full of light and life.

Of course, I hadn't known back then that the Kline family might as well have owned the whole town for as much power as they had over it at that time. Her dad was the manager and a major player in the biggest local bank, and her mother had come from an old-money family who owned most of the real estate worth a damn in the county. It was strange to me that, even with all their cash, they would choose to stay somewhere like Redwood Cove, but I would soon come to figure out that they liked it precisely because they were big fish in a small pond.

My family, we were about as far away from that as we could possibly be. It's not that I didn't love my parents, because I did—they had worked their asses off to make sure that my siblings and I had everything that we needed—but we came from the rough part of town, the part that didn't come from old money. Or even new money for that matter. Or money at all, to be honest. But we made do with what we had. My dad owned a little mechanic shop, and he worked hard to provide for all of us. Mom handled the paperwork side of it and took on little cleaning jobs here and there where she could find them. We were usually scraping to get by, but it never bothered me that much. It was just the way life had to be.

But when I met Marjorie, I realized that wasn't the case for everyone in this little town. We became friends through other friends – I was too nervous to go up to her myself and was glad when I discovered that Cady, a friend of mine from middle school, had gotten close to her and thought we would hit it off. And we did. Almost right away.

Looking back on it, it was kind of crazy how badly I had fallen for her in such a short time. By the end of sophomore year, I knew that I was in love with her. I didn't even really understand what love was, but I knew that it was what I felt for Marjorie. I had no idea if she felt the same way about me, too stupid to read the signs, until we went to a dance as friends at the start of junior year, drank a couple of shots of cheap whiskey, and kissed outside the hall while everyone else was still hanging out inside.

From that moment on, we had been inseparable, and I had been happier than I ever had been before in my life. I knew I was in love with her, and now I was sure that she loved me back, too. She was sweet, smart, beautiful – Oh God, she was so fucking beautiful sometimes it made my heart hurt just to be around her. My family loved her – I had been worried that she might find our lifestyle a little weird, given the money she had grown up with, but she had thrown herself into helping out any way she could. One of my favorite things to do with her was babysit Carla, my baby sister, and make out on the couch while the baby was sleeping. I could kid myself that this was what it was going to be like when we had a family of our own.

"Where do you think we'll live?" she had asked me once as we lay there on the couch together. I was holding up one of her hands, winding my fingers in and out of hers, marveling at how well they seemed to fit together. Sometimes it just seemed crazy that I had ever held back on my feelings for her at all. She was so obviously the woman that I was meant to be with; I couldn't believe that I had doubted it for a second.

"I think we'll live in the middle of nowhere," I told her. "With loads of dogs."

"Dogs, yes, I like the sound of that," she agreed. "And cats?"

"As many as you want."

"And a little garden where I can grow my own food?"

"You got a green thumb I don't know about?" I asked, and she laughed and wiggled her thumb against mine.

"Well, how hard can it be, really?"

I smiled and pulled her closer. I knew that a lot of people would have looked at what we had and called it nothing more than a teenage fantasy, but I didn't care about that. It felt real enough to me; it felt real enough to her. What did it matter what anyone else out there happened to think about it?

Planning our future together was so exciting to me. I knew I wanted to work in medicine, though at that point, I was still unsure just what part of it I wanted to make my career in. She was interested in fashion design and had a few connections across the state, a few designers who were always jumping at the chance to dress her family for this event or that. The world seemed so fresh and free and open when she was with me, as though there wasn't a thing we couldn't do.

Unluckily for me, though, her family hadn't felt the same way about me. Her father, Gareth, especially always had a problem with me and my family.

"So what do you intend to do with your life, son?" he asked me the very first time I came around to meet Marjorie's parents. Marjorie had warned me that her father could be kind of an asshole, and she had squeezed my hand under the table when he hit me with that question.

"I'm going to work in medicine," I told him firmly, and he snorted with amusement. The sound seemed to echo through the cavernous dining room, filling the space and ringing around my head at the same time. I clenched my fist at my side, trying not to let him get a reaction out of me.

"I'd be surprised if your family could afford to put you through medical school," he remarked. "Thought that kind of thing is pretty expensive."

"I'm making it work," I replied, trying to keep my voice steady. He seemed to know just which buttons to push to get me to lash out with irritation, and I hated that he was actually putting me in a bad mood.

"I'm sure you will," her mother told me, and she smiled in my direction. At least she seemed to think I wasn't a total waste of space. That was a start.

That was the attitude her father had held toward me for as long as I could remember, though. No matter how much Marjorie told me that he would cool off and calm down eventually, he just seemed to increase his dislike of me, making sure that I was well aware of the fact that he didn't consider me good enough for his daughter. Most of the time, he would just slide in these snide comments that were meant to undercut and upset me, but other times, he would be a little more blunt about it.

"I think you need to show me that you're actually going to be able to provide for my daughter," he told me one day, crossing his arms across his chest and raising his eyebrows pointedly. Marjorie was out with her mother, and I was picking her up from her house as soon as I got the chance; I had arrived a little early, and that meant that I had to deal with her fuckwad of a father for the time being, instead. How Marjorie had managed to become such a sweet, non-judgmental person when this man had a hand in raising her was beyond me. It just didn't make any damn sense.

"I've seen the way your family lives," he told me, a warning edge to his voice. "I've seen all the kids your parents have. They can barely afford them, not with your father's little shop—"

"My father worked hard to get that place off the ground," I told him, a barbed edge to my voice. He raised his eyebrows at me.

"And it's going well, is it?" he asked. "Running smoothly, is it?"

I didn't reply. Running the bank meant that he had an inside track on pretty much everyone's financial status, and he liked to make sure that everyone knew that. This was a small town, and it was in everyone's best interests to keep their heads down and hope that this asshole didn't expose them if they crossed him in some way.

He knew that the shop wasn't doing well. It wasn't doing well at all. In fact, we were going to need to take out a loan to make sure that it stayed open – a loan that Gareth would have the final say over. And I couldn't think of anyone worse to be the one making the decision whether or not our family business stayed open.

But still. As long as I was with Marjorie, I knew that everything would work out. Gareth might dislike me, but he wasn't going to wield that against my family. He wasn't a monster. At least, that's what I had told myself, so many times over the words had stopped making sense.

Business at the shop grew worse and worse. I could have sworn that someone was spreading some questionable stuff about it around town to make sure that we started to fail. It wasn't like we had a lot of savings; I put in the college fund I had been adding to with part-time building jobs, but it wasn't enough to keep the wolf away from the door for much longer.

I knew that it was real when I came downstairs to find my mother crying on the couch in the living room. She normally never showed any strong emotion in front of us kids – too much for the little ones to take, and she didn't like to worry me on top of everything else that I was dealing with.

"Mom?" I asked her quietly, and she looked up at me. She didn't even try to wipe away her tears.

We couldn't get the loan. The bank wasn't going to give it to us, for reasons that they didn't seem too keen on elaborating on. I knew exactly what this was about, though I couldn't exactly throw that at the bank to get them to give me what I wanted. I *knew* that this had everything to do with the man who hated me so much, the man who wished his daughter had chosen someone, anyone else to spend her life with.

I couldn't take it any longer. I went over to their palatial house when I knew that Marjorie and her mother were going to be out shopping, and I confronted her father about it.

"You made sure that we couldn't get the loan, didn't you?" I demanded, as soon as I found him looking over the morning paper in the dining room.

"What are you talking about?" he asked.

I slammed my hand down on the table. I was done with him playing dumb, acting like he'd had nothing to do with making this happen.

"Just be straight with me," I ordered him. "You're the reason that my father couldn't get the loan he needed, aren't you?"

"Well, they said it was for the shop, but I know they're going to have a hard time paying for your schooling on top of that," he pointed out. "I didn't think I would see it back in good time. You understand? It was just too much of a risk ..."

I closed my eyes for a moment. I needed to gather myself. I hated this man so much that it was making my blood boil, but he was the person I needed to help get me through the mess that my family was caught up in. God only knew how much I wished it could have been someone, anyone, else, but it was him. And I would just have to live with it.

"What do you want me to do?" I asked him quietly. "To get the loan. What do you need from me?"

He leaned back in his seat and eyed me for a long moment. This was what he had wanted. Power. Men like him always wanted power, no matter how pathetic it was, no matter how underhand the tactics they had to use to make sure they got it.

"You need to leave Marjorie alone," he told me. My stomach dropped. It felt like the world was shifting out underneath me. I wasn't sure I could do that. The thought of not being around her, of not having the woman I adored so much by my side ...

"I'd be more than happy to give your family the loan if you could promise me that," he explained. "And enough to cover a year of your medical school, too, if that's what you need."

I pressed a hand to my forehead. I couldn't do this. What sort of guy did he think I was? I wasn't going to sell out Marjorie for some money ...

But then, I remembered my mother crying on the couch. The sound of my father working late into the night in the shop to try and make enough money to pay the food bill for that week. The fact that Annie and Elsa, my two little sisters, were having to stay with their school friends any chance that they got because they could actually afford to keep their houses warm.

And I knew what I had to do.

"What are the terms?" I demanded, trying to bite back the swell of grief that was already taking me over. He smiled widely, but it didn't reach his eyes. Like he had finally got what he wanted and was glad he had managed to get me on board.

Everything that came after that is something of a chaotic rush. He drew up the contracts in secret and got me to sign all of them. The deal was that I left Marjorie at the end of the school year, going off to college and never contacting her again, as long as the contract was in effect – and that would last as long as we were both still kicking. I didn't get to tell her why I was leaving her or give her any warning. I just had to go and reject all attempts she made to get back in touch with me.

Somehow, counting down the days until I had to say goodbye to her was worse than actually saying goodbye. I tried to pull away a little, to let her get used to the thought of me not being around, but I was just too in love with her to allow that to happen. I adored her, every part of her, every inch of her, and I never wanted to let her go. The grief of letting go of what I had thought was going to be my future was agony. Not being able to tell her the truth behind it was even worse. I wanted to gather her up in my arms and tell her that I was sorry and that I only did this to save my family, and that if there had been any other way, I would have jumped on the chance to take it.

I left for college in a blur, refusing to give myself the time to look back and wonder what might have been – what could have been if I had let it. My family got the loan, and the business stayed afloat for as long as it took them to get back on their feet. I often suspected that Gareth had had something to do with the initial failure of the place, but I had no proof of that and would have preferred not to give that asshole any space in my head, anyway.

And that was how I ruined things with Marjorie for good. She tried to reach out to me, over and over again, tried to reconnect with me in every way that she could, but I had to keep shooting her down, blocking her, ignoring her calls. I cut off contact with most of my friends from back home because they were too close to Marjorie for my liking, and I didn't want to be any nearer to her than I utterly had to be.

Not to mention the fact that, as I got older and established my business, I had that contract hanging over my head the whole time – if I broke it, Gareth was entitled to come for 75% of my holdings, which would leave me all but destitute. There had been many nights when I had laid in bed and thought about what it would be like to hear her voice again, to just talk to her and listen to her and tell her that I was sorry, but it wasn't worth it. It would have been unfair to everyone around me, including her, to pull her back into my life after so long vanished.

But now, she was back. She had just walked into my office out of nowhere. I was pretty sure I couldn't be penalized via the contract for that, but I would have to check. I didn't want to get fucked over just because she booked an appointment with me ...

I had given her my number. I'd hardly thought twice about it when it happened. I just wanted her to know that she could reach out to me any time she wanted and that I would be there for her, no matter what. It was, in my roundabout way, an attempt to make up for walking away from her twelve years ago.

She had been married since then. She wasn't any longer, but she'd had a whole life that had nothing to do with me. She had opened that store, by the sound of it – I would have bet it was one of the best in the whole city. She always seemed to know what people wanted as if she could read their minds with ease. Marjorie had to be one of the most incisive women I had ever met. Even when she was sitting opposite me at this desk, I had felt like she could get inside my head.

She hadn't asked about anything that had happened between us. She probably didn't even think about it any longer. It had been so long, and she'd constructed a whole life for herself that had nothing to do with me. How arrogant could I have been to think she still gave me a speck of space in her head?

Either way, though, I was going to refer her to another doctor. To Jason, probably. Even though this had been nothing more than an innocent mistake, I wasn't going to put my livelihood on the line – I still sent a lot of my monthly income back to my family, a way of supporting them the way they had supported me. I wasn't going to see her again. I couldn't, even if I wanted to.

And, even though the decision was firmly made inside my head, I couldn't help feeling a pang of sadness about it. Because I wasn't ready for this to be over. She had only just walked back into my life – and there seemed something terribly wrong about casting her out again so soon.

Chapter Seven – Marjorie

I hadn't been able to stop thinking about him.

"You look giddy!" Terri exclaimed to me when I came into the store the day after my appointment with Blake. "What's going on?"

"Oh, nothing," I replied, waving my hand. I had told Terri and Stephanie the story of my teenage heartbreak, and I had a feeling that if they caught wind of him being in town, they would be all too quick to storm down to that office and give him a piece of their minds. Or maybe just torch it, I wasn't sure.

"You had your appointment thing yesterday, didn't you?" Stephanie called from the storage room. "Did it go well?"

I hesitated for a moment before replying. What was I supposed to say? *Well, I still have no idea about this whole having-a-baby thing, but the man I thought was the love of my life was there, and now I'm pretty sure the universe is telling me to get back together with him.* They would think I was crazy. They didn't know me when I was with Blake, when I was carefree and treated everything with whimsy. It was his leaving that had brought me crashing down to Earth, for better or for worse.

"I think so, yeah," I agreed, and Stephanie emerged from the back room with a smile on her face.

"That's brilliant," she told me warmly. "So, shall I order that toddler collection, or ...?"

"Okay, okay, slow down." I laughed. "I don't think I'm quite there yet."

Something about keeping my encounter with Blake a secret made it all the more exciting, a little treat that I could give myself. It had been a long time since I allowed myself a crush on anyone – I was married up until a couple of weeks ago, after all – but it would have felt odd not to be crushing on Blake a little bit.

He had changed a lot, of course, but his energy was just the same as it had always been. He still had the twinkle in his eye, the one that I fell in love with on first sight when we were teenagers. I was way too nervous to go up and talk to him, so I had enlisted a mutual friend, Cady, to drop some hints about me to try and figure out whether he was actually interested in me or not. And, lucky for little old me, he was.

As romantic as it was to look back on our history together, I was deliberately skipping a pretty huge portion of it. The part where he stomped all over my heart. I still hadn't been able to figure out just what happened, and God knows I spent a long time trying to put the pieces together. When he told me that he loved me that last time, had he been lying? Did he know it was the last time? When he kissed me goodbye, did he think that he would be kissing me goodbye forever?

These were the questions I was never going to get the answers to because I didn't have the nerve to ask him. He was my doctor now, anyway, and I didn't want to drag our complex history back into play here. I would be surprised if he even remembered the reason he had left me. He'd been heading off to college – hell, he probably just wanted to play the field a little bit and didn't want to have to do that with some high school girlfriend in tow. That was how it worked, right? You dated in high school for the experience, and when you got out into the world, you had a handle on how this dating thing worked. You had to get past your first love to move on to one that actually worked for you.

But I still had so many damn *questions*. That break-up had gone on to define so much of how I negotiated the rest of my relationships. I had held back for so long, fearful of being burned again, and it had been scary opening myself up to anyone, knowing that they could pull the same stunt that Blake had. I couldn't just come out and ask him, no matter how much I wanted to. No matter how crazy not knowing was driving me. But we were working together now, and that meant that we had to stop letting anything about our pasts get in the way of that. No matter what it was.

And I would have been happy with that, really, I would have. I would have been able to do it, though it would have been tough. And yeah, it might not have been ideal, but I could make it work. But that was before I got that phone call from him – the phone call that brought everything grinding to a halt inside my head once more.

I answered as soon as I saw that it was the clinic calling, and I couldn't help smiling as I lifted the phone to my ear. Yes, I knew it was tacky and a little silly, but I was looking forward to hearing his voice.

"Hey," I greeted whoever was on the other end of the line, and I realized that I sounded a lot more flirty than I had intended to. What if it was just his secretary or something? I glanced around the store, making sure that nobody was there to listen in to the conversation, and thanked God that I had sent the two of them home a little earlier than normal – it would give me the peace to carry out this phone call in private.

"Hello," Blake's voice came down the line, and I practically shivered when I heard the sound of it once more. God. Had he always sounded this good? His voice was deep and seemed to fill the negative space around me until there was no room left for anything else. I forgot for a moment that he must have been calling about something to do with my appointment; I would have been happy to just let him read me the weather with that voice.

"I hope you're doing well," he told me, and there was a careful removal to his tone, as though he was trying to put some space between himself and what he was about to say. My stomach dropped. Oh, no. I had hoped that now that I had found him again, I wasn't going to have to bother with losing him. But this ... this felt wrong. I felt fearful all over again. Which was seriously crazy because he was just my doctor, and even if he didn't want to see me anymore, I would find someone else who could take me on and ...

"I am," I replied, trying to keep my voice even. "Is everything okay? Are you calling to reschedule my appointment? Because if you want, I'll be able to ..."

"No," he replied, cutting me off as I spoke. "I'm calling because I wanted to let you know that I'm assigning another doctor to your case."

I stopped dead in my tracks. It was stupid, and I knew it, but I couldn't fight the feelings that were rising up inside of me, those feelings of rejection, of being left behind the way I had been when we were in high school. I hated this. I clamped my hand into a fist and tried to pull myself back to reality. I needed to get my shit together and stop letting the past define how I was going to deal with this.

"I'm sorry to have to change this on you since we already got started on things," he continued. "But I think it would be for the best if you worked with someone else for the duration of your time with us. I have a large workload at the moment, and I wouldn't want you to receive anything but the most expert, dedicated care."

"Of course," I muttered, and I rubbed my hand over my face. He was palming me off, getting rid of me. Just the way he had done before. But this time he had the nerve to actually say it to my face – that was something, I supposed, even if it felt like nothing.

"I'll get my secretary to call you up with the details of your next appointment," he told me, and just like that I could feel him slipping through my fingers again, This man who had been gone from my life for so long, was going to slide right on out of it again. I was going to lose him. I was going to lose him for good, and there would be nothing I could do after that to bring him back to me, no matter how much I wanted to.

"Thanks for letting me know," I replied, automatically, letting my emotions get masked behind a wall of politeness. I had been working in customer service for too long; this was my response to getting hurt by someone, to just smile and nod and let them walk away from me.

"Okay, well, I'm sorry that this didn't work out," he told me, and I could feel him wrapping up the call. He had bigger and better things to deal with, that was for certain. But I needed to speak to him. I needed to see him. I needed to look him in the eye and get an explanation for everything that he had done to me. The universe had offered me a chance to find all that out, once and for all, and I needed to take it.

"Blake?" I said his name quickly, scared that if I didn't come right out with it, I might forget how to say it at all.

"What's wrong?" he asked, concerned. Even after all this time, he could still tell when I was upset. He still knew me well enough to remember that, at least.

"I – I want to see you," I blurted out to him. I couldn't believe I was doing this. Any other day and I might have just let him get rid of me and let that be the end of it, but this month, I had been through a divorce, I had moved out of my house, and everything that I had taken as real had just slipped away from me in an instant. I would be damned if I let that happen with the man who had been the very first to break my heart.

"What do you mean?" he replied. "As I said, I'll refer you to another doctor, one that I have complete confidence in–"

"No, not like that," I told him quickly. "I want to see you. Like ... I want to have dinner with you. If you're up for that."

I could practically hear the shock coming off him in waves. He could just say no if he didn't want to see me again, and I would accept it. I got that. I knew how it was. He probably didn't want to have to look back on the version of himself that had hurt me, let alone try to give me an explanation for why he had done it in the first place. But yet, as the silence pulsed between us, I found myself hoping, praying that he was going to say yes. Because I needed to know. I needed to know everything.

"Just dinner?" he asked. My heart leaped. He was actually considering it.

"Just dinner," I assured him. "It's been so long since we last saw one another, it feels like we have a chance to connect again, right?"

"Right," he agreed. I began to pace back and forth in the store, covering as much ground as possible in as little time as I could. I just wanted to hear him say *yes*. I just needed to hear those words come out of his mouth. Because I knew that staying in this city and knowing there were two men out there who had broken my heart with no good reason was going to drive me a little crazy.

"That actually sounds fun," he agreed. "I'm not sure when I'll have an evening free, but I'll let you know, alright?"

"You better not be blowing me off," I warned him playfully, and he laughed. God, his laugh sounded just the same as it always had. All of this was such a mindfuck; I could still remember how it felt to be close to him in the ways that I missed so badly, and yet there was still all this distance and all this time separating us.

"You know I know better than that," he replied, and I could hear the smile in his voice. I leaned up against the counter, finally ready to stop pacing.

"You better," I warned him, and for a moment it was like no time at all had passed. He was still the man who made me laugh and feel so loved when I was a teenager. The man I still desired, the man who I had seen grow up. I knew that there was no way he would embody all of that for me now, not in the same way, at least – he had to have changed in the last twelve years, or else there would be something wrong with him, but I still craved who he used to be, before he broke my heart. Before all of this had gone so very, very wrong.

I gathered myself and decided to end the call there before I got any more attached to the idea of what came next.

"I'm really looking forward to seeing you," I told him, and I meant it, I really did. I could already picture his face, sitting opposite me, at a table. It would be like a first date. Apart from the fact that we had already slept together, we had known each other for about fifteen years, and this was really a rescue mission for the teenage version of my heart that he had broken so utterly and completely.

"Me too," he replied warmly, and both of us lingered on the phone like we were waiting for something else to be said. I knew what I wanted to hear from him, but it was ridiculous of me to expect something like that from him. I couldn't expect an apology, an explanation, after all this time. He had probably all but forgotten why he split with me in the first place and didn't want to dredge up all that bullshit high school drama. But still – I knew that I had to hear the truth.

"Okay, I'll speak to you soon," I told him, and I hung up the phone before I did or said anything else that might have landed me in trouble.

I tucked the phone away in my pocket again and closed my eyes. I had a date. A date with a man that I had loved for a long time. Was that dangerous? Probably, but I was finding it hard to give a damn. I was just happy that I would get the chance to see him again. That I hadn't been foolish enough to let him slip through my fingers once more. Even though he had tried to get rid of me, I managed to get out there and find a way to meet with him. And I, for one, was keenly looking forward to finding out what he would have to say about everything that had passed between us more than a decade ago.

I busied myself tidying up the store; no point lingering on that now. I would have to wait until I saw him in person. Which, hopefully, I wouldn't have to wait too long for now.

Chapter Eight – Blake

I gathered myself as best I could, looking at myself in the mirror and trying to figure out if this was a good idea. Or a really, really fucking bad one.

When I'd told Jason what I was doing, he practically tried to lock me in my office to keep me from going through with it.

"Dredging up these old memories is never a good idea," he warned me. "You know that, don't you? It's only going to end in tears for both of you ..."

"We're just going for dinner," I protested. "I'm not about to propose to her. It's been a long time. She's been married since then; I doubt she's even thinking about anything like that."

"She wouldn't have invited you out if she was really not thinking about *anything* like that," he pointed out. "She wants something from you. You should be careful with her."

You should be careful with her. Those words ran around and around my brain as I prepared to head out to dinner to meet with Marjorie again. I knew he was right, but that didn't mean that I was in any great rush to admit it.

When she suggested dinner, I had tried to listen to the voice in the back of my head that told me this was a stupid idea. I would be breaking the rules of the contract, technically, by meeting up with her. I would be seeing her out of choice. But I could already come up with a million excuses to defend myself with, already come up with all the ways in which I could prove that I was the one in the right. I had been rolling them over and over in my head since I accepted her invitation. She was the one to invite me, and besides, we were talking twelve years later, more than a decade since all of that had gone down. There was no way that she would actually think of me as anything other than a relic from her past, a curio she was interested in pulling out of the display case just to see what memories it held.

But what about me? What was I doing this for, then? I was having a hard time justifying it to myself, even though I had been rolling it over and over in my brain trying to come up with a good reason why I had agreed to see her again. I should have just shot her down, said no, told her that it wouldn't be a good idea and that I was too busy anyway. But I didn't. As soon as she had brought it up, I had known that I was going to be helpless to say no to her because I did want to see her again. I wanted to be close to her, to look her in the eye and find out everything that had happened in the time we had been apart. A lot of life had passed by, a life that I had nothing to do with. I would have been lying if I said that I wasn't a little curious to find out where it had taken her.

I called her up and suggested a restaurant, and she agreed at once, as though she had been waiting by the phone all this time for me to do just that. I wanted to stay on the line with her longer, to listen to the sound of her voice, to try and figure out what it was she was searching for when she suggested that the two of us get together. But I could do that when I got there.

Of course, I found myself overtaken by nerves as soon as I walked through the door. I had chosen a hip little Asian fusion place, about as far removed from anything our hometown had to offer as possible. There was some part of me that wanted to prove to her that I had really changed – that the person she knew back then was nothing even close to the one that I was now. I had moved on and improved myself and changed my life. I wasn't the guy who had abandoned her.

What if she brought that up? She hadn't mentioned it over the phone or at our first meeting, but surely that had to be some of the reason she was so keen to see me again. I knew that if the same thing had happened to me, I would have been crazy with all the questions as to why I had just walked out of her life after promising her that I would spend the rest of it by her side. That didn't happen without leaving some scars.

But the contract had determined that I wasn't allowed to say a word to her about what had happened between her father and me. I couldn't tell her why I left without a trace. I couldn't be honest and say that if I could have stayed – if there was any way that I could have made it work, I would have done it in an instant. I couldn't tell her that ever since then I had been pushing away every other woman who so much as got close to me because the thought of letting someone down again the way I had let her down was too much for me to take. Not to mention the fact that I compared everyone who came into my life to her and none of them had even come close to the power of what we had shared.

I was just seeing her as a friend. Nothing more than that. I kept repeating that to myself in the hope that I might actually start believing it. But I was craving my hands all over her body, her touch on my skin … The memory of her kiss was fresh and powerful as it had ever been.

I headed out to the restaurant a little early remembering that Marjorie didn't like to be kept waiting around. I arrived a little before her – a new one for the books, given that I was usually the one running late before. I was taken to our table and glanced around at the other people in the restaurant. They all looked like they were out on dates, most of them comfortable, laughing at something their companion had said. I had come straight from work and was still feeling a little uptight like I was stuck in the office for some reason.

But then, I saw her in the doorway, and all of that just seemed to fall away.

"Marjorie," I murmured, even though she couldn't hear me, and I got to my feet. She was wearing this delicate black dress with what looked like shimmers of blue all wound through it, a dress that looked as though it had been made for her and her alone – well, she ran that store of hers, maybe it actually had been. She smiled when she saw me and made her way over to the table. I could see a little nervousness in her eyes, and I was relieved that I wasn't the only one trying to quell some nerves over the course that this night would take.

I kissed her on the cheek in greeting. Her skin still smelled the same. Not the perfume, but something underneath it – something that defined her so utterly and completely as her own woman. When I pulled back, she looked a little shaky on her feet, and she sat down quickly and picked up a menu.

"This place looks really good," she remarked.

"I thought it might be nice to come somewhere we never could if we'd stayed at home," I replied.

She smiled and nodded. "You know, you have a point there," she conceded. "Back home people would think this place was some sort of godless alchemy chamber."

"That just sounds like a good time to me," I replied, and she laughed. She had the most beautiful laugh I'd ever heard; I'd thought that even back when the two of us had first been dating. When she laughed, everything seemed to pause for a moment, everything in the world narrowing down to the two of us.

"So, what do you recommend here?" she asked, furrowing her brow as she looked down at the menu in front of her. "I haven't been out to eat a lot recently; I guess I've fallen behind with what all the trendy foods are meant to be."

"I'll split some appetizers with you if you like," I suggested. "That way you can try a little of everything."

"I like the sound of that," she agreed, and we turned our attention back to the menu to focus on what the two of us were going to eat. We chatted a little about the food, about the places we liked to eat – about the bars we'd liked to drink at when we had first moved to the city. I could see that some of her divorce was still weighing on her pretty heavily, judging by the way she seemed to flinch when I brought up certain locations. Had those been places that she frequented with her ex? Maybe she had met him at one of them. I felt a flicker of jealousy, even though I knew I had no right to. I had been the one to break things off; I had been the one to end it.

The food arrived, and we started to eat. The conversation turned, as it was destined to, back to everything we had shared back in our hometown.

"You remember that spot under the bleachers?" She laughed. "The one we used to sneak off and smoke at?"

"The one with all the chewing gum stuck to the seats above it? I think that's burned into my nightmares," I replied with a grimace. "Jesus, I don't know what's more stupid, smoking, or the fact that we insisted on doing it there of all places."

"Yeah, I feel you," she agreed. "Good thing we always got the cheapest, disgusting cigs we could find, right? I think that put me off smoking for good."

"Oh, I don't know, I can still be tempted after I've had a couple of drinks," I reasoned, and she raised her eyebrows at me.

"If you're offering, then the least you can do is give me one too," she replied.

"I thought you said that you didn't anymore," I pointed out, and she shrugged.

"There's a lot of stuff that I stopped in high school that I've been rethinking lately," she replied, and the way her gaze bored into mine, I knew just what she was talking about.

I knew that I couldn't come out and give her the answer that she wanted to hear. I wished I could just tell her that it had been a mistake and that I was sorry and that I hoped I hadn't hurt her too badly, but I knew all of that would have been pointless. The damage was already done.

"So, you were married, right?" I asked her once I was a couple of glasses of wine in and feeling a little looser around the edges.

She nodded and glanced down at her hand, as though she was still getting used to the reality of not having the ring right there where she could see it. "I was married," she agreed softly. "Feels like a long time ago now, though."

"I'm sorry," I told her.

She shook her head and gathered herself once more. Nothing to be sorry about," she replied firmly. "Better that it's all behind me now, that's for sure. Didn't want to be stuck with him any longer."

"Sounds like you're better off without him."

"Much better," she agreed. "Not to be all Stella Got Her Groove Back, but this is the best I've felt in a long time, actually."

"That's good to hear."

"What about you? You ever walk down the aisle with anyone?" she asked, pointing her fork at me playfully.

I snorted and shook my head. "Not really my thing," I replied. "Never found anyone I wanted to do that with, anyway."

"You always said that the two of us would get married one day," she replied, trying to keep her voice light and failing. She glanced up at me, clearly waiting for an explanation as to *what* the hell happened between us that rendered that so far from reality.

"Yeah, guess that must have changed over the years," I replied vaguely, hoping that I could keep her from diving too deep into what had kept us apart.

"Guess so," she agreed, and she grinned at me. "Or was the bachelor life in this city just too much for you to resist?"

"Okay, okay, so that might have had something to do with it," I joked back, enjoying her lightness of touch. It was clear that she knew how to make people comfortable – it came with her job, I assumed, and she was seriously good at it.

She cocked her head at me for a moment, eyeing me from across the table.

"What is it?" I asked.

She shook her head and drew her eyes away from me. "I was just ... thinking," she replied. "About how long it's been since I last saw you. But ..."

I knew what she was trying to put across. I felt it, too. I didn't know how it was that we could have spent all this time away from each other and yet felt the same sharp chemistry between us. The distance between our bodies was nebulous like I could have moved forward an inch and held her in my arms. The whole restaurant was packed now, but I could hardly see anyone else in there, not when she was right in front of me.

"It's so good to see you again," I murmured, without thinking about how flirtatious those words would sound coming out of my mouth.

She fluttered her eyelashes at me, and suddenly she was the teenage version of herself again – all of this new to her; the two of us learning it together. "You have no idea," she agreed, and she caught her breath like her imagination was taking her places it shouldn't have been. Places that I was keen to visit with her.

We finished the rest of our food, and I managed to quell the desire that was pulsing through me. It was just a sense memory, nothing more than that. Her pheromones locking in with mine and making me think that there was something there between us once more. I was just responding to all the history we had together, not to anything that actually existed between us now. Right?

She told me about her store, and I talked to her about my work and the whole time it was clear that we were just dancing around a central point that both of us were too nervous to look in the eye and confront. I didn't know if I should be the one to say it, but we wanted each other. No matter what the contract said, we wanted each other, and I knew that fighting those feelings was going to be too painful to resist. If she so much as opened the door a single inch to that notion, I would be powerless to resist her.

Not powerless. I wasn't powerless in front of anyone. I had control over this, over the way I functioned, over what I did. But I wanted to strip that responsibility away from myself and hide from it, just so that I would have the excuse to take her the way I was craving so badly.

The conversation flowed with ease, and before I knew it, we had finished dessert. There was no reason for us to carry on with the rest of this night, not really. And yet, the way she was looking at me, I would have done anything to make it last just a few more minutes.

"You have to work tomorrow?" I asked.

"My staff is covering for me at the store," she replied. "I can stay out as late as I want."

"No curfew now, I guess, huh?" I remarked, and she grinned and nodded.

"And we don't have to bother with fake IDs," she pointed out.

"I still like to keep mine around so I can pretend that I'm younger than I am," I replied.

She laughed. "I don't know why you'd bother," she shot back. "Growing up suits you."

"It does?"

"It does," she said. "You look a lot more ... I don't know. Last time I saw you, you were a teenager, and now ..."

She let her eyes travel over my body, and I could see the naked lust in her gaze. She wanted me. She wanted me bad. I felt that heat between us and tried to pretend it wasn't there. Letting that flicker grow into a flame would have been dangerous for both of us, even if she didn't know it yet.

"Now I'm all grown up," I replied. "Like you."

"Oh, I don't like to think of myself as an actual grown-up." She laughed, waving her hand to dismiss it, as though it was an accusation I was throwing in her direction.

"You've been married," I pointed out to her. "Wouldn't you consider that the peak of grown-up-ness?"

"I would consider that being able to invite you back to my place for a glass of wine."

For a moment, everything stopped. This was the moment I made the choice. This was that very second that I should tell her no, not now, it wasn't right, I should be getting back to my place and making sure she got home okay. It should have been easy for me to turn her down.

"I would love that," I agreed.

We caught the subway back across the city, talking the whole time as though we could fill the space between us and pretend this wasn't about just the feeling of her body against mine. She chatted about clothes and her business and oh my goodness, how sorry she was that I was going to have to see her tiny little apartment and that I would have to forgive her for it because she was just getting it set up and still didn't have it the way she wanted it. I could hardly focus on any of it. I was too busy wondering if her pussy still tasted the same as it had all those years ago.

When we got to her apartment building, she unlocked the door and led me up the stairs – in the half-light of the stairwell I could see the way her hair curled around her cheek. Without thinking about how it would look, I reached up and brushed it away from her skin. She closed her eyes and let out a low noise that told me she liked it when I touched her that way. I moved behind her, close enough that our bodies were nearly touching.

"You want to come in?" she asked softly, giving me one last chance to back out of this and see it for the stupid idea that it was.

But instead, I slipped my hand around her cheek and brought her face around to mine. I didn't want to speak an answer to her when I could tell her in a way she couldn't fail to understand. I lowered my mouth to hers, and as soon as our lips met, something clicked into place. Something that I had been doing my best to ignore since the moment I watched her walk into the restaurant. Fuck, since I had seen her there in my office. She arched her back and pushed herself against me, kissing me back, letting me know that she was as eager as I was.

She unlocked the door, and we practically fell into her apartment – I had to catch her to keep us from tumbling over. Laughing, she turned to kiss me again, slipping her arms around me as I kicked the door shut behind us. The rest of the world could wait. I was with my woman again, and there wasn't a thing in the world that I was going to let disturb me right now.

"Should we really be doing this?" Marjorie breathed in my ear.

"Do you want to stop?"

"No ..."

That was all the invitation I needed to keep things going. I pushed her down onto the couch that was right next to the door, the one that was pressed up against her bed – this place really was as small as she'd said it was, but I didn't care. As far as I was concerned, this was just a cocoon for the two of us, away from the real world. I wanted to hide out here with her for as long as I could. I wanted to stay, to forget that there was anything beyond these walls and beyond the feeling of her body beneath mine.

I ran my hands down her shoulders and across her waist, feeling her out; it was strange because she was both familiar to me and brand-new at the same time. I could still feel some of the same dips and curves she had when we had first been together, but her body was fuller now, more womanly. I was already obsessed with it. I wanted to find every change that had taken place over the years and remind her that I adored it, every inch of it, every single part of her gorgeous body. Was she doing the same for me?

She pulled off my blazer pretty quickly, tossing it aside and unbuttoning my shirt with slightly shaky hands. I kissed her hungrily, our tongues coming together once more. If I gave myself even so much as a second to think this through, then I might think better of it. And the straining in my pants told me that was a bad idea.

She wrapped her legs around me, and her dress fell away. I ran my hands up her bare thighs. God, she felt so fucking *good*. Had she always felt this good? When we had first been together, there was always this niggling in the back of my mind, this voice that told me that whatever we had wasn't going to last forever because we were teenagers and teenagers didn't fall in love for good. My parents had always told me that – that the love I had now wasn't the love I would have forever, that I couldn't rely on the tininess of this town to take care of everything I would need for the rest of my life.

I hooked my fingers around her panties and ripped them off her in one swift motion. I wanted her bare, naked; I wanted her body to belong to me again. She might have been married in the time that we were apart, but that didn't matter now. Now, it was like she had been waiting all this time just to be with me.

I wound my arms around her tight and just held her for a moment. This was the intimacy I was craving, that I had lacked for so long. I had pushed that away from me, trying to keep it at arm's length, trying to hide from the reality of what it would bring into my life. But being with her it was impossible not to let myself give over to it. Fuck, I had missed her so much. How had I made it through the last ten years without her?

"Fuck me, please, fuck me ..." she groaned. I had planned to take my time, but hell, if I was going to be spending the night here, I had all the time in the world to explore this, right? I was going to give her what she wanted. God only knew how much I wanted it, too.

I unbuckled my pants and pushed her skirt up and took my cock into my hand. She arched her back from the couch and wriggled back and forth slightly, a move I remembered from way back when. It was what she did when she was seriously horny; when she was so keen for me to take her that she couldn't do anything but move her body to let me know. Her fingers sinking into my shoulders, she looked deep into my eyes, and finally, I pushed myself inside her for the first time in more than twelve years.

"Oh," she groaned, and I covered her mouth with mine. She felt incredible – warm and wet and tight, her body responding to mine like it had before. There was something that felt *right* about what we were doing, about the fact that she was so keen to let me have her again. She had been the first woman I'd ever done anything like this with. It would have been wrong to never come back to see how it had aged, right?

I grasped her thighs and pulled them up and used the leverage to pound into her more deeply. I had been waiting for this all evening, even if I hadn't wanted to accept that side of myself. I wanted her, needed her, *craved* her, and now that she was mine again, I couldn't imagine ever letting her go. I had been with plenty of women in the time we had been apart, but none of them even came close to the way she was making me feel. I pushed my head into her shoulder, but she caught it and guided it back up so she could look at me. Her eyes were on fire, her gaze blazing bright with all the want that she had for me. She just looked at me for a moment before she kissed me once more, rocking her hips back to take me as deep as she could.

I lost myself in her then. Nothing else mattered but this moment and how fucking good it felt to be with her once more. We had each other. Against all the odds, we had managed to find each other once again.

I kissed her and looked at her and touched her all over, feeling her sweet, soft body beneath my own. She was a full-grown woman now, with everything that came with that aging, and her new body was so fascinating to me; I found new things to explore with every caress.

I could feel her cresting, getting close. It wasn't just the way she was moving her hips, or the way her thighs were tightening around me, but rather something in the way she was breathing. Like her breath was catching with every inhale. I remembered it, vividly, from before, and it took me back to being with her then, to loving her more than I had ever loved anyone in my life. And it was that, at the end of it all, that took me over the edge and into my release.

I filled her and held her and felt her as we came at the same time – the sounds in my ears blurred together until I couldn't tell the difference between her breath and mine, and she pushed herself onto me like she never wanted to let me go. Her body was shivering and shaking as I held her close, still moving in shallow thrusts into her, and she moved with me like she was rolling with the waves of the ocean.

When I eventually pulled out of her, she curled her knees to her chest and closed her eyes, wrapping her arms around herself and clinging on tight.

"You okay?" I asked her gently, and she nodded.

"Fuck, yes," she assured me. "It's just been a long time since I got fucked as good as that."

The crudeness of her words stirred something in me again. I had always liked it when she talked a little dirty to me; reminded me that there was far more than just the good girl hidden away inside of her.

"Oh, yeah?" I asked. I might have just been looking for a little ego boost, but what was wrong with that? It had been a long time since we had been together, and I wanted to make sure I was still doing a good job when I was with her.

"Oh, yeah," she agreed with a sigh, and she laughed and clapped her hand over her mouth.

"Damn, I can't believe I really just did that." She giggled. "I didn't think ... not with you, anyway ..."

"Hope you're not regretting it already."

"Not when it felt that good," she assured me. "By the way, if you need to get home, I'm not going to be offended. I get it."

"I'd like to stay, if you don't mind," I replied, and she raised her eyebrows at me.

"Really?"

"Really," I replied, and I slipped down on the couch next to her. "Even if I don't have to sneak out through your bedroom window like before."

"Well, I'm sure I can see my way to letting you stick around a little longer," she agreed, and I nuzzled into her neck, making her laugh again.

"Good," I murmured. "Because I am *so* not done with you yet."

Chapter Nine – Marjorie

When I woke up the next morning and turned to see a man in my bed beside me, I couldn't help smiling.

It was the first time I had woken up to anyone in a long time. First time I had woken up next to a man since my ex had moved out of the apartment. And the first time I had woken up without any doubts in the back of my mind about where this man might rather be.

I couldn't believe that Blake was really right there in my bed beside me. Blake. As in, actually, literally, really, Blake, the man I had been sure I was never going to see again. I reached out to touch his cheek, and he shuffled in bed and let out a little snort. Yes, that was him alright, firmly and truly here beside me and ... mmm.

I wriggled down in bed and pulled the covers up over me. It was still early, early enough that the streets hadn't started to fill with sound yet, so I could lie here for the rest of the morning if I wanted to. Which, you know, probably wasn't a bad idea, given how exhausted I was after everything that happened last night.

We had stayed up nearly all night long, just fooling around with each other like we had in the old days. Truth was, I had forgotten how nice it felt to just be intimate with someone without the goal of sex hanging over my head. When I had been with my ex-husband, everything we had done was always done with the assumption that it would eventually take us to making love, but with Blake, I could just enjoy what he was giving me at the moment and let that be the focus of my pleasure. By the time he had tired me out, it was pitch-black outside, the streets quiet, and it felt like we were the only two people in the whole city.

I had asked the girls to cover for me today – I hadn't told them why, of course, because I knew that any mention of a date would get them way too interested, and I didn't feel like deflecting any of that today. I wanted this to be mine and mine alone. Maybe that was a little selfish, but it felt like the healthiest thing for me in the here and now.

Or maybe it was just that I knew how concerned they would be if they found out that I was fooling around with a man who had broken my heart so long ago. I was just out of a marriage that had crushed my self-esteem, after all – anyone would have looked at what I was doing here and seen it for an attempt to salvage some of the ego I had cultivated before everything had gone down with my ex. Maybe they would have been right. Or maybe, just maybe, this was the universe giving back to me after spending so long fucking me around. Blake had come back into my life right at the moment when I had needed him. That couldn't be a coincidence, now, could it?

Listen to yourself. This wasn't who I was, the believer in the great unknown, in the promises of what the universe would give me. And yet, as I let those thoughts run through my head, they made something close to sense. Yes, this was my apology letter from the world at large. I was getting paid back on all the pain from before.

I laid there with him for a little longer but found myself restless and full of energy, ready to get up and do something. I didn't want to wake him so soon, so I got out of bed and had a shower. As I touched myself, I couldn't help remembering where he had put his hands the night before. God, it had been like he hadn't been able to get enough of me. I knew how that felt. From the moment he kissed me outside the door, I had known, known deep down in my guts, that this had been the right choice for me to make.

I slipped into something cute but comfortable. I didn't want to stir him too early, but it wasn't like I had a lot of room in this studio to do much else. I had to sneak around like a teenager returning from a house party, all the while trying to stifle the giggles that were threatening to bubble up and over. I was giddy, giddy with excitement, giddy with lust, giddy with the thought of what came next ...

But I had to keep reminding myself that he hadn't given me an answer for what happened when we were teenagers. I had tried to approach the issue a few different ways in the hope that he would come clean, but he ducked the question every time I got close to it. Was he ashamed? Did he just want to get me into bed, and thought that explaining the truth behind his actions might get in the way of that? I had no idea. Maybe I should have been blunter with him last night. Maybe I should have demanded the truth and refused anything else until he gave it to me.

But I hadn't. I just wanted some fun for a change, and now that I'd gotten it, it was hard to argue, even in my own head, that it had been a bad idea. We'd had fun! Shit, how long had it been since I had just allowed myself to have *fun?* Everything had been so heavy lately, and God knows how much I needed to blow off some steam. The weight of everything felt a little easier to carry now that I knew I still had the capacity for pleasure that I'd always had. It was amazing what a few good orgasms could do to brighten your outlook, huh?

I made myself some breakfast and figured that the least I could do would be to cook him something as well. I was honestly surprised that he had taken me up on the offer to stay the night. I assumed that he had some fancy place all to himself that he would want to retreat to as soon as he got the chance, but he had been pretty insistent about staying over, and I certainly wasn't going to pass up the chance to have someone fill out this tiny little apartment with me. I didn't expect it to become a regular occurrence, which meant I had even more reason to enjoy it while it lasted.

"Morning," his bleary voice came from the bed, and I turned to see him just waking up. He was naked, and when he stretched his arms above his head, I could see the muscles of his shoulders rippling beneath his skin. I quickly pulled my eyes away from him. I'd felt them last night, sure, but seeing them in the light of day was something else entirely.

"Good morning," I greeted him, as I tended to the eggs in the pan. "You want some breakfast? I was just making myself something to eat."

"What are you having?"

"Eggs," I replied, and I heard a snort of laughter from behind me. I turned around and raised my eyebrows at him. "Sorry, is there something funny about eggs?" I asked, smiling, waiting to be let in on the joke.

He shook his head and started putting on some of his clothes. "Nothing at all," he assured me. "I just had a ... uh, an unfortunate experience with eggs recently, that's all."

"I suppose, in your line of work ..."

He burst out laughing again. "Not those kind of eggs," he replied, and he pulled on his boxers and came over to join me. "Those look good. I'd love to have some if you're offering."

"I'd say grab a seat, but you kind of made a mess of the couch," I pointed out, and he hooked his chin over my shoulder and hugged me close. I froze for a moment, not quite sure what I was meant to do with his sudden nearness to me. It had been a while since anyone had expressed that kind of off-the-cuff sweetness to me, and it was a little more than I was ready to take. But after a moment, I found myself relaxing back against him, enjoying the feeling of his arms wrapped around me. He was so strong. He had always been wiry and athletic back in the day, but now it felt like he was a solid wall of muscle, like nothing bad could possibly happen to me as long as he was here to take care of me.

"Maybe I could run out and grab some coffee?" he suggested. I hesitated for a moment. Was he going to use this as a chance to ditch me?

"Take the keys," I suggested, hoping that he wouldn't be enough of an ass to make off with them. He nodded and headed for the door, and I smiled as it shut behind him. This was all so comfortable. So easy. It was just like it had been before–

No, I couldn't let myself start thinking that way again. It wasn't like it was before. We had a betrayal between us now, twelve years unaccounted for, a marriage on my side and God knows what else on his. Our lives were different, and I needed to remember that. No matter how nice it was to have him around again, he had hurt me, and I didn't want to get hurt again.

I finished cooking up breakfast, and he arrived back a few minutes later.

"You still take it black with two sugars, right?" he asked, as he handed me my cup. "I couldn't remember, so I just had to take a shot."

"Yeah, that's right," I agreed, and I took the cup from him and smiled shyly. How was it that I had spent all of last night with this man and yet I was feeling all fluttery and nervous like this was the first time that I had ever met him?

"I got us some bagels, too, because they looked really good and I figured we could use something to go with the eggs," he replied. He smirked again, clearly amused by whatever had crossed his mind before.

"You going to tell me what you keep grinning about?" I asked, nudging him with my foot, and he shook his head.

"You'll just have to live in mystery," he replied, and I served up the eggs onto the plate and grabbed some sauces to go with them. We flopped down on the couch together, and I had a vivid sense-memory flashback to doing just this with him after some big house party in high school.

"Does this remind you of ...?" he began, but I jumped in before he could finish.

"Lindsay's graduation party when we were seventeen?" I filled in for him. "Yeah, totally, I was just thinking that."

"Man, I think that still stands as the worst hangover I've ever had in my life." He laughed. "And trust me, I've put in my time there."

"I'll bet you have," I agreed as I took a sip of my coffee. It was a little too hot for me to drink yet, but honestly, I needed the little jolt back to reality to remind me that I shouldn't get too invested in whatever the hell was going on between us.

We chatted a little, about the area I was staying in, living by myself again – he asked a couple of questions about the divorce, and I did my best to deflect them, wanting nothing more than to forget about all of that while I was with him. The real world could wait, as far as I was concerned. Hell, it could fuck off entirely. I ate my breakfast and drank my coffee, and we looked back on the best and worst parties we went to when we were in high school. We were still dancing around the point, of course, skipping out on the years between then and now, but I was just glad for the company. Especially the company of someone who had known me so far back.

After my father passed away, it had been easier for me to just try and let go of my history. There was too much in my past that didn't make me happy. He had been the start of it, really – the start of coming to terms with the fact that everything wasn't always going to be easy, that people were going to lie to me and that they were going to hurt me if I let them get close enough. It had taken me a long time after he was gone, to accept any kind of love back into my life. And then, when my fucking father ran off with another woman, I had been reminded of why I didn't trust anyone, not completely. Why I wouldn't hurry to let people into my life. Apart from the women I worked with, I was perfectly happy by myself. Well, not perfectly happy, but surely, I was better off keeping people at a distance than inviting them in ...?

Even though that was exactly what I had done with him the night before. I had been the one to suggest that he come back to my place. He wouldn't have pushed me for it, I knew that. And yet, the thought of just letting him go, letting him leave, that stung me too badly to really consider it. I didn't know if he would ever make the time to see me again. The way he talked about his job, it sounded like he was pretty constantly busy, and I didn't want to put too much pressure on him to meet with me again. But the reality of all of this had sunk in and I had, with the help of the wine, jumped at the chance to bring him back here. That wasn't exactly sticking to my motto of protecting myself at all costs, was it?

"What are you thinking about?" he asked me, and I quickly smiled and shook my head, hoping that my thoughts hadn't been readable on my face.

"Oh, nothing," I replied, keeping my voice light. "Just thinking about how you have to show me where you got these bagels. They're amazing. You seem to have found the best bakery on the block, and you only stayed here one night ..."

"I guess I just have a knack for good bagels," he replied with a shrug, and the playful look he gave me reminded me, at once, of the boy he'd been before. The boy I had known before he broke my heart. The boy who had loved me, or at least the boy who had claimed that he loved me. The thought of it stung, but in a good way, the memories flooding through me in a way I hadn't let them in a long time. Normally, I didn't let myself linger in them, but being so close to him again was making it hard to deny how I felt. No, how I *had* felt. This was in the past. The love we had for each other was behind us now, and that was the way it was.

At least that's what I would have to get myself to believe. One way or another.

We sat down and ate together, and luckily, I was able to detach a little from the nerves and actually just have a good time. I felt so bright and flirty like I had been shot through with a fresh energy that I had lacked before – I could almost feel it fizzing from my fingertips, and I wanted more. I could still remember how good his mouth had felt on mine yesterday when we'd slipped into bed together, and I was so, so ready to pick up where we had left off.

But in truth, there was something else on my mind, as well – something more important than just sex. When he had called before, when we made this date, it had been to tell me that he couldn't be my doctor any longer. Well, I wanted him to rethink that because I knew that he was the best in the city, and I wasn't going to step off quite so easily.

"Blake, there's something I wanted to talk to you about," I admitted to him, and he cocked his head at me, raising his eyebrows as an indicator for me to go right ahead.

"And what might that be?"

"It's about ... it's about my treatment," I explained, fiddling with the last piece of the bagel that I hadn't been able to finish.

His face dropped. "I was hoping we could skip out on talking about work."

"Sorry," I apologized. "But you said ... you said that you couldn't be my doctor any longer. Do you still think that?"

"Look, it's not that I wouldn't want to work with you," Blake explained with a sigh. "I think you'd make an amazing mother; I've always thought that. But I don't want any old feelings getting stirred up alongside this; you get me?"

"I get it," I replied. "But you must know that you're the best in the city, Blake. And I don't want to go work with anyone else on this. You know me, you know what I can handle, you know what's good for me–"

"We haven't been around each other in years," he reminded me, and I could feel the sharp edge to his voice like he was letting me know that he didn't want to be having this conversation. "You don't ... you don't know ..." He got to his feet. He seemed irritated – angry, even.

I stood up and looked him in the eye, daring him to lash out at me again. Instead, he sighed and rubbed his hand over his face.

"Shit, I'm sorry," he muttered.

"It's fine," I replied, and I meant it – somewhat. "I didn't mean to ... I didn't want to push you. That wasn't why I invited you back here, for the record, I actually ..."

I stopped myself in my tracks. What was I planning on telling him? That I actually wanted him? Yeah like he wasn't well aware of that already. He'd spent all night with me, making me come, watching me writhe and gasp and moan under his touch. I just wished I could convince him that there was something to be said for us working together, too. What I was doing, making a baby, it was so intimate. I wanted to do it with someone I trusted utterly and completely, and it was like the universe had handed Blake back to me as the obvious answer to that question.

But he shook his head once more. "Look, I'm sorry, but this just wouldn't be right," he told me. I noticed that he seemed to be avoiding looking me in the eye.

I furrowed my brow at him; what was his problem? I couldn't get him to look at me.

"I think that we're too close for this to actually work," he continued, speaking quickly like he was trying to convince himself as much as he was me. "We know ... well, we've been through too much. I wouldn't want anything from our pasts getting in the way of what you want for your future."

"But that's just what you're doing," I pointed out. "You're saying that what we had means that you can't get involved with me as a doctor. Doesn't that seem a little crazy to you?"

"I'll refer you to someone who'll work with your budget and what you need," he assured me, and I could hear him sliding into the same tone of voice that he used when he was at work. This was Blake the professional I was dealing with now, not the Blake I knew, not the Blake I had grown up with.

"But it wouldn't be professional for me to continue seeing you in a medical context after ..." he replied, and he gestured towards the bed. The place was so small that he could be standing next to the door while he was still just a few feet from where we had been making love all night long. That stung, I wasn't going to lie.

"I'll speak to you later, alright?" he told me, but I could tell that he didn't have much intention of doing so. I watched as he grabbed his coat and his coffee and slipped out the door, leaving me standing there and feeling like a full-blown fool for believing that anything good could have come of that date.

I hadn't gotten an answer to any one of the questions that I'd needed a response to. How could that be? How stupid was I? Had I really just let him ... just let him sweet-talk and charm me into forgetting about everything he had done? No wonder he had gotten out of here so quickly, he probably couldn't believe his luck and wanted to hit the streets before I started asking harder questions.

Ugh. And now he wasn't even going to give me the help that I needed for my fertility check-ups. A connection like him could have made everything so much easier to handle, but of course, I had to blow it by hooking up with him. How stupid could I be? I wanted to go back in time and remonstrate with the past version of myself, tell her off for thinking for a second that any of this was a good idea.

But as I cleared away the stuff from breakfast, I couldn't help running through what he had said before he'd made such a swift exit. It had been like he was hiding something from me. Talking about the past, talking about what used to be. Was there something that he wasn't telling me? Well, there must have been – must have been something that he was keeping from me, given what had happened all those years ago. I could have sworn that he was teetering on the brink of telling me there for a hot second, but I must have been wrong. Whether I liked it or not, he was still the same guy he had always been, and I just had to find some way to come to terms with that.

Or did I?

As I tidied up my place, I let my thoughts wander in a different direction. Just one more time. One more time seeing him. Would that be so wrong? I had to find the truth of why he left me. I deserved that much, didn't I?

I was going to do my damndest to prove to myself that I deserved better than this.

Chapter Ten – Blake

I should never have gone home with her.

I mean, any idiot could have told me that much, but now it had happened, I couldn't help turning it over again and again in my head. I shouldn't have gone home with her. Damn, it would have been so easy for me to just cut myself off before anything happened, go home, go to bed, pretend that the thought had never crossed my mind.

But no. I had to give in to how I felt about her. How could I not? When I saw that softness in her eyes, when I saw the way she reacted to my touch, it was like I was hooked again, all at once. I couldn't have stopped if I tried. Muscle memory took over, my need for her a reflex that I couldn't deny myself.

I could have snuck out while she was asleep, of course, but I had enjoyed sleeping next to her far too much for that. Every moment when I should have got up and left, I failed to take, and I only had myself to blame for what happened as a result.

As soon as I woke up and saw her making me breakfast, I knew I was in trouble. Not because I wanted to go, but because I wanted to stay. When I found out it was eggs, I couldn't hold my amusement. She had no idea what had happened to me with that chick a few days before when I freaked out at the thought of anything more than sex and a sleepover.

And she didn't know that with her it felt so different. She was just doing what she had always done, taking care of me, looking after me, being what I needed her to be; she would never know how grateful I was for all the kindness she had shown me. When I had been growing up, everything had been so hectic that sometimes I felt like I got lost in the mix. But she always seemed to be able to find me, no matter what I was going through, no matter what was in my way. And the relief of knowing that there was someone out there who saw me, saw all of me, was greater than anything else I had ever felt before.

It was so easy to slide back into that place with her. Too easy. Fuck, even the thought of her now was tempting, while I was sitting in my office at work, doing everything I could to keep her out of my head and in the back of my mind.

Jason had no idea what had happened between us. Better I kept it that way. I felt as soon as I spoke the words out loud, I would be making it real. No denying it then. I wanted to keep it hidden away in the back of my brain, and hopefully, the thought of her would wither and die on the vine, and I could get on with my life, and she could get on with hers. She had likely already forgotten about me. She was freshly single after a divorce; she would have men beating down her door to get her anything and everything she wanted. Soon enough, I would just be a vague, distant memory, one in a long line of dudes who she enjoyed her singledom with.

But I didn't want that to be the case. Even the notion of it sent this bullshit little flare of jealousy through my system. I didn't want her to forget about me. Even though I had fought for so long to get her out of my head, I wanted to be in hers again. Fuck, I was already hooked on her. I wanted her back, or at least some part of me did. A part of me that didn't take well to being reasoned with.

Fuck it. One more time, right? Just one more time to get her out of my system. I'd had a taste, and now I needed to prove to myself that I wasn't hooked. I could have her and walk away if I wanted to.

I dialed her number without thinking about what I was doing. This was crazy – batshit crazy. I needed to stop myself before I went any further. I tapped my fingers on the desk as I waited for her to pick up. I needed to hear her voice again, to see her face – I could only think about her and her touch and her kiss and how badly I needed all of them again, sooner rather than later.

"Hello?"

"Hey, Marjorie?" I greeted her. The sound of her voice was like a salve to my ears. It had been two days since I had seen her, and I was already jonesing for another taste.

"Oh," she replied. "I didn't expect to hear from you–"

"Me neither," I agreed. "Could I see you?"

"Right now?"

"Right now," I repeated after her, and there was a pause at her end of the line. She was measuring up the plus and minus sides to what I was offering her. I knew she understood what I was getting at. I waited for her to respond. She could just say no, then all of this would be over, and we could go back to our real lives and pretend none of this had even happened at all.

"Where are you?"

"My office," I replied at once.

"I'll be there in twenty," she told me, and she hung up the phone. I ran my hands through my hair and tried to figure out if I had really just done that. I was the one who had told her that this was wrong, that we needed to call it off before it went any further, and yet I had just invited her to my office. And she damn sure knew what I wanted when she got here, too.

I cleared my schedule for the next hour and waited outside for her to get here – as soon as she did, I took her around the back and into my office so that nobody would see her walking in. She greeted me curtly, not even asking what this was about. She already knew.

As soon as the door was shut behind us, I moved toward her. I slipped a hand around her waist and just looked at her for a moment, letting my eyes linger on her face, letting myself get lost in this brief moment. And then, I kissed her. And I forgot about all those good reasons I had to keep her away from me.

She moaned into my mouth, and I knew then that I had no chance in hell of resisting her. I backed her toward the door to check that it was locked, and as soon as I was certain that it was, I picked her off her feet and planted her down on the desk.

I had never done anything like this before – yeah, I had thought about how hot it would be to just fuck someone in the office, but I had known that I would need to actually date somebody for that to happen. With her, though, it was different. There was just this understanding between us. And besides, we had done enough crazy shit in crazy places when we were teenagers that hooking up in an office was actually pretty low on the list. You had to make do when you didn't have a place of your own, right?

She was wearing a pair of pants, sleek and tight to her body. I unzipped them and let her lift her hips so she could wriggle out of them. I sank my fingers into her bare ass greedily – God, she'd always had the best ass I'd ever come across, thick and shapely. She pressed her lips to my neck, and I wondered just what she had dropped to come running to me so quickly. I had to admit, the thought of her dumping everything she had to do for that day just to be with me was seriously turning me on.

I ran my hands up her back and pulled down her shirt, letting it roll down beneath her breasts so that I could taste them. We hardly said a word to each other, but this had always been the way we communicated anyway – with touch, sensation, feeling. I pushed down the cups of her bra and leaned down to take her nipple into my mouth, letting my teeth graze roughly against the exposed skin. She breathed in sharply – trying not to make a sound, aware that at any moment someone could come in and bust us in the act. Somehow, that just served to turn me on even more.

I reached around to unhook her bra and tossed it aside so that I could have all the access to her that I needed. Her fingers were running through my hair, and her nails were on my neck, and I wanted to feel everything she had to give me – I wanted to feel the pain, the pleasure, all of it. I didn't know if I would ever get up the nerve – or push down my own internal logic enough – to do this again. If this would be the last time, then I sure as hell was going to make it one to remember.

She was almost naked, and I saw no good reason for her to have any more clothes on her body at that moment. I stepped back and looked at her, at her panting, keening form, and I knew what I wanted.

I sank to my knees and ripped off her panties, tossing them aside so that I could see her properly; she spread her legs like she knew exactly what it was I was craving, and I looked up at her to see the want in her eyes. I planted a kiss to the inside of her soft thigh and inhaled the scent of her skin once more. I brushed my lips across her, toward her pussy, letting my mouth trace the puff of dark hair on her mound. And then, at last, I lowered my lips down to her and tasted her.

"Fuck," she groaned, and she reached down to grasp hold of my shoulders; I didn't have so much as a sound in me, my body trying to process how good it felt to have my tongue against her clit once more. She was the first girl I'd ever gone down on and, in the days before we consummated our relationship, I had grown pretty skilled at knowing what she wanted. Now, to see if I had retained all that ability ...

I slipped my hands beneath her ass and pulled her eagerly toward me so that I could taste every part of her; swirling my tongue in a circle, I reminded myself of the feel and the shape of her. She was already shaking. Had she sat there in the cab on the way over here, thinking about what we were going to do, waiting, waiting, waiting to take what she wanted? I hoped so. The thought got me even harder than I had been.

I found her clit and let my tongue linger there for a long moment, softening it so that I could coax it to swell between my lips. Her thighs tightened around my head, and I knew I was doing something right. Her fingers were in my hair, stroking, smoothing, touching me, and I could feel her fingertips on my scalp, finding those nerve endings that lit up when she was around. Soon, she was slowly rocking her hips back against me to meet me, letting me taste her properly – her wetness coated my chin and my mouth, and I wanted nothing more than to soak myself in her.

I got lost in going down on her – I forgot that we were in the office, forgot that I was doing something that could land me in serious trouble, forgot all of it. How could it matter when we were together again? She was moaning softly, every breath growing more and more needy, and I knew she was getting close. I wanted her to come, wanted to make her come with my mouth, wanted to remind her what she had been missing all this time.

She was grinding herself back against my face, and I reached up to grab her thighs, holding her close, not letting her get away from me – I wanted this, I wanted her, and I wasn't going to stop till I got both.

When she came, I felt it before I heard it – felt the contractions of her muscles, then the way her body seemed to slacken above mine, felt the way she gave in to it like it was all she had ever wanted in the world. I looked up at her, and her eyes were closed, her head tipped back, her body trembling from top to bottom. She reached down and pulled me to my feet, not opening her eyes once, and kissed me, kissed me so that she could taste herself all over me. I kissed her back, eager, hungry, my cock swollen and pressing almost painfully up against my pants. She'd had her fun – and now it was my turn for a little of the same.

"Turn around," I growled to her, and she did as she was told at once. I unzipped my pants and took my cock in my hand, and she arched her back as she felt me guiding myself toward her once more. I could hardly breathe as I watched my cock slip inside her for the first time. At her place, it had been in the dark where I could hardly see her, but now I could make out every inch of her body, and I was already obsessed with it.

I took her hard – I knew that it was only a matter of time before someone noticed my absence and came looking for me, and I wasn't going to hold back a moment longer, I wanted her so badly. She clamped her hands onto the desk and arched her back, pushing toward me so that she could take me even deeper. I couldn't believe how good she felt – slick and warm and tight. I closed my eyes and gritted my teeth and tried my best not to make a sound, even though all I wanted at that moment was to let out a cry that would alert everyone to what we were up to.

I looped an arm around her waist and pulled her a little more upright, twisting her head around so that I could kiss her once more – her lips parted for me, and our tongues met, greedy, grasping, needing each other. I thrust hard, our hips coming together loud enough that our skin made a sound. She was reaching for me any way that she could, grabbing hold of me, gripping tight to me, her nails on my skin, her fingers tracing shapes against my body. I pulled back an inch and just looked at her, watched her face, her eyes squeezed shut as she tried to take in the rush of feeling that was moving through her. I knew how she felt. I always knew how she felt. Often, it seemed like we were moving on the same wavelength, the two of us coming together in a way that just made sense – silent words exchanged but never spoken out loud.

I didn't know how long the two of us were at it like that. I knew I had an hour, but time seemed to fall away as I gave myself up to her. She just felt so fucking good. I slowed my roll after a while, really savoring the feeling of her body against mine, in no great rush for it to be over. The sound of her breath mingled with mine, and I could focus on nothing but the fact that I had her, I finally had her. After so long. Too long.

Eventually, I could hear that telltale rasp to her voice, and I knew that she was getting close again – I felt a tingle deep within me, telling me that I was almost there, too. I thrust once, twice, three times more, and I felt myself unleash inside of her.

The release was beyond anything I had ever felt before in my life. It was like someone had unlocked something deep inside of me that I didn't even realize I had been trying to keep hidden away even from myself. I held myself there and groaned, and moments later, I felt her tight pussy contract around my cock as she came for the second time. I moved slowly, letting myself stay inside of her, fill her up. I didn't want this to be over. I had told myself that this was where it ended, but I knew that it wasn't going to be that easy, not when I knew how incredible it could be between us.

Slowly, eventually, I pulled myself out of her, and she grasped the table for support. Her legs were trembling beneath her, and I put a hand on her hip to support her and make sure she wasn't about to keel out right in front of me.

"You okay?" I asked, and she nodded. Her eyes were closed like she was trying to take this all in. Or maybe because, like me, she couldn't believe she was letting this happen once more. Couldn't believe that it was with me. And couldn't believe, above all else, that it was still so damn good after so many years apart.

"I should be getting ..." she mumbled, the words trailing off. She didn't have the energy to finish them.

"Right, right," I agreed. "You want me to call you a cab, or ...?"

"I can manage it myself," she replied, and she waved a hand at me vaguely. I smiled. It was a little funny, I had to admit, to see her like this. I could still remember all those amazing sessions we had when we were dating when the teenage hormones and the newness of what we were doing were enough to keep us up all night long.

"Didn't think you still had it in you," she remarked, as she went to gather her clothes. I held my hands up.

"Okay, that sounds like you're trying to tell me something about my prowess here ..."

"No, nothing like that." She laughed. "But just ... yeah. I didn't think it would still be that good."

"Guess there are some things you never forget," I replied.

"Like riding a bike."

"Hey, what did you call me?" I joked – but before we could take it any further, there was a knock at the door, and Marjorie's eyebrows shot up so fast I thought they were going to fly right off her face.

"Blake?" Jason's voice came through the wood. "Blake, you in there? I need to go over some numbers with you ..."

He tried the door, but I had locked it, thank fuck. I turned to Marjorie and jerked my head in the direction of the back door, the one that I had brought her in through.

"Come on," I hissed. "I don't want anyone to know that you're here."

"Way to make a girl feel special," she whispered back as she hopped back into her pants. But she wasn't looking to stick around any longer – in fact, she gestured for me to go ahead of her and lead her back outside, and we hurried her around to the front of the building once more.

"Well, that was ... something." She giggled, and I realized that I was smiling, too. Something about sneaking around like this made it all the more exciting. To think, life had just been going on in the office as nothing had changed – nobody knew that I had been fucking her over my desk just a few moments before.

"That really was," I agreed, and I reached up to swipe a strand of her hair that had fallen out of place back where it belonged. I wanted to say, *see you,* but I had no idea if I could actually back that up at the end of the day. Or if she wanted me to.

"I hope you don't get in too much trouble with that other guy," she told me, and before I could stop myself, I planted a quick kiss on her cheek.

"Worth it," I replied, and she grinned at me happily.

"Yeah," she agreed. "It really was."

And with that, she was gone – hurrying across the parking lot to get back to whatever real-life had been offering her before I had rolled up out of nowhere and disrupted her day. I watched her as she left and felt the instant and overwhelming urge to go after her, which was annoying. I had done all of this with the hope that I would actually be able to let her go once and for all – that I could put her out of my head. But it seemed like I wasn't going to get so lucky. She was still stuck in my head like a record on repeat. And if anything, this little encounter we just shared only served to make it a bit harder.

Chapter Eleven – Marjorie

"Wait a damn second." Terri stopped me in my tracks, raising her hand to get me to quiet down so she could wrap her head around what the hell I was telling her. "We're talking *the* Blake?"

"The Blake," I agreed, taking a sip of my coffee and leaning on the counter. It had been a slow day at work and finally, I just cracked and came out with it, telling the two of them what was actually going on so I could get it off my chest.

"The Blake who dumped you with no explanation when you were in high school?" Stephanie asked. "The very same one?"

"The very same one," I admitted and felt a little flush of nervousness. The way they were both looking at me, it was like they thought I was batshit crazy. And honestly, truly, maybe I was because there was no way in hell I should have been doing anything I was doing right now.

It had been about a week since I went on that date with him, a few days since I had seen him last – when he had called me into his office where the two of us had some *crazy* hot sex together. I still couldn't believe that it had really gone down like that. Well, that he'd gone down like that. When he called me, I did everything I could to talk myself out of believing that he was really looking for another hook-up, but as soon as I got through the door, he made his intentions pretty damn clear.

"I can't believe it," Terri replied, shaking her head. "This is the guy who fucked you over, right? The one who got away?"

"He's not the one who got away," I replied, waving my hand to dismiss that notion. "It's just ... things were different then, that's all."

"And he's explained to you why he dumped you back then?" Stephanie asked. "I mean, I assume that if you're dating now ..."

"We're not dating," I protested. "At least, I don't think we are. I mean, I wouldn't be totally against it ..."

"Oh my God, you totally want to date him," Terri replied, her eyebrows vanishing into her hair. "You *totally* want to date this guy."

"I honestly don't think that I do," I replied, but I knew I wasn't exactly selling it. Terri and Stephanie exchanged a look that told me just what they thought of my attempts to spin.

"Come on, don't give us that bullshit," Terri exclaimed. "We know you better than that, don't we, Steph?"

"Yeah, we do, and we don't want you to jump into something with someone when you've barely even sealed the deal on your divorce," Stephanie told me. I could hear the concern in her voice. It was ridiculous, even though I was the oldest of all of us, she was always the mom of the group. That came hand-in-hand with all the responsibility she'd had to take on, I supposed.

"I'm not jumping into anything, so you don't have to worry about that," I promised them, and I went about arranging one of the shelves near the window. Neither of them said anything, and I could feel their eyes stuck on me.

"You going to say something?" I asked, shooting a glance over at them.

"At least give us the juicy details," Terri replied, and Stephanie nodded.

"I suppose it has been all doom and gloom from my end for a while now," I conceded.

"Yeah, least you could do is fill in the fun stuff," Terri replied, and she crossed her arms over her chest and leaned back on the counter.

I took a deep breath. Where did I even start? There wasn't that much to tell, but it felt like so much had happened already. Maybe because I had spent such a damn long time running it over and over in my head in an attempt to make some sense of it all.

I caught them up on the whole story so far – that we had met at his office, that he had told me he couldn't be my doctor, then the date and the sex and the *second* time we had sex, and the fact that I hadn't heard a word from him since then. I could see the furrow in Stephanie's brow getting deeper and deeper as I told them the details, and I knew she wasn't pleased with what I had been up to. Sometimes, it felt like she was on the brink of imposing a curfew on me.

"I mean, at least the sex was good, right?" Terri remarked when I was done. "Been a while since you've had a taste of any of that ..."

"Yeah, you're right," I agreed.

"But you think that's all it is?" Stephanie cut in. "I mean, you don't have any feelings for him anymore?"

"I wouldn't say I have *no* feelings for him anymore," I replied, glancing away from her for a moment. "I mean, what we shared when we were together before ... they say that the first person you're in love with, it never really goes away, right?"

"Yeah, they do," Stephanie agreed. "Which is why jumping back into something with your high-school ex is hardly encouraged in getting over a divorce."

"Oh, I'm over the divorce," I replied, waving my hand. "Just because it was only official recently doesn't mean I haven't put it behind me already. I'm so ready to get on with my life; I'm not going to wait around for him to come back or see the light ..."

"And even if he did you would kick him to the curb, wouldn't you?" Terri asked. "I mean, that asshole doesn't deserve even the sniff of a second chance with you."

"I'll make sure to put him in contact with you directly if he tries to pull anything like that." I laughed. I appreciated how protective they were over me. Sometimes, it felt like I just wasn't able to do that for myself the way I should, and God only knew how much I could use that protection once in a while.

"Oh, I'll keep him right," she replied, clenching her fist demonstratively.

"But just because things are over with him doesn't mean that you have to go out looking for the next guy," Stephanie reminded me gently.

"That's the great thing, though. I didn't go looking for him," I told her. "The universe just handed him over to me. Don't you think that's a sign? Don't you think that means I should give things a try?"

"Look, I am a hopeless romantic at the best of times, you know that," Terri cut in. "But this guy ... it's been one date, right? And he left in a hurry the morning after? And then he called you into his office, and you hooked up again?"

"Yeah," I replied. When she put it all like that, it didn't sound quite as dreamily romantic as I might have hoped.

"It doesn't sound like you're headed towards something super serious, is all I'm saying," Terri finished up. "Don't get me wrong; I think you should go out there and have all the fun you can now that you're single again. But just don't ... don't end up getting yourself hurt, alright? We care about you. We don't want to see that happen again."

"Neither do I," I replied, a little defensively. But I was only being so spiky because I knew she had a point. I had put myself through enough with men lately, and I didn't want to throw myself into something else that would only end with me getting stung once more.

"Did you at least find out what happened before?" Stephanie asked with interest. "You know, when the two of you were back in high school?"

"No," I admitted, shaking my head. I felt stupid, confessing all this to them, but they were the jolt of reality that I obviously so sorely needed. They exchanged a glance.

"Just promise me something," Terri told me, and it seemed like she and Stephanie had exchanged a silent psychic message with that glance.

"Yeah?"

"If you get a chance to see him again, at least find out what the fuck he was thinking dumping a catch like you," she replied. I laughed.

"I'll make sure to phrase it in those exact terms," I assured her. "Maybe you could write it down for me; I can mail it to his office."

"Don't tempt me," she said giggling.

"Oh, shit, the delivery's here," I remarked as I saw a familiar van pulling up outside. "Terri, can you give me a hand unloading stuff? Stephanie, you have the invoice, right?"

"Yeah, right here," she replied, as organized as she ever was. Sometimes, when we got in new clothes like this, I found myself wanting to ask her why she didn't put in some designs of her own, but I knew that she had her shit just the way I had mine. The less poking around I did in her life, the better for leaving my own stones unturned.

The rest of the day went by pretty much as normal; we stocked the shelves, dealt with a few customers, and chatted to a regular who was in for a pair of shoes for a fancy event she was going to with her new boyfriend. It was nice to tap into someone's life in such a positive way. It was one of the things I liked about working here so much; for the most part, I got to see everyone's good side.

When we were done for the day, Stephanie hung back to help me tidy things up.

"You don't have any hot plans for the evening?" I asked.

She laughed and shook her head. "Not everyone can have a life as interesting as yours is right now," she shot back.

"I don't think interesting is the word ..."

"Well, half of me thinks that it sounds like something out of a fairy tale, and the other half thinks that you're just going to wind up getting yourself hurt," she told me. "I don't want to say which one it is yet, but ..."

"But I'll keep an eye out for myself either way," I finished up for her. She leaned over and gave me a quick hug.

"It's going to be fine; I know that," she promised me. "You know how to handle yourself, right?"

"Hey, you're talking to a woman with a whole divorce behind her," I joked. "I think I know how to do relationships, don't I?"

"Of course," Stephanie agreed, and the two of us chatted as we finished closing up for the night.

But as I walked home, I couldn't stop thinking about the way the two of them had reacted. They were my friends, after all, and they had my best interests at heart. If they thought that something was wrong, well, then there was a pretty good damn chance that it was. And when I told them about what was happening with Blake, they had both reacted like I had told them I was thinking of taking up heroin as a hobby.

The city was buzzing with activity that night, and I found myself pushing through crowds of people and trying to figure out what I was supposed to do now. I had his number. I could call him again, invite him around – but for what? I had no clue what my endgame was. Just for sex? I wanted more ... Didn't I?

It had been so long since I had been in a relationship that was just for *fun*. You know, one where I could just kick back and blow off some steam and actually have a good time instead of being caught up in what it meant or where it was going. Ever since I met my ex-husband, it felt like everything had been pedal-to-the-metal, all of the time – like everything was running at double-speed as I tried to catch up with where I thought I was supposed to be in my life. I knew it was stupid, knew that it was only myself I was competing against, but that didn't make it much easier for me to dismiss out of hand.

Was that what was happening with Blake? Was I just attaching too much importance to something that he could walk away from at any moment? Honestly, I didn't know. I had no idea what a casual relationship looked like now that I was an adult. Was I even capable of one?

It wasn't like I could just call up Blake and ask him what the hell was going on between us. That would have been the adult thing to do, but I didn't have it in me, not even a little bit because the thought of being shot down again after everything that had happened ... yeah, I knew that I wouldn't be able to handle that with grace. I just wanted him to tell me that he still felt the same way that I did, and that I wasn't crazy for feeling it too, and that he wanted me back, and that we could ...

Oh. I didn't know what I wanted. Was this just a rebound? It had been so long since I had done anything like this that I honestly had no memory of how these things went. Wasn't it meant to be more fun if that was all it was? I was quite sure of that aspect of it if nothing else ...

I shoved it to the back of my mind as I grabbed the groceries I had kicking around at the back of my fridge and threw something together for dinner. I wasn't going to give him any more space in my head. He already had quite enough, as far as I was concerned.

But then, just as I was sitting down for something to eat, my phone rang. I fumbled to grab it out of my pocket. Was it him, wanting to see me again? I could be across to his office in a half-hour – I didn't know where he lived, but if he'd wanted me back there, then I would have been happy to run over to his place, too. I lifted the phone to my ear and answered the call.

"Hello?" I asked breathlessly, so ready to hear his voice coming down the line.

"Hello, Mrs. Kline?" a woman's voice greeted me. I sank back into the seat, rubbing my hand over my face.

"Yes, it's me," I replied. "And it's *Ms.* Kline now."

"Ms. Kline," the woman repeated, and then she launched into her spiel. "We heard you have a small business, and we wanted to reach out to you about the offers we have for you today ..."

I closed my eyes and let her spill all the details about these new offers that even she sounded pretty bored to be giving out, and I hoped that I was giving her just enough so as not to seem rude as I ate the sparse pasta dish I had tossed together for myself a few minutes before. Honestly – and I was well aware of how pathetic it was – it was nice to have some company over dinner, even if I knew she was just doing it for her job.

I politely turned her down when she was done, and she less-than-politely hung up on me, and I tossed the phone to the other side of the room and let out a sigh. My appetite was fading fast. I was so irritated with myself; I could hardly think about eating.

I had been so ready and so willing right then and there to drop everything so I could go be with him. I thought this time after my divorce was supposed to be a chance for me to re-evaluate, to settle into the new person I was becoming and figure my way through that. Instead, I was sitting around waiting for a call from a man I didn't even know liked me or not.

I was sure you couldn't share the connection we did without there being something more to it. And I knew that we had a history, a past, a story that connected us more than almost anyone else I had ever been with. But was that making me crazy? Making me read into things that weren't there? I had no idea. I felt like my head was going to straight-up explode with all the damn *questions* that were running around inside it. I was only just back on the dating scene, and it was already tiring the life out of me. How on Earth did people do this?

Chapter Twelve – Blake

I swear, it was like I could sense her walking into the building. As if her very presence was enough to set off sensors in my brain that she was getting near. As soon as I heard her voice outside my office, I got to my feet at once and cracked the door so I could see if she was really there, or if I was just imagining things. I peered through the crack, and there she was, the woman of the hour herself – Marjorie Kline. My heart skipped a beat or three when I saw her, and I did my best to calm myself down.

It had been a good week since I'd last seen her, and I had been going back and forth about reaching out to her so that I could see her again. God knows I wanted to – far too many times I had found myself staring at her number in my phone and wondering how wrong it would be to just call her up and tell her to get her ass down here again so we could fool around. And yeah, the physical impulse to just give in to that and let it happen was strong, no doubt.

But there was more than that, too. It was impossible to deny that we had some serious chemistry going on, and there was nothing I wanted more than to explore it. How did it work now that we were adults? I had no idea. I wanted to find out. I hadn't felt this way about anyone in a long time – not since we were teenagers, at least. I was craving her, thinking about her all the time, wondering what she was doing and if she was thinking of me. My body craved hers in a deep, visceral way that I had never felt before, even more than when we had been teenagers. Now, I had so much more to compare her to, and it was even clearer to me that she was the best I was ever going to have.

But there was no point in risking it. I knew what I would be putting on the line if I was to go after her again, and it wasn't fair. Not for me, not for her, not for Jason, not for anyone who was involved with this. I still had no clue whether she knew about what her father had done, and I had no intention of coming out and asking her. If she knew, then she probably thought of me as weak and pathetic for giving in to it. And if not, when she did find out, it wouldn't be long till that was the only way she could see me.

But yet here she was, back again. I took a deep breath and stepped out of my office, figuring that there was no harm in finding out why she had come back, right? I was interested. We were old friends. At least, that's what I kept telling myself, no matter how much bullshit I knew it to be.

She glanced up when she caught sight of me and started when she looked me in the eye, as though she hadn't expected to see me here. I mean, I did co-run the place, so I wasn't sure why she'd imagine she could avoid me. She gathered herself in an instant, though, smoothing any expression from her face and rolling her shoulders back.

"Oh, hello," she greeted me.

"Hey," I replied. "What are you doing here?"

"Booking an appointment with your partner," she told me. "You mentioned getting me set up with a colleague, and since I didn't hear from you, I guessed I had to do it myself."

Shit. It wasn't that I had forgotten, but rather that I knew if I so much as heard her voice I would be helpless to stop myself from inviting her to my place so I could make her come again. Not that I could exactly announce that in front of a waiting room full of people.

"Yeah, sorry about that," I replied, and I hoped I didn't sound too hostile. It was like I had to put walls up when I was around her or else I was going to give in to that burning desire to have her once more.

"I've heard he's the best in the city," she remarked coolly – she had used that exact same descriptor for me, and I knew she was wielding it to try and get a reaction. I didn't give her one. I wasn't in the mood to play those games.

"Yep, one of them," I agreed. "You need help getting anything set up? If you want, I can call—"

"No, I think I'm perfectly capable of handling it myself," she told me, and though her voice was almost pointedly calm, I could hear a little waver in it. I felt a twist of guilt. Had I put that there? Had I been the one to make her feel this way?

I took her arm and led her away from the reception area so I could talk to her for a moment. She didn't so much as twitch as we walked, as though she had known that this was coming.

"I'm sorry I haven't been in touch since—"

"Since you booty-called me in the middle of the day so you could get yours?" she finished up for me. I was a little taken aback. I didn't realize that she'd felt that strongly about it.

"Since that," I replied, trying not to let her sharpness faze me. "I know I said I'd get you set up with another doctor. I'm sorry I left it so long, it was just that—"

"Look, Blake, I don't want to hear any of your excuses," she told me sharply.

"I didn't realize I had anything to excuse myself for," I shot back. So, I was a little defensive. She was coming at me way harder than she needed to, and it was throwing me the fuck off. I was sliding back into the mode that came when I was trying to get out of some woman's apartment without her throwing eggs at me.

"Yeah, well, of course, you don't," she fired back.

I clenched my fists at my sides. I didn't much care for being spoken to like that, but there wasn't a lot I could do about it, not here in the middle of my workplace, at least.

"Let me get you set up with an appointment with Jason," I asked her. "Least I can do. I'll get him to put you top of the list; you'll be the next person he sees—"

"No, I can handle this myself," she told me, and with that, she took one last look at me and then walked away. I was left standing there, staring after her, wondering what in the name of holy hell had just happened in the middle of a perfectly ordinary workday.

I headed back to my office, shooting a last glance at her to see if she had softened a little – she hadn't. I couldn't believe this. Where had she gotten the nerve ...?

I made it back to my office before I let out a little snort of annoyance at how she had just spoken to me. A week or so ago, she had been sneaking in here so we could fuck, and now, she was coming at me like I was the second coming of Satan? It didn't make sense to me how she could cycle so quickly through her attitudes toward me. I sank into my seat and, now that I was away from her, I could clear my head a little and actually make sense of it.

From her perspective, I supposed, the way I had treated her wasn't exactly the sweetest thing in the world. I mean, it made sense from where I was coming from, given that I had everything with her father to think of. She wasn't aware of the fact, I assumed, that I stood to lose as much as I did if I wanted to make something happen with her. Even if I did, I already knew her family didn't like me. There was no point in risking more than I had already put on the line for her.

But *damn,* if it didn't hurt to know that she thought of me like that. I had dealt with my fair share of pissed-off women over the years. But in those situations, I'd felt like I had done everything I could to make it clear to them where I stood. My cards had all been on the table, and I hadn't been trying to fool anyone into thinking this was any more than what it seemed to be on the surface.

With Marjorie, I hadn't had the luxury of being so blunt. I should never have agreed to dinner with her, but I knew that I couldn't say no – too intrigued, too interested to see where things could go from there. Maybe I should have told her about the contract. Surely, she would have taken my side about this whole thing, seen how crazy-unreasonable her father was being and taken a step back from him?

Yeah, but he was family. Even when it came to the irrational, blood ties were usually enough to clamp that down. You never turned your back on your family, not if you could avoid it, even if they were being outright irrational. And it wasn't like I had given Marjorie many reasons to think that I was the better option here. In her eyes, I had just led her on only to let her down again the first chance I got.

There was a knock on the door. I cleared my head, set my face to neutral.

"Come in!"

Jason opened the door and stepped inside, looking a little confused.

"I saw you talking with that woman out there," he remarked, jutting his chin back in the direction of the waiting room. "Seemed pretty serious. Is everything okay?"

"Everything's fine," I promised him. "Just a misunderstanding, that's all."

"You sure?" he pressed. He knew me better than almost anyone else did, so he could see that I was lying to him. Still, I wasn't about to fill him in on all the gory details of what had happened between me and that woman over the years. There was too much I was too ashamed of. Not to mention the fact that he would chew me out if he knew that I had brought that drama right into the office.

"Well, you need anything you let me know, alright?" he asked. I nodded. Honestly, I just wanted to be rid of him so I could take some time to digest what the hell had just happened in here. I was still trying to wrap my head around it, struggling to make sense of it all.

"Will do," I replied, and he paused for a moment, as though giving me the space to bring up something else if I wanted to. I raised my eyebrows at him, daring him to come out and ask me what he wanted to, and he shook his head and left me to it. He knew I was way too stubborn to bother arguing with when I got in one of these moods.

As soon as the door closed behind him, I let out a sigh of relief. I needed to be alone. I needed a fucking second to figure out what the hell I had done to deserve that because I felt like I had done everything as well as I could, given that I was still dealing with the nightmare that her father had dumped in my lap a long-ass time ago ...

Shit, I just wanted to be able to tell her about that. I wished I could fill in those blanks for her. If I did, everything would make a little more sense to her; I had no doubt. Maybe she would even take my side over it. Maybe she would reject what her father had done ...

I pushed those thoughts to the back of my mind. Even if she did, that didn't void the contract. I would still lose everything I had worked so hard for, for so long. I wasn't interested in ruining my career over some woman.

Not just some woman, though, not if I was honest. The woman that had meant more to me than any other woman in my life. Marjorie Kline. If there was anyone worth blowing up my entire life over, it was her.

But I couldn't. I was pretty sure she hated me now anyway given the way she had just spoken to me. I doubted that she ever wanted to lay eyes on me again, and I could hardly blame her. No, I had led her on and then pushed her back with no damn explanation for anything I was doing. She was being sensible for protecting herself. And now, I just had to focus on doing the same thing. No matter how much I would have liked to be passing the time with her, instead.

Chapter Thirteen – Marjorie

Ugh.

I sat there in my apartment, in that tiny space, and looked around and tormented myself with the memory of everywhere Blake had been when he was here. In the bed, on the couch, drinking coffee ... and then out the door, as though the last thing he wanted on Earth was to be here a second longer. And I had been foolish enough to go back and try to figure out if there was something there between us.

I hated myself. No, I hated *him*. I hated him for coming back into my life when I was vulnerable, and sleeping with me, and making me feel all those things that I had done my best to push down and hide, even from myself. I hated him for making me love him again, if just for an instant, and then having to go through the pain of losing him once more. And I still didn't *fucking* know what it was that had pushed him away the first time. All these mysteries were still in place, all these questions still left without answers, and I had just smiled and waved my hand and let it all happen. I couldn't believe that I had been so stupid.

I had decided to skip out on telling Stephanie and Terri what happened. I didn't want their sympathy about this. I was having a hard enough time dealing with it all by myself, and the thought of pulling other people into the mix would just make it all the more ... real. I had never been a person who would go out looking for sympathy or support, and I supposed that wasn't exactly a good thing, but I didn't care. I just wanted to pretend that none of this had happened and that I could move on with my life without looking back or wondering what I could have done differently. Hell, if I could have gone through the whole divorce without anyone else actually having to know about it, you better believe that I would have done just that. I hated the thought of anyone being in on my personal shit like that.

Maybe I was just being stubborn. I had done so much by myself in this life. I had come to New York, I started the business, I built myself a marriage and a life here – a life that recently fell to pieces of course, but I didn't need to think about that. Perhaps now was the time to accept that I could really use some support. That I needed people outside myself to help me through. Terri and Stephanie would come over in an instant if they thought I needed them, and maybe I should take them up on that.

I was sure it had something to do with Robert. He was someone I'd actually allowed to get close to me – well, clearly, since we had married and that was sort of part of the deal. I had allowed him into my life, and it had been good for such a long time, good to have someone so utterly and completely on my side, good to have someone who cared for me first and only.

And look at what happened. He broke my heart. He had lied and cheated and left me because he'd found someone he liked better. A younger model who didn't have the same weight of the world on her shoulders. He had chosen her over me, and I just had to live with myself knowing that even the man who stood in front of me and dedicated his life to me would rather be with someone else when the chance came up.

I sighed. I was mad at myself for letting these men into my life in the first place, both Blake and Robert. I had been sure that I loved them and that they loved me, and all they had done was break my heart and move on and leave me wondering what the hell was wrong with me to earn such horrible treatment.

But I had to keep reminding myself – it wasn't me, it was them. I had done nothing wrong. I had just tried my hardest to love and find love and give love, and it had all ended with me getting stomped all over like I was nothing. I knew that I had been cold to Blake when I saw him last, but what did he expect? Me to come rolling in there all smiles and acting like I hadn't been stung by the way that he treated me? Yeah, maybe his other hook-ups were cool enough for that, but I sure wasn't. I was thirty, and I was divorced, and I was sick to fucking death of having my heartbroken.

My phone buzzed. I didn't care who it was; I was going to talk to them about this. Even if it was that guy who had called before about the special deals they had on curtains, I was going to spill my guts out and let him know that I had a terrible love life and I was mad at myself for it. Hell, maybe it could even be the start of something beautiful, a torrid affair ...

I checked the number – didn't recognize it. Maybe one of the girls calling from somewhere they didn't usually go? They weren't sitting around at home feeling sorry for themselves, they were actually out on the town living their lives and having a good time. Unlike me.

I answered the call, and as soon as I heard the voice at the other end of the line, my heart stopped.

"Hello? Margie?"

It was Robert. I would have recognized that voice anywhere. I got to my feet at once, trying to gather myself. Should I just hang up the phone? I had no clue how I was supposed to react. His voice sounded heavy, full of feeling, and I would be lying if I said I wasn't a little curious as to what the hell was going on. I hadn't heard from him since we sealed the deal on the divorce, and I hadn't expected to, either. Both of us were moving on with our lives. We didn't talk anymore, not really. And yet ...

"Robert?" I greeted him, though it came out sounding more like a question than anything else. He had called me by the nickname that he had always used, the nickname that usually made my heart warm, but for some reason, I didn't feel even a speck of reaction to it.

"Is it you? I couldn't remember if I got the number right," he went on. I nodded, then remembered that he couldn't see me.

"It's me," I replied. What the fuck was he doing calling me this late in the evening? What the fuck was I doing answering the phone and giving him the time to speak to me? This was crazy. I was acting crazy. And yet, there was a part of me that was far too intrigued to hang up the phone.

"I need to speak to you," he told me, somewhat redundantly. "I made a mistake, baby," he continued, and the words caught me by surprise.

"What?" I demanded. He was calling me baby again. This couldn't be good. Or maybe it was just what I had wanted all this time. I had no fucking clue. My mind felt like it was turning inside out.

"I ... Joanne and I, we split up," he explained. "We weren't together for that long, even. I just ... I didn't know how much I would be leaving behind when I ended things with you. I thought I knew what I wanted, but I didn't. I want you, Marjorie. It's always been you. I was just too much of an idiot to see it before now ..."

He kept talking, but there was a ringing in my ears that covered up my ability to hear a word that came out of his mouth. What the fuck? What in the actual holy fucking fuck? Was he really telling me that he wanted to get back together? I must have been hearing this wrong. Or maybe this was a prank call. Maybe this was all some sick joke at my expense, and he was leading me down some painful path for his own sick, twisted amusement. I couldn't imagine what he would get out of it, but I could imagine him and that girl he had run away with, sitting there, snickering ...

"Marjorie?" His voice spoke my name again, and I came back to the conversation. Could I really call it a conversation when it was just monologuing from him? I didn't know. And I didn't know if I cared.

"Yes?"

"I'm so sorry that I put you through all of this," he continued, and it was like he was reading from cue cards – he had never been good at big conversations, and I supposed that he had rehearsed this all in his head before he picked up the phone.

"I needed to be apart from you to realize just how much I really *loved* you," he explained, and at once, my bullshit detector launched into action. How did that work? You didn't get to go off and cheat and then act like it had been some pious act in protection of your relationship.

"Do you understand what I'm saying?" he continued, and I honestly had no clue what I was supposed to tell him because yes, I understood what he was saying. I knew the words that were coming out of his mouth, and I knew that they were directed at me and that they were about the marriage that we had shared for all those years.

But I couldn't make sense of them because his actions did nothing to back up his words. He had left me, for goodness sake – he'd had all the time in the world to figure this out before now, but it was only when his girl left him that he began to think about what he had left behind? No, that wasn't love. That wasn't marriage. That wasn't what he had promised me.

"Marjorie, I want you back," he told me, speaking slowly, as though he was sure that I couldn't understand what he was saying.

A flare of annoyance ran through me. He had always been like this, always been so patronizing, acting like I didn't have a mind of my own when I didn't fall in line with what he wanted right away. He spoke to me like I was an idiot. This wasn't the first time, either, though I had been able to ignore it before because it was easier to sit back and simper than it was to accept that my husband was treating me like I didn't have a brain in my head.

But he wasn't my husband any longer. He had nothing to do with me. And he had no right to be calling me up and acting like he had any right at all to claim my attention. Or to expect me to come back to him. I hadn't been sitting around on my ass this whole time, politely waiting for him to come home. I had been out there and living my life. And yes, I had wound up getting hurt, but I wouldn't have swapped it for anything, because those were my experiences, everything that I had chosen to do with myself.

"I don't want you back," I told him bluntly, and I was shocked by the sound of the words coming out of my mouth. I hadn't expected to be so blunt with him. But then, he had hardly held back when he had dumped me for that woman, had he? Maybe honesty was the best policy. If he was expecting me back, then the least I could give him in response was my stone-cold honesty.

"What?" he blurted out, and it was as though the thought of me giving him this kind of answer actually hadn't crossed his mind. I took a deep breath, gathering myself, preparing to deliver the death blow to any hope of a relationship that he might be hanging onto.

"You left me, remember?" I reminded him. "You didn't feel any of this when you left me. And you had all that time, through the divorce, you had all that time to figure this out and stop it before it went through. And you know that I would have dropped everything to be with you again ..."

I caught my breath. I had imagined him coming back to me and begging me for another chance more times than I cared to admit, and every time in those fantasies, I would so sweetly invite him back into my life, and the two of us would fall in love all over again and live happily ever after.

But now, I wanted nothing to do with him. I didn't care that he was coming on strong with all of this shit. He could keep it. I had a life now, a life that had nothing to do with him. And yeah, okay, it might not be perfect, but it was mine.

"You have to listen to me, Marjorie," he pleaded. "We're meant to be together. I only saw that when I was apart from you–"

"Well, too late," I replied, firmly. "I'm not interested. I've moved on. I suggest that you do the same."

"You can't be serious," he snapped, and he actually sounded pretty mad about what was happening. Something about that delighted me. Yeah, it was childish, but he had hurt me in ways he would never understand. He deserved to feel like this, to feel the burning pain of knowing that he couldn't have what he wanted.

"We're married, Marjorie, come on," he implored me.

"We're divorced," I corrected him. "And besides, I'm dating again now. I don't have time for you."

"You're dating?" he exclaimed. "You didn't wait long, did you?"

"You didn't even wait till the marriage was over," I reminded him. "At least I had the decency for that."

And with that, I hung up the phone, and tossed it to the other side of the couch, and stood there, staring into space, wondering what the hell I had just done.

And then, I burst out laughing. All of this was so obviously and utterly crazy. My ex-husband, calling me up, begging to get back together because he had been dumped by the younger woman he left me for. She had probably gotten tired of his bullshit; she saw through it before I did – good for her. I meant that – good for her. I hoped she was out there living her best life, forgetting all about the man she'd dated for a few months. I might have been foolish enough to spend a few years with him, but that was firmly behind me now. I was moving on. Moving out. Moving up. And nothing was going to hold me back.

A few months ago, I would have dropped everything to be with Robert again. I would have done anything to unwind the mess he had made of our marriage, to convince myself that there was still really something there between us, but now I could see that all of that was just wishful thinking. I'd wanted what he promised me when we started out together, not what he had actually given me. When we married, it had been a life, a family, a world that we could explore by each other's sides. Well, now I was going to do that all by my damn self.

The sound in his voice when I had told him that I was dating. I mean, sure, he didn't have to know that my dating life had been so spectacularly crappy, did he? He just had to know that I was out there, hanging with other men, spending time with them, letting them make me feel wanted in a way he had failed to do for such a long time now. If he could have his life, then I could have mine. And I knew, now, that I didn't want him anywhere near it, not anymore.

I could do it myself if I had to. That family? Yeah, I could make it happen. That might have been what got me in contact with Blake in the first place, but I had made it as clear as I possibly could the last time I laid eyes on him that I didn't want him as part of my life any longer. There were other people who could help me in this city. The place was full of opportunity, and I just had to step up and take it.

A family. I could make a family for myself. For so long, I had been waiting around for the men in my life to give me what I needed, what I wanted, and they had all come up short. Well, now was the time that I stepped up to the plate myself. No more hiding. No more holding back. No more waiting around. I had a life to live, and I would be damned if I was going to spend another moment holding back on actually getting out there and living it.

It was time to turn my attention back to me. Not any other man – just me. I was going to start a family, and I was going to do it all by myself, and there was nothing anyone could do to change my mind on that. With renewed resolve, I felt a swell of excitement in my chest. Yes. I could do this. More than do this. I wanted to do this. And I was going to make damn sure, no matter what, that it got done.

Chapter Fourteen – Blake

"No, really, it's fine. I've just got some papers to fill out anyway," I assured Jason, as I justified why I would be spending the day at home. The last thing I wanted was to come into work that day, especially knowing who had her appointment that very afternoon.

"You sure? We could use you around, you know," he told me, sounding a little surprised, a little concerned.

"I'm sure," I replied. "I'm feeling a little rough today; I could use some time to rest up. I don't want to get anyone sick."

"Fair enough," Jason replied, but he didn't exactly sound like he was sold on my charade. I considered throwing in a demonstrative cough, but he would see through it. That was one of the only problems in working with someone who'd gone to medical school.

"I'll come by later, and we can catch up, alright?" Jason suggested. "There's some stuff I need to go over with you."

"Yeah, yeah, sure," I replied, and I hoped that I had done enough to get him off my back for the time being because the last thing I needed right now was to have to be around anyone else.

I hadn't been able to stop thinking about Marjorie since that last encounter when she told me off and looked at me like she never wanted to see me again. And I got it; I did, because I had put her through so very much, so very much that she still had no context for. I hated myself for dragging her through all of it, but the thought of stepping back, letting go ... yeah, that was equally as painful a notion to me. I was stuck in a rut, and I couldn't get out, and I had no clue what I was supposed to do with myself now.

I think what hurt most was the fact that I had allowed myself to think about a future again. Whether or not I wanted to accept it, when I was younger, I had all these fantasies about what a life with her would look like, how it would be for us once we grew up and got out of our small town and struck out into the world. Typical teenage lover stuff. But it had always felt so damn real with her. So real, it seemed, that I had never been able to fully let go of it.

What we had back then ... it was real. I knew that now. I guess a lot of people looked back on what they had in high school and saw it as nothing more than a wannabe-romance, rather than testing the reins of something you would actually take on when you grew up. But it had been different with us; it had always been different. I had known from the moment that the two of us got together that it was different. When I looked at the couples around us, the jocks and the cheerleaders making out next to the bleachers, all I saw were people who were together because circumstances had encouraged them to be. They were dating because they wanted to date, and these were the only people they could find.

But I loved Marjorie, fiercely, passionately. When I looked at her, I saw a future. I saw someone who could parent my children. I saw someone I would have followed anywhere in the world just as long as I got to be at her side. And I knew that she looked at me and saw the same thing.

Or at least, that's what I'd felt about her. Could she have really felt the same way if she had gone on to marry someone else? I mean, I had never expected her to wait around the rest of her life for me, but perhaps all she had seen me as was an experiment. We were dating because we wanted to date, not because she felt something for me like I felt for her.

Fuck. It was all just such a mess that I had a hard time keeping track of it. I had made a mess of it by signing that contract for her father, and ever since then, everything had rolled away from me. If she'd never come into that office … if I'd never laid eyes on her …

But I didn't want that. I didn't want to pass up what we had shared this time around. I didn't want to hide from it, to lie myself out of it, to move on from it. You couldn't fake that kind of passion. It just didn't work like that. People might try to capture that a dozen different ways, try to convince themselves that they could have something close to what we did, but I knew, deep down in my gut, that it wasn't that easy.

And I had passed it all up because I needed to save my family business.

I never told them about it, of course. That would have been just too cruel. I knew that they would want to try and make it up to me. But there was nothing that they could do to make it better, nothing that they could do to change it. I just had to live with the reality of knowing that, no matter how much it hurt, no matter how much it pained me. No matter the fact that I would have done anything to get her back.

I tried to focus on my work, and it did a somewhat passable job of filling in the blanks in my brain – it was mindless stuff, easy to keep myself distracted with, even if she was there, pulsing at the back of my mind the whole time. I had carried all of this with me for such a long time, and I knew – I *knew* – that I was going to blurt it out to someone one way or another. I needed to talk about this. I needed to get this off my chest.

I made it through the rest of the day until Jason was due to stop by. I was sure that he had caught onto the fact that something was going on with me; we had worked together long enough to make it all but impossible for him to miss when something wasn't right. I didn't know how the hell I was going to go about filling him in on all this – but I had to start somewhere. I had to speak to someone about the truth of everything before I lost my fucking mind trying to keep it all under wraps.

By the time he arrived, I had managed to sort through some of the mess that was going on inside my head. Not all of it, of course, but at least enough that I could tell him the truth that had kept me so distracted from work.

He arrived with coffee and a grin on his face – I didn't know how he managed to keep his energy so high after a whole day of work, but he always seemed to be bursting over with it.

"Hey," he greeted me as he stepped through the door – he had a key to my apartment for a long time, mainly to kick my lazy ass out of my bed when I was too hungover to get up for work. He was carrying a coffee with him, and he handed it to me carefully. He scanned me from top to bottom, taking me in, and then grimaced.

"Alright, so are you going to tell me what the hell is going on?" he asked, closing the door behind him and leaning on the counter.

"I don't know," I confessed. I wanted to, but emotional openness was hardly something that I had a whole lot of practice with. He might have been my best friend, but when it came to the shit that mattered, I was fiercely private and liked it that way.

"Because you don't look so sick to me," he remarked. "But you did crap out of coming into the office on the same day that the woman you were talking to was in again."

"Right," I sighed, and I looked up at him.

"Something you need to tell me?" he asked, coaxing it out of me, clearly not willing to wait any longer for me to catch up with his schedule.

"Marjorie," I told him, and even saying her name out loud sent a jolt through my system. "That woman you're talking about, that's Marjorie Kline."

"Yeah, I know, I treated her earlier today," he reminded me. "Seems like the two of you have a history, am I right?"

"You're right," I agreed.

"But you've slept with plenty of women in this city; I don't see how she—"

"It was more than just sex, Jason," I told him, and it was like I was admitting it to myself for the first time, too. "It was way more than that."

"Okay, you need to tell me what the fuck is going on here," he told me, and he planted himself down in the seat next to the counter. I put my head in my hands. I didn't even know where to start, but I knew I had to start somewhere because I had been hiding away from all of this for long enough. I was finally ready to talk.

I told him about Marjorie and me – that we had dated in high school. About the future we had planned together. How much my family loved her and how much her family hated me. About the garage, and about how it was struggling, and about how I saw my family fighting just to keep food on the table and a roof over our heads and that I felt responsible, as the oldest, to do anything I could to help them.

And then I told him about the contract. It was the first time I had ever admitted to that. I had been too humiliated to even bring it up before, but here I was, finally speaking the words out loud, finally admitting that I had been stupid enough to give this man what he wanted. I could have stood against him, that would have been something. But instead, I had pretty much held my hands up and let him do what he wanted because he didn't think I was good enough for his daughter.

"And then we met again when she came into the office," I continued. "I knew it was her right away. Turns out, she was married, but they split up recently, and so the two of us went out a couple of times, and ..."

"And let me guess, you broke the terms of the contract a few times over?" he replied. I nodded.

"I called things off with her a couple of weeks ago," I explained. "I just stopped getting in touch with her. She didn't take it well – she went off on me in the office that one time, and we haven't seen each other since then. I figured it was best to stay out of her way while she was coming in today."

"You know, if she's going to be one of our clients, you can't avoid her forever," he pointed out.

I shrugged. "I can until I actually stop thinking about her all the time," I replied.

He grinned and shook his head. "You know that's not how this works."

"You don't want me around her," I warned him. "If her father finds out ..."

"Then we could lose everything we've been working for," he finished up for me, bluntly. "Yeah, I get that. And trust me when I say that I'm as unhappy about it is as you are."

"I'm sorry that I didn't tell you about this sooner," I confessed. "I should have come clean to you about it—"

"Yeah, but you didn't, and I doubt that I would have believed you if you had," he replied. "We just need to figure out a way to make this work now that all the cards are on the table."

"So what the fuck do we do?" I asked. I was glad to finally have someone else in on this whole mess. Jason had always been a voice of reason when everything going on in my life seemed batshit insane. I was grateful to have him around – always would be. And man, did I need someone to come out and help me right about now because there was no game plan to take on what I was looking down the barrel at right now.

"Look, I don't like this any more than you do, but I think you've got to put some space between you guys," he said. "I can tell that you still have feelings for her—"

I opened my mouth to protest, but he just lifted his hand and stopped me dead in my tracks. He knew me too well for me to lie to him about this.

"But we'd be risking so much if you were to go after her," he finished up. "And I'm sorry, but I can't let you pull everything I've worked for into that. Not to mention the fact that I don't want you to end up shooting yourself in the foot over this. You've worked hard; you don't deserve for some uppity asshole to come sliding in and take it all from you."

I nodded. I knew he was right. Didn't want to admit it, for sure. But he was right.

"You need to make sure that there's nothing in that contract that's going to land either of us in trouble," he said. "Okay? And then we're going to take it to the lawyers and have them go over it and see if there's any chance at all for us to find a way out of it."

"Right," I agreed, and I let out a breath I didn't know I had been holding. *Jesus.* I didn't realize how much I had been holding in until I let it all out. My whole body felt lighter.

"And in the future, you need to tell me when you're getting caught up in shit like this," he warned me. "I don't want anything else coming out of the woodwork to surprise me, okay?"

"Okay," I promised him. And I meant it. I didn't want this to go on a moment longer. No more lies, no more hiding, no more anything. But, above it all, no more Marjorie.

But even the thought of that was enough to make my heart sink.

Chapter Fifteen – Marjorie

I looked over the files that were splayed out on my living room table. Something was holding me back. Something I couldn't quite put my finger on.

In front of me, in theory, was everything I would need to know about the man who was going to father my child. Well, was father the right word? I had no idea. I had collected the sperm donor files from the office that Jason referred me to earlier in the week once all my fertility testing had come back normal, and now I should be picking out what guy I wanted to do this with.

"You should just go for the hottest one," Terri had told me when I came clean to her and Stephanie about what I was doing.

"No, no, you want to go for the one who's got the best job," Stephanie replied, shaking her head. "That way, you know they're going to have ambition ..."

"And how can you know whether or not he just got that job because of family money or something?" Terri protested.

Stephanie cocked an eyebrow at her. "Well, because I doubt that anyone with that amount of cash is going to donate sperm to try and scrape rent together," Stephanie pointed out.

Terri shrugged. "Still, at least it shows that he's got a little imagination," she replied. They both looked over at me. I was staring off into space, trying to take in everything they were saying, and feeling like I was going to collapse under the weight of it all.

"You okay, Marj?" Terri asked me, and I nodded quickly.

"Oh, yeah, fine!" I exclaimed, probably a little louder than I had to. Terri and Stephanie exchanged a look. Yeah, I had been *way* louder than I needed to be.

Stephanie took me aside later in the day – I supposed she was still trying to wrap her head around this just the same as I was. I had sprung this on them out of nowhere, the fact that I was going to try for a baby with some mystery sperm donor, but I knew I needed the accountability of someone else knowing about it. I would have just kept stalling, kept putting it off otherwise, and I was so ready to move on with my life for a change. I felt like I had been in stasis for so long, and that call from Robert had shocked me out of it.

"I think it's amazing, what you want to do," she told me. And I knew I was in for one of her polite but forceful delves into what was going on in my head. She cared about us, so much that she had the nerve to stick herself in the line of fire when she thought that we were making a choice that wasn't going to work.

"But you seem a little freaked about it," she remarked. "Are you sure this is what you want to be doing?"

I eyed her for a moment and chewed my lip, glad that she had come to me with these concerns. Because there was something inside me that was holding me back, and I couldn't for the life of me figure out what it was – or why I was allowing it so much space in my brain.

"I know that it must have been hard with Robert getting in touch," she continued gently. "But you don't need to prove anything to anyone. You do things at your own pace, alright? Don't rush yourself into it just because you think it's where you need to be."

"I know," I replied, and I was grateful for her reaching out to me like this. But in truth, I didn't have the words to put into speech the way I was feeling right now.

"Besides, you don't want that jerk to have a say over anything about your life anymore," she continued.

"Who, Blake?" I replied, confused.

"No, Robert," she corrected me. "But now you bring it up, him too."

"Right, of course," I agreed, and I could feel my cheeks growing a little hot when I realized that I had just brought Blake up out of nowhere. We hadn't been speaking about him, and yet, there he was, at the front of my mind, just like he always was.

I hadn't seen him since that day in the clinic when I told him off for the way he'd treated me. When it happened, I felt powerful and in control, like I was the one in charge of my fate. But it really just left more questions unanswered, more words unspoken. Yes, I had had the last word – but I didn't want there to be nothing more to say between us. I still had so many questions. What was wrong with me that had scared him away? Was it still there, deep down inside of me? Was that what had caused Robert to go looking for someone else ...?

"You alright?" Stephanie asked as she saw me vanishing down a wormhole of insecurity and panic.

I managed to smile, hoping that it looked something close to believable. "Yeah, I'm fine," I replied. "And thanks. I know, I'm not doing anything for him anymore, don't worry."

"Well, in that case, you know that you've got our support no matter what you want to do next," she told me. "You know Terri and I will be there to help you through whatever happens."

"I know," I replied and smiled at her. "You have no idea how much that means to me, really. I couldn't have gotten through any of this without you guys ..."

And I meant it, I did. But in truth, I knew that this was a choice that I had to make all by myself. It couldn't come from them, or Robert, or anyone. If I was starting a family, then I had to do it on my terms. And I had to be ready. Nothing else could be standing between me and what was to come, between the future that I could see for myself.

But the truth was, I had never imagined doing this without a partner there at my side. And I know that probably made me a bad feminist, but the thought of being a unit, raising kids together – yeah, that was what I had always wanted. Someone to do this with. Someone to help me with the hard parts. Someone I could share all of it with because the thought of doing this all alone ...

I had pictured Robert as the father for a long time. Of course I had because he had been my husband. But now that he was gone, I felt like there was an empty space where he should be. A gap that needed to be filled.

Except that I already had someone to fill it. Someone who had filled it in my head for more than a decade now. The first person I had ever allowed myself to feel that way about. The person who had found his way back into my life as a direct result of all this happening.

Blake.

Blake, Blake, Blake, the man I couldn't shake. Well, it rhymed, so it had to be true, didn't it? When I was a teenager, I had imagined our life together, the way our worlds would intertwine to fit around one another. I had imagined holding his baby in my arms, and it was so vivid it had to be real. It had to be some vision from the future, meant to guide me to make the right choice for myself. Maybe that was crazy, but perhaps it was just my brain trying to tell me that the right guy had been here all along – and that I had just been too damn stupid and obstinate to accept that he was the one.

I hated that I couldn't get him out of my mind. I had worked so hard for so long to make myself a life – to make myself something that I could be proud of and I could be happy with, something that didn't need any man to fill out. But there were questions, still questions, always questions about what I had left behind. About why I hadn't been enough for someone who had told me that he loved me. Who had promised me a future and then ripped it away before I had a chance to take hold of it.

I had to know why that was. I knew that it was crazy and that I should have left him behind by now, but it wasn't that easy – hell, if it was, I could have let go of it already.

Before I moved forward with this new version of what I wanted my life to be, I had to take a step back and think about what had gotten me to this point in the first place.

I had promised myself that I would never see Blake again, not if I could avoid it, but that wasn't an option anymore. I had to get him out of my system, and the only way I could do that was if I finally confronted him and got the truth. I had to know. I couldn't move forward until I left that part of my life behind. It was ugly, and it made me unhappy, but if I knew the truth, my past couldn't impinge on the life that I wanted anymore. I needed to find some way to let it go before I got dragged down into the mire of it and never escaped.

I couldn't help thinking about my father. He had always been the kind of man to live in the past, in what came before – he always wanted to uphold what he saw as the nobility of our family, to make sure that nobody who could smear that even got close. I knew that was why he had always hated Blake; he had never seen him as good enough for me, no matter how much I tried to convince him to the contrary. And look where that had got him. His obsession with upholding the history of our family had landed him dead, with nothing to show for it but a life that even he didn't seem to like living most of the time. I would be damned if I was going to let that happen to me. And I was going to be *damned* if I let that same attitude pass down to my children. If I was bringing a family into this world, I was doing it without anything weighing me down or holding me back.

I looked back at the piles of files on the table that were supposed to guide me into my future. I was almost ready. Almost.

I grabbed my phone and scrolled through the numbers. I had decided to hang on to Blake's for reasons that I hadn't been able to put my finger on, but I knew now that it was the right choice. Because through him, I was going to get the closure that I needed for so long. Through him, I was going to let go and move forward. I was finally going to get the answers I had been searching for since he abandoned me over a decade ago.

Chapter Sixteen – Blake

She was the last person I expected to see, though not the last person I wanted to.

Jason burst into my office just before she arrived – he'd obviously been on high alert for her appearance, and there was a panicked look on his face as he strode into the room.

"What's wrong?" I asked, furrowing my brow. It wasn't often that I saw this man flustered, but it was clear that something had seriously gotten under his skin.

"She's here," he told me, and it took me a moment to figure out who he was talking about. Who would have shaken him up so badly? But then, it hit me.

"Marjorie?" I asked, and he nodded. I got to my feet. I wasn't sure why, or what I was intending to do now that I was up, but I needed to move around.

"She's in the office, and she says she wants to speak to you," he told me. "I can get security to take her out if you want, or–"

"No, let her in," I told him.

He stared at me for a long moment. "You know what you're risking if you let her come in here, right?"

I nodded. My mind was made up.

"And you're willing to put all that on the line just to see her again?"

I nodded once more. I could tell that he was shocked, but he had asked for the truth, and I had given it to him. I saw no reason to lie to Jason. I had avoided her as best I could, but if she was here, if she was looking for me, then that wasn't going to work much longer.

"I know her," I explained. "If she's here, then it's because she's got something serious she wants to talk to me about. We're not going to get rid of her by just ignoring her and keeping our fingers crossed and hoping for the best."

"Ten minutes," he told me. "You hear? Ten minutes, and then I'm getting rid of her. I'm not letting you put this place at risk for her."

"Fine," I agreed. "Ten minutes. Now, can you send her in so I can actually speak to her?"

He eyed me for one more moment, as though he was waiting for me to change my mind and back out of this. But I simply looked back at him, coolly, knowing that he knew there was no point in arguing. With that, he tossed his hands in the air, defeated, and headed back out to get Marjorie.

I found that my pulse was racing as I waited for her to come in. I knew that I shouldn't let myself get so panicked, but how could I fight it? Had something happened? Had she found out about the contract and was now here to tell me that she thought I was a spineless bastard who should have fought for her when I had the chance? If she came in declaring all of that, I could hardly argue with her.

She appeared in the doorway, and I swear I had to catch my breath as soon as I saw her. How was it that she could be so absurdly and outrageously beautiful even when she looked like she wanted to pop my head like a grape? Maybe it was something to do with that – I had always loved how passionate she was about everything. When she was committed to something, she was seriously committed to it, and that meant that she had to be committed to me and this and whatever the heck was going to come with it.

"Marjorie," I greeted her, and I extended my hand to greet her, playing like this was just the same as any other meeting we might have had. "How can I help you?"

"Oh, drop the bullshit," she snapped. "This is serious."

"Serious enough for you to come to interrupt me in the middle of my workday?"

"Don't start with me on that," she said, and there was an aching sadness to her voice that made my heart hurt. I used to be the one who could take that pain away, but now I was quite sure that I was the one who had put that pain there in the first place.

"Then what can I start with you on?" I demanded, raising my eyebrows at her pointedly. "You're not exactly giving me a lot of options here ..."

"Fuck," she muttered, and she rubbed her hand over her face in distress. I felt bad for her. Even now, after all this time, all I wanted to do was reach into her head and find some way to convince her that this was all going to be fine. The attachment ran deep and powerful, stronger than I cared to admit. Even after everything that had happened between us.

"Okay, calm down," I told her, and I took her arm and guided her into the chair opposite mine at my desk. I expected her to shake me off and tell me to leave her alone, but instead, she let me show her the way. She sank into the seat as though she was glad to finally take the weight off for a moment. I wondered how long she had been rushing around on this passionate journey of something-or-other that I had to assume I was a part of.

"Can you tell me what you're doing here?" I asked her as gently as I could. I didn't want to set off another rolling wave of anger in my direction, but the time we had was limited.

She put her head in her hands, took a deep breath, and then looked back up at me. "I need to know why," she told me, softly, finally.

It felt like someone had ripped the ground out from underneath me. This was the question that I had been straining to avoid all this time – the one that I would have given anything to put to the back of my mind for the rest of my life. But now she was here, looking at me, needing that answer. The tremor in her voice spoke to years of wondering, waiting, holding back, hiding.

And, after all this time, I felt like she deserved an answer. But that was part of the contract. If I told her, and she went to confront her father, I would be fucked – totally fucked. There was no way out of this that didn't end badly for me one way or another. I just had to choose my poison.

"You wouldn't tell me before," she continued, speaking slowly. "I know I should have been more direct, but I thought – well, I thought you would be sticking around a little longer. But then you were just gone, and it left me wondering what the fuck I did to deserve this, twice over."

She was gazing up at me, waiting for a response, and I had no idea what I was going to tell her. I opened and closed my mouth, searching for the words that would give her what she wanted. The least I owed her was the chance to move on, surely?

"Okay, let me be a little more specific since you can't seem to remember what I'm talking about," she snapped to me. She planted her hands, palms down, on the table, and fixed her eyes on me.

"I want to know what I did when we were teenagers that made you just run off and leave me like that," she told me. "I want to know how badly I fucked up that you were happy to promise all that stuff to me, and then just walk away like none of it had ever mattered to you."

"Marjorie, it's complicated ..."

"I don't see how that's possible," she replied bluntly. "You just stopped caring about me, right? That's the only explanation that makes sense. And when I came back into this office, you saw a chance for a quick fuck with someone you knew had never got over you ..."

She caught her breath like she had given away too much. I stared at her. She hadn't gotten over me? I had never imagined that. I knew that my connection with her sustained, but I had assumed that she had swiftly gotten over me. She had been married, for goodness sake. You couldn't do that if you were still hung up on somebody else ...

"So I think the least you fucking owe me is the truth," she finished up, gathering herself once more. I could hear her voice shaking slightly. I felt so fucking guilty, so guilty for putting her through all of this, and for being too much of a coward to just tell her what had really happened.

She dragged her gaze away from mine and shook her head, snorting, as though she couldn't believe that she had allowed herself to think that she would get what she wanted from this meeting. "Jesus Christ," she muttered, rolling her eyes. "You really have nothing to say for yourself? You really don't give a shit?"

"I care," I told her, fiercely. "Don't you ever think for a second that I don't care."

"But not enough to let me move on from this?" she demanded. "I can't let go of this, not when I don't know what I did to ... to make it so you didn't love me anymore."

I took a deep breath. How could I tell her it was never to do with how much I loved her? That I had loved her more than I ever loved anyone since? It hurt to hear her refer to herself like that, to the love that I had for her in the past tense. I wished I could draw it back up to the here and now, that I could make her see just how crazy I was about her, just how crazy I had always been. But I was being silenced by that contract, by that fucking contract.

"I know you can just fall out of love with people," she told me, her voice shaking – I wondered how long she had bitten back those words, how long she had fought the urge to say them to my face. I thought back to all

113

those moments on the dates that we'd had together when it had seemed as though she was on the very brink of coming out with something. Had this been what was on her mind then? Maybe. More than maybe.

"I know because that's what happened with my father before he died," she went on. "I know that he just stopped being in love with my mom, and–"

"Wait." I held my hand up and stopped her in her tracks. I hadn't even thought to ask about her father. I had just assumed that he was still alive and kicking and determined to make the contract he'd built with me stick, no matter what. It hadn't even passed through my brain to think that he wasn't around any longer.

"What is it?" she snapped back. "You finally got something to say for yourself?"

"Your father's dead?" I asked, bluntly. She winced, and I realized how harsh those words must have sounded coming out of my mouth.

She hesitated for a moment, and then she nodded. "Yes," she replied quietly. "Yes, he's dead."

That changed everything. That contract only lasted as long as we were both still alive. And if the contract was over, that meant ...

"Marjorie," I asked her before I could find a way to talk myself out of it. "Will you come to dinner with me? Tonight?"

"What for?" she replied, her arms crossed over her chest.

"Because there's something I need to tell you," I replied, and I reached out to take her hand. She actually let me.

"Fine," she replied softly, and I squeezed her hand tight. I would have told her right then and there, but I needed some time to figure out what I was going to say, and how I was going to make it up to her.

"Thank you," I told her, and I meant it. This was my last chance to make things right with her, and I knew that this time, I wasn't going to fuck it up. This time, I was going to make it stick. This time ... this time, everything was going to be different. And fuck, what a relief it was to think that I could finally tell the truth to the woman I loved.

Chapter Seventeen – Marjorie

I was stupid for giving him another chance.

I knew that's what everyone would say if they could hear what I was about to do. I had declined to tell Steph or Terri because it just seemed way too much like jinxing it to invite any more speculation into the game.

I had been running it over and over in my head enough for the three of us, anyway, since he invited me out to dinner. Something seemed to change in him when he heard that my father had passed, and I couldn't help thinking that maybe, just maybe ... maybe I was going to get the answers I had been searching for all this time.

But that was just stupid hope again. The same hope that had gotten me into this mess in the first place. I should have known better now, known to let go and move on, but it just didn't work like that. Not with him. Never with him.

I fidgeted at the table and wondered if everyone in this place was looking at me. Probably. It felt like they were judging me for being back here again. It was the same place we had come that first night when I had invited him back to my place and this whole mess kicked off.

I had arrived early, and I was still waiting for him when the clock ticked around to seven, the time we had agreed to meet. Was he going to stand me up?

But then I caught sight of him walking through the door, and my heart jumped, and my head tried to calm down, and everything felt like it was twisting into circles. I smoothed my skirt over my legs and checked my nails. I had to make it look like I didn't give a damn.

He made his way over to the table; I looked up at him, waiting for him to lean down and give me a kiss on the cheek or to say my name or to greet me or something, but he didn't. Instead, he took his seat opposite me and looked at me.

"I'm sorry," he said. "I wanted to tell you that first. I'm sorry that I put you through all of this. You have no idea how much I want to go back and change everything. If I could ..." He stopped himself, probably figuring that going any further wouldn't be as good to me as just hearing, once and for all, what the fuck had been happening all this time.

"I wanted to tell you before now," he explained, and he reached into his bag and pulled out a wad of papers. "But I had to hold back. There were these contracts; I could have lost my business ..."

"What the hell are you talking about?" I asked. I felt desperate, honestly – I needed to know one way or another what was happening, and all of this seemed like a bigger mess than I could take on.

He pushed the wad of papers across the table toward me. "Look at these," he told me.

I frowned and did as I was told, picking up the papers and starting to leaf through them. It was all small-type, legalese – an agreement made between Blake Mathieson, and ...

"Why do you have a contract with my father?" I gasped. This didn't make sense. The two of them had hated one another, and there wasn't a chance in hell that Blake would ever have agreed to work with him ...

"This was the paper he made me sign so that he could get me to leave you alone for good," Blake told me. I dropped the papers. They scattered around the floor surrounding us, like fresh snow. The waitress dived down to help me pick them up, but I couldn't move a muscle.

"What the fuck are you saying?" I asked, as quietly as I could. If there was ever a moment that I thought I was being conned, it was right now. Because there was no way it could be real.

"It was back when my family was struggling," he explained quickly like he didn't want to drag this out any longer. "We needed the loan. And he was the one who had to sign off on it. He knew that we didn't have the money to support all of us, as well as my studies, and he took advantage of that ..."

"You're telling me," I began, slowly, surely, making sure that I hadn't fucked this up, "that my father got you to sign this contract so that he could ...?"

"So that he could make sure that I didn't see you again," he told me, and he grabbed one of the papers and pointed to it. "Look. It says here. He made me promise that I wouldn't contact you. He never thought I was good enough for you, not ever, and we needed the money so much ... Jesus, Marjorie, if I could have done this without hurting you, you know that I would have, in a second ..."

He trailed off, and I could feel his eyes on me. I wanted to say

116

something, but what the hell was I supposed to come out with? It had to be a lie. My father could be an asshole, but surely he never would have gone this far. Not really. That was insane.

"This doesn't make any sense," I muttered. I didn't know what else to say. I was looking over the contracts and searching for something in them that would render all of this a lie – something that would expose this for the bullshit that it was. But I couldn't find it. Those were my father's signatures, that was my family's address, every single detail down to the very last letter told me that this was real.

Contracts. Money. That loan. My father had paid him off to leave me. But what choice had Blake really had? I knew how much his family had struggled, and I knew that he hardly had a choice in all of this. He was a teenager, he was a kid, and he was handed this level of responsibility. He was handed a choice between me and his family, and he had taken the one that nearly anyone would have taken in his position.

"I can't believe this," I breathed. But the worst part of it all was that I could. My father had been a good dad to me in many ways, and he'd been an awful man in many others. When it came to getting things his way, he would have done anything to make sure it happened. Blake was right. My father had always despised him, even when he pretended otherwise. I thought that he had sucked it up for my sake, but no – he had made sure that my heart paid the price for his hatred.

This was all too much. I put my head into my hands and felt the tears running down my cheeks. This was insane. I had carried this pain for years, for more than a decade, and this secret had been hidden out in the middle of it. Everything that had happened had started here when I had been led to believe that the man who had promised to love me for life had left me without a word of explanation as to why.

"Marjorie? Are you okay?" Blake asked with concern.

I looked up at him and shook my head. "How the fuck am I supposed to be okay with any of this?" I demanded. "It doesn't ... it doesn't make any sense ..."

"You don't believe me?" he asked worriedly.

I shook my head. I wanted to think that he was lying to me, but in truth, I knew my father too well to think that this wasn't the kind of thing he would go for. "I believe you," I replied, and I gestured to the papers scattered across the table in front of me. "Doesn't look like I have too much of a choice, really ..."

"I didn't want to tell you like this," he told me, and his voice was hard-edged.

I didn't know what to feel. Yes, there was some part of me that was angry, but there was another that was confused, another still that was upset, and some others that were just baffled that any of this could have come to be at all. It all seemed like ... it all seemed impossible. Like someone had come up with this specifically to anger or confuse me.

It hurt, even more, to think that it had been my own father who put this on me in the first place. I'd known that he was a selfish man as soon as he left my mother for someone younger and more refined, but I had never imagined that he would have worked this hard to hurt me when he knew how I felt. He had stripped me of the most important thing in my life. I felt a flare of anger pulsing through my veins, fury that he had thought that he had any right to define how my life unfolded.

"I was risking so much just seeing you as it was," Blake explained quickly. "I knew that it was too dangerous for us to start dating again – with your father around, I mean. I thought that he would try and call in the contract, maybe take my business given that so many of my assets were tied up in that. I spoke to my partner about it, and he was just as freaked as I was."

He was still talking, but I could barely hear a word coming out of his mouth. I wanted to listen to him, I did, but how could I do that when my brain was running through everything that this had revealed about my family? Had my mother known about this? Had they both conspired to keep me from this man that I loved? I looked at him across the table, and I searched for the words to tell him what he needed to hear.

"I don't blame you," I told him, at last.

His chest deflated as though he had been holding in all this tension from the moment he'd walked through the door. "I'm still sorry," he told me. "If I could take it back ..."

"You can't," I replied, bluntly. I knew that was harsh, but I didn't want him dragging this out any further. It took a damn lot of nerve to come here and tell me such a difficult truth about my own family. The kind of nerve that I would have expected from the younger version of him. The one that, now, I could see gazing back at me from the other side of the table.

And I felt a swell of joy rush through me. He had never gone, not the way that I feared he had. He had never left me. I had been so sure that the man I loved before was nowhere to be found, but I could see that it had just been a figment of my imagination. As he gazed at me, waiting for me to speak again, a smile spread across my face.

"You can't take it back," I told him. "But you've done what you can. And you have no idea how much of a relief it is to hear that I wasn't losing my mind this entire time."

"What do you mean ...?"

"I thought you just stopped loving me," I admitted. "You'd been so sure about me before, and then you just dropped off the face of the Earth like it was nothing, and I felt like I was never going to see you again."

"I think that's how your father would have had it if he could."

I waved my hand. "Fuck him," I replied, and I meant it. I had known he'd been a shit before, but this was above and beyond. This was an attempt to control me in a way that he never had before. All this time, he had known, and he had lied to me ...

"I don't want you to hold this against him," Blake told me. "I don't want you to look at me and think of what he did."

"It's going to take a while before I can forgive him," I admitted. "But it's ... I can still see you. It's hard, but I can still see you."

"God, I missed you so much," he told me, and he reached over and clasped my hands tight. The sudden gesture made my head spin. His touch was unfettered by our past now. When I looked at him, I didn't see all the questions that I was still clinging to, the words that had gone unspoken, all the wondering I had done.

"I missed you too," I admitted. " All this time, I thought you just left me ..."

"I would never have done that, not if I had the choice," he told me fervently. "I felt like I was between a rock and a hard place. I had to lose you, or I had to put my whole family in danger for something they didn't even get a say in."

"I don't blame you," I replied. "I can't imagine what that must have been like."

"You can't," he agreed, and he shook his head and winced. "I didn't think I could do it, not really – I kept on thinking that I was going to have to go back and tell you so I could make things right, but then all this time passed, and I couldn't imagine that you would ever want to see me again as long as you lived."

"I thought that too," I admitted. "I really thought that everything would be easier if I could just never see you again. But then I walked into that office ..."

"Shit, yeah, you have no idea how it felt to see you like that," he replied with a chuckle. "I was sure it couldn't be you. I was sure there had to be some mistake. It all just seemed ... too fucking crazy. After all this time ..."

"I don't know if I believe in fate and all that stuff," I told him. "But it seems like too much of a coincidence otherwise, huh?"

"Too much," he echoed. He was still holding my hands. I couldn't stop looking at his fingers wrapped around mine. This felt so good, so right – all this time apart, and finally I had the truth, and finally I could look at him as the man I had known when I had loved him. Not a liar, not someone who fled from me when things got too much. The man I wanted more than anything.

"Does your family know about any of this?" I wondered suddenly.

He shook his head. "I just kept it quiet," he replied. "I hadn't told anyone else, actually, until I spoke to my partner about it a few weeks ago."

"You've been carrying this all by yourself, all this time?" I murmured. I could hardly imagine how heavy it must have been.

"Yeah, I have, but not anymore," he told me with a smile on his face. He seemed so much lighter like a weight had been pulled from his shoulders.

"If I could have done this differently, you know that I would," he continued. "But as long as it means that I get to be with you now ..."

I jolted in my seat. Did he still want that? I had been so close to being ready to move on, and now he was pulling me back in. He was looking at me, and he was telling me that he wanted to be with me, and the life I had imagined for us suddenly came slotting back into place. It might not be how I imagined this going down, but I would take it, I would take anything I could get as long as he was there to share it with me.

"If you want that," he finished up, seemingly sensing some of my reticence. I didn't have the words to tell him how wrong he was about that; I wanted it, I wanted him, I wanted the future that he was offering me. But it was all coming in so hard and fast that I was having a hard time keeping up with it. My brain was racing trying to keep up with what was going on, and the only anchor I could find was in his eyes, holding me down to Earth, to reality.

"I ..." I whispered, and he pressed his lips together as though he was holding in a breath. Everything we had been through came down to this moment – came down to me admitting whether or not I actually wanted him back. Because I knew that if I told him no, he would leave me alone. He would respect that, even though I knew that it would kill him to be apart from me again because he loved me. He had always loved me, and it was just that the words to speak that love out into the world had been taken from him. But now, now that he knew he could say them out loud again, he wasn't holding back, and his presence, his sureness, his certainty reminded me how good it was to be loved by him once more.

"I think you should come back to my place," I told him, finally. I didn't know what I wanted to say to him, not yet, but I knew that everything that needed to be said couldn't be declared in this restaurant full of people. I needed him all to myself, and I needed him to listen to every word that came out of my mouth. I needed this to be between us and us alone. Nobody else. Not my father, not his partner, not my ex, not anyone.

"Then let's get out of here," he said. He got to his feet and offered me his hand.

I took it at once. And I knew that this time, everything was going to be different. It had to be. I couldn't wait to see what that difference looked like. And I couldn't wait to tell him everything that had been on my mind for the last twelve years.

Chapter Eighteen – Blake

I knew what was going to happen before we so much as got back to the apartment. Yeah, we could have talked, maybe should have talked instead, but that was so much less interesting than what I really wanted from her. We were free from the binds of the contract, and I wanted to celebrate that by taking in her body every way that I could with no fear that it was going to come back and bite me in the ass.

She held my hand as we headed back through the city to her place, and I marveled at the fact that we could actually do that together now. I didn't have to worry about anyone seeing us; I didn't have to worry about being busted in the act of being with her. I was free. Totally free.

I took her into my arms before the door to her apartment building had even closed behind us, and she smiled into the kiss. I knew that she had been waiting for this just as long as I had, and it was hard to remember any reason good enough to keep this from ourselves. I kissed her and kissed her and kissed her and pushed everything else to the back of my mind.

One of her neighbors opened their door, and we sprang apart, caught in the act; Marjorie burst out laughing and clapped a hand over her mouth to silence herself, and the two of us, still snickering, made it the rest of the way through her apartment door.

We tumbled over it together, still giggling, and she dragged me straight to the bed – no reason to hold back, no reason to stop, we could just have each other the way we wanted all this time. I kissed her like my life depended on it, and she kissed me back as though I was her only source of oxygen, and I climbed on top of her and pushed her arms above her head so I could watch the way that her body reacted so easily to my own. God, she was perfect. She was *perfect*. Every inch of her, every part of her, everything that lay hidden in her depths. I wouldn't have changed a thing, except how long we had spent apart from one another.

I ducked down and kissed her again, and she moved her hips up to meet mine. I was already hard beneath my pants, and I needed to be inside her. I needed to feel her around me. I let go of her arms, and she meshed her fingers into my hair, pushing them over my scalp, her nails scratching and her fingers digging and her body arching and aching and calling out for mine any way that it could. She didn't need to say a word; she just needed to be there, and I could read her like a book.

"I want you inside me," she breathed in my ear, her tone tense and taut, and I had no intention of keeping her from what she craved.

My hands were quick as they undressed her, and I wondered if she had been thinking about this as much as I had – if she had lain awake in bed picturing the two of us together, all those memories running together until she couldn't tell the difference between what had happened and what she wanted to happen.

I smoothed her hair back from her face once I got her naked underneath me, and she looked up at me, her eyes wide and glowing with all the promise that had been taken from us all those years ago. For a moment, I was overwhelmed with emotion; I felt so much for her, so much that I hadn't had a chance to tell her, but I knew that would come later. We had all the time in the world. For now, we just needed our bodies to speak into one another, and to forget that anything had ever drawn us apart.

I rolled beneath her and undressed myself as she helped out as best she could. Our breath was mingling together, the space between us dipping and falling away until there was nothing but the sound of her and the sound of me and the sound of us together. I pulled her on top of me, and she parted her legs and hovered herself above me for a moment; I just took her in, took in that strong, beautiful body, that body that had been through so much and still remained as gloriously perfect as it had ever been.

Slowly, she planted her hands on her chest and let herself down on top of me. The moan that escaped her lips seemed to fill the small apartment completely, leaving no room for anything but the way she looked at that moment. I closed my eyes and took it in, the feeling of her pussy around my cock, and gripped hold of her hips so that I could pull her down even further.

"Fuck," I groaned, and she just panted in response. I knew how she felt. When we were together, everything else seemed to slow and still around us. How could I even think about anything else? Her skin, the feel of her body around mine, the revelation that we had been made to fit together ... I reached up and linked my fingers through hers, and I held her hands as she began to move on top of me.

It was then that I just let the feelings take over. Not just the physical sensation, though of course she felt amazing – but the emotion, too;

knowing that this was mine now. All the walls that had been thrown up between us had fallen down, and we could just *be* now, no more lies, no more questions, nothing but the two of us, the way it was always meant to be.

I pushed myself up from the bed and wound my arms around her, holding her in place as I thrust up into her. I could feel her nails on my back and her breath on my ear, and I kept moving, harder, harder, harder, listening to her moans as they grew more insistent. I wanted her to come. I wanted to remind her how good we were together.

When she gave in, I could feel it – even if she hadn't let out a loud cry that filled the entire room, I could feel her pussy tightening over and over again around my cock. I held her in place as best I could, even as she writhed helplessly and let the pleasure careen through her, holding her down, holding her to me, reminding her that even when she felt out of control, I would be here to hold her and keep her safe.

As soon as I felt her come back down to Earth again, I flipped her over and pushed deep inside of her, winding my fingers around hers again, looking at her and watching her and taking her in as she let me take her. I leaned down to kiss her and tasted her again, feasting myself on the way that she felt against my lips. I would never get tired of this. I would never get tired of her. If there was one thing I was sure of, above all else in the world, it was that.

"Come inside me," she moaned into my ear. And that was all the permission I needed – I hadn't realized how close I was until she said that, and I felt myself give out inside of her, my cock twitching as I filled her up with my seed. The intimacy of sharing that with her was something I had never experienced before, and I held myself inside of her deep, not wanting to pull out, not wanting this to be over quite yet.

Slowly, we unwound from each other, and I slipped down on to the bed beside her and reached my arm out over her stomach. I wanted to be close to her, even though we were done – I wanted to feel every inch of her body. It was something I had never felt with anyone else. For such a long time, I had tried to manufacture the intimacy that I shared with her with other people while I knew; I *knew* that I couldn't do that. It was only now that I was near her again that I could see how futile an attempt it had been.

Once she caught her breath, she reached a hand over and let it rest on my back. It was as though she was just making sure I was still there. I knew how she felt. After all this time apart, it was hard to believe that we were both really here, that this was really happening, that I wasn't going to have to crap out and flee in the morning for fear of losing everything I had.

"That was fucking incredible," she murmured.

"Or incredible fucking," I replied.

She laughed and shook her head. "You never could resist wordplay, could you?"

"You still remember that?" I asked, surprised that it had stuck in her mind. She nodded.

"Of course I do. I remember all of it. I remember being in love with you," she admitted, softly, her words tangled with nerves. "I remember how that felt. I don't think I ever really forgot it ..." She stared at me for a moment longer like she was waiting for permission to keep going.

I decided that I had to be the one to say this first – I had to be the one to come out with it. "I never forgot, either," I confessed, and I reached over and touched her cheek. "I don't think I ever really stopped loving you, actually."

She sucked in a sharp breath, surprised, and for a moment, I thought I had gone too far. But then I saw her expression mellow, and I knew that it hadn't been too much for her. In fact, it had barely been enough.

"I love you," I told her. "I've always loved you. Really, I have. I didn't know that anyone could love someone as much as I love you, but I do. And I don't think I'm ever going to be able to stop."

She closed her eyes for a moment like she was letting those words sink in. I needed a second, too. I might have known they were true, but it was the first time I had admitted them to myself, let alone anyone else. Let alone the woman I thought I would never get to say them to.

"I love you, too," she replied at last, after a pause to gather herself. "I love you so much."

I reached over and pulled her against me, savoring the sweetness of having her body so near to mine. Jesus, what a gift it was to just let this happen at last. For so long, I had run from it, sure that being with her would ruin my life, but all this time I had been too blind to see that it was being apart from her that was ruining things for me.

"I missed you so much," I told her, and I briefly let my nose rest against her head. She was here, really here, truly here. I could have stayed in this spot for the rest of the night if she'd let me.

"I missed you too," she murmured back, and she nuzzled herself into my chest and let out a long sigh, as though she was expelling everything she had been carrying with her all this time.

"Can you stay tonight?" she asked.

"I thought you were never going to ask," I replied. "I have to get to work tomorrow, but maybe we can get breakfast before I go out?"

"That sounds awesome," she agreed. "And then I have to start figuring out what to do now that I know about the contract ..."

"Anything I can do to make that easier on you, you know you just have to ask," I told her.

She squeezed herself against me. "I know," she agreed. "And I'm going to need you to help me. But I just want to enjoy this right now; is that alright by you?"

"More than alright," I murmured, and I wrapped my arms around her and closed my eyes.

Chapter Nineteen – Marjorie

"You know, you don't have to come with me for this," I told Blake, but he waved his hand and dismissed my protests at once.

"I don't have to, but I really want to," he replied, and he pulled my hand to his lips and kissed my knuckles. I smiled. He was such a romantic. He couldn't keep his hands off me; he would take every chance he got to touch me or hold me or kiss me whenever he could.

I knew how he felt, though. We had wasted so much time being apart, and I couldn't imagine wasting another second of it now that we were together. The last few weeks had been a rush, but I had savored every single second I got to spend with him.

I had needed time to myself, as well, of course, because I was still trying to wrap my head around everything I had found out about my father. I knew that he had pulled a lot of shit over the course of his miserable life, but this was above and beyond anything that I ever could have predicted.

It fucking *hurt* to know that the man who was supposed to protect me above all else was the same one who had taken the most important thing in my life from me. I supposed that I hated him, at least for a little while, he had done this to ruin my life. I wished I could confront him about it and get an answer as to why he made it happen. But I couldn't. I supposed in some ways it was better that I would never get the answer that I craved so badly. He could never give me anything other than his own, selfish reasons, the same reasons he had thrown around when he hurt my mother so badly, the same reasons that he used to justify so many of the awful things he had done in his life. Those weren't good enough for me, not really. Nothing would be good enough.

All I could do was know that it had happened, know that it had driven me and Blake apart, but understood that it had drawn us back together, too. It was through Blake's brutal honesty that I had managed to trust him again, an honesty that I would never have believed him capable of.

The more time that I had to take it in, the more I realized that it might have been ... maybe calling it a *good* thing was too close to a lie, but it had given us both time to grow up as people before we came together once more. The future I had wanted for us when we were eighteen was a fantasy existence, no matter how appealing it might have been to me then. It was built around the notions of what I thought I *should* want from my life, not what I knew I did. Who's to say if we would ever have gotten out of our hometown, ever come to this city, ever gotten off our asses and chased down the dreams that had fulfilled us?

And now the two of us were in a place where we could actually do what we had always dreamed of. Settle down. Set up a home together. It was early days yet, and neither of us had actually come out and said anything about moving in together or starting a family, but it didn't need to be said. That was the glorious thing about having so much history; we didn't have to run over every little detail because we already knew what was going on between us. I could see from the look in his eyes when he woke me in the morning that he was thinking about what it would be like to do this when we were old and grey. And when he kissed me on the cheek as I was making breakfast for the two of us, I could almost feel the image of doing this with a family by our side pass from his imagination to mine. We had a connection that burned bright, impossible to hide from or deny.

Terri and Stephanie had been a little concerned for me when I first told them everything, but then they met him, and all of that just fell away. They could see how crazy he was about me and how crazy I was about him. It took them a while to believe that the contract story was anything other than a crazy fabrication, but when I showed them the copies, they took him at his word.

"I just can't believe the two of you are really doing this again," Terri had remarked, leaning on the counter as she watched me practically dancing around the store while I did a restock.

"Yeah, well, me neither," I replied. "It's the last thing I expected."

"Oh, come on." Steph laughed. "You've wanted this right from when you first saw him again, don't lie."

"Was it that obvious?" I asked, grinning at her.

"Well, if my blind ass saw it, it was pretty obvious," Terri teased, and she hopped off the counter and came to help me with a box.

"Guess so," I agreed. "You guys don't think it's totally ridiculous, though, do you?"

"Of course we do," Stephanie replied. "But if it makes you happy, that's all I care about."

"You guys are more than I deserve," I told them, and I was suddenly overwhelmed with emotion. It had been happening a lot lately actually, these rushes of feeling. It was as if everything I had been trying to contain all this time was bubbling up and over and I could feel again – feel everything that I had fought so hard to hold back. It was a little scary in some ways, but more than anything, it felt liberating to know that I could actually have emotions again.

I was carrying on with the fertility check-ups, though it was really more a formality than anything else. Everything had been going well so far, and I was happy knowing that all the time and effort I had put into taking care of myself had paid off. I had thought that I would be doing this with Robert, of course, but it turned out that the universe had a totally different plan in mind for me.

And now, it was the day of my final exam – nothing serious, just a quick ultrasound to make sure there was nothing that might get in the way of me conceiving. We hadn't talked much about it, but I was sure that Blake was at the same place I was with it. I was sure that he wanted to have this baby with me just as much as I wanted to have it with him. That was why he had insisted on coming to all these appointments with me; he was making sure that there was nothing he needed to do to keep me safe and happy and healthy for us to start a family. We had a whole lot of time to catch up on, and neither of us intended to waste another split second waiting around any longer.

He drove me down to the clinic where they were conducting the exam and held my hand all the way, as though he could sense how nervous I was. I had been freaking out since I got up that morning, even though I knew there was nothing to be worried about. I had been feeling a little funny down there lately, and I was concerned that this exam was going to turn something up that I didn't want to deal with.

We got out of the car, and I could have sworn that I felt a little wobble around my knees. He put his arm around me and guided me toward the office.

"Is everything alright?" he asked gently.

I nodded. "Everything's fine," I promised him. "Just a little nervous, that's all. I want to get this done with, and then we can ..."

"Then we can get down to starting a family," he finished up for me. I beamed at him. He had read my mind.

The scan was taking place at a clinic that worked with Blake and Jason, and the doctor conducting my exam greeted Blake warmly and led us into the room where it would be taking place.

"And this is just a general check-up, right?" the doctor asked as he snapped on a pair of gloves and Blake helped me up into the seat that I would be chilling in for the remainder of our time here. I nodded.

"I just want to make sure that everything is in good working order down there," I replied, and Blake squeezed my hand tight. He knew how much this meant to me. Even though I knew that thirty wasn't that old to be having a baby in this day and age, there was still a part of me that was freaking out that I had left it too long and that I was going to pay the price for that.

"I'm sure it is," the doctor replied warmly, and he and Blake chatted a little about their work – I tried to listen, but I was too jittery to think about anything but how this exam was going to go. Blake, seeming to sense that I was feeling a little out of sorts, kept tight hold of my hand the whole time.

"Okay, so I'm just going to ask you to roll up your shirt so I can apply this gel," the doctor explained, and his deep, authoritative voice calmed me down a little bit. I was in good hands. No matter what happened here, I knew that Blake would support me. Nothing was going to scare him away or get him to think any less of me.

I winced as the doctor applied the gel – it was cooler than I had thought it would be, and my toes curled in my shoes. I was going to have to get used to this if I was actually going to have a baby, wasn't I? I watched as the doctor reached for the machine and wondered how many times I would come in here – how many times I would get to look inside myself and see the little creature that I had made. Not that there would be anything there to see this time around, but soon, soon enough, I would have a child in there ...

"Alright, so it looks like everything is where it needs to be," the doctor told me as he squinted at the screen. "None of your tests came back with anything that we were concerned with, so I'm not looking for anything–"

And he stopped dead in his tracks. My heart fluttered in a panic.

"What? What is it?" I demanded, peering at the screen to try and see what it was that would have made him fall silent like that. Something was wrong; I could hear it in the tone of his voice ...

"Hold on," Blake murmured, and he leaned forward to get a better look at the screen. "That's not ...?"

"I think it is," the doctor replied, and his eyebrows shot up. "Well, I can safely say that's the first time anything like that has happened here."

"What is it?" I demanded again. They didn't seem as worried anymore, but they knew what was going on inside me and I didn't, and I wasn't sure that I liked that one little bit.

The doctor turned to me, glanced over at Blake, and a huge smile spread over his face. "You're pregnant."

"What!" I didn't even phrase it as a question – a question would have implied that there was something for them to answer because there was no way in hell that could be real. I couldn't be pregnant. Could I? I looked at the screen, and there it was, the little wriggling blob that was my baby.

"Not too far along," the doctor continued, as though he hadn't just dropped the biggest bombshell imaginable directly into my lap. "Maybe four to six weeks? Depending on when your last period was ..."

Everything fuzzed out in my ears as the doctor and Blake continued to chat over the top of me. I couldn't take this in. I couldn't believe this. It felt like my head was going to explode. My brain ... Jesus Christ. No way. No way, no way, no way, no way could I actually be pregnant.

"I think we need a minute," Blake told the doctor, and he nodded and cleaned the gel off my stomach before he left the room. The image on the screen stayed right where it was, as though it wasn't burned into my memory already.

"This is really happening," I murmured, mostly to try and convince myself that it was real. I had dreamed of this moment for so long, for so many years, and now it was just ... here?

"This is really happening," Blake repeated to me, and I turned my attention to him, slowly meeting his gaze. A big grin spread out over his face as soon as I looked at him.

"Do you want this?" he asked me.

I paused for a moment – "Are you kidding? Of course I want it, you knucklehead," but I smiled at Blake as I said it. I knew this was the universe's way of saying to me that he was the one – I could have gotten knocked up by Robert before this, but it hadn't happened, because it wasn't meant to. My body had known. It had been waiting for Blake to come back to me at last.

"Jesus, you have no idea how happy that makes me," he murmured. "Is that crazy? I didn't mean this to happen, but ..."

"But maybe it's perfect that it did," I finished up for him.

He leaned over and pressed his forehead to mine. "Marjorie, you have no idea how much I wanted this ... even when we were apart, I couldn't stop thinking about how much I wanted this with you. Is that crazy?"

"It's a little crazy," I teased him. "But it all came back round to this, didn't it? It's time. And I don't want to waste any more of it."

"You're perfect," he told me, and he kissed me, before leaning down to plant a kiss on my belly. "And so are you, little one."

"Hey, we've still got a long way to go yet," I warned him. "We don't know–"

"You're with one of the best fertility doctors in the city," he reminded me. "Everything's going to be just fine, alright? You have nothing to worry about."

I felt myself begin to relax. "We're really doing this," I told him, and it was the first time that I actually let myself believe it – the first time that the weight of it, and the joy of it, fell into me all at once. I felt the tears prick my eyes. I couldn't believe it. I couldn't *believe* it.

"We're really doing this," he promised me, and he kissed me again, and I laughed and cried all at once, the mess of emotions consuming me. Above all, I was happy. I knew this was right. It might have been more than I had expected right now, but it was everything that I had ever wanted, and it was happening, it was really happening.

The two of us turned our attention toward the screen again, where the little nub of our baby was still waiting. I reached out to touch my fingers to it, my child in pixels, and I whispered my very first hello.

"Hey there, little buddy," I greeted them. "I can't wait to meet you in person."

Epilogue – Blake

"Annie, come over here!" I called our oldest daughter as she went rushing into the kitchen. I didn't know where she got all this energy from; I felt wiped out most of the time, and that was just running around after her, not actually *being* her. But then, I supposed, she was a kid – she was a full-time rocket of energy. That was her job right now.

"Catch me!" Annie called back, but before I could say another word, I saw her appear over the counter as Marjorie scooped her up into her arms.

"I already did," her mother teased, and she kissed her on her big, chubby round cheek and cradled her close in her arms. Annie wrapped her little arms around Marjorie's neck and hung on tight, just the way she always had since she was a little baby and could lift her arms all by herself. She was so perfect; sometimes it made my heart ache just to look at her. Had done since the first time I had laid eyes on her in that doctor's office when she had been nothing more than a nub in her mother's belly.

"Okay, okay, I think she asked *me* to catch her," I told Marjorie in a faux-scolding tone, heading over to lift Annie out of her arms. Marjorie had to feed Veronica, and I knew that our youngest wasn't going to respond well to not being the center of all attention. Especially when it came to dinnertime.

I gave Annie a big kiss, and the two of us watched as Marjorie got a bottle for Veronica – it was funny, in appearance, Annie and her sister couldn't have been more different, but in personality, they were more or less the same human being. I knew they were going to be so close when they grew up. Maybe they would clash, too, but I could tell that they were going to adore each other above and beyond anything else.

It was hard to believe that nearly three years had passed since that appointment where we had found out that Marjorie was pregnant for the first time. We'd always referred to Annie as our miracle baby – the baby that the universe gave us because of all the time we had lost, all the time we had to make up for.

Marjorie had been scared when it first happened – we had both been freaked the fuck out about what it would mean now that we were actually going to be parents. I had never intended for this to happen to us, not so soon at least, and the shock of it was almost more than I could handle for a while.

"Are you sure you want to do this?" Marjorie asked me one evening, maybe two weeks after we found out. I looked over at her, and there was no doubt in my mind, not a single scrap of it, that this was the right choice for us. Other people might have called us crazy for diving into this so quickly, but they didn't know what it was like to want something for so long and be denied it all that time.

"Of course I am," I told her, and from that moment on, I have been committed to the power of what we were doing together. It was wild, in some ways, but in others, it just felt ... natural. I had spent such a long time convincing myself that this was what I wanted, and then she had been torn away from me. But now she was back we were more in love than we ever were before when we were kids.

There was something profound about the thought of coming back to one another after all this time. It might seem cheesy to some people, but to me, it just made sense. If we had gone from that small town straight into a life outside of it, we never would have had a chance to grow apart. Marjorie had needed the time to get her shop off the ground, and I had to focus on my career to make sure that I could support myself. We had loved and lusted and lived outside of each other, so when we came back together, there was nothing in the way of regret, or fear that we had missed out on something. I had lived without her by my side, and I knew that having her right here next to me was better than anything I had ever been through without her.

The first time I held Annie in my arms it had been a bittersweet moment because I knew that I would have gotten to it sooner had I not been so quick to give in to Marjorie's father. But as the days went by, all of that fell away, and it was simply what we had now that mattered.

I knew that it had taken Marjorie some time to get over what her father had done to her. In fact, I would have been surprised if it hadn't. Though she told me that she had moved past it a long time ago, I knew her too well to fall for that one quite so easily; I could tell that she was still freaked about it, about the control that she had allowed him to have without even knowing about it.

"It just hurts sometimes, you know?" she said to me one evening after a couple of glasses of wine too many when Annie was actually asleep for a change and we could steal some time together.

"I thought that he trusted me to make my own decisions," she explained. "But he didn't. He thought I was going to mess it up so badly that he had to get involved ..."

That pain lingered on for her for a long time, no matter how much I tried to make it easier. I helped her focus on motherhood, on parenting, on building our lives together, but I knew that it wasn't enough for her to let go of everything in its entirety. In fact, it wasn't until she got pregnant with Veronica that she seemed to find some closure.

"You know, I think I'm starting to get it," she told me, as I rubbed her feet after a hard day at work – I had tried to get her to take some more time off, but she had rolled her eyes at me and reminded me that she didn't get where she was by slacking off, even if she did happen to be pregnant.

"Get what?" I asked.

"My dad," she explained. "I don't agree with what he did, don't get me wrong, and I never will. But there's ... there's something to be said for wanting to protect your babies. I mean, I haven't even held this little girl in my arms yet, and I know that there isn't anything I wouldn't do to keep her safe. Maybe that's what he was trying to do with me, in his own fucked-up way."

"Hey, no cursing in front of the kid," I joked with her, and I reached over to plant a hand on her stomach. "But I get it," I agreed. "It's hard to think about letting anything bad happen to her. But I guess she might have a hard time agreeing with us on what exactly a bad thing is, right?"

"Exactly," she replied, and she looked down at her belly. "I don't think I would ever go that far, but he was just trying to take care of me. I don't want to hold that against him anymore."

"Then consider it gone," I told her, miming like I was plucking the thoughts right out of her head.

She grinned and cocked her head at me, looking a little misty-eyed. "You know, you're a really amazing dad," she remarked softly. "I knew you were always going to be, but damn, it's good to be proved right about stuff."

"Glad you're on board." I laughed. "Though I kind of thought that you might have believed it after you agreed to have another baby with me."

"Well, I needed two to make sure, didn't I?" she shot back playfully.

I leaned across the couch to give her a kiss. I was so happy with her; it made my heart spin sometimes. She was still the woman that I had always loved, still, the woman I had always needed. So much of her had remained the same, and I knew those were the fundamental parts of her, the parts that would never change; she would always be Marjorie, and I was grateful to have the chance to know her all the way through her life.

"Have you got her?" I called through to Marjorie as she went to feed Veronica, as I bounced Annie on my hip; she made a face at me, and I made one right back, and she giggled and buried her head in my shoulder. It was funny, I had seen so many couples over the years so delighted with the kids they had brought into the world, but I had never been able to truly wrap my head around what it was like to have one until I was holding my own baby in my arms. Now, I could understand why the work that we did was so important to so many people. Having a child that you could call your own; it made everything in the world feel a little brighter, run a little deeper. Every step you took was for them, and everything you did had more purpose knowing that it was going to impact them.

"I've got her," Marjorie called back, and she emerged back into the room with little Veronica in her arms. Annie reached out for her little sister, and I brought them together so she could say hello. Marjorie, though tired, smiled widely as she saw them interacting. Maybe I was fooling myself, but I felt like they were already the best of friends.

"And I've got you," I told Marjorie, leaning in to give her a kiss on the cheek. And at that moment – surrounded by my family, by the woman I loved and our two daughters – I knew that everything had turned out just the way it was supposed to. And I couldn't have been happier if I had tried.

THE END

Book 2: The Second Chance

Chapter One – Stephanie

It was the strangest atmosphere in the room.

Something between sadness and excitement. I had never been to the reading of a will before, but this was going to be something intense, I knew that much. I sat there, in the seat by myself, arms wrapped around myself, as I waited for the lawyer to arrive.

Nate and Patty were leaning in the doorway, the two of them chatting away like they hadn't got a damn care in the world. Lucky for some, I guessed. The two of them were confident that they would be the ones to land this line, after all, and I supposed that if I thought I was about to come into a company as prestigious and enriching as this one, I would feel the same way, too.

I checked my phone to see if there was anything that had come up that could get me out of this. Nothing but a message from Marjorie and Terri telling me that they were thinking of me and that they would take me out for a drink when all of this was done. I smiled. I was lucky to have friends around me who looked out for me, even when things were hard, like they were now.

In fact, I felt a little bit of a fraud calling this hard. Because I had never really known my grandmother Amaya all that well. She had come over to America just a couple of times, usually too busy with her work back in India to bother with the round trip, and both times that I had met her I had been totally intimidated by her bold attitude and outgoing nature. I had no idea how anyone could be around her without feeling insecure. She had this solidness to her, like she was bound to the Earth by sturdy roots that kept her upright no matter what. I could only dream of having her confidence.

To be fair, we had bonded over our love of fashion – it was funny, even though I had never met her as a kid, it felt like she had influenced some part of me, the part that had always been fascinated with clothes and what they could mean and everything they could announce about a person before they had so much as opened their mouth.

"I like this," she had remarked, tugging on the bright red scarf I had wrapped around my neck. I smiled, averted my eyes from her, as though looking at her too hard for too long would reveal that I wasn't as bold and brilliant and she was.

"Red is a good color," she told me. "Outgoing. It says a lot about you if you can walk into the room wearing something bright red – not an outfit, of course, but an accessory or something. This looks wonderful on you."

I smiled at her and thanked her for her kindness. Even back then, at twelve, I was already starting to find myself drawn to clothes and fashion and accessorizing. I didn't have much money for it, of course, but I would count out my cents and go to thrift shops to find little details that I liked to add to my outfits. I was the most stylish pre-teen on the block. I mean, the rest of the pre-teens around me might not have agreed, but I was all about pleasing myself with the way I dressed.

I was sure it was her influence that had gotten me to apply to New York's Fashion Institute, even though even then it had been a heck of a long shot for me. I had no idea how I got in, but I did. I needed my family to support me, of course, because living out in the city by myself was far too much to handle alone, but that was okay – they were more than willing to make sure that I kept up my studies there. More than willing to support me, if it meant that they could boast a little to whoever was listening about how terribly successful I was becoming.

That was, of course, till my brother threatened to have a whole lot more success than me. And after that happened, all the support that I had laid claim to went right out the window. Not that I let myself think about that too much, because if I did, I had a habit of getting seriously angry. And that was the last thing I needed right now.

Amaya had passed away a few weeks before, and in the rush of getting everything organized and all the family who could afford it back to India for her funeral, we had only just gotten around to the reading of the will. My parents were calling in through video chat, having been amongst the few who could make it across the world on such short notice. It was just me, my brother, and his wife actually in the room, waiting for the lawyer to turn up, and to find out what was going to happen to Khatri Limited.

The fashion label was one of those things that I always wished I'd had more of an excuse to engage with over the course of my life. Think how wonderful it could have been to connect with my parent's culture like that;

there was plenty that I did to remind myself of my heritage where I could, but there seemed no better way to do that for me than with fashion. That was my major passion, after all, that was what I had built so much of my life around; it would have been the perfect way to get to know that side of my family, maybe even fly out to India and see the work in progress.

But soon enough, the company would be handed off to my brother and that would be the last I would see of it. He got everything that he wanted, always had, always would. I didn't even know what I was doing here, not really. I was sure that the lawyer had just invited me along as a polite formality, knowing that if he didn't it would look particularly cruel on his part.

I had serious doubts that Nate was going to keep the company in the family. He probably took one look at it, at all the clothes and the customers and the international connections, and saw it as too much trouble. He was a man, after all, who liked things to be obvious and easy. That was the only reason I could think of for him marrying someone like Patty; they had met when he was twenty, and he had just decided that *this* was the woman he was going to marry, and that was the end of anything that might have led him into the real world. It made me a little sad to think of him taking that place over and just tossing it out the first chance he got to finance another fancy holiday, but there was nothing I could do about it. If this was what my grandmother had wanted, then this was what I had to respect, no matter how bad an idea I might have thought it was.

Finally, the lawyer entered, and my brother greeted him with a warm handshake; I could give Nate one thing, he could be very charming when he wanted to me. He had his arm around Patty's waist, and the two of them together looked every bit the all-American couple who deserved to earn the family business. I shook the lawyer's hand and then returned to my seat, and wished that there was some way I could get out of this. I didn't want to have to be here when I watched a family business that had brought so much success to us was handed over to someone who wasn't going to appreciate it for a moment. Nate didn't much believe that fashion was worth his time or effort; I supposed I should have been able to guess that from the chinos and button-down shirt that he was wearing, looking more like he was heading out to a garden party than to a lawyer's office.

"Thank you both for coming here today," The lawyer, whose name had been on the office door and whose name I had also totally forgotten already, announced as he took his seat. Patty and Nate joined me in sitting down, and I tucked my phone away and reminded myself that I had drinks with my best friends as soon as this was over. I could make it through a lot if I just had the promise of that on the horizon.

"I understand that the main focus of this reading is what's going to happen to Amaya's business," He continued, and Nate nodded. I could practically hear him salivating at the thought of getting his hands on it. I shot him a look, telling him to settle down, but he ignored me. I had overheard him and Patty talking about what they were going to use the money for the sale for once they had it in their account, and I would have been lying if I'd said that it didn't upset me a little. Maybe I was just too sentimental for my own good, but I didn't like the thought of something that our grandmother had worked so hard to build over the course of her life just sold off to the highest bidder to pay for an extension on their already-tacky house outside the city. They didn't need any of that stuff, but they acted like it was the most important thing in the world, and I knew there would be no talking them out of it.

"Yes, of course," Nate replied, barely containing his excitement.

"Well, I know this might come as something of a surprise," he went on, and he glanced over at me. "But the business has been left to Stephanie."

"What?" Nate exclaimed. I knew that I should have said something, but I had no clue what the hell I was meant to say. As soon as I heard those words come out of his mouth, the lawyer seemed to blur to uselessness in front of me. There must have been some mistake. There was no way – there was just no way that this could be happening. Stuff like this didn't happen to me. I wasn't the one in the family who got this side of things. I wasn't the one who came first for the good stuff. That was Nate, it had always been Nate, as long as I could remember, and it felt like some profound disturbance in the balance of things that it had suddenly, all at once, shifted to me.

The lawyer was still talking, and I did my best to quell the ringing in my ears so that I could actually tune in to what the hell he was saying. I felt like my head was going to explode, but I needed to hear the rest of this, just to make sure that it wasn't some odd joke at my expense.

"...Obviously, this comes with a few stipulations," The lawyer went on.

"But we can run through all of those in more detail when you're feeling a little more...Ms. Khatri-Locklear? Are you alright?"

"I need to get a glass of water," I muttered, and I managed to get myself to my feet and head down the corridor to a water fountain to take a drink. I needed it. The cool water in my mouth was enough to ground me once more, and I realized that I was trembling slightly. There was still some part of me that thought this was all some mistake. I never got this treatment, not in my family. I got what Nate didn't want, and I knew for a fact that my brother had wanted this with every fiber of his being. What had happened? How did I fix it? Did I want to fix it? Did I really want it to change?

I made my way back down to the office. Whatever I wanted, I was going to have to figure it out soon, because the moment I walked back in there I was going to have to deal with my brother and his wife freaking the hell out about not getting their hands on what they thought was rightfully theirs.

"And you're sure there's not been some kind of mistake?" Nate demanded, planting his hands on the desk and glaring at the lawyer as I made my way back into the room. The lawyer looked back up at him calmly, not shaken – I checked his name on the door as I came back in, figuring that I should at least know it. Johnathan, okay. I just had to remember that.

"I'm sure," he replied coolly, and Nate tossed his hands in the air and turned to his wife.

"Come on, Patty, I don't see any other reason for us to be here," he announced, and she grabbed her tacky handbag from where she had stashed it under her chair, got to her feet, and let him lead her on out of there. He slammed the door behind him, ever the adolescent, and I winced as the glass wobbled in the window.

"Sorry about that," My father's voice suddenly cut in, and I about leapt out of my seat as I remembered that they were actually there. The computer that contained them was propped up on the edge of the table, so they couldn't quite see me from where they were sitting.

"But you have to understand, this isn't what we expected at all," he continued. "Stephanie means well, but she doesn't have the guts to handle something like this. She never would..."

Without saying a word, Johnathan tilted the laptop an inch or two further so that they could see me sitting there in front of them. I saw my father's eyes widen, and a moment later, the call dropped; no doubt he would come up with some excuse for it later, but I knew he was just ashamed to have been caught talking so badly about his only daughter. Not that I hadn't overheard him share the same sentiments with my mother before, exactly around the time that they had pulled me out of college. *What's she going to do with a degree anyway?* They had probably just told themselves that to feel better in the face of what they were doing, but the words were still burned into my head.

"So, to the matter at hand," Johnathan continued, smoothing down what I was quite sure was a toupee on the top of his head. "The business is now all yours, with a couple of stipulations..."

"I don't know if I can handle this," I blurted out. I wasn't even sure if that's what I actually believed, or if, rather, that was just what had been drummed into my head at every turn since I was a kid. All my life, I had lived under the shadow of my brother, under the shadow of all the things that I was told that he could do better than me. And yeah, maybe at this point, I had started to believe a few of them. Whether that was fair or not I wasn't sure, but it was the truth of how I felt, and there was nothing I could do to shake that so quickly.

"Your grandmother certainly thought that you could," he pointed out gently. I let out a long breath. When he put it like that, it made me feel a little stronger. I had only met her a couple of times, but she wasn't the kind of woman I would have ever accused of being lacking in taste or skill.

"And trust me, there's a good reason that she didn't want your brother anywhere near it," he continued, and he glanced around as though there might be some vestiges of Nate left behind to hear whatever it was that he was going to say next.

"She didn't trust him," he continued. "She was sure that he would just sell it the first chance he got."

"She was right," I murmured. I wondered how she had picked that up from so far away – but then, she was a perceptive woman. There were things she could get a read on that I could only dream of wrapping my head around.

"Exactly," Johnathan agreed. "She wanted this business to stay in the family and she saw you as a way to guarantee that."

"I'm worried I'm not going to be able to handle it," I blurted out again. I didn't want to take this on if I was just going to fuck this up. Sure, I wasn't going to sell it the first chance that I got, but that didn't mean that I wouldn't find some other way to make a mess of it and let her down. I didn't want to let her down, that was the main thing; if she had gifted this profound and precious thing to me, then I would have done anything to protect it. I just wasn't sure how I was meant to go about enacting that protection.

"I'm sure that's why she put in this stipulation on the will," he continued, and he pushed a sheath of paper towards me. I looked down at it with something close to fear; I didn't even know where I was meant to start going about reading through something like this. When it came to the technical stuff, I had never been the first pick in the draft.

"What stipulation?" I asked, and I reached for the papers and started thumbing through them nervously; all of that looked pretty scary to me, and I knew that I was going to have to find some way to wrap my head around all of it without losing my mind. Maybe Marjorie could help. She was always the smart one out of the three of us.

"You're aware of a Mr. Jon Wallace?" He asked. The name sent a shock down my spine. Of course I was aware of him. I was vividly aware of him, even though I hadn't seen him in a good few years now. He had been close with my brother, after the two of them had met setting up a new distributor for Amaya's clothes – back before the wedding, back when my brother actually acted like he had a moment of interest in anything beyond what would give him money in the here and now. I had been a teenager then, and yeah, sure, I would have been lying if I'd said that I didn't have a little, passing crush on the guy. He was cute and I was young and it wasn't like I had much of a chance to meet with a lot of men, given that my parents seemed intent on keeping me locked in the house as much as they possibly could. I doubted he would even remember who I was. But I knew him. I knew him better than I would have cared to admit.

"I'm aware of him," I replied, trying to keep my voice and my face neutral and probably failing dismally.

"Well, your grandmother did a lot of work with him while she was alive," he explained. "A lot of her connections in the States came through him. She wants to carry that on now. She wants you to work with him in expanding the business over here now that she's gone."

I sat back in my seat. I had walked in here thinking that this would be nothing more than a formality, and now, I was going to walk on out carrying with me the weight of a whole business on my shoulders. It wasn't exactly how I had imagined that this would go. And working with Jon? I didn't know if I could handle it.

"Can I have some time to think?" I asked him, and he nodded, reached for the papers that he had pushed across the table towards me.

"Of course," he replied. "I'll be happy to pass along all of this information to your lawyer, if you'd like?"

I smirked briefly; I didn't have a lawyer, but I had the image of Terri, with a silly wig on and a pair of studious glasses, posing as one to make me look more legit.

"I don't have one," I admitted. "But I'll be back soon, okay? I just need a little time to think over everything..."

"Take your time," he replied. "None of this is going anywhere. She wanted you to have it. No matter how long it takes."

"Thank you," I replied, and I shook his hand, grabbed my stuff, and managed to make it out of the room before I felt that wave of dizziness hit me again.

I couldn't believe this. I couldn't believe that this was happening to me. I was never the one who got this treatment, never the one who got the first call for something as exciting as this. It had always been Nate. But Nate was probably out on the highway by now, angrily driving badly and yelling to Patty about how he couldn't believe that they had chosen to hand the company off to someone like me. The thought of that brought a smile to my face, though I knew it was childish of me to enjoy it.

I had a lot to think about. A lot of pieces to put together. And I needed to figure them out sooner rather than later. I strode out of the office, trying to keep my head held high, acting like I thought a woman who had just come into possession of a whole-ass business would act. And trying my very hardest not to think about the fact that I might just be working alongside the man who had been the focus of all my teenage fantasies for years on end.

Chapter Two – Jon

"Shit," I muttered, as my phone buzzed in my pocket just as I made it back into my office. I closed the door behind me and took the call quickly; I didn't have time for this, whatever it was. If this turned out to be a marketing call, then whoever was on the other end of the line was going to some serious-

"Mr. Wallace?"

"Yes, this is Jon Wallace," I replied. "How can I help you?"

"I'm calling on behalf of the estate of Mrs. Amaya Khatri," the voice on the other end of the line continued.

"The estate?" I replied, freezing on the spot. I checked that the door was shut, and started pacing back and forth in the small office space.

And with that, they filled me in on everything – Amaya's passing, the business that she had left behind, and the fact that she had named me in the will as one of the people she wanted to run it in her absence.

"One of the people?" I asked.

"Yes," The man told me. "The other is Stephanie Khatri-Locklear. Her granddaughter? I'm not sure if you've had a chance to meet, or..."

Stephanie. Damn. Now, there was a name that I hadn't heard in a long time. I knew her, for sure, but I wasn't sure that the version of her that I had known back when she had just turned eighteen would have much in common with the woman that she was seven years later.

"I'll reach out to her," I told him. "And thanks for letting me know about Amaya. Pass on my condolences to her family, alright?"

"Will do," The lawyer replied, and with that, he hung up the phone – and left me sitting there, trying to wrap my head around what the fuck I had just heard.

I had worked with Amaya on and off for nearly ten years now. She was a badass woman, one of my first clients, one of the only people who had kept coming back to me for help even when she could have gone to bigger firms and gotten the whole red carpet treatment. We had worked together for years, and I had helped her get set up with some of her biggest and most significant clients; what she put out there was so important to the community that she was a part of, the families that wanted to maintain their connections to what they had known in the past, that it was never hard to find people willing to stock her work. Not to mention the fact that it was exceptionally high-quality, and that it came with the seal of approval from one of the foremost designers from all of India.

I was sad to hear that she was gone, I really was. The world would be a worse place without her. She was someone who had always been totally committed to the idea of supporting the people who helped you get where you were in life – it was why she had always come back to me for help, even when she started to blow up over here. And now...

Now, she had left me the company.

I could hardly wrap my head around that. A few times, when we had been video-chatting, she had made a comment about me working one end of the business for her, but I had always put that down to speculation or just straight politeness, not anything that she was actually planning on following through on.

I had spent so fucking long in this industry. Marketing, working my ass off to get myself off the ground, to make a name for myself and the people I worked with. I was a freelancer, a lone wolf, but I had often thought about what it would be like to settle down with something more solid. Of course, that had always been a long way off in the future, something for me in a few years or a few decades to give real thought to. But now, it was right here on my doorstep. And I had no idea how to feel about it.

If I had been the kind of guy to buy into that sort of stuff, I might have called it a sign. A sign for me to stop pushing myself so hard and take a step back and focus on something more grounded, an industry that I could actually root myself in. But, luckily for most of the people who worked with me, I didn't much believe that the universe was offering me an out from my current situation. This was just an opportunity. A chance for me to change things up. And my curiosity, I was sure, was going to get the best of me.

Stephanie came as part of the deal. I wasn't sure how to feel about that one. I mean, yes, sure, I got it – there was no way that Amaya was just going to kick her family entirely out of the equation. She had always been connected to her family, her heritage, the things that mattered to her, and there was nothing that would have led me to believe that she had anything other than the utmost love and respect for her family.

But it had to have caused more than a little stir that she had given this to Steph and not Nate. I had been friends with Nate back in the day, when I had first started working for the family, and talk about golden child. I was pretty sure he could have dropped his pants and taken a dump on the dining table and his parents would have applauded him for it. He had been alright when I had first met him, but it hadn't taken him long to drop into this strange, difficult attitude that just made him come across as a moody asshole who thought he knew better than everyone around him. Sure, he came from a good family, but that didn't mean that he just absorbed all their skills and knowledge by default as a result of that.

And, okay, yeah, I would have been lying if I'd said there wasn't a part of me pissed that he had all these opportunities laid out in front of him and chose to do next to nothing with them. When we had met, we had been working together on a project for Amaya's company, but he had swiftly lost interest and left me in the lurch to pick up the pieces of what he'd left behind. He had told me it was a family emergency, and I had been naïve enough to believe him, but I found out later that the girl he was dating had just invited him to her family's home in the Hamptons. Family emergency, my ass.

I'd had to work hard my whole life just to get anywhere, and this guy – this fucking guy just swanned around like he expected everything to be handed to him. And the worst part was that it normally just was. He had no idea what toil or sweat or hard work actually looked like, because he'd had no reason to. I knew that I couldn't get mad at someone just because they'd lived a life with more privilege than me, but damn, if he didn't make it hard to stick to that rule.

And I'd always felt sorry for his sister, Steph. She was just a few years younger than him, but she felt like she had so much more maturity than he ever would. Just the way she carried herself, the way she moved through the world, she made it clear that she had been through much more than him. Just not being the family favorite when he was so lavished with attention must have been tough enough. But she had always been gathered, smart, and probably a million times better off taking on a family business than her dead-end brother might have been. Jesus, he had asked me to be his best man when he got married to that girl of his – we had barely been talking at this point, but he must have pushed enough of the people around him to make sure that nobody would be willing to step up to the plate when the time came. I sure as hell wasn't going to go out of my way to do it. I wondered if he was even still with that girl. Marriages like that tended to last ten minutes or ten centuries, no in-between.

But yeah. Stephanie. I had always felt a little sorry for her, but I doubted that she would much care now that she had the company. Was this what she had wanted? Maybe she had asked Amaya to take control of it after she passed. Or maybe she was as shocked as I was about this.

It was strange – it wasn't that she had never crossed my mind in the years since I had seen her, but I had assumed that I was never going to get the chance to see her again so I just hadn't allowed her a whole lot of space in there. Last time I had seen her, she had just graduated high school and was about to head off to study – what was it? I couldn't remember now, but she had her heart set on this prestigious college in New York. I was sure she would have gotten in, I couldn't imagine much out there in the world that would have held her back if she could help it.

And even though there had been a good few years between us, I had noticed that she was growing into a beautiful young woman. She was just past eighteen, and honestly I hadn't so much as noticed her before then, but there was something about her that caught my eye when I ran into her at their family home stopping by to pick up some papers that Amaya had faxed over. She was a buzz of excitement then, and maybe it was just her effusive energy that had attracted my attention, but I could have sworn something had shifted inside of her. Something that I very much liked the look of.

Still. She was probably all settled down by now. What would she be, twenty-five? Her family were pretty traditional, and I imagined that she would have found some willing dude who wanted to marry into her prestigious family and get his hands on this gorgeous, accomplished woman to boot. No point wondering....

No point wondering anything. I shut down those thoughts before they could even go anywhere. Not a chance in hell. If she even wanted to work with me, which I had no promise that she did, then it wasn't like she was going to be throwing herself out me like something out of a porno. It would be strictly professional.

And besides, I was never the guy who hooked up at the office. I was never the guy who hooked up with women that he had to see more than once, to be quite honest. There were too many women in this city to worry about getting caught up with one in particular. Besides, with how much I travelled for work, it wasn't like I had a whole lot of time or energy to focus on nurturing a relationship when I got back. I was a busy man, and I had swiftly discovered after coming to New York from the middle-of-nowhere Iowa that women were looking for more than just a call once a week and a date whenever I could fit them into my schedule.

Didn't mean that I didn't know how to have a good time, though. Didn't mean I didn't know this city's nightlife like the back of my hand. Work hard, play hard might have been trite, but in my case, it was true and always had been. The only way that the balance worked was if I threw myself full-force into both sides of my life. No holding back. No half-measures. Why would I bother with a thing like that, when there was so much that this city had to offer me?

And now, it seemed, it had Stephanie to offer me. Which was something that I hadn't been prepared for. I would need to reach out to her and figure out how she wanted to move forward with all of this – hell, just get to know where she stood after all these years, how much of the girl I remembered was still true. And, against all my better interests, I couldn't help but feel a little flare of excitement at the thought of seeing her once more.

Not that this was going to be anything other than professional. Even if she did want to work with me, then we were going to keep it cool, calm, casual, nothing more than what it had to be.

I leaned back in my seat, and I couldn't help but grin as I thought about everything that this phone call had changed for me. It had been the last thing I had expected to receive today. And yeah, I was sad to hear that Amaya, one of my first and favorite clients, was no longer with us. But this was something I had never expected – this was something that I could never have predicted. And I was keenly looking forward to finding out what could happen now that I had my hands on an actual company of my own. And, on top of it – a chance to see a woman I hadn't seen in a long time, too. I could hardly wait. Though for what, I wasn't sure quite yet.

Chapter Three – Stephanie

Okay. Okay, okay, okay, a million more times, okay. I could do this. I was totally capable of doing this. I was *good* at this. Probably. I mean, I had no idea, but I probably wasn't bad, right?

I stood there, at the door of this building, and gazed up at the enormous office in front of me. How bad could it really be? I had talked myself around in circles but now I was here and I was going to *do* this, once and for all.

"You have to!" Terri had exclaimed to me, as soon as I had told her what was on the table here. I looked over at Marjorie, the voice of reason, even more so since she had gotten pregnant.

"I think she's right," Marjorie agreed. "This is your family that you're talking about here, and it's a fashion business. I don't see why you wouldn't be well-qualified to take it on."

"Also, it's your grandmother's company," Terri cut in, throwing in a little of the emotion once more. "Think how much she would have wanted you to have it, right? She must have really believed in you if she gave this to you..."

"I guess so," I agreed, and I bit my lip. It had been two days since my meeting with the lawyer, and I had been talking myself around and around in circles about what the hell I should do about it. I kept on bouncing between the urge to just shoot down the whole endeavor and tell everyone that there was no way that I could do it, and diving head-first into it without holding back. Even just to spite Nate. I couldn't stop thinking about the look on his face when he had found out that he wasn't getting what he wanted, and I would have been lying if I'd said that that alone felt like a good reason to go ahead and take the position.

"You won't mind that I'll have to take some time off of work?" I asked Marjorie, and she squeezed my shoulder and shook her head.

"Not at all," she assured me. "You take all the time you need. We're always here when you get back, alright?"

"You better be," I tried to joke. It came out a little more high-pitched than I had intended.

"As long as you give us first dibs on the clothes you bring over," She remarked, flashing me a smile.

"Oh my God, that would be so cool!" Terri exclaimed, her eyes widening as she clearly started putting together all of this stuff in her head. "We could have a special display just for clothes that your grandmother made...and you could come by and help dress people and stuff..."

"Bold of you to assume that I know how to wrap a Sari," I laughed, and Terri shrugged, never once put off.

"We could learn together," she suggested happily. And I couldn't help but find her enthusiasm a little infectious. I needed this support from them, because sometimes I felt like I didn't get it anywhere else. Not least from my family; the comments my father had made when he had found out that I was getting the company were still ringing in my ears, a reminder that nobody seemed to think that I was suited for this. There was a part of me, a childish part for sure, but a strong one that told me to push through all of this just to prove them wrong.

"We could," I agreed, and it was then that the decision was made. I needed other people to get excited about this for me, so that I would stop damn second-guessing everything that came out of my mouth and go for what I knew I wanted.

And so, I called up Jon's office and booked a meeting with him. He sounded like he was busy, but he made time for me. He must have been as surprised as me that Amaya had involved him in the ownership of the business. Or maybe he had been expecting it? Maybe they had already discussed it. I had no idea. I hadn't seen Jon in so long, I didn't know where he stood with the rest of the family.

I knew that he and my brother didn't talk much anymore, if at all – if they had, then Nate might have gotten a heads-up on the way that this company was going to go. They never had a real falling-out that I was aware of, but they didn't need to; Jon had probably just seen through all of Nate's bullshit and dropped him like everyone did at some point or another. I was surprised that Patty had gritted her teeth and stuck around for as long as she had, but then, I supposed, she had the money to soften the blow when things got difficult. The rest of us just had to find some way to navigate it because he was family and that was, apparently, enough to tie us to them for life.

I had been sad when Jon had dropped out of the family – I mean, yes, he was still involved with the business, but we didn't see him around anymore, and I had missed his presence. I was sure he saw me as nothing more than a gawky, slightly awkward teenager who felt bright red and stuttered when she was around him, but he had always been sweet to me, treated me like a real person, and God knows I didn't get enough of that when I was growing up.

Yes, I'd had a crush on him. Okay? I could admit that to myself now. I had been young, and it wasn't like I came into contact with many guys in my day-to-day life, not ones that my parents weren't blatantly trying to set me up with, anyway. He was something...different. Just a few years older than me, handsome, charming, smart. Even though he was young then, he always seemed like he had everything together. He was confident, knew how to carry himself, walked and talked like he knew what the world owed him and he wasn't afraid to take it. Would he be the same way now? I could hardly imagine him having lost that over the years. People changed, but if he had shifted, I got the feeling that it would only have been to embrace an even more certain version of who he had been back then.

I picked out my outfit for our first meeting, changed my mind, and then changed it back again. How was I meant to dress now that I had embraced ownership of this company? If someone could have come along and given me a few pointers, that would have been handy. I decided to settle on something smart, but something that I could be comfortable in. Last thing I wanted was to be distracted all the way through our first meeting because I had a wire or strap prodding in to me from a strange angle.

And now, here I was; standing outside the building, about to walk in and meet with him for the first time. Well, not the first time ever, but the first time since I had really felt like myself. Thinking back to the girl I had been before, the one who was nervous, nervy, tripping over her words and herself as she tried to think of something smart to say, I could hardly recognize her now. I was better than that. Greater than that. I was going to show him just how much I had changed, and I was going to prove to myself that I was more than capable of taking on this business.

I marched into the building, a shared office space that was made up of professionals from a wide variety of industries; once upon a time, I could have seen myself occupying one of these offices, hanging out behind one of these doors and running my own clothing company. That was when I had imagined that my career would have come before my brother's marriage, of course. Silly me for getting stuck on a thought that was so obviously wrong.

I found myself outside his door all at once, and I stood there for a long moment, just staring at his name on the brass tag screwed into the wood. *Jon Wallace.* I repeated it again and again in my head, trying to cool myself off. Not that there was anything I was getting heated about – oh, for goodness sake. I was letting all of this go to my head. I knocked on the door, not giving myself another second to overthink this, and marched inside.

And there he was.

It took me a split second to gather myself after I laid eyes on him again. It had been so long that I had to re-calibrate everything about the memory of him that I'd had inside my head. He was – well, he was just as handsome. But his slightly overgrown dark hair had been cut short into a sharp cut that served to draw the angles of his face out beautiful. Had he always had that sharp a jaw, those cheekbones? His grey-green eyes flicked up to meet mine and I felt like I was going to swoon on the spot. *Hold it together, Stephanie. This is meant to be a business meeting, remember?*

"Stephanie?" He asked, and he got to his feet and extended his hand towards me. He was dressed in a sharp navy suit, and looked like he could have rolled out of some TV drama about life in an office. Where he would have played the romantic lead, of course.

"Jon," I greeted him, and I took his hand. As soon as his fingers closed around mine, I felt like the ground was swaying slightly underneath me; I wasn't sure what it was, by the warmth of his touch made everything feel a little unsettled, as though my brain was twisting in two trying to make sense of it all.

"It's so good to see you again," he told me, and the smile on his face suggested that he actually meant it. I had expected a lot of smooth-move niceties meant to catch me off my guard and get me to give him everything he wanted, but he at least made it feel like he meant it. Maybe that was part of the game. Maybe I should stop trying to guess the game and calm the hell down...

"You too," I replied, and he gestured for me to take a seat – I thought he was reaching for my hand again, and realized a split second too late that he wasn't, once I had already shaken his hand with my other one.

"Oh, shit, I'm sorry," I muttered, and I felt a heat running up my cheeks. This wasn't off to a good start. How was I meant to convince him that I was a worthwhile business partner when I couldn't even figure out how to shake hands properly?

"It's fine," he replied, and though I couldn't quite bring myself to look him in the eye, I could hear the smile in his voice. He must have been amused by me.

"Thanks for coming in today," he told me. "I have to admit, I wasn't sure what to expect when I got that call from Amaya's lawyer. I mean, I know she liked working with me, but I had no idea just how much."

"Me neither," I admitted. "I didn't expect – I mean, everyone thought that Nate was going to get hold of it instead."

"Now, give Amaya a little more credit than that," he remarked playfully. "She knew better than to give over her life's work to someone like her grandson."

I couldn't keep back the snort of laughter. Clearly, there was no love lost between the two of them.

"And I thought you two were meant to be friends?" I pointed out. He shook his head.

"Not for a long time," he replied firmly. I would have to get the story of that out of him some day. If I saw him again after this, that was.

"I wanted to let you know," I began, running through everything that I had rehearsed in my head on the way over here. "I want to...I want to give things a go. Give running this with you a go, that is."

He raised his eyebrows at me, and a smile curled up his lips.

"Well, that's what I assumed," he replied. "Didn't see much reason for you to come down here otherwise."

"Fair point," I agreed, and I felt that flutter in my chest. I planted a hand there to soothe myself, and took a deep breath.

"Hey," he murmured, noticing my nerves. "You have nothing to be worried about. I don't bite."

Suddenly, my mind was filled with images of him biting me. That wasn't helping. I felt my cheeks grow a little redder again. Damn my imagination.

"Uh, of course," I replied. "Sorry, I've just never done something like this before. Business isn't really my thing."

"Well, you're going to have to make it your thing," he remarked. "If we're going to get this off the ground, right?"

"Right," I agreed, and I forced myself to calm down. I looked at him again. I swear, every time I looked into his eyes I felt like I was spinning out of control, back to being that teenager who found herself fluttering with nerves every time he got close to her.

"I thought that we could start with a three-month trial," I explained. "Both of us working together. I know that I'm going to need some hand-holding to get me through this, but I want to be as involved with it as I can be. What is it you did for my grandmother, exactly?"

"I helped her find distributors in the US," he replied.

"Right, so you know how all of that stuff functions? At least stateside?" I asked. He nodded.

"Yeah, I do," he replied. "But there's a lot more to think about than that. We're going to need to look at how we'll uphold production out in India – I know she wouldn't want us to move it out of all those workshops she got set up – and touch base with the suppliers out there too."

"Right, of course," I agreed, and I massaged my temples. This was already starting to sound a hell of a lot like hard work. Which I had expected, of course, but the sheer weight and enormity of everything that we had to take on was more than I had been ready for.

"I don't know if we'll get everything in place in just three months," he warned me. "But I want you to know that I'll work as hard as I have to in order to keep this company above water. It's going to take a lot from both of us, but I know that Amaya must have picked you to take over for her for a reason."

"Yeah, because she had no idea how crap I was going to be at it," I replied without thinking. He burst out laughing.

"Okay, that's not exactly what I dream of hearing from the person I'm meant to be running a company with," he remarked. "Where's your confidence?"

"In industries that aren't this one," I confessed. "Look, I have to tell you the truth, I'm not exactly...I don't have a clue of what I'm doing when it comes to this. I've worked in a store for most of my adult life, I haven't taken on anything like this before."

"But when you got your degree-"

"I didn't get my degree," I cut him off before he could finish. Too painful to allow him to come out with the rest of that statement. I didn't want to have to tell him the truth. He already disliked my brother enough as it was, and it looked like he was going to have to work closely with the family again. I didn't want to cause more trouble there.

"It's a long story," I replied. "But what I'm saying is, I'm going to need as much help as I can get."

"I'm willing to give you that help," he replied, and there was a sureness this voice that made me believe that I could actually do this. Shit, I had no idea if I had it in me to actually pull this off, but I had to give it a go, didn't I? He grinned at me, and the look on his face made the hair on the back of my neck stand up. There was such a certainty in the way he was looking at me, as though he was already figuring out all the ways that he could get me to do everything that I wanted him to. Not that it would have taken a hell of a lot of convincing on his part. Even just sitting there, opposite him, I felt like I could have gone along with anything at all that he suggested to me. Maybe I even wanted to.

"Then we have a deal," he announced. "Three months, okay? Then we can take a step back and figure out where we want to go from there."

"That sounds good," I agreed. I was terrified, but also a little elated, too, like if I stood up my feet wouldn't quite have been touching the ground. Was that how it felt? When you made a deal? I had never done it before, I had no idea. But if this was what it was, then I could get used to it. I smiled at him, and felt a weight lift from my shoulders. The deal was done. Now, all that remained was for me to find some way to follow through on it.

Chapter Four – Jon

"You ready for our first day, partner?"

"Ready as I'll ever be," Stephanie replied, and she drummed her fingers on top of the coffee that she had brought in with her that morning. She had been buzzing with audible nervousness since she had arrived, and I was just doing what I could to take the edge of it. I wasn't sure that much that I was doing was actually helping, though.

"I'm sorry," she apologized. I was sure this had to be about the half-dozenth time that she had done so since she had come in that morning, and it would have almost been funny if I wasn't trying to convince her that she had every right to be here.

The office was only just big enough for the both of us, but she had moved in some of her stuff and we were ready to get going. This was the new headquarters of the business Amaya had left behind, and I was damn sure that we were going to do everything we could to make it work.

I still couldn't believe that this was happening. She had only come in to meet with me for the first time a few days before, and now we were getting started on this for real. It was the strangest thing – I had had to put my other clients on hold, and I would have been lying if I said that it didn't come with a little anxiety. All my life had been built around getting them together, making sure that I had everything around me that I would need to keep me in work for the next year. For the time being, it was just this, only this. That was a lot of pressure to put on my newest venture. Which meant that I had to make sure it worked.

Stephanie had been pretty upfront with the fact that she didn't have a lot of experience when it came to this, but I could live with that. I was more than happy to help her through these first few weeks. It would be the first time that I had been working with someone else so closely in such a long time, I was glad that I wasn't going to have to deal with someone swaggering in here and acting like they knew better than me. She was nervous, skittish, but open to me teaching her, which was all that I could ask for.

"So, I thought we should start by consolidating the contacts we have out here," I told her. "Letting them all know that they're not going to be dealing with Amaya anymore, let them know what's going on and how we plan to move forward."

"Right, of course," she agreed. "I have a friend in the city, actually, she said that she would want to stock a few of her outfits if we could get them to her. I know it's just a small store, but..."

"But every little helps right now," I promised her. "Well, put her on the list. We'll make sure to reach out to her as part of our rounds. I'm going to get us a collection of numbers and then we can go over everything that we need them to know, alright?"

"Alright," She agreed, and she leaned up in the doorway; the door was still open, as though she was half-planning to bolt when she had the chance.

"And maybe you could grab a seat," I suggested. "So it doesn't look like you're waiting to get out of here the first chance you get."

"Right," She replied, and she managed a smile. Though she had changed in so many ways since I had last seen her, there was still some of that nervousness to her, like she didn't believe that she could really do this. I wanted to tell her that she could, that anyone who told her that she couldn't was crazy, but she was just going to have to work it out for herself. That was the only way you could improve your confidence with this stuff. Nobody else could give it to you.

Speaking of the ways she'd changed. I had to admit that she was far removed from the young girl that I had last seen her was; there was no denying the fact that she was hot as hell now, even if I wasn't sure that she knew it. Her hair was long and thick and swayed down her back in a long ponytail; she dressed conservatively but not prudishly, in crisp white shirts and fitted pants. Her make-up was minimal, but drew attention to her huge brown eyes and the soft olive tones of her skin. She was gorgeous, no doubt about it. I hadn't had a chance to ask about a boyfriend yet, but I figured that there was no way someone like this didn't have a guy hanging on her every word. Maybe I was even a little jealous of him. In fact, there was no maybe about it.

Not that there was any way that I was going to let that get in the way of what we were doing here. I had better things to think about than how hot she happened to be. Sure, okay, she was sexy, and yes, we were going to be working close together for the foreseeable future, but that didn't mean anything. I was a grown-ass man with a grown-ass man's self-control, and nothing else mattered.

I went through a list of all the clients that we had to reach out to, and I was impressed at how well she seemed to take to the spiel I had put together to give to all of them. I listened in on the first couple of calls, not letting her know that I was paying attention, but she seemed pretty confident on the phone – more so than she did in person, for sure.

By the time she had finished up her third call, I had actually just stopped to take a moment to listen to her. She spoke well, quickly and clearly, and she seemed to have the answers to all the questions that they threw in her direction. She even managed to crack a few jokes here and there, and she laughed with the would-be clients on the other end of the phone. They must have been charmed senseless by her. I knew that I was, and she had hardly turned that attention on me yet.

She hung up, and noticed that I was just sitting there look at her. She raised her eyebrows at me, clearly a little thrown by all my attention.

"Did I do something wrong?" She asked nervously, and I shook my head at once.

"Not at all," I assured her. "You're doing really well. You should be pleased with yourself."

"I'll be pleased once we actually have some distributors locked in," she replied, and there was a sturdy sureness to her voice that made me laugh; she turned to me, surprised.

"What are you laughing at?"

"You just sound so business-ready," I replied. "I didn't think you would take to it so quickly. It's hard work, this side of things, but you seem to find it easy."

"I just know that we don't have a lot of time to get all of this off the ground," she replied, and she ran her finger down the list of contacts I had given her and furrowed her brow. "How many more of these do we have to go through?"

"About a dozen," I replied. "And I know we're going to find people who want to keep us around, really. I'm sure of it."

"If they don't think that when I start the call, they will when I finish it," she replied with a crisp certainty. "By the way, why have you stopped calling? You should be keeping up with me, right?"

"Right, boss," I replied, saluting her playfully. She shot me a look.

"Hey, I'm not good with being the one in charge," she warned me.

"Don't give me that opening, alright?"

"You like me to be in charge?" I asked teasingly. She flushed a little. God, when she flushed, I felt something brewing inside of me, something that certainly should not have been anywhere near us right now.

"I think it's for the best for now," she replied, and she quickly picked up the phone and took the next call, and I did the same thing. We worked alongside each other well, and I was glad for the company for a change; it had been a long time since I had worked with anyone else, and having someone to split the load with was actually kind of a relief after all this time. Not to mention the fact that she clearly knew this side of the industry better than I did. She talked fashion and fabric and design with confidence, the same confidence that I had heard from her grandmother. Had she inherited that knowledge from her, or come to it herself? I was curious.

Once we had finished the entire list, and left our new information with distributors and investors we were hoping to start work with soon enough, she sank back into her chair and let out a long sigh.

"I'm not used to spending that much time talking," she admitted.

"I thought you worked at a store...?"

"Yeah, but most of the time the other two girls who work with me, they're the ones dealing with customers," she explained. "I generally just hang around the back and ring up the customers when they've had a bunch of stuff sold to them."

"You know so much about fashion, though," I pointed out. "You must have spoken to a few people about it one time or another."

She sighed. It seemed as though a bunch of her energy just leaked from her as soon as I said those words. I scanned her face, looking for an explanation, but I couldn't find one.

"Sorry, did I say something wrong?" I asked her, and she shook her head quickly.

"No, no, nothing like that," she assured me. "It's just...yeah, I did used to speak to a lot of people about this stuff."

"But not anymore?"

"Not anymore," she agreed, and her eyes glazed over as she gazed off wistfully into the distance, like she was looking back on something that she had long-since put behind her.

"What happened?" I asked bluntly. I had never been one for beating around the bush and I was hardly going to start now. She glanced over at me, clearly surprised that I was showing any interest at all.

"You really want to know?"

"I really want to know."

She let out a long sigh, and ran her fingers through her hair.

"You remember when we last saw each other?" She reminded me. "I was just about to head off to college then."

"Yeah, of course I remember," I replied at once. She had seemed so bright then, so fresh with the promise of what was to come; so far removed from the woman that I saw sitting in front of me now.

"Well, I went off to study fashion design," she explained. "In New York. I really loved it, I really did, I thought that I was going to be able to make a career out of it – I had never found anything before that made me feel so excited. You know that feeling?"

"I do," I agreed. It was the same way I felt when I nailed a deal, that thrill, that feeling of wanting to punch the air and tell the world to go fuck itself because I had things just where I needed them. And if someone had tried to take that away from me...

"Well, I was there for a few months, a couple of semesters," she explained. "It was all just introductory stuff but I was feeling pretty solid about it. I felt like I had found my thing, you know? Found my people. It just made sense for me to be there, surrounded by all these creative types. I had never really thought of myself as one of them, but I realized that this was just where I fit."

I stayed quiet. She was gazing off into the distance again, like she was trying to press down on some particularly heavy memory. She looked as though she was in pain. I didn't want to push her, but I was curious to know what she was carrying around with her that had given her so much joy but that now seemed like a source of nothing but grief to her.

"My parents were supporting me," she continued. "Since my brother didn't go to college or anything, they were giving me everything I needed to get by. And I appreciated it so much, I really did – I was going to make them proud, I told them that all the time. I was good at this stuff. I had never been much for studying before, but when it came to that school, I felt like everything just stayed in my head. I didn't have to put in any effort to keep it there, it all just hooked in and stayed there."

Her voice was starting to shake a little now. I couldn't tell whether it was with sadness or anger or some odd mixture of the two, but it was heavy and obvious to me. I wanted to reach out to take her hand and do something to soothe her but I knew that was far from my place. I had to play it cool. She was just sharing this with me, not inviting me to get involved in the story.

"But then Nate got engaged," she continued, her voice edged with bitterness. "And as soon as I heard, I knew that there was no chance that I was going to be able to go through with the rest of the course."

"What are you talking about?"

"My family, they poured all their money into making sure that this was the wedding of the year," She went on. I wasn't even sure if she'd heard me.

"I think part of it was it was that they were just glad that someone had actually agreed to take him on after all that time, and they didn't want to wait, so they jumped into it really quickly," she explained. "I don't know if you've ever tried to book flower arrangements and stuff last-minute, but it's expensive. Expensive enough that they didn't have anything left for the rest of the family. And especially not me."

"What are you saying?" I asked her.

"They pulled the funding for my course," she finished up, finally, her voice heavy with sadness. "That was it. I couldn't get the money together in time to pay for the next couple of semesters, and they needed it upfront – couldn't find a loan in time, either, and even if I had, I wouldn't have been able to pay it back."

"So you had to drop out?" I replied. I felt a flare of anger pulse through me. Okay, I knew that Nate had been my friend at one point, but that didn't mean that this didn't make me mad as hell. I knew Nate, knew that he was essentially a waste of space and that I could already see that his sister was way more than he could ever dream of being. And they had given up on her, for what? For his wedding?

"Yeah," she replied, with a heavy sigh. "I had to drop out. That's how I got the job at the store, I had to find something to support myself after I got kicked out of dorms. I lived in the crappiest apartment for a while, you should have seen it, I shared it with four other people and the rooms were about the size of closets..."

She shook her head, and slowed herself down, as though she knew there was no point in going on any further.

"But yeah," she rounded off her story. "That's why I know so much about fashion."

"That's bullshit," I told her bluntly. "You must be able to see that it's bullshit, right?"

"I try not to think about it," she replied gently. Her voice had a benevolent tone to it, but I couldn't imagine in what world she was able to handle knowing that all that had happened to her. If my family had ripped away something that I was passionate about, something that I was talented at, in that way, I wasn't sure that I would ever have been able to forgive them. Just the thought of it was enough to put my hackles up, and I had just heard the story, not lived through it.

"We should go out for a drink," I suggested. I needed to get out of this office and I sure as hell wanted to do something for her after she had let me in on the story of her life so far. She deserved it, after the bullshit that her family had put her through.

"Shouldn't we get some more work done here first?" She asked, and I shook my head and waved my hand.

"We're not going to get anything done today, not more than we already have, at least," I told her. "You need to take some time off and get yourself together, and then we can get back to work."

"That doesn't sound very professional...."

"You've worked all day long," I pointed out to her. "You need some rest, seriously. Get you head back in the game for tomorrow, yeah?"

"Well, when you put it like that," she replied, and a smile spread across her face. I was glad to see it there again. Even more glad that I had put it there.

"Something to celebrate the two of us working together," I suggested.

"Just like Amaya wanted," she replied, a little tinge of sadness to her voice. But she soon pushed that down, put the smile back on her face, and kept her head up. I wondered how many times she had been forced to do that with her family, put on the game face and make like she wasn't in pain from what they had done to her. I wished I could have been there when it had all happened; I might not have had a lot of cash then, but I had been smart enough to see that she was a far better investment than Nate was ever going to be.

"Right," I agreed. "Come on, I know a place not far from here. They do cheap wine and good cocktails, if that's your thing-"

"Wait, we're going now?" She asked, a little surprised. I nodded.

"I don't see why not."

"I'm not sure that I'm ready..."

"You're ready," I promised her. "Come on, let's get out of here. I want to go get several beers."

"Agreed," she replied, and she got to her feet and stretched; she looked so long and lean when she moved like that. For the briefest moment, I wanted to reach out and touch her hip, just that spot where her shirt had ridden up and exposed a strip of flesh. It would have been so easy to just make her stop in her tracks, feel her skin beneath my own; I had no idea how she would react to my touch but I doubted that it would be anything particularly good.

"Okay, I'm ready to get out of here," she agreed. "Show me where we're going. I want a drink."

And with that, our first day together was over with – and our first night together was just beginning.

Chapter Five – Stephanie

I looked at myself in the mirror of the bathroom of the bar that Jon had taken me to, and giggled at my own reflection.

What was it about having a couple of drinks and then seeing your reflection that always made you look so goofy? I'd only had a couple of drinks and I felt like all my features had shifted slightly, rendering everything just slightly wrong. In the funniest way possible, of course.

I washed my hands and dried them under the wimpy dryer and smoothed down my hair. I couldn't believe I was actually doing this. I should have just gone home, really, should have gone and relaxed and gathered myself after the day that we'd had. But when he had suggested a drink, well, I had been helpless to resist him.

Maybe it was because I had spilled the truth about what had happened with my studies to him; maybe I felt like I could do with something after recounting the reality of that. Sometimes, when I thought about it too hard, it was enough to make my chest ache with the thought of all those opportunities missed. I didn't know why I had gone into so much detail and told him everything, but sometimes, it felt good to get it off my chest. To be reminded, by someone else, that what had happened back then had been totally ridiculous and that I was right to still see it that way.

The bar he had taken me to wasn't the fanciest place in town, but like he'd promised, the drinks were cheap and the atmosphere was good. I was a couple of Cosmos in, a drink that I rarely allowed myself these days; too sugary, the hangover too grim for me to deal with. But something about putting in an actual day of work at that office made me feel like I deserved it. Not that I didn't work hard at the store, but that felt like more play than work since I was doing it alongside two of my best friends in the world. This was actual work, office work, calling up people and trying to get them to see it from my perspective kind of work. And I needed something sugary and boozy to take the edge off of it.

By the time that I returned to the table, Jon had gotten us a third round of drinks; I knew that we were heading into slightly dangerous territory, but that was fine. I was two drinks in and that meant that any apprehensions I might have had had long since gone out the window.

"You trying to get me drunk?" I asked him, as I joined him at the small table once more. The place we were in was quiet, just a dozen or so other people filling out the spaces around us, but that was fine by me. I didn't do well around lots of people, and besides, it made me feel like we were in some exclusive club that only we knew about. It excited me to think about all the parts of the city that he knew that I had never come across before in my life; a whole new world, a whole new side to New York that he would be able to show me.

"Trying to get you to blow off some steam," he replied. "Besides, I wanted another one, and I wasn't going to leave you in the lurch, was I?"

"Your mom raised you well," I replied, and I picked up the glass containing my drink and took a long sip. "Mmm, you were right by the way, this place does do amazing cocktails."

"I told you," he agreed, a smile spreading over his face. "You like it?"

"So far, yeah," I replied. "I don't come out drinking a lot, though, so maybe you've got a win on your hands there already."

"Maybe," he agreed, and there was this brief silence between us when he was just looking at me and I could feel this overheated rush pulse through my system, and I could have sworn that the world slowed down just for a moment. He smiled at me and it lit up his whole face, and I tried my best not to let my eyes linger on him for too long. And this was just why I didn't drink around men. Way too dangerous. Well, maybe that was just true when I was drinking around him.

"So, how long you lived in the city for now?" He asked me curiously. He had been peppering me with questions all night long, and I was still having a hard time working out if he was just being polite or if he was actually interested in me.

"About nine years," I replied. "Shit, I can't believe it's been that long myself. Feels like I only arrived here last week..."

"Yeah, I feel you there," he agreed. "But you grew up around here, didn't you? Not far from the city?"

"Yeah, in the state," I replied. "But my parents never really let me come down here by myself. It was always their version of New York, you know? The one that they approved of."

"And let me guess, that version isn't all that fun?" He suggested. I grinned at him.

"Nowhere near fun enough," I replied. Was I flirting with him? I had no idea. Actually, I knew exactly what the answer to that question was, but I just wasn't ready to face up to it yet. I wasn't the girl who went out and got tipsy and flirted with some guy she had only just met again after years apart. I was the one who went home early and made sure that they had their meals prepped for the rest of the week. I had some fried rice ready for me to dive into as soon as I got back to my place, but in truth, I wasn't feeling that hungry. Or if I was, it was for something other than food.

What the fuck! I couldn't believe that I had even allowed that sentence to cross my mind. I was working with this guy for goodness sake, and there was no way I was going to let something as silly as an old crush get in the way of that.

We chatted a little while longer, but the whole time, I found that rush of want towards him pulsing at the back of my mind. It was making it hard to concentrate. And I got the feeling that it was going to keep being a problem as long as we were working together.

"So, you come here a lot?" I asked him, gesturing around the bar. "I would have guessed you had somewhere fancier to take out all your lady friends."

"Hey, how do you know about all of them?" He asked playfully, cocking his head to the side and eyeing me for a moment. I shrugged.

"I didn't," I admitted. "Just got the feeling that you probably had a few. And I'm right, aren't I?"

"I guess you might be," he agreed, and a smile licked up his face. "Why, you jealous?"

"Jealous?" I laughed out loud. "No, I don't think I'm jealous."

"You only think you're not jealous," he pointed out. "Sounds like you're having some doubts."

"Okay, well, I know I'm not jealous," I offered back. "Does that make it clearer for you?"

"Yeah," he agreed. "A little more of a let-down, too."

"Why, you really want me jealous of the women you're dating?"

"For one, I don't think you could call what I'm doing with any of them dating," he replied, waving his hand like the very thought of it was crazy to him.

"Oh, no?" I shot back. "And what exactly would they call it?"

"I think they're in the same mindset as me," he replied firmly. "I don't think any of them would exactly be in a rush to consider me their boyfriend."

"You don't think of yourself as the boyfriend type, huh?"

"I think it's more that none of them see me as that," he replied, with a grin. But he didn't exactly look down and out about admitting it.

"No wonder you didn't want to be at my brother's wedding," I teased. "You probably would have combusted the moment you walked into the church, right?"

"In my defense, I'm not that bad," he replied. I could feel that little fizz of excitement building inside of me. I tried to ignore it but it didn't want to be ignored.

"So you didn't come to the wedding because...?"

"Because I was standing in solidarity with you getting fucked over by your family," he replied. "Shit, sorry, I shouldn't say that about them-"

"You can say whatever you like," I replied. "You're right. They did fuck me over."

"It's funny hearing you curse," he remarked. "Can't think of the last time I heard you do it."

"Well, don't get used to it, because it only happens when I'm a few drinks deep," I replied.

"In that case, I'm going to have to keep you permanently tipsy so that I can hear you speak your mind," he replied. I held up a hand, a warning shot.

"Hey, I'm not sure you want me to speak my mind all the time..."

"Why, what's on it?" He fired back, his voice edged with curiosity. I opened my mouth, about to blurt something out, but I bit it back before I could get ahead of myself. No need for me to act out so early on into us working together. I had to keep myself under control. Booze or no booze. Though I was starting to think that the booze had been the best, worst idea I'd had in a while.

"I don't know if I should say," I replied, knowing that he was going to coax it out of me now that I had laid down the gauntlet like that. He rolled his eyes skyward and grinned.

"Oh, come on," he protested. "I feel like I didn't bring you all the way out here just for you to hold back on the good stuff, right?"

"Who says it's good stuff?" I replied. He cocked his head to the side.

"Well, then, maybe I need to hear it even more," he replied. "Make sure you're not holding a total grudge against me without me knowing."

"Does that happen a lot?" I asked. "People hating on you without you knowing about it?"

"Most of them have the good sense not to come out and say it to me, but I can tell," he fired back. It felt like this conversation was one we had been having for weeks; we bounced off one another easily, comfortably. He wasn't afraid to have a little fun and I was more than happy to give as good as I got. It was how things always were when I was with Marjorie and Terri, anyway, so it was just what I was used to with the people I worked with. Though, if I was being honest, the way I felt about them had nothing on everything running through my head at that moment.

"Why are you so interested in my dating life, anyway?" He asked. "You jealous?"

"Of all the women you're not dating? Nah, I think I can live with it," I replied. I trailed my finger around the glass, then realized what I was doing and stopped myself in my tracks. Oh my God. I needed to get myself together. I felt like my brain was going to pop. I looked into his eyes, and I couldn't draw my gaze away from him.

"Can I be honest?" I blurted out. He smiled.

"Of course you can," he replied.

"I totally had a crush on you in high school," I admitted. I couldn't believe I had just said that. I wanted to bite back the words as soon as they'd come out of my mouth, but then I saw the look on his face and I knew that he was glad to hear them.

"Really, now?" He remarked.

"And I figured it's better to just get all this stuff out there now," I continued, speaking quickly, feeling the heat rush up my neck and over my cheeks. Why was I saying this? Was there time to back out of it? Even if I could have, would I have wanted to?

"I mean, if we're going to be working together, then we need to make sure that we don't have secrets," I went on, speaking faster, so fast that everything seemed to be blurring together. "And, I mean, I don't have anything for you anymore – no feelings, I mean, but just in case it came up-"

169

And then, before I could get another word out of my mouth, he slipped his hand behind my head and kissed me.

It was just a soft kiss, just for a moment, and it seemed to be more to quiet me down than it was anything else, but it made my head spin as soon as I felt his lips on mine. Everything about him was suddenly more than I could handle; his touch, his mouth, and the taste of the liquor he had been sipping on. I felt my toes curl in my shoes, and the tipsiness I had been hanging on to seemed to explode and increase a thousand-fold. Like he was getting me drunker.

When he pulled back, I kept my eyes closed for a moment longer, letting the kiss wash through me. It wasn't like I had never been kissed before, but there was something about that one that had just...*wow*. Okay, now I was starting to understand what it was that women seemed to like so much about him.

"There," he told me, grinning as he leaned back. "Now you had a crush, and I had a kiss. And it's out of the way. All in the past, right?"

"All in the past," I breathed in response. And I could just about convince myself that it really was.

I finished my drink and said my goodbyes to him, and headed out on to the street to make my way back to my apartment. I was exhausted, and totally confused after what had happened. He gave me a hug and told me not to be too hungover to come into work the next day, and waved me off. And I was a little ashamed to say that I actually turned to watch him walk down the street away from me.

I couldn't stop thinking about the way he had kissed me. I had been kissed before, but it had never made me feel like that. I wanted him to kiss me again, the whole night through. Even as we moved on to other things, I found my eyes darting down to his lips, intent on finding another one from him one way or another.

It wasn't far back to my place, but I took my time, letting the cool evening air scrub out the last of my boozy tipsiness from my system. I needed to be sober tomorrow. Though I wasn't sure how I could feel even remotely normal when I was around him after what we had just done.

I needed to talk to someone about this. Terri? No, Terri was hardly the most sensible person in the world, she would have gotten way overexcited and would have fed into the thrill that was going through my system right about now. I needed someone who could remind me of what was important.

I dialed up Marjorie, held the phone to my ear, and dawdled a little, not wanting to be home yet, not wanting to have to admit that this night was over and done with and that I needed to get back to reality. He had said that it was behind us now, but how could he feel that way when the memory of it was so fresh?

Marjorie picked up after a few moments; she had been sleeping badly since she had gotten pregnant, and was usually up at all hours.

"Hey," she greeted me.

"Hey, sorry, I didn't wake you, did I?" I asked, fretting at once.

"Nah, you're good," she promised me. "My bladder got me up anyway. What's going on?"

"I just...need you to tell me not to be stupid about something," I told her, sighing heavily.

"Okay, that doesn't exactly sound good," she replied. "What's going on? Are you okay?"

"Yeah, I'm fine," I replied, assuring her as best I could. "I just had a...thing. And I need some advice on it."

"A thing? With who? Or what?"

"With...Jon."

"Jon?" She exclaimed. "Like, the guy you're meant to be working with Jon?"

"The very same," I admitted. "We had our first day together today, you know, working, and then we went out for a drink..."

"Okay, so already off to a bad start," She remarked. "What happened to freak you out so much?"

"We were just talking," I protested. "And I really didn't expect anything to come of it, I didn't. But I got a little tipsy, and I told him that I used to have a crush on him when I was younger..."

"Oh my God," she muttered. "You didn't really, did you?"

"Yeah..."

"And what happened?"

"He kissed me."

Marjorie fell silent for a long moment and I chewed my lip. I had no idea if she was about to cheer for me actually getting some action, or tell me off for letting something like that happen with someone I was working with.

"He kissed you."

"Yeah, just once," I replied, protesting the point even though I knew there was no reason to. "And he said it was just so we could put it behind us."

"But the fact that you're calling me suggests you're not exactly in a rush to put this behind you, huh?"

"Guess so," I agreed quietly. Just speaking to her was helping get my head a little more clear, and I was so grateful to have her voice of reason feeding into my brain right now.

"What were you talking about that something like that came up?"

"We were discussing his dating life."

"And how is it?"

"Well, he says that he doesn't really date at all," I confessed. "He just...sees women, I think. We didn't really get into why, but I didn't want to push or anything."

"So you just let him kiss you instead," She replied bluntly.

"Hey, don't you judge me for this," I laughed. "It was just a kiss. I just need you to remind me that that's all it was, okay?"

"That's all it was," she assured me. "Maybe he's right. Maybe you needed that to get it out of the way."

"Hmm..."

"But don't you go getting feelings for him, alright?" She warned me. "You know better than that. You're smarter than that, right?"

"I mean, I like to think so," I replied, and she giggled. She had such a girly giggle, you would never have imagined that it could have come out of the mouth of a woman who was as pulled-together and adult as her.

"If he's seeing a lot of girls," she continued, once she had calmed down. "Then you make sure that you just keep everything totally professional, right? Sounds like he's got enough complications as it is right now, you don't want to become one of them yourself."

"That's true," I murmured, scuffing my foot at the sidewalk below me.

She was speaking the truth, but I wasn't certain that I wanted to hear it right now.

"If you need me to come down to the office and kick your ass to remind you, just let me know," She offered. "These pregnancy hormones are just making me so angry, I'd be more than happy to have someone to take it out on."

"Damn, now I feel bad for leaving Terri alone with you," I teased. She snorted with laughter again.

"Are you walking home now?" She asked.

"Yeah..."

"Text me when you get back to your place, okay?" She ordered me. "So you don't have to make me worry all night long."

"You know you're going to be a great mom, Marj," I told her.

"I sure will," she agreed with confidence. "Come on, get yourself home and to bed. Make sure you're fighting fit when you go in tomorrow, okay?"

"I will," I promised her. "Thanks for talking with me, Marjorie."

"Anytime, Stef. You know that."

With that, we said our goodbyes and I hung up the phone. I made it the rest of the way home without much thinking about Jon, or the kiss, or anything that had happened in that bar while we had been out together. And yeah, when I got through the door, I found myself wishing that he could have been right there with me. But he wasn't. And that was just fine. We were working together, nothing more than that. No matter how tempted I was to pursue something outside of the office.

Chapter Six – Jon

I had no idea what to expect when I came into the office the next day.

I knew that she was going to be there, and that I was going to have to look her in the eyes and find some way to not think about the way her mouth had felt against mine the night before. A kiss that short had never left an impact this long on me, and I was having trouble thinking of anything other than the way it had felt to kiss her at last.

At last? Yeah, because if I was being honest, I had been thinking about it since the moment I had seen her again. And when she had told me that she used to have a crush on me when she was growing up, well, it would have seemed rude not to steal a quick kiss from her as a thank-you for her sweetness.

I hadn't been thinking about how I would justify it when I had leaned in for the kiss, but by the time I pulled back, I knew that I would have to come up with something. I couldn't just admit that I had kissed her for the sake of kissing her, because the thought of not feeling her lips on mine for another moment was way too much for me to handle right in that instant. By the time that I had pulled back and looked her in the eyes, I had figured it out – managed to spin some story about putting all this behind us so that we could move on with everything once and for all. Which she seemed pretty happy to just go right along with, thank fuck.

But I had kissed her. I had kissed her and I had forgotten that we were meant to be working together and not...well, not doing anything else together. Get a couple of drinks in her, though, and Stephanie was way different than the version of her that I had gotten to know so far. She was sharp, spunky, and flirty – yes, flirty, I was sure of it. She had been the one to bring up my dating life, after all, not me, she was the one who had wanted to know what my situation was when it came to women. If that wasn't hitting on me, then I had no idea what was.

I had thought about her all the way home that night. Half-tempted to invite her back to my place, actually, but I had figured that the kiss had already been an overstepping of the mark. I had to hold back, play it cool, and make sure that I didn't let my instincts get the best of me. Even though my instincts were telling me that as soon as I saw her again, I should pull her into my arms, and...

"Morning," Stephanie announced as she entered the office, and I quickly pushed everything that I had been thinking right to the back of my mind. No need to get hung up on any of that, right? I grinned and nodded in her direction.

"Not too hungover, then?"

"More a sugar hangover than anything else," she replied, pulling a face. "But I can survive. Just going to need a few more coffees than normal and I'll be fine."

"Relief," I replied. "I thought I was going to have to make it through this day all alone."

"You really thought I would leave you in the lurch this early on in the game?" She replied, and she shook her head. "Damn, I was sure you thought better of me."

"Must just be a hangover from working with Nate..."

"Hey, no mentioning his name in here," she warned me, waving her finger in my direction. "I'm nothing like him. He's not relevant here, okay?"

"Noted," I agreed. "So, you ready to get back to work?"

"What exactly is it that we're doing today?" She wondered aloud. "We did all those calls yesterday, I assume there's not much that we can follow up on-"

"No, but I want to get together a list of the new clients we can reach out to," I explained. "It's going to be hard work, but we just need to sit around on our asses and do nothing but scroll through internet searches. You think you can handle that?"

"I think that's all I can handle right now," she agreed, and she took a sip of the coffee that she had brought with her and planted herself down at the small corner of desk that I had cleared for her. Opening up her laptop, she looked over the email I had sent her with the links where she could start looking for potential new clients, and she got down to work.

And I kept on stealing little glances over in her direction. What was she thinking about? Was she thinking about me? If she was remembering our kiss from the night before, then she was doing an excellent job pretending that she wasn't. I found my eyes drawn to her mouth more than once, drawn to the shape of them, the way they looked, the memory of the way they had tasted. A small furrow appeared in her brow when she was concentrating, and it was the cutest thing in the world to me. I wanted to reach out and smooth it over, to calm her down and cool her off.

She jumped when her phone leapt back to life once more, and she pulled it out at once. Looking down at the screen, her jaw dropped.

"What is it?" I asked curiously.

"It's one of the people I was speaking to yesterday," she explained quickly. "Desi Designs? I thought they sounded pretty bored by the whole thing, but she wouldn't be calling back so soon if she wasn't..."

"Stop trying to guess and answer it!" I urged her on. She blinked at me, and then nodded in agreement.

"Right, right, of course," she murmured, and she snatched up the phone and took the call.

She got up and headed out of the room while she was on the call, and I fought the urge to get to my feet and listen in at the door to catch what was going on out there. I needed a win here. Not just because it would have been good for the business, but to remind me that this was where we worked best. Not kissing in bars after a few too many drinks, but working together, working to make this company work the way that it needed to.

By the time that she came back into the room, she had a huge smile on her face and her eyes were shining with a barely-contained excitement.

"Oh my God," she breathed. "You won't believe it..."

"I think I will," I urged her. "Come on, tell me what happened!"

"They want to order a huge shipment," she explained. "I told them that we were still getting sorted with our distributors and stuff, but they said that it didn't matter. Said they'd buy up what we have left in stock right about now, and then when we start manufacturing again, they'll be the first in line to buy from us."

"Fuck," I muttered. I was already crunching the numbers inside my head.

"That's going to be enough for us to look into the new factories, hire some new employees," I murmured. "This is what we needed. Shit, Stephanie, you saved our asses here..."

"I know," she laughed, and she dropped her phone back into her pocket. "I know! I didn't think we would hear from anyone so soon, but they seem really enthusiastic."

"That's all on you," I told her. "You know that? I heard you yesterday, it was hard not to get excited just listening to you talk about all this stuff.

You should be so proud of yourself, you've already done something huge for the company and it's only your second day here."

"I just can't believe it," She murmured again, and she seemed so utterly and totally stunned that there was nothing else she could come out with. I clasped her face in my hands, and looked deep into her eyes.

"Well, you better start," I told her firmly. "Because you did this. You hear? You did this. You get to be proud of this."

"I guess so," she replied, and suddenly her gaze was fixed on me again – just like it had been back in the bar. Her mouth parted a little, and her gaze travelled down, and suddenly I knew just what she was thinking about – just what was going through her mind. It had taken a while for me to click into this place with her, but now I was here, I didn't want to go.

I thought about kissing her again. For a longer moment than I would have cared to admit to. My hands were still on either side of her face and I knew that she was thinking about it, too. How could she not be? We were so close, so near, the two of us so close to one another that either one of us could have moved an inch and made this happen.

But then, before I could let my mind linger there a moment longer, she pulled away from me.

"I, uh," she blurted, stammering, and she bit her lip. Fuck, I wish that could have been my teeth on her. I wanted to see if she would flinch when I touched her that way, or if she would like it and beg for more.

"I should go get myself another coffee," She remarked, loudly, like she was trying to extinguish the last of the flame that was still there between us.

"Do you want anything?" She asked. I nodded.

"Just something black and strong," I replied, and she nodded at once. She hovered in the door for a moment before she went outside, and she flicked her gaze up to meet me once more.

"I'm sorry," she murmured. And though I knew she had nothing to apologize for, it made something jolt inside of me – because that she was apologizing meant that she had felt this, too. And it seemed like either of us acknowledging that was a little too much for me to handle.

"What for? Getting us a client who's going to let us profit off our backlog?" I replied, pretending that I had no idea what she was talking about. She smiled.

"Yeah, of course," she agreed. "I'll be back in a second."

"See you," I replied, and I kept the smile on my face until she had closed the door behind her and walked out. As soon as she had, I slumped back down into my chair and let out a groan.

What was it about being around a woman that I knew I wasn't meant to have that made it so hard to keep my fucking cool? I could have gone out and picked up anyone I wanted, couldn't have hit up a bar and made myself feel at home in any woman's bed for an evening or two. But now, I wanted her. Now, my head was stuck on the way that she made me feel. I hadn't had something off-limits to me in a long time, even something that I had just marked off inside my own head as not on the table. I didn't like to restrict myself where I could avoid it, and this felt markedly like restriction.

But there was something about her. It was more than just the way she looked, though I obviously thought that she was hot as hell. Something about the way she carried herself drove me crazy. This budding confidence that I could see blooming there right in front of me – God, it was a gift to get to see it in action. I knew she was only just starting, too, that it wouldn't be long until I got to see her at full force, in full flow. I couldn't even imagine what she was going to be like then, in her final form. Given that she was already so awesome right now.

But maybe it wasn't my place to know. Maybe I just worked with her, gave her the space to do what she needed to do, supporting her along the way. I could see it when it came to work, but when it came to her, I would have to accept that she didn't owe me anything. I was lucky to have someone like her working next to me. That was where it ended. Sharing coffees, not cocktails. Celebrating wins at work, not anywhere else. Last night had been a mistake, one that I wasn't planning on making again any time soon. At least, that's what I had to convince myself.

Chapter Seven – Stephanie

"Well, well, well, if it isn't the rich, successful businesswoman!" Terri greeted me as I rolled a rack of clothes through the door.

"Hey, I don't know about rich," I laughed. "Or successful yet..."

"Successful enough to get stocked in here," Marjorie remarked, nudging me and winking. Her belly was starting to look so swollen, and every time I laid eyes on her, I found myself just swooning a little bit more at the thought of holding my perfect little niece or nephew in my arms when the time came.

"Yeah, well, I've got an in with the boss," I joked. She grinned.

"Fair point," she agreed. "But I think I'd have taken these anyway. They're gorgeous, really – I don't think we've ever had anything like this before."

"Yeah, they're really beautiful, aren't they?" I agreed, a little wistfully. They were from the last collection that Amaya had designed in its entirety – she had been interested in marrying more traditional fabrics with more modern shapes, and some of the stuff she had come up with was just stunning. These gorgeous, tailored pants, printed with red and gold; loose, flowing tops that would have looked so chic tucked into a pair of jeans or smart pants.

"You're lucky you got in touch with us in time," I continued, distracting myself from the melancholy that had threatened to take control of me when I thought about Amaya. I knew she would be looking down on this display I was setting up with happiness; this store was well-attended by the people who knew where to look for something different, and I was sure they were going to eat this up.

"We had someone buy up the last of the stock back in India just a couple of days ago," I explained. Terri, hopping down from the counter where she had been waiting for me, clapped her hands together.

"That's amazing!" She exclaimed. "You guys are already doing so well. You must be so excited, right?"

"Yeah, I am," I agreed. "Glad to have the money to pay for the set-up for the next stage."

"And what does that look like?" Terri asked with interest. I waved my hand.

"Honestly, I don't really want to talk about that right now," I admitted. "I've spent way longer than I would have like to lately going over all this stuff, I just want to forget about it for a while."

"Well, I'm sure we can help with that," Marjorie assured me, as she guided the rack behind the counter and started going through the clothes I had brought in for her to stock. It was so good of her to agree to share Amaya's stuff with the world like this, but then, these guys always had my back – I shouldn't have expected anything different.

"How are things going with Jon?" Terri asked, and I glanced over at her. That wasn't exactly what I had been expecting, to be honest. I noticed that Marjorie had gone a little red, and I raised my eyebrows at her. Had she spilled the beans as to what had happened with Jon and me on that night out?

"What about Jon?" I asked, a little more on the defensive than I exactly had reason to be. Terri cocked her head to the side and eyed me.

"Oh, I think you know," she shot back, a grin spreading over her face.

"Okay, yes, so I kissed him," I admitted, and I tossed my hands in the air. "Or he kissed me. I'm not even sure which way round it was, not really..."

"Hmm," Terri replied, tapping her finger on her lip. "Well, from the way Marjorie described it..."

"And bear in mind that she was describing it based on what I told her," I pointed out. "Not first-hand."

"But from what she told me, it sounded like he kissed you after you told him that you used to have a crush on him," she pointed out. "Wouldn't you say that's the case?"

"You sound like a detective," I teased her, but then I sighed and nodded. "Yeah, I think that's closer to what actually happened. I mean, I'd like to think that I was the in control of all of that, but..."

"But he just swept you off your feet," Terri finished up for me, clasping her hands to her chest as though she could hardly take the intense romance of it all. I laughed.

"I don't think I'd go that far," I replied, shaking my head. "It was just a kiss. And he said it was just so that we could put all of this behind us, so that we didn't have to think about-"

"If he'd really wanted you to be able to move past it, he wouldn't have kissed you," Marjorie interjected. She had been tending to the dresses for a little while, but she had been clicked into our conversation, and it was obvious that she was no great fan of what she was hearing.

"What do you mean?" I asked, and she raised her eyebrows at me.

"I mean, if he really wanted you to be able to forget about all of this," she pointed out. "He would have just laughed it off and kept going like he'd never heard it. The fact that he kissed you...well, those aren't the actions of someone who wants to just leave it behind, put it like that."

"And so what if he doesn't?" Terri remarked. "Nothing wrong with our girl having a little fun for a change, is there?"

"For a change?" I protested. "Is that really how you guys think of me?"

"No, not at all," Terri assured me. "Just that...you know. You've never..."

She trailed off and left the words unspoken, but she didn't have to say what was on her mind. It was clear to me. She was talking about the fact that I was a virgin.

And yeah, I did get that it was a strange thing for them to try and get their heads around. I was meant to be this strong, empowered woman, after all – and strong, empowered women didn't exactly sit around waiting for permission to go out and enjoy their lives to the fullest. But it was hard to shake off the memories of how you were treated for pursuing what you wanted, and I was in no place to get over the upbringing that had told me that I was a slut for so much as thinking about having sex.

And by the time that I had learned that there wasn't anything wrong with me for having these needs and desires and stuff, I guess it had already been drilled into me that I shouldn't bother pursuing them, and I had pushed down my libido so far that I could hardly dig it up again. How was I meant to just click out of that mode when I had spent so long thinking that way? It wasn't that easy.

I had met a few guys here and there, had even gone on a few dates, but I had never gone past making out and I had never much felt the urge to, either. It was just that, after hanging on to it for so long, I felt oddly protective of my virginity. I didn't want to just give it away to anyone. I wanted to make sure that it was something utterly and completely perfect, and maybe that was what had been getting me to hang on to it all this time.

Or, maybe, that was just an excuse to make sure that I never had to follow through with any of the guys I had been seeing before. It was easy to pick these minor flaws here and there, to realize that I didn't like the way he talked or the way he chewed his food or the way he kissed me that one time, and call the whole thing off in my head. I didn't want to toss it away, and that had led to me carrying it about for so long now that I couldn't ever imagine not being without it.

But I would have to get rid of this damn thing one time or another. I was letting nerves hold me back, had been for a long time now, and where had it gotten me? It had gotten me to the age I was now, still a virgin, still freaked out about the thought of actually letting someone that close to my body. I had been the only person to see me naked in a long time, and the thought of someone else laying eyes on my naked form like that...no. No way. What if they thought I was ugly? What if I was, and didn't know it?

Not to mention the fact that being a virgin at my age was hardly something that people expected. I guessed there was a certain type of guy who would have been happy to come prowling for women who had never had sex before, but I didn't want anything to do with that kind of man. I wanted the kind of man who would know that about me, accept it, but wouldn't make it some big thing.

"Of course you have fun," Marjorie promised me. "But you know how it is, guys can be strange if you haven't done what they think you have..."

"And you think that any guy looking at me is just going to assume I'm a full-blown sex vixen?" I asked, smiling, half-joking. Terri pinched my elbow playfully.

"Well, duh," she replied. "Look at you. Anyone could see it."

"Of course," I agreed. "But...but you think I should go after that? With him?"

"With Jon?" Marjorie cut in. "No damn way. You never want to get involved with someone you work with."

"Wait, is that what's been getting in the way of our passionate love affair all this time?" Terri asked, clasping her hand to her chest. "I can't believe it. If only I'd known sooner..."

"Very funny," Marjorie laughed. "No, but you see what I'm saying, right? You don't want to jump into something with someone you're going to be working closely with for the next three months, it just wouldn't be smart-"

"Yeah, but that's how you met your man, wasn't it?" Terri remarked. She had a point. Marjorie shrugged.

"Yeah, I guess so," she admitted. "But the two of us weren't stuck together for three whole months. I could have tapped out any time I wanted. But with you guys..."

"It's only three months," Terri reminded me. "So if something doesn't pan out then you can just peace out when it's all over, can't you?"

"And if it doesn't work out before you get to the three-month mark?" Marjorie asked, planting her hands on her hips and giving Terri her best mom-friend look. I almost laughed out loud; the two of them were constantly disagreeing, and sometimes I wondered if there was a single thing that had come out of Terri's mouth that Marjorie hadn't had something smart to say about. But I knew the two of them loved each other like crazy; Marjorie had just been even more protective about the two of us lately, probably because she knew that she would be having her baby soon and wouldn't be able to keep as much of an eye on us.

"Then they'll find some way to figure it out," Terri replied. "Come on, it could be fun. Right, Stef?"

I hadn't said a word in a while; wasn't sure what I was meant to say, really. This was sex and dating and relationships, all the stuff that I had been so careful to avoid getting into in deep detail before. But now, they were debating the merits of my dating life, and I had no clue how to feel about it.

"I guess," I admitted, but I didn't really sound so sure. Because I wasn't - I had no idea if this was what I actually wanted or not. It felt...heavy. Difficult. Something that I had never really thought about before, if I was being honest, something that I had never really *wanted* to think about, either.

"See, she's not sure about it," Marjorie pointed out. "You don't have to do this, Stef, you really don't. If you want to take your time losing it-"

"Can we stop talking about my virginity?" I asked, suddenly. I usually didn't mind so much conversing about my lack of boyfriend, but there was something about today that just flicked a switch. I didn't want to have these conversations with them any longer. Wasn't this meant to be personal? I was pretty sure I should have been keeping this to myself.

"Sorry," Marjorie apologized. "I didn't want to make you uncomfortable."

"Yeah, sorry, babe," Terri murmured to me, and she gave me a quick hug. "I guess we're both just shocked that you've managed to hold on to it for so long. I mean, look at you..."

She trailed off, probably sensing that I was more than done with this conversation as it stood. It wasn't that I didn't appreciate the compliment, but I felt like I had better things to be doing with my time than listening to how pretty she thought I was. It was sweet to hear that they thought I was that beautiful, but I was starting to feel a little uncomfortable, and that wasn't something I dealt too well with.

"Hey," Marjorie reached out for me, and squeezed my arm. "Consider it dropped, okay? Why don't you tell us a little more about your grandma's designs?"

I perked up at that offer; I was always happy to do a little more talking on that subject. We talked some more about the clothes and the looks and the way that we could style it on the mannequin that stood in the window, and soon, I had all but forgotten about the conversation that we had been having up until that moment. It didn't matter. It was behind us now, and I wanted to forget about it for the time being.

It wasn't until I walked out of the store at the end of the day that my mind flickered back to what we had been discussing before. Maybe Terri had a point — it was strange for me to still be hanging on to my virginity after all this time. I should have let go of it by now. It wasn't like I hadn't had the offers over the years, and in all honestly, most of the guys I'd thought about doing it with had probably been totally acceptable candidates.

But I wanted something special. Something different. Maybe that was naïve of me, I had no idea, but it was all I could think about when it came to this. I wanted to make sure that when I lost it, it was to someone who knew what they were doing — somehow who I could be sure would do a good job, who would open me up to the world of sexuality in a way that I would never forget in my whole life.

And if anyone could do that, it would be Jon. I mean, judging by everything that I had heard from everyone in this city, anyway. He had enough of a reputation that I had to believe at least some small part of it was well-earned. He was the kind of guy who got around, and you didn't manage to do that if you were terrible in bed.

And that kiss. I couldn't stop thinking about that damn kiss. It had felt like my feet had drifted off the ground for a moment, and I couldn't stop thinking about how amazing that sensation had been for me. How much better would it be if I was to take that to the next level? If I was to let him...well, if I was to let him do everything that he wanted to me?

I swear, I hardly noticed the rest of the city around me as I imagined it. I had no idea how I would get to that point, only that I would get there, and that when I did, it was going to be amazing. I could just imagine it – yes, we would slip into bed together, and there would be that look on his face that told me that he wanted every little thing about me, and I would be helpless to resist. I would whisper to him that it was my first time, and he would kiss me again and assure me with that kiss that he was fine with that. That he was honored by the chance I had given him to be the first person to take me to bed. Mmm, even the thought of that...

"Excuse me, Miss?"

I looked up, and realized that I was just standing in the way of three older tourists who looked like they were annoyed by the hold-up. I gasped, and quickly stepped aside, ducking my head down in apology.

"Sorry, sorry," I muttered, and I headed past them and felt my face getting hot. Okay, so maybe thinking in great detail about this while I was wandering about the city wasn't the best idea. They gave me a funny look and walked on by me. Probably wondering why I was walking around the streets like such a complete ditz.

It was because I had a crush. If I was being honest, that was the reason. I had a crush on Jon just the same way I had had a crush on him when we had been younger. Except this time, I wasn't an awkward teenager – this time, I was a fully-grown woman. A woman who knew just what she wanted.

And maybe I wanted – well, him. I couldn't be sure of that yet, and I felt like I never properly would be, but I had to give myself some space to think that I could be. I had always doubted my instincts and my ability to be certain when it came to stuff like this, but perhaps, just perhaps, maybe, there was a chance that all of this was just what I had been waiting for.

There was a reason Amaya had put the two of us together to run the company. She knew us better than we knew one another. Perhaps there was something there that she saw, something that we hadn't figured out yet...?

By the time I got back to my apartment, I had all but convinced myself that Amaya had set the two of us up with every intention of us getting together. Which was a little crazy, when I put it like that, but maybe it was true, somehow. Or maybe I was just looking for an excuse to finally climb into bed with a man, and lose what had been weighing me down all this time.

The thing was, I did see myself getting married and settling down in the future. And what man was going to want to be with a woman who hadn't even lost her virginity yet? They would think I was crazy, that there was something wrong with me, and I had no intention of putting off a perfectly good prospect just because I was struggling to get my shit together when it came to losing it. I had to get this out of the way before it caused a bigger problem in my life than it needed to, didn't I? And that meant just leaning into it and getting it down before I let it grow any bigger in my head.

And look at what had happened for Marjorie. She had done something like that, and it had turned out so well for her. She had fallen in love, gotten pregnant, she had found the perfect guy for her. Maybe, just maybe, I would be lucky enough to get the same thing from all of this-

I stopped myself in my tracks before that line of thought went any further. Nope. Nope, nope, nope. I had to be more careful than that. I couldn't let the rush of what I wanted to happen with him turn into a certainty in my head. I had to hold back and make sure that I knew that this was just going to be sex. Because Marjorie had had a history with her guy, but me and Jon – well, we might have had a history, but it was hardly the kind that you could build a relationship on. The last time he had seen me, I had been an awkward teenager crushing hopelessly on an older man.

I just hoped that he would be able to see past that and to the person that I was right now. I knew it was going to be tough to convince him, but I was sure I could do it. After all, he had been the one to kiss me. He had been the one to want me in the first place...

I went for a shower to try and cool myself off and stop all of this taking over my head. I needed some time to think, much as it was tempting

to just text him and tell him to come around here and fuck me at last. But I would see how I felt about it in the morning. No rush. Take my time. I had already taken twenty-seven years to get to this point, and I certainly wasn't going to hurry to lose it even if I thought I had found the guy that I wanted to do it with.

As I lay there in bed that night, all by myself, staring at the ceiling, I wondered if he was thinking about me. I didn't know where he lived in the city, but somehow, I could feel him as though he was close by. Which was crazy, I knew that, but it felt so powerful to think of him so near to me. As though I could just reach out and close the gap between us, make it so that there was nothing keeping us apart any longer. Nothing between us. Nothing holding us back.

And in that moment, I knew that I wasn't going to have to wait till the morning after to make my choice. I was ready. I was ready, and I knew it was him I was ready for. There was no more doubt in my mind. It was time. And it was time to do it with him.

Chapter Eight – Jon

The last thing I expected when she marched into the office that morning was what came out of her mouth.

"Hey," I greeted Stephanie, glancing up from the papers I had been looking over when she had arrived. "You doing well?"

"Yeah," She replied. "I dropped off the garments at the store yesterday, so they're all set up and ready to go..."

I noticed that there was a slight tremble in her voice, and I looked up at her and furrowed my brow.

"Is everything alright?" I asked her, and she looked at me, really looked at me, as though she was weighing up the pros and cons of something in her head. Finally, she nodded.

"Everything's fine," she replied quietly. She closed her eyes, took a deep breath, and planted her hands down on the table in front of me.

"Jon, there's something I really need to ask you," she announced. I raised my eyebrows at her.

"Anything, you know that," I assured her. "We have to be honest with each other, right?"

"Right," she agreed, and she looked down at her hands for a moment and took another deep breath. It was like she was taking a run-up at something, ready to plunge over the edge and free herself from whatever she was holding back.

"I've been thinking about something," she confessed.

"You know you can tell me anything," I promised her, and I furrowed my brow as I looked into her eyes and tried to figure out what it was that was on her mind. There was sure as hell something bothering her, that was for sure, but I couldn't imagine what it might have been. Everything had been going well lately, and unless there had been an issue with her dropping off the garments at her friends store-

She sat down in the chair opposite mine, and I knew in that moment that it was something that had nothing to do with the business. Something way more intense than that. She didn't take her eyes off me the whole time, and I could see something pulsing at the back of her brain, something that she had been nervous about coming out with. I wished I could just reach in there and find out what it was, but she was holding back from me, holding back this secret, whatever the hell it was.

"What's going on?" I demanded at once. "Has something happened?"

"Jon, okay, listen to me," she began, and she took one last deep breath and then launched into it.

"Please just let me get all of this out, alright?" She pleaded with me. "I know it's going to sound crazy, but you just have to trust me with all of this. It sounds like a lot and it probably seems like a really stupid idea, but I could use your...help, I guess, when it comes to all of this."

"What's happening?" I asked her, a little more gently than last time.

"I need you to fuck me."

"What?" I exclaimed. I was sure that I must have heard her wrong. Must have pasted in what I wanted to hear over what she actually said because there was no way in hell-

"Okay, sorry, I shouldn't have opened with that," she corrected herself. "I mean to say – I mean to say that I need to get something out of the way, and I figured that you're the man who can help me with it."

"What do you need to get out of the way?" I asked, confused. She sighed, closed her eyes for a moment.

"Okay, so I'm a virgin," she confessed. My jaw just about dropped.

"What do you mean?"

"I mean, as in, I've never had sex," she admitted. "It's been...uh, not that the opportunity hasn't arisen or anything, but I...I just never got around to doing it."

I stared at her for a long, silent second. There had to be some kind of mistake. There was no way in hell someone who looked like that, who moved like that, who acted the way she acted, there was no way that some guy hadn't snapped her up already.

But then, maybe it wasn't about the men, I reasoned with myself. Maybe it was about her. What she wanted. What she felt comfortable with. And it was clear that, even talking about it now, she was far from comfortable.

"Okay," I replied, nodding, trying to keep my face neutral and my voice clear of any judgement over what she was telling me. "And why are you letting me in on this?"

"Because I need you to help me get rid of it," she told me. "I mean, if you want to, I mean. If you don't, I totally get it, but it's just that-"

"Stephanie, you're going to have to be a little blunter with me about what you actually mean here," I told her, lifting my hand to stop her in her tracks. "You want me to...?"

"I want you to have sex with me," she replied, and she finally looked me in the eye, and just hearing those words come out of her mouth was enough to send this shockwave of want all the way through my system.

"I see," I replied, trying to keep my voice and my face neutral and not give away the sheer excitement at the thought of what she had just said to me. She bit her lip, and I remembered, uninvited, just how good it had felt to kiss them. And she was asking me to do it again. To do it again, and more. God, that would be so fucking hot...

"I know that it sounds crazy," she admitted. "Trust me, I do. But it's not like I'm going to have a chance to meet many other people since we're spending all our time at the office, and I just want to get rid of it once and for all, and I'm not going to be able to do that with someone I know anytime soon because you're the only man I actually really know outside my family and-"

"Stephanie," I stopped her gently in her tracks. She caught herself, and shook her head.

"Sorry," she apologized. "I just don't really know how I'm meant to go about this whole...thing."

"Me neither," I agreed. "So let's take it slow, huh?"

"Okay," she replied. "I'm sorry to just spring this on you, and I get it if you don't want to do it, but I figured that we're spending most of our time together anyway, and I need to get rid of this thing that's hanging over my head, so why not just...just get it out of the way for good?"

"That's very business-like of you," I laughed. I had to admit, this whole thing sounded crazy to me, but if it was what she wanted then I was more than happy to give it to her-

In fact, was I? Yes, I was attracted to this woman, there was no doubt in my mind about that, but we were also meant to be running this company together. Her family company. If we hooked up and things didn't go exactly as we planned, then what could that mean for the rest of the time we had to spend together?

It was only three months, though. I could survive three months of just

about anything. If things got awkward, then I could just bail when it was done, get her an office of her own to work in, forget that any of this had ever happened in the first place...

I was already talking myself into it. Already taken with the idea of being with her. Even as she sat here opposite me, I was thinking about everything I wanted to do to her, all the ways I wanted to strip her down naked and run my hands over that perfect body. I wanted to kiss her again, and this time, do it properly – I wanted to do it with my hand between her thighs so I could feel how wet she was getting from my attentions, and I wanted to make sure that her first time would be the time that she would never forget.

I knew that now she had put the offer down on the table that I wasn't going to be able to say no to it. I had to take her up on this. If I didn't, I would spend the rest of the time that we were working together wondering how amazing it would have been if I had just gone ahead and said yes. I would never have been able to forgive myself. And she was a grown-ass woman; if she wanted to do something like this, then who was I to deny her of that?

"So, do you think you can do this for me?" She asked. "Just a one-time thing, that's all. I don't want it to get complicated between us, and I know that sounds crazy given what I'm proposing, but-"

"I'll do it," I promised her, and, at once, a huge smile spread over her face. She planted her hand on her chest.

"Oh my God, I was so sure you were going to say no and then I was going to have to leave the city out of humiliation," she remarked. "Are you sure? You sure you can do this?"

"I'm sure I can do this," I replied. She was talking like this was some great trial that she had asked me to take care of for her. Did she know how fucking sexy she was? Any man out there would have jumped at the chance to be with her in that way. And she was talking about it like she was asking me to give up some of my precious time for something that was a pure indulgence to her. She really had no idea how fucking hot she was, did she?

"Good," she replied, and she took a moment to gather herself. "Sorry, I didn't think – I guess I didn't really believe that you would say yes to this."

"Well, here I am, saying yes," I assured her. "And I mean it, really. I want to do this for you. If it's going to help."

"I can't believe we're sitting here in the office just talking about this," she remarked, glancing around as though she half-expected the ghost of Amaya to rise from the grave and tell her off for not taking this seriously enough.

"Well, we've got to talk about it somewhere, right?" I replied, and she nodded.

"I guess so," she agreed. "But can we just...shall we just leave this behind us for now? We can come up with a time and place, and then we can just make it so we don't think about it until then. Does that sound good to you?"

"Sounds good to me," I agreed, and she beamed widely. She had the most beautiful smile, the kind that lit up her whole face. It made my heart beat a little faster thinking about seeing her wearing only that smile.

"So, when and where?" She asked, and she pulled out her phone. "Let me just check when I have some time free..."

I couldn't help but laugh at the sight of her putting our hook-up into her calendar like it was just another business meeting.

"What is it?" She asked, glancing up at me. I shook my head.

"Nothing," I assured her. "When works for you?"

"How about this Saturday evening?" She suggested.

"That's perfect," I agreed. "At my place? I can text you the address..."

"Yeah, that sounds great," she replied, and she paused for a moment, biting her lip and just looking at me. I could see that she had a whole lot of questions she wanted to throw my way, but she had the sense to realize that this was best left till the time actually came. Till the time came for *her* to come, that was.

"Thank you for doing this for me," She murmured, and she seemed to mean it. Did she really think that being with her in that way was going to be some kind of trial? I wanted to land a punch on the guy who had made her believe that she was anything other than totally perfect the way she was. Though, I supposed, it might have been to do with her family; they could be old-fashioned in their way, and it might have been their influence that kept her from embracing what she should have allowed herself.

"So, the deal's done?" I asked her, and she extended her hand to me.

"The deal's done," she agreed, and I reached out to take her hand. As soon as our skin touched, I knew that we had made the right choice. This might have sounded crazy to anyone else, and maybe it even sounded a little crazy to me, but I was ready to do this. Ready to give her what she wanted so badly. If she needed a favor from me, then who was I, as her partner in this, to say no to her?

"I'm going to go get a coffee," she told me, as she withdrew her hand from mine. "Do you want anything?"

"Nope," I replied. "But thanks for the offer."

She smiled, and I watched her as she got up and headed for the door. I wondered if she could feel my eyes on her or not, given that she swung her hips this way and that in a little over-the-top strut as she made her way out of my office. God, she was so fucking sexy. I couldn't wait to get my hands on her. When I had come into work this morning, this had been the last deal that I had expected to make – but maybe it was the one that I should have been gunning for from the start.

I was already planning out every detail of what we were going to do together. It was going to be so much fun. She had never done this before, so she would be looking to me for guidance and support on all of this, guidance and support that I would be more than happy to gift to her. It had been such a long time since I had lost it that I had nearly forgotten what it had been like not to know what to expect from an encounter like this, but I was sure I could pull myself back there, get myself into that state of mind once again to give her everything that she needed for this.

I leaned back at the desk, and locked my hands behind my head. Yeah. Yeah, this was going to be good. Maybe I should have been more careful not to let my dick run the show – or maybe giving myself over to my most primal desires was the best thing that I could do right now. Ever since that kiss, I hadn't been able to stop thinking about her. And now, it seemed, we were both going to have the chance to get over each other for good. By getting under each other at last.

Chapter Nine – Stephanie

I had checked my hair precisely twenty times in the mirror before I had left my place, and I was still sure that I looked awful.

I wasn't sure that this was a good idea. I had been having second thoughts about it since we had agreed to it a few days before, and I was certain that I was making some kind of mistake. My brain felt like it was overstuffed with all the panic and nerves that had come with losing it, added to the fact that I was doing it with a man that I was meant to be working with...yeah, I was sure that pretty much anyone out there would have told me that what I was doing was stupid. And maybe they had a point.

I hadn't breathed a word of this to anyone else before I had gotten out there, and there was a good reason for that. I didn't want anyone else getting involved and having something to say about what was going on between us. I was nervous, sure, and I could have used some advice to make things a little easier, but I had to make this entirely my own choice. Not something that came from anyone or anything else.

He had given me his address, and I had been thinking about it ever since we had walked out of the office on Friday. I wanted him, there was no doubt in my mind about that, I wanted him badly, but there was some part of me that was beginning to doubt if this was really how I wanted him. I mean, I had spent my whole life trying to make sure things ran exactly as I wanted them to, and now I was treating losing my virginity like that as well. Could it really be that easy? I was worried that I was turning this into too much of a chore when I should have been allowing myself to get lost to the raw, real passion of the moment.

That was what I had waited for all this time. Spontaneity. And I had never been able to let it happen because I had never once allowed the moment to just take me. I had been sure that it was the best way to keep everything carefully-controlled in my life, but maybe, just maybe, I was wrong about it this time. Maybe it needed to come out of nowhere.

I took my time getting to his place; he lived in a nice part of the city, and he had promised to have wine ready for me when I got there so that we could take the edge off of my nerves together. But by the time that I arrived outside his door, my nerves had all but swelled to take control of me. I didn't know if I could do this...

And I didn't know if I could back out. I mean, how dumb would I look if I pulled out of this now? I didn't want to run away from something that I had been so forthright in getting off the ground in the first place. What would he think of me? Would he imagine that it had all been some kind of joke at his expense? That was the last thing I wanted, and yet...

Someone bumped into me, and made a little noise of irritation, and I realized that I was just standing there in the middle of the street like an idiot getting in everyone's way. I had to go up there. I had to see him face-to-face, and then I could work out what the hell I was going to do next.

I buzzed on his door, and a moment later, the latch clicked and I headed inside. I was wearing this dark dress that was tight around the hips, and it meant that I was a little hobbled with every stride. I tried not to think about how silly it was going to make me look. I held my breath until I arrived outside his apartment, and I found myself hovering outside the door for a moment, not sure what I was meant to do now.

And then, it opened right in front of me, and I was faced with him, the man I hadn't been able to get out of my head since we had kissed for the first time.

"Jon," I breathed, his name like wine on my lips. And with that, I moved towards him, and I felt his lips on mine, and everything else just seemed to fall away like it had never existed in the first place.

His mouth was soft and eager, and he parted my lips with his tongue quickly, pulling me over the threshold and into his apartment before I so much as had a chance to take it in. His hands were on my waist, pulling me in close, and I arched my back to push myself against him. How was it that his touch could make me so crazy? I felt like everything was finally coming together the way it was meant to after all this time, and I could hardly keep my head straight, my brain felt like it was overflowing with the intensity of wanting and being wanted like this...

He pushed me back against the door as soon as it was closed behind me, and kissed me again, harder this time, his hands pressed to the wood on either side of me like he was pinning me in place. I didn't care. Even though I knew I should have felt trapped, I felt safe; I knew that if I told him that I wanted all this to stop right this instant, he would do that for me without a second thought. I was so lucky to be with someone who was so understanding, who seemed to get me on such a fundamental level. What had I been nervous about, again? It was hard to remember.

His mouth was eager and hungry on mine, his lips parting my own like he couldn't get enough of me. I was already addicted to this, to the way it made me feel. I had never in my whole damn like felt as desirable as I did when he was kissing me. All the other men I had been with, they had treated me like I was this delicate thing, careful not to break me, but he – he was different. He came at me like he could hardly resist me, and there was something so painfully hot about that I could hardly handle it.

His hands stroked down my sides, over my hips and my waist, tracing the shape of me under my clothes, until they came to rest on my thighs beneath the hem of my dress. I could feel him breathing hard as he moved his mouth from my mouth to my neck, the intensity of the moment getting the better of him just the same way it was getting the better of me.

"Fuck," he groaned in my ear. "You have no idea how long I've been waiting for this..."

I could only moan in response, all ability to actually talk out of my head for good. How could there be words when all I could think about was him? How could there be anything other than just the way that he made me feel? I needed to know, needed to understand, needed to wrap my head around it, but there were no answers, only the feel of his fingers guiding up the hem of my dress.

My breath was coming harder now, my heart pounding, and I felt like I was getting a little dizzy. All of this was happening so fast, and I didn't want to stop it, but I had no idea what came next. I didn't like feeling out-of-control, but maybe this was what I needed – maybe this release is what I had been searching for all this time.

"Is this okay?" He asked softly, as his fingers skimmed up the inside of my thigh, tracing the shape of me all the way up to the black cotton panties I had slipped on before I'd left the house. I nodded.

"Tell me," he ordered me, and there was no room for argument in the way that he spoke to me.

"Yes," I replied, and I meant it. He was being careful with me, giving me every chance to stop if I wanted to.

He slowly let his fingers move a little further up, and he cupped his hand around me for a moment – God, the pressure of his fingers even through the fabric that continued to separate us was more than I could take.

I had to catch my breath for a moment, and he looked into my eyes, taking in my reaction. He knew just what he was doing to me. He knew just what he was doing to me, and he liked that he had me so utterly aroused that I could hardly even speak any longer.

"I want to taste you," he told me, softly, and the sound of those words coming out of his mouth – fuck, I had been wet before, but it had never felt like this, not in a million years. I wanted to plead with him to go ahead and do it, but I had no words left in the vault of my head right down. The best I could manage was to grab his hand and push it beneath the fabric of my underwear. He grinned, and kissed me again, then moved his mouth to my ear so he could whisper right against it.

"I'll take that as a yes?"

I nodded, and with that, he scooped me from where I stood, and carried me over to the couch in the middle of the room.

He placed me down on the middle of the couch, and knelt down between my legs, pushing my thighs apart like he had been starving for this for as long as he could remember. Reaching up, he hooked his fingers around my panties and tugged them off, slowly, taking his time - I watched his face as he undressed me, and I hoped to God that I wasn't going to do anything that would let him down. I knew it was crazy to think that way that he had made it pretty clear that he was attracted to me and that he didn't want to hold back from this, but still. I had been with men before, at least some of the way to the full shebang, and none of them had exactly acted like I was the most desirable being in the world.

He rolled up the hem of my skirt slowly, taking his time, pushing it over my hips, and he let out this low growl when he had me as naked as he wanted me. He lowered his mouth slowly to the inside of my thigh, and closed his eyes as he brushed it up my skin; I could feel his warm breath on that most intimate part of me, and my toes curled in the heels I was still wearing. I had thought they would be the sexiest thing about me, given my lack of knowledge about all of this stuff, but the way he was touching me and caressing me, I knew that he disagreed.

"Can I go down on you?" He asked me, as he reached the crook of my hip, the line that led down towards my pussy. I looked down at him, at this perfect man, and nodded.

"Yes," I breathed. And that was all the invitation that he needed.

He pressed his mouth to me for the first time, and I let out a helpless cry as he tasted me; fuck, that felt so incredible, it was almost more than I could take. I gasped as I felt his tongue brush against my clit, and I found my hips pushing up to meet him. I couldn't hold back, I didn't want to – I needed to feel him, every part of him, every inch, all of his mouth as he went down on me like it was the only thing that mattered to him in the entire world.

I reached down and ran my fingers through his hair, tentative at first; I wasn't sure how I was meant to touch him or what I was meant to do now that he was there. But I figured the best thing was to just let my instincts take control, and so I let that happen. I balled my fingers in his hair and pulled him on to me, and he let out a groan of pleasure as I took a little of the control from him. So, he liked that, huh? I felt a jolt of desire rush through me. I wanted him to want me just the same way that I wanted him. I needed it. I needed to know that he was as into this as I was.

I tipped my head back on the couch and let the feeling rush through me, nothing but the feeling. It felt incredible to just let him do this to me; it had been so long since I had allowed myself to give myself over to something as selfish as this, and my body had needed every moment of it. His tongue flattened gently and he lapped at me like he was starving, and I felt my toes curl as the rush of it took control.

That was it. From that point on, I could hardly remember anything else that happened, apart from the sheer intensity of the pleasure that he sent pulsing through my system as he went down on me. I had never had anyone go down on me before, and I had thought that it would feel a little strange – and maybe it would have, if it had been anyone other than him. But he seemed to know just what he was doing, just what I wanted, even before I did. He gently slipped a finger inside of me, and I gasped; I had thought that it might come with a little pain, someone else doing that for the first time, but instead, it felt...good. The mesh of sensations were incredible, powerful.

I could feel myself getting close already – God, so close I could hardly handle it. My breath was coming harder and faster than it had been before, and my skin was aching, every inch of it prickling as I pushed myself further and further towards the release that I needed so badly. I had never come with anything but my own hand before, but the feeling right now, as he took me to the edge – I knew that I was close to getting where I needed to be. God, the feeling of it, the sensation, it was like I was going to explode just trying to keep every inch of this pleasure in.

And that was when it all hit me.

The pressure that it released in that moment was more than I could stand. How could I hold it back any longer? I cried out so loudly that the sound seemed to fill the whole apartment around us, as everything clenched tightly for a moment and then released. I had come plenty of times before, of course I had, but none of them had ever felt like this – none of them had ever felt like they exploded through every inch of me, commanding my attention like this one did. I swear, my vision started to get a little blurry around the edges, and then I came back into my body, back to the pleasure, back to the moment.

He pulled his mouth back from my pussy, and looked up at me; his eyes were burning with desire, and he got to his feet and kissed me again. I could taste myself on his lips. A reminder of where he had just been – and I loved that.

He sank down on to the couch and pulled me on top of him, and I sank into his arms as I kissed him back. Where I had been feeling that intense lust just a few moments before, all I could think about now was the exhaustion that was consuming me. I had been so tense and so nervous and now that it was over it felt like all of it had leaked out of me.

"Are you alright?" He asked me, smoothing his hand gently down my back and looking at me intently. I nodded.

"More than alright," I replied. "That was amazing."

"If you want to leave it there," he murmured, and he kissed my cheek; it was almost a sweet gesture, had it not been for the fact that I was naked from the waist down. I looked at him for a moment, really thought about the question he was asking me – and realized that I couldn't do this. Not now.

"I think...I think I need to," I admitted. I felt a flush of humiliation over my body, and my toes curled again this time out of nervousness. I was so mad at myself for letting my feelings get the best of me, but maybe this was the right choice.

"It's fine," he promised me, but I could feel his hardness pressing against me, and I knew that he must have been mad at me pulling back when we had already gone this far.

I slipped from his lap and reached down to pull on my clothes once more. I couldn't believe that I had done this. I had come in here acting so sure, and now there was something else coming over me. A doubt. A fear. All of that breeding that I had grown up with, all of it was swelling up to take control of me, and now I couldn't go on and I needed to stop and-

"It's okay," He assured me, and he put his hand on my back; I jerked away, unable to feel his touch right there right now. I felt like I had let him down. I had promised him so much, and now I was pulling away and – I only had myself to blame for all of this.

"I need to go," I blurted out, as soon as I was dressed enough to get out of there. I was ready to get out of this place. I needed to. I couldn't sit here and continue to let him down when I had let him go that far with me, and then...

"I'm sorry," I told him. "I'm really sorry. I didn't think – please don't-"

"You don't have anything to be sorry for," he promised me. But I couldn't even look him in the eye. I had to get out of here, I had to be gone, and I had to make sure that there was nothing that would even hint that I had been here in the first place. Go, go, go.

I headed for the door without so much as looking back at him. This wasn't how I had seen this night going. I had pictured us curling up together, smiling, and holding one another. I had pictured me, happy, a little shocked at how good it had been, how easy it had been. I wanted it to go like that, but here I was, running out of there before he had been inside of me. I couldn't believe I had let this happen, couldn't believe it had gone so wrong...

By the time I made it out on to the street, I could feel the tears pricking my eyes. I had fucked this up. I had let him down. And it wasn't like I was just going to be able to brush this off so easily now that it had gone so badly wrong – we had to work together now, and I couldn't get out of it so easily.

People were filling out the streets outside by the time I got out there, and I was relieved that I had gotten out of there; I usually didn't like being surrounded by so many people, but right now, at least I could fade into the background and pretend that nobody had seen me in the first place. I could pretend that I was one of these people, people who had never been silly enough to think that they could take control of their own lives and then watched it blow up in their face. I would bet that none of the women here were fleeing from the apartment of the man who they were supposed to lose their virginity to before things got too intense for them to handle.

I considered calling Marjorie on the way back, but the thought of her kind sympathy to me was more than I could handle. She would be kind and understanding and I needed someone to tell me what an idiot I had been and that I should never have been as stupid as to do what I had done. The same thing that was rushing around and around my head right now, those same angry, furious thoughts that came to fill my brain.

I made it back to my place, and I pulled off my clothes and climbed in the shower. I kept the water cool, hoping it would serve its job to calm me down after what had happened. It didn't. Instead, it only serve to chill me to the core, and remind me that I had to go in to work on Monday – and face the man that I had just walked out on with no explanation.

Chapter Ten – Jon

She hadn't been in to the office all week. But that didn't mean that she could just check out of this job for good.

I hadn't been able to stop thinking about Stephanie since the two of us had had our aborted encounter a few days before. It had been incredible, but as soon as she had come for the first time, I had felt that doubt coming out of her in waves. She was worried, nervous – I could feel it. And I didn't want anything to do with a woman who wasn't one-hundred-percent committed to doing everything that I wanted to do with her.

She had left as soon as I had given her the chance, and I couldn't say that I was surprised by that. I mean, she had seemed so into it when we had been starting out with this, and I had certainly enjoyed it, but it was as though something had just switched inside of her as soon as it had come to what came next.

I was glad that she'd felt safe enough to say no when the time came, but I would have been lying if I'd said that I wasn't a little let-down about this. I had wanted her so badly, and now that the switch had been flicked inside of me, it was hard, if not impossible, to flick it back.

Since that night, she had been finding excuses not to come into the office, and I couldn't say that I blamed her. If I had been the one to walk out the way she had, I wouldn't have been able to show my face again, even if I knew that I had done nothing wrong. Really, Stephanie should be proud of herself for being strong enough to be clear on what she wanted. But at the same time, I doubted her upbringing allowed her much space for pride.

But I really needed to speak to her. We had a meeting coming up that was going to require us to go travelling together. And I knew that there was no way I could do this by myself, but I didn't want it to come across like I was trying to get her alone again.

I had tried calling her a couple of times, but to no avail; she had been exchanging emails with me, making excuses why she couldn't come in. She had been spending a lot of time down at the store that we had first stocked at. Which wasn't a bad use of her time, not really, but I would have rather she was here so we could talk this out and get it over with.

Because I knew that the only way that we were going to get through it was if we acknowledged what had happened and moved on. We didn't have a choice. It had been a mistake – a fun one, for as long as it had lasted, but a mistake nonetheless and I was ready to put it behind us.

If only so we could jump into the next deal that had come our way. A group from New Jersey had reached out to us – apparently they were looking to try stocking a few of our clothes when we got the factory moving again, and we needed to lock that down and get a contract signed so that we could make the money to make the clothes again. I knew that I couldn't do this without her, or else I would have gone down by myself and taken care of it already. She knew the fashion side of this better than I ever would and that was what we needed right now. Someone who could talk about this stuff with the passion that I had heard from her.

The passion. I had felt that passion come from her in waves when the two of us had been together in my apartment. And God, I wanted that again – I wanted it so badly that it hurt. I could feel the need for it burning inside of me, the intense rush of it that insisted that I take notice of it. My need for her was more than anything that I had ever felt before for anyone, and maybe that was because I had had her and then she had taken that away. If I'd just been able to make her mine once and for all right there, then I could have gotten past it. But because we were unfinished...

Suddenly, the door to my office opened – and I found myself looking at the object of my fantasies right there in front of me.

"Oh," She squeaked, looking away from me at once, instantly flushing bright red. "I'm - I'm sorry, I didn't think you were going to be in right now."

"Well, somebody's got to hold down fort here, don't they?" I remarked. It came out a little more barbed than I had intended it, and she winced. I instantly wanted to apologize and take it back, but I knew that was just going to make it more real, so I allowed it to skim on by.

"I'm sorry," she told me again. "I didn't mean to be out of the office for so long. It's just been so...busy, you know, down at the store..."

I let her trail off, and allowed the words to hang in the air between us. She knew she was lying and I knew she was lying but neither of us were going to come out and say it. It was slightly ridiculous, but at the same time, I got where her fear came from. She didn't want to admit to what had happened between us, because if she did, then something might change, and she couldn't handle that. She wanted to go back to how things had been before, and I wished I could just let them.

But looking at her right now, it was impossible for me not to think about her, legs spread on my couch, pushing my head into her pussy so that I could taste every part of her. She had been so hot for me in that moment, so hot for me in a way that I could never have predicted; I had thought that, being a virgin, she would be a little reticent and would want to hold back, but instead, it seemed like everything in her was driving her on, driving her to desirous heights that she had never reached before. When she came, it was as though I could actually feel it pulsing out of her. God, I wanted more of that. I wanted all of that that she would give me, all of that that she would let me have...

"There's something I need to talk to you about," I told her, getting to my feet and drawing my eyes away from her carefully. I couldn't look at her without thinking all of that, it was just too difficult, and I had to focus on work. We had to get back to where we had been before, had to make sure that this didn't get any further for our original goal.

"Okay?" She replied, a little nervous. She was likely worried that I was about to jump down her throat about what had happened. Which was tempting – well, it was tempting at least to ask if there was any chance that she would let me bend her over this desk and fuck her raw right here in the middle of the office – but I had more important things to deal with right about now.

"We need to go out to New Jersey," I explained. "There's a company out there, they're thinking of working with us. But we're going to need to head out there together and meet with them to make sure that we lock it down. I can't do it by myself, I need you there to talk the fashion side of it with them, or else I'm going to look like I don't care about any of this stuff."

She held her breath for a moment, and let it out slowly. I could see that she was annoyed, or maybe just a little upset at the thought of being alone with me again. Was it because she thought she couldn't control herself around me? I hoped so. I knew that was selfish, but I hoped so.

"I want to get us a hotel out there," I explained. "Stay over for the night. Show that we're serious. We're not going to be on our best form if we're dealing with jetlag or just tiredness."

"Separate rooms?" She asked nervously. I nodded.

"Of course," I promised her. "Separate rooms."

She screwed her face up for a moment, like she was trying to work out the upsides and downsides to all of this. Whatever she came up with, she must have known that she had to go. We couldn't back out of something like this. We had to jump at every chance to take this to the next level, no matter what was going on between us.

"Okay," she replied with a nod. "Do you want me to book the rooms, or...?"

"I have them ready to book up," I replied. "And I hope that we get that deal, because I'm dropping a lot of money on this."

"Well, don't worry, I guess I could manage coach," she joked, and there was the flicker of a smile on her face. She was kidding around with me again – that had to be good, right?

"Good to hear," I replied. "I'll book it for over the weekend. You ready for it?"

"I will be," she promised. "Like you said, we don't have a choice. We have to get this off the ground, right?"

"Right," I agreed, and she opened her mouth as though there was something else that she wanted to say. But then, she thought better of it, and shook her head.

"Let me know when and where, okay?" She told me. "And pass along anything that I'll need to know for the meeting. I'll do some research on the company and hopefully by the time we get out there I'll be all up to date."

"That sounds good," I agreed with a nod, and I pulled up my email to put everything that she needed to know into a message. A few moments later, it was all sitting in her inbox waiting for her.

"There, all sent," I replied. "Let me know if there's anything else you need, okay?"

"I will," she promised, and her eyes softened a little. "And I won't be as long away from the office this time, alright?"

"You better not," I joked. "Your employee evaluation is coming up, and I can be pretty brutal."

"Guess I better get my ass in gear then," she remarked, smiling at me. I could feel some of that chemistry coming back, but I ignored it. That was the last thing we needed right about now.

"Guess you better," I agreed, and the two of us just stood there for a moment, taking each other in, as though we were trying to figure out what the hell was actually going on here.

"I'll catch you later," she told me, and with that, she turned and walked out the door, leaving me sitting there and watching her as she went. I remembered when she had walked out of here after she had first thrown that deal down on the table, how excited I had been – and I realized that I was still feeling that same way now. Excited. At the thought of being alone with her again, so far from home. It wouldn't be a vacation, but it could be a new start. And damn, after what had happened between us – I felt like we both deserved it.

Not to mention – what happened in New Jersey, stayed in New Jersey. Right? No matter what happened there. And, while I had no ideas in my head about what was going to go down – it might be a chance for both of us to have a little well-deserved fun.

Chapter Eleven – Stephanie

"Oh my God, It's so much busier than I thought it was going to be," I muttered to Jon, keeping my voice low and hoping that my nerves weren't completely evident and written all over my face.

"You're good," he assured me gently. "I've dealt with a lot more people than this. You just have to keep the game face on and make sure that you don't let them see through you, right?"

"Right," I agreed, a little grimly. I had no idea if I was going to be able to make that work. I was just so on-edge – and it wasn't only to do with the fact that we were putting in a showing at this conference.

I had checked in with Terri and Marj over what they thought I should do about this trip away. Both of them had been totally in favor of me going for it.

"I don't think you have much of a choice, do you, really?" Marjorie pointed out. "I mean, you have to get back to normal with him. Even if you guys...."

"Hooked up," Terri filled in the blanks bluntly. Marjorie shot her a look.

"Well, they didn't go all the way," she replied, and Terri shook her head.

"I don't think it would have made much of a difference if they had," she pointed out. "The damage is done, in a way."

"I don't think it was damaging..." I protested, a little weakly. Terri shook her head.

"No, I didn't mean like that," she assured me. "It's just that – well, you've already been together. And you already know how good you are together. That's going to be a hard thing to shake, isn't it?"

I sighed. She was right. Much as I didn't like admitting to the fact that she was right.

"I guess so," I replied. "But what am I meant to do about it?"

"Please tell me you at least sprung for separate rooms," Marjorie asked, and I nodded.

"Of course we have," I replied.

"Then you're going to be fine," she replied. "Just make sure that you keep out of his way as much as possible, stay in your room when you can, and don't indulge in too much of the free drinks, alright?"

"Alright," I agreed, and in that moment, I could just about believe it. But now that we were out of town and all alone together...

No, we weren't alone together, that was the thing. We were just spending some time together as part of the job that we were trying to do. The last thing I needed was for sex to get in the way of this business. I didn't want to let Amaya down, and that meant staying focused on the task at hand here.

"So, where are we going first?" I asked him. We were already booked into our very different rooms, and now we had come down to the conference floor in the hopes of finding a few clients to take on our clothes. I had a portfolio tucked under my arm, and was protectively holding it against me like it was armor to deflect anything that he might have thrown in his direction.

"I think we should stick together," he replied. "We'll cover more ground apart, but I think we're best when we're coming at this stuff as a team."

"Agreed," I replied. I didn't like the thought of being cast out here to handle all this by myself – there was a reason that I had never considered taking part in the business arena before this, and I was still lacking in a little confidence when it came to that.

"Okay, so, you talk clothes, I'll talk business, and hopefully we'll find some people to sign on?" He suggested. I nodded.

"Okay, lead on," I replied. And he did.

It was a good reminder, actually, of just how solid a team we made when we were dedicated to working together like this. He was impressive in the way he moved around this place, as though he had been here a hundred times before and knew just what he was meant to do. I was glad for his presence, because I would have been totally lost trying to figure out somewhere like this. But he was utterly in control, and I was grateful for it.

And other people seemed drawn into his actions, too – it didn't take long until we had a couple of people who had handed over contact information with a view of taking some of the new batches of clothes that we were planning to put together, and then a couple more on top of that. By the time we had finished making our rounds, we had a half-dozen people that we had been asked to reach out to when we got the chance, and I felt like that was worthy of some sort of victory.

"You know, they do two free drinks for everyone at the conference at the bar," he remarked. "You want to grab something, to celebrate?"

"Sure," I agreed, and Marjorie's warnings played at the back of my mind – avoid the free booze, spend as little time together outside what was called for as possible. And I heard them, and I politely decided to ignore them for now. Because the buzz in the pit of my stomach at everything we had just pulled off was too strong for me to deny, and I didn't want to put it out by going back to my room alone quite yet.

I got a glass of wine, promising myself that it would just be one, and he sipped on a scotch. Around us, other people who'd had less successful outings at this conference were drowning their sorrows. I was grateful, for once, that I actually got to be with the winning side for once.

"We did a really good job out there," I told him proudly. "I couldn't have done it without you."

"And you know I would never have been able to pull it off if it hadn't been for you," he replied. "The way you talk about those clothes, I'm close enough to putting money down to buy a few, and I'm the one selling them."

"You're too sweet," I replied, and I felt a little smile curl up my lips. I knew just what was going on, and I had no intention of stopping it, even though I really should have been adult enough to do better, to think better of it all.

"So, you want another?" He asked as soon as we were finished, and I nodded.

"Just one more," I replied. "And then I have to get to bed."

"Of course," he agreed. "But we deserve a little fun, don't we?"

"Sure thing," I replied. "Though are you trying to imply that I'm not fun the rest of the time?"

"Far from it," he assured me. "But there's...well, since..."

He let the words trail off, didn't bother filling them in, but I knew just what he was getting at. I felt my cheeks flush with a redness, and I knew that it had nothing to do with the wine. I was a little tipsy, yes, but nothing close to actually drunk. It was just being around him, having him

209

acknowledge the reality of what had happened between us that was doing this to me.

"Have you thought about it?" I blurted out, before I could stop myself, the curiosity far and away getting the better of me. He cocked an eyebrow.

"How do you mean?"

"Since we...well, since we did that," I explained. "Have you thought about it?"

"Of course I have," he fired back. "All the time, actually."

"I'm sorry I let you down like that..."

"You didn't let me down," he told me firmly, as though he didn't even want to hear that train of thought coming out of my mouth. "You were amazing, Stephanie. If that's all you ever wanted to do again, I think I would feel pretty damn good about it."

"Really?" I replied, surprised. And a little aroused. I could feel that heat, the familiar heat that I had been trying to deny since we had been alone together, starting to rise between my thighs. I just wanted him. Was that so wrong? I wanted him, and I wanted him to want me, too. And maybe Marjorie had been right about the wine because I could already feel it starting to take the edge off the part of me that had been sure that I was stronger than to give in to this.

"Really," he told me, and his eyes locked with mine and I swear I nearly combusted on the spot. I knew that he meant it. I could feel the pressure of his mouth against me just the way it had been when we had been together before, and I wanted it again, wanted it more than anything I had ever wanted in my life. I was surprised that nobody around us was stepping back to get out of the way of the heat that was pulsing between us. Because surely, I couldn't be the only one noticing it.

"I thought about it a lot, too," I confessed. "It's been on my mind a lot."

"Well, that's not right," he replied, his voice dropping to a different tone, a different register, one that sent a shiver down my spine. "You're meant to be thinking about work, right?"

"In theory," I agreed. "But it's hard, when..."

I let the words hang in the air between us, unspoken. I knew he knew just what I was getting at, and I didn't have to go any further than that.

"In that case, we should clear it," He told me, and suddenly, his hand had slipped on to my knee. His touch secured it for me – we had to do this. He was right. There was no way that we were going to be able to move on and get down to work again when this unfinished business was hanging in the air between us. I felt my breath catch in my throat, and the pressure between my legs rose to nearly unbearable levels. If he didn't touch me there again in the next five minutes, I felt like I was going to explode.

"Take me to your room," I told him. "Right now."

He grinned, as though he had won out at a game he didn't even realize he had been playing, and he got to his feet. His arm was tight around my waist as he led me out of the bar and towards the stairs, and I felt giddy at his touch once more. I knew this was wrong. But how could it be so wrong, when it just felt so right?

He took me back to his room, and before the door had even shut behind us, he was kissing me again. God, it felt good to kiss him – I had missed this so much. I had missed it and I had hardly had a chance to get used to it in the first place. There had to be something wrong with that, wrong with me, but I would be damned if I didn't just let myself enjoy this and have a little fun while I could. When we were out of town, I could pretend, at least for a little while, that the real world didn't exist, and that's just what I intended on doing.

He pushed me back against the door and slipped his hand between my legs, cupping me through my panties, and I let out a long grown of need. He knew just how to touch me, that was the crazy part. Even though I didn't even fully know how I liked to be touched yet, when he laid hands on me, it felt like everything just made sense. I didn't have to worry about it, I didn't have to hold back, because I knew that he was the one in charge and in control and that I could trust him to give me what I wanted.

"I really want to fuck you," he growled in my ear, the words simple but powerful enough to make my knees feel like they were buckling beneath me. And this time, there was no doubt in my mind – I wanted this, too. I needed this. I had needed it since the moment I had walked out of his apartment before. I had been scared then, but now – now, it was different. I was ready.

"Then fuck me," I breathed back to him. The words sounded so sweet and seductive coming out of my mouth, I could hardly recognize myself as the one saying them. But it must have been me, because he grabbed me by the arms and pushed me back to the bed and set about undressing me like the thought of not seeing me naked right away was going to make him drop dead on the spot.

His hands were quick but careful, and every part of me that he exposed, he touched or kissed in some way, as though he was letting me know how much he wanted every part of me. And God, it was hot watching him appreciate my body like that. I had never seen anyone so engaged with the way I looked, the way I felt, and it allowed some part of me to just let go and enjoy what was happening right in front of me.

"You're so perfect," he breathed, as he kissed down my stomach, pulling down my stockings as he went. It was all happening so quickly that I hardly had time to feel nervous about the thought of him seeing me like that; in fact, I wanted him to, I could feel that desire burning inside of me. It was something I had never felt before, that certainty, and I knew that it was enough to take me over the edge and into what I had been waiting for all this time.

He undressed himself quickly and lowered himself down on top of me, and I wrapped my arms around him and marveled at the weight of his body on top of mine. It felt good, warm, comforting, as though this is what I had been waiting for all this time without even knowing it. I knew that that was crazy, but it was just the truth of how I felt. I wanted him. I needed him. My body had called out for him for so long now that actually having him felt surreal, as though it had to be taking place inside a dream.

I could feel his hardness pressing up against my thigh, but instead of sending nerves through my body, all I could feel was excitement.

"Are you ready?" He asked, voice low. And I knew that if I had told him *no* in that moment, that he would have accepted it and let this go. That knowledge was what told me that I had made the right choice – that I had chosen the right man. Because I could trust him, utterly. And now, I could trust myself in being sure that I was ready.

"Yes," I breathed. And with that, he pulled out a condom, rolled it over his erection, spread my legs, and slowly guided himself inside of me for the very first time.

And yes, there was a little pain as he slipped into me. No, not pain, that was the wrong word – it was something else, a shift, like my body was just getting used to the feel of having someone penetrate me like that. I sucked in a sharp breath and did my best to let my body relax into it, and he kissed my shoulder and whispered in my ear.

"Are you alright?"

"Yes," I replied. And I wasn't just saying it because I knew that's what he wanted to hear from me. I knew that it was true. I parted my legs a little wider, shifted my hips down on the bed, and wrapped my arms around him tight, and just like that, he was moving inside of me – really moving, filling me up, and taking me like there was nothing in the world he could imagine wanting more.

I closed my eyes and let myself get lost in the feelings that were coursing through me. How could I have waited this long for something that felt this damn *good?* The feelings that were rushing through me were more than just physical – there was an intense mental aspect to it as well, as though my brain was hurrying to find some way to wrap itself around the fact that I was really having sex with the guy I'd crushed on for years in high school. And he was as good as he had been in all the fantasies I had spun about him – as tender, as careful, as sweet.

And before long, I started to feel that swell of passion in my belly, the one that told me I was getting close. I hadn't expected to come so quickly, but I supposed that my body had been waiting a long time for this release even if I hadn't been aware of it at the time. I found myself pushing my hips back against him, driving him deep inside of me, needing more, craving more, my mouth parting as my breath came faster and faster, and soon, all too soon, I was tipping over the edge and...

"Oh," I gasped, and he kissed me as I felt my pussy tighten around him, the rush of the orgasm sending shockwaves through my system. It was unlike anything I had ever felt before in my life – and I was pretty sure I liked it. No, scratch that, I was pretty sure that I loved it. I groaned and shivered in his arms, and a few moments later I felt him reach what I assumed was his own release inside of me. He let out this sharp noise that told me that I had been correct, and I felt a little shudder of excitement knowing that I had been enough to get him there.

He held himself inside me for a little longer, as though he wasn't quite ready for this to be over yet – I knew just how he felt, the intensity of what we had been doing was too much to just let go of. But, slowly, he drew himself out of me, and I lay back on the bed, staring at the ceiling, trying to catch my breath.

"Are you alright?" He asked softly, as he got to his feet and disposed of the condom. I nodded. Well, it was the most I could do given that the power of speech had basically vanished for me.

"Good," he replied, and he slipped back into bed beside me, and wrapped his arms around me tight. I closed my eyes and let him hold me. I knew there was a lot that this was going to bring up, now that we had actually done it, but for now, I just wanted to lie here in the glow of finally having been with a man who I truly wanted. And finally having divested myself of my virginity.

Chapter Twelve – Jon

"Well, good morning."

I greeted Stephanie as she walked into the office for the first time since our encounter in New Jersey, and I couldn't help but smile when I saw the way she blushed bright red as soon as I spoke to her. It was nice to know that, after what we had done, I still had some kind of passing effect on her.

"Morning," she replied, and she couldn't keep the smile off her face as she headed to her desk. We hadn't talked about the fact that we had finally had sex at the conference since it had happened, but I figured that it was going to need to come up sooner or later.

When we had woken up together the next day, still curled up in my bed, she had lifted her head from the pillow and offered me a soft, quiet little smile.

"I think we have some work to be getting on with," she had told me, and I had only been able to nod back in return. I knew that there was still a lot for us to figure out, and I wasn't going to push her beyond the point that she could handle it. I just wanted to make sure that she was happy, comfortable, and that she didn't feel like she had made a mistake with what we had done.

And, in all fairness, I was pretty confident that she wasn't feeling anything like that, at least from what I could tell. We had worked together again on the conference floor and I was feeling good about the form we were on. It felt like we had connected on a whole other level, and now we could wrap our heads around each other in a way we'd never been able to before. I could get used to that feeling. I could get addicted to it, in fact.

And now, we were back in New York, and I was having to give some thought to the fact of what came next. It wasn't like we could just carry on pretending that we had been chaste all weekend.

"So," I remarked, as she took her seat and pulled out some of the papers she had come into work with that day. "Are we going to talk about it?"

She bit her lip and looked up at me.

"I honestly don't know how," she confessed. "This is all new to me, remember. I'm not...well, I don't have experience in stuff like this..."

"That's okay," I assured her. "But I think we need to get it out in the open, right?"

She nodded, though I could tell there was still an edge of discomfort to this for her.

"So, how do you feel about it?" I asked, and the smile practically spread from ear to ear over her face.

"I feel good about it," she replied at once. "Really good. I still can't really believe that it happened, but...but I'm glad that it did."

That was just what I had wanted to hear. I knew that losing your virginity could be a big deal for some people, and the last thing I would have wanted was for her to feel anything other than totally good about it. I knew that I sure as hell did, but that likely had something more to do with the fact that I had slipped into bed with one of the most stone-cold sexiest women I had ever seen in my life. It would have been a little odd if I had been anything other than totally chill about it.

"And do you want to do it again?" I asked, bluntly, figuring that the best way to get this conversation down with was if we were both as honest as we could be. She bit her lip. And then she nodded.

"I think I do," she confessed. "Is that totally crazy? I know we said it would just be to get it out of the way, but..."

"But it was way better than either of us expected it to be," I filled in for her. "Yeah, I feel that. And I want you again, if you'll let me."

The bluntness of my words brought a deeper hue to her cheeks. I liked that I could have that kind of impact on her. It was hot as hell to know that her mind was going just where mine was right about now.

"I think I can swing to that," she replied, and though she tried to keep her voice steady, I could hear that little quaver in it that told me that she was already hot for the thought of me.

"But we have to keep the rest of this strictly professional," she replied, straightening up a little and gathering herself for a moment. "I don't want this to get in the way of what we're doing here, alright?"

"Of course," I agreed. "But this could be a good way to balance the work and the play, don't you think?"

"You really have a way of selling this stuff, huh?" She remarked, a little smile on her face.

"I think it could be good for us to make sure we're not getting too caught up in work," I replied, and I got to my feet; I could see her catch her breath as I moved across the room towards her, closing the distance between us. There was so much that I wanted to do with her, to her, that I hardly had a clue where to start. I pressed my hand against the door behind her to make sure it was shut.

"In fact, I have a few ideas right about now," I murmured, and she moved a little closer to me.

"Really?"

"Really."

"In that case..." she breathed, and I tucked my hand behind her head and lowered my mouth down to hers again. Kissing her was like drinking from the fountain of life; it was as though I had been holding my breath all this time, but now I could finally breathe once more.

And yeah, okay, I knew that this was sort of going against the rule she had just put in place to make sure that we kept this firmly on the professional side of things. But who was I to deny the pleasure that we were both craving right then and there? We wanted each other, and it was going to be tough to focus on work if we didn't get this out of the way. Not to mention the fact that I was curious to see just how loudly I could make her moan when we were right here in the middle of the office. Call it an experiment, call it whatever you want. But I was going to make her come. And I was going to do it right here, right now.

Chapter Thirteen – Stephanie

"Jon!" I protested weakly, as he leaned down to plant a kiss on my neck. He knew that was my weak point; when he went there, I was basically helpless to resist him. Even now, knowing that we had a meeting about to take place, it was hard for me to deny the rush of need that pulsed through me as he brushed his tender lips over my skin.

"Oh, sorry," He murmured, winding his arms around me from behind. "You just looked so good, I forgot that we even had a meeting coming up..."

"You know, that excuse doesn't work when you keep on using it," I warned him, and I tried to sound stern and failed utterly.

"Hmm," he murmured, as he nuzzled his mouth against my neck. "You're just totally distracting. I hope you know that."

I grinned. It had been nearly a month since the two of us had hooked up at the hotel in New Jersey, and ever since then, I had been struggling to find a way to balance my desire for Jon with my desire for this business to take off. Which was about the best rock and a hard place that I had ever been stuck between.

I loved spending time with him, no matter what form that time might have come in. He was smart and funny and he worked hard and he cared about me – he listened to what I wanted, no matter how those wants came about. And yeah, maybe we had agreed to keep this out of the office for the most part, but the lines between the two sides of our relationship were getting more and more blurred with each passing day.

Not that I minded. I had never felt a connection that had run this deep with anyone before. I knew part of it was because I was having sex with him, and I had never actually had sex with anyone else before, but I wasn't lovestruck enough to see that there was more to it than that. We had a good chemistry even out of the bedroom, and that was obvious to everyone who met us. Even the clients who we held meetings with would occasionally offer comment on the fact that they had never seen a couple of business partners so close before, and were surprised when we told them that we had only been working together for a couple of months now.

And hell, the impact we had made on the company felt like it should have stretched a little further than a couple of months, too. We had been working our asses off and it was really starting to show on the numbers we were getting back. We had finally been able to find another factory to help produce fabric for us, and had restarted the workshop that Amaya had run out in India; I had plans to go down there and visit at some point, something I would have been way too nervous to even think about doing before I had gotten started in all of this. I felt like a new version of myself, one that was surer and stronger than ever before. And I was proud to be able to claim her as my own. She had a lot going for her, this new version of me, and I was proud that I had finally been able to give her shape and life of her own.

It hadn't all come from the sex, of course, but I would have been lying if I'd said that that wasn't a major part of it. I suddenly had this ability to accept my body for what it was, for the pleasure that it was able to give me, as opposed to constantly beating myself up over it not looking a certain way or not reacting the way that I wanted or needed it to. It was amazing what you could forgive your body for when it gave you so much pleasure, and I had stopped nit-picking every little detail and started just enjoying everything that it could give to me.

And yes, there was something powerful that came from being wanted so much by someone I felt that same level of want towards. I was totally obsessed with the way that he made me feel, and it seemed like he was utterly in the same place when it came to me. I loved the way he touched me, the way he held me, the way that he made it clear that he couldn't bear to keep his hands off me at any given moment because I was just way too gorgeous for him to handle.

And I felt the same way about him. In fact, so much so, that I had even been emboldened enough to go the extra mile and give him something that I had never imagined I would have the nerve to give anyone.

"What's on your mind today?" He had asked as soon as he'd seen me that morning. He'd been able to tell that I had that little devilish glint to my eye, and he already had a good idea of just what that might have meant for him.

"Close the door," I told him, and he did as he was told. I glanced around, as though making sure that there was nobody hiding out inside the small space of the office, and I wound my arms around him and kissed him.

"This isn't very professional," he murmured, but, judging by the way he was stroking his thumb lightly over my hip, I doubted that he cared that much. I smiled at him.

"You think you can stay quiet?" I asked.

"You going to give me a reason not to be?" He shot back. God, he knew just what to say to get me going – sometimes, just a word or a look would be all it took to send that sharp start of want down my spine.

"Let's see," I murmured back, and with that, I dropped to my knees and started undoing his pants.

I had gone down on him a couple of times before, but I was already worried that I was doing it wrong and that I was going to hurt him in some way – but a couple of drinks with Marjorie and Terri, and some serious girl chat later, and I was under the impression that the best thing for me to do was to just go for it. Both of them had told me that the best port of call was to be enthusiastic, careful, and make sure that I kept everything wet, and I wanted to show him just how much I had learned about what turned him on.

I slowly reached into his underwear and wrapped my fingers around his cock; he was so impressively long, and I loved the feel of him when he was hard, loved knowing that I had been the one to do this to him.

I stroked him a couple of times and looked up at him, and I could see that tightness to his jaw that told me that I was seriously turning him on. God, was there anything hotter than knowing that he wanted me like this? I moved my mouth towards him, hovering it just an inch over his head, a trick I had learned from him – he would always do this to me before he would dive down between my legs for good, and it felt like it was going to make me crazy each and every time.

Finally, I flickered my tongue out against his head, tasting the barest hint of his pre-cum that was already there and waiting for me. He let out a long groan as I sealed my lips around his tip and drew him deeper into my mouth, and I let the rush of it move through me – God, it sometimes felt like more than I could handle when I had him like this, utterly at my mercy.

"You look so good like that," he murmured, and I flicked my eyes up at him playfully. I knew he liked watching me, taking in my reactions when I was doing this for him, and while I had been a little nervous at first, I was getting better and better about just letting this happen. About accepting that I was sexy to him, and that the hottest thing that he could see was for me to embody that sexiness when we were together.

I took him as deep as I could, and then wrapped my fingers around his base so that I had all of him taken care of. I ran my tongue up the underside of his erection, feeling that seem that ran from the top to the bottom, and found my own heart beating a little faster in my chest. I knew that if someone came to the door, or even just walked right on in, that they would catch us in the act, but I didn't care. In fact, some deep, dangerous part of me actually found the thought of that even hotter. He was so into me that he was willing to allow me to do this to him when it could land the both of us in trouble.

I began to move my mouth up and down his length, matching it with the movements of my hand, making him good and slick with my saliva so that I could move with ease. God, there was something so sexy about it, having him like this – I felt like I was so powerful I could have taken on the world in that moment. I loved the way being with him made me feel. For so long, I had been told that having sex would be to give up some fundamental part of myself and hand that power over to somebody else, but now, I could see that all those had been were lies meant to keep me in my place. And I wasn't going to let them consume me any longer.

And with that, I knelt there in our office, and I made him come with my mouth. I was amazed to find how easily it came to me – after all this time that I had spent holding back and trying to hide from the lust that I really felt, I had assumed that I would have to work double-time to catch up on those skills. But it turned out that there was some natural talent built into me that had just been waiting for him to come out and play. As I blew him, carefully, letting my tongue and lips tease every part of him, I knew that he was the difference – he was what had changed in my life. I had always had this in me, but it had been waiting, holding back until he got here to show itself.

"Fuck, yes," he groaned, and he pushed himself a little deeper into my mouth; I was surprised to find how easy it was to take his length like that, even though I would have been sure just a few minutes ago that I couldn't. But he seemed to be losing control, unable to hold himself back, and I was the one who had taken him there, I was the one who had done it for him. How many women had he been with over the course of his life? And now, he was with me, and not one of them mattered.

I grabbed hold of one of his thighs, holding him in place, and I applied a little light suction pressure to his length; it was that that seemed to take him over the edge, and within seconds, I could feel him twitching in my mouth. I had never let him finish there before, but it only seemed natural to take him in that way. I wasn't going to pull back now, not when I had already come so far, done so much. This felt like a triumph, and there was no part of me that wanted to give that up.

So I swallowed him, taking every drop that he gave me; I held him in my mouth until I could feel him starting to get soft once more, and I tasted the slightly salty, slightly sweet taste of him as he finished in my mouth.

I slowly pulled back, flicking my tongue over my lips to get the taste of the last of him off my mouth; that day, we didn't have much to do in the way of meeting up with other people, but that didn't mean I wanted to spend it with the taste of him on my tongue. Not least because it would have been way too tempting to just go ahead and do it all again.

He reached down and pulled me to my feet, and wrapped his arms around me, planting a kiss on my exposed collarbone.

"That was amazing," he murmured. "Thank you."

"Think you can pay me back in kind sometime soon?" I teased him lightly, and he pulled back and grinned at me.

"I thought you'd never ask..."

And yeah, okay, maybe we didn't get a lot of work done that day after all. But I didn't mind. There was something about being with him that made everything else just fall away, as though it had never even mattered in the first place. I was obsessed with him, and I knew that it was starting to go a little past casual.

I was home alone, spending the evening by myself, mostly to make a point about how easily I could keep myself together and that I didn't need Jon to entertain me in my spare time. But all it had done was served to underline the fact that I was already missing him like crazy.

Maybe I should have called Marjorie or Terri – yeah, but then they would have been the first to tell me that I needed to keep my feelings to myself for now, until I had a better handle on just what they meant for me. And I knew they were right, at least that they had a point; I couldn't deny that I wanted to spend more time with him, but there was also no doubt in my mind that it was dangerous for me to accept that. We were toeing the line dangerously close to the edge of what we had agreed on, and I needed to work hard not to let myself tip all the way over the edge.

Maybe this was just what it was like the first time around. I mean, I had no point of reference for any of this – perhaps it was some chemical reaction that attached you to the person that you had slept with for the first time, something as simple as that. Most people got over it when they were teenagers, but it had taken so long for me that I was acting this all out now as a grown-ass adult. Well, something close to an adult, anyway.

But Jon, Jon couldn't be feeling the same things that I was. He was already well-versed in these games, in sex and love and attraction and everything that came with it; I would have been an idiot to believe anything else. He wasn't falling for me the way I was falling for him, because our circumstances were just so utterly and completely different that there was no way the connection could exist in the same way. I wanted it to, of course, God knows I wanted it to, but I didn't think that I could actually expect him to reflect my feelings back at me.

And besides, we had to think of the business first and foremost. No matter how tempting it might have been to let myself get caught up in this fling, or whatever it was that he wanted to call it, we had to think about Amaya and her company and making sure that it survived these first few months without her. She had left this to us because she thought that we were the best people to keep it alive, and I didn't want to let her down in any of that.

Because it was one of the only times in my life that I had been treated like I might just have been as good as my brother. Maybe even better. I knew that, deep down, the people in my family had never really seen me as an adult the way that they saw Nate was one; they didn't like the idea of accepting that, maybe because it meant that I would have to be out there doing adult things and some of them were just a little *too* adult for my family to consider. But Amaya, Amaya had seen me differently. She had seen that there was something in me that was mature, grown-up, ready to take on the world, and she had wanted that part of me at the helm of the business she had loved so very much. And I would be forever grateful to her for that.

That's what I tried to keep in mind when I went back into the office the next day – this wasn't about me and Jon, this was about me and Jon running this business and making sure that it stayed above water no matter what. And I honestly had that sealed in my mind right up until the moment that I had walked through the door, and laid eyes on Jon there waiting for me.

He was wearing this clean-cut suit with a pale blue shirt underneath, and he looked so handsome – like he belonged on the red carpet, not the scrubby blue of this office. He smiled as soon as he saw me step over the threshold, and got to his feet.

"Okay, morning," he greeted me, and he came around the desk and I could see that excited look in his eyes, the one that told me he had a whole lot of plans for the day ahead. "So, I was thinking-"

Before he could say another word, I wrapped my arms around him and kissed him. The door was still open, but I didn't care – most of this office building likely knew what we were getting up to in here, anyway. He caught me in his arms and kissed me back, and I wondered if someone Amaya had known that we would be such a good fit for one another – if she had been able to see it, somehow, read it into both of us even though I doubted she had seen us in so much as the same room before.

But before I could give that any more thought, I heard a voice. A voice speaking my name.

"Stephanie?"

I sprang back from Jon at once, ready to apologize to whatever client had happened to walk in on the two of us together – but instead, I found myself looking straight into the eyes of my big brother.

I sprang back from Jon at once, but the damage was already done – he had already seen us together, and I knew there was no way that I could convince him otherwise. And, before I could lunge out of the office and stop him in his tracks and beg him not to tell anyone in our family about this, he shook his head at me, turned on his heel, and walked away. Leaving me with nothing but the creeping dread that I might have just ruined things for good.

Chapter Fourteen – Jon

"Stephanie, nothing's going to happen," I tried to assure her, as she marched back and forth over the small space of our office like she was trying to burn off the calories of the donuts she'd eaten that morning with her coffee. I had hoped some food would be enough to calm her down, but it looked like it had only made things worse. She had been distinctly green around the gills since she had arrived in to the office this morning, and frankly I had some serious questions about what she actually thought was going to happen.

"You don't understand," she replied. "My brother, he's going to use this against me any way that he can. And it's not going to be hard for him to do that when all my family think that I'm not fit for this anyway..."

"Yeah, but it's not like they can just get rid of you after all the work you've been doing for this place," I pointed out. She shook her head again. Every time I tried to soothe her, she would just come up with another way that I was actually wrong, and I would have to try a different approach to make her feel better. I just wished there was something I could do to calm her down, but ever since Nate had seen the two of us together, she had been in full-blown freakout mode, and nothing was enough to calm her down.

I wasn't sure what all her panic was about, not really. I mean, yeah, her brother knowing about us wasn't ideal, but her family surely wouldn't give that much of a damn about what she was doing with her personal life, would they?

She seemed convinced to the contrary, and it was like nothing that I could say or do would change her mind on that. Well, maybe I needed to accept that she had a point. Her family had insisted on coming by the office to meet with us, under the guise, at least, of checking out how we were running the company; I had welcomed their attendance, glad to have an excuse to show off everything that we had been doing here, but she seemed certain that it was a portent of major doom.

It was about an hour until they arrived, and she had been drinking coffee and rushing about all morning to keep herself busy. I had been trying to keep her calm, but she wasn't having any of it.

"You don't know what they're like," She had tried to explain to me, after she had attempted to go after her brother only to find out that he had already made it out of the building.

"Then tell me."

"It's hard to explain if you've not been through it," she replied with a sigh. "But...but everything Nate does, it's totally fine, and even if I'm doing exactly the same thing, then it becomes this whole big debate about whether or not I'm doing the right thing."

"But surely Nate dated before he got married," I pointed out. "I mean, I know he did, I was there for a lot of it..."

"Yeah, and if you tried to bring any of it up then my entire family would pretend that you were speaking a different language," She shot back. "They don't want to hear any of that stuff. As far as they're concerned, he's done everything right his whole life, and I would have done well to follow in his example."

"That's bullshit."

"Tell me about it," she agreed, and she finally stopped pacing and slumped into a chair at last, giving herself a moment to catch her breath. "But that's how it works with them. That's how it's always worked."

"But Amaya gave you the company," I pointed out to her. "So she can't have thought of you like that."

"Yeah, and she was very much the exception," She explained. "They're probably going to try and claim that she was senile close to the end and that's why she left the company to me instead of Nate."

"That's crazy," I replied. "They must be able to see how good a job you're doing with it now. Nate could never-"

"Yeah, but that's not what they think," she answered me. And I knew that everything I tried to use to explain away what she had been through was just going to wind up getting deflected back at me. She had been through this for years, and I supposed that she understood it better than me. Because, in my eyes, this sure as fuck didn't make any sense at all.

When they finally arrived, I put on my best game face and tried to come across as the coolest, calmest guy in the room. It was just her brother and her father, Ethan, and I greeted them both formally.

"Great to see you both," I told them, but Nate hardly even nodded in my direction; his eyes were already roving around the office, like he was planning what he was going to do with the place once he had it all to himself. I tried not to let the bristle of irritation at his actions show on my face.

"You too," Ethan replied, at least able to treat me with a small modicum of decency. Neither of them had so much as looked at Stephanie since they had walked in, as though she wasn't even there. I wanted to put my arm around her, pull her to my side, make it so that they had no choice but to acknowledge her presence there, but I got the feeling that she would have rejected me if I'd tried anything like that. So I kept my hands by my sides, and gestured for them to take a seat.

"Thanks for meeting with us today," Ethan told me, once again ignoring his daughter as though he couldn't even see her there. I tried not to let it get to me. It wasn't my business to get up in arms about the way they treated her, and I knew that she wouldn't thank me if I did.

"Not at all," I replied. "So, you mentioned wanting to go over the state of the company – I have a few details about our new clients, plus some of the factory background for the new-"

"No, I think perhaps you've misunderstood," Nate cut in, and there was a sneer to his voice that set my hackles on edge. God, if there was ever a man who could have used a-

"We're not here to check in on the company," he explained. "We're here to take it from you."

"What?" Stephanie gasped. I was too shocked to even come out with something like that. Ethan nodded, his mouth set in a hard line as he focused on his daughter for the first time since he had walked into the room.

"Obviously, we don't want the company to be associated with the sort of behavior that you are exhibiting," he went on. "I understand that you're an... adult woman now, and you're going to act out the way you want, but we don't want the family name attached to that."

Stephanie was just staring at him. The shock was evident, written all over her face, and she couldn't come up with anything to say back to him. Luckily, I wasn't feeling quite so reticent.

"I'm sorry, what the hell are you talking about?" I demanded, shaking my head. "This is what Amaya asked for in her will, you don't just get to change that up because you don't like what Stephanie has been doing in her personal life."

"We do," Nate replied firmly. "It has do to with the image that this company has in public. I mean, we sell traditional garments, I don't think a lot of people are going to want to purchase from you if they know that the person running things behind the scenes is...doing what you're doing."

I clenched my fists under the table. I knew that Nate had spent a hell of a lot of time fooling around with various women when he had been younger, before he had been married to his current girl, but there was no way that I could prove that right now and if I threw it out there with no proof it would be easy for him to just brush that off as me trying to get him looking bad in front of his family.

"You can't do this," Stephanie pleaded with him – it was a statement, it was her begging so that she could hang on to what she had worked so hard for. I wanted to reach across the table and grab Nate by the lapels and demand to know if he understood just how ridiculous he was being.

"I'm afraid we can," Ethan replied, and there was something about the fact that he actually sounded sorry. He had the choice to stop this, but he was going on and pushing it forward. I wanted to scream at both of them. I couldn't believe they were doing this. Not just to me, but to her – to this woman who had shown that she could do so much for this business.

"How?" I asked him. "How can you overrule the contract like that? That was what she said in her will, wasn't it? That she wanted to leave it to the both of us?"

"Yes, but that's only as far as it works for the business," Nate cut in. "We checked it out. If there was something big that was getting in the way of you doing a good job, then we have a right to come in and change that."

"And you think this is a big enough deal."

"We do," Ethan agreed. I shook my head.

"But nobody has to know about this if you don't tell anyone," I pointed out. "You...you're the only ones who know about it. Why wouldn't you just leave it at that?"

"Because these things have a habit of getting out whether you want them to or not," Ethan replied, coolly, his voice taking on a slightly pissy edge. He had obviously thought that this was going to be easy, but he hadn't counted on me putting up a fight. But if he thought that I was just going to roll over and take this, he had another thing coming.

"No, they don't," I shot back. "Not if you don't want them to. And you can't really believe that this is destined to come out."

"We do-"

"And even if it does, I doubt any of our clients are going to care," I cut in. "This isn't like it was when Amaya started the business, and even if she did think that this was a bad idea then, I don't think she accounted for how much people would change their minds on this stuff in the meantime."

"No," He replied, bluntly. Ethan had crossed his arms over his chest, and suddenly I could see where Nate got his stubbornness from. I could see it written all over their faces. The two of them looked so eerily similar, so strongly set in their ways, that it was almost a little discomforting. I didn't know how Stephanie could deal with it, deal with the two of them sitting there and all turned against her. I would have gone crazy. Fuck, I had only dealt with them for a few minutes at the same time, and I felt like I was struggling to keep my cool.

"At least let us meet with a lawyer," Stephanie asked. Her voice was quiet, but sure, and I was relieved that she had finally gotten back the power of speech.

"What do you mean? What for?" Nate asked, and he sounded a little panicked. He hadn't figured for this in the plan of how he had thought this would unfold.

"I mean, I want to make sure that this all above board," She replied, coolly. "If this is going to happen, then the least we can do is be certain that this is happening as it should be."

Nate just looked at her for a long moment, and the silence seemed so heavy that I could almost feel the weight of it pressing down on my shoulders.

"Fine," Nate snapped back after a long pause. "Fine, if that's what you want. You bring along anyone you want, it's not going to undo what we know you've been up to."

The anger was hard to hold in right then; I knew that it wouldn't help anything if I was to swing for Nate, but damn, I wanted to. His smug fucking face-

"Fine," Stephanie replied, and she got to her feet and extended her hand, almost robotic in her movements, as though she had divested herself of any emotion just to keep herself safe. They took her hand and with that, the confrontation seemed to be over. By the time the door closed behind them, Stephanie was standing ramrod-straight, holding herself upright as though if she let go of an inch of the tension in her frame, she would go to pieces at once.

"Oh my God," she gasped, as soon as the door was shut. "I can't believe...I'm so sorry, Jon. You have no idea."

"It's not your fault," I assured her, and I wrapped my arms around her. "I had no idea that they were going to take it this far. I mean, when you said it to me, I thought it had to be a joke or something..."

"But now you believe me?" She asked. I nodded.

"Now I believe you."

Chapter Fifteen – Stephanie

"Are you sure there's nothing else I can get you?" He asked, and I shook my head. I was staring off into space, feeling stupid, feeling like I had just been emptied out beyond repair, and I had no idea what I was meant to do to fix that feeling.

That meeting with my family...I had been through a lot with them over the years, that was for sure. But that had been more than I had been prepared for. I mean, yes, I knew that they were going to try to cast some aspersions on whether or not I was actually any good for this company or not, but it was one thing to suggest some doubts, another thing entirely to...to just come in, and make it clear that they didn't think I had any right to be here at all.

I put my head down between my knees, perched on the edge of my couch, in an attempt not to let myself throw up on the spot. It was hard to keep my cool when it felt like everything was tumbling down around me.

Well, not everything. I still had Jon here. And that had to count for something, didn't it?

He had been pacing back and forth over my apartment floor all this time, the sound of his footsteps almost like a pendulum. He couldn't believe any of this had happened, and he wasn't afraid to make that very clear.

"I'm going to do everything I can to fight this," He told me seriously, as soon as they had left the office. "I'm not going to let them get away with it, alright?"

Before I could come out with an answer that made any kind of sense, I felt my face crumple as the tears started to come all of a sudden. I had done a good job keeping them in until that moment, but now that my family were out of here, I felt like I had unlocked a great groundswell of feeling and now I needed to deal with it one way or another.

Jon had never been the guy who had dealt brilliantly with emotions, if I could remember correctly; he was good with the fun stuff, not so much with everything else. And as soon as he saw me start to cry, I could see that this had freaked him out. But instead of making his excuses and getting out of there, he wrapped his arms around me and pulled me tight against him.

"Let's get you out of here, alright?" He suggested gently, and I nodded, unable to say anything, I was crying too hard for that. I just needed to be far from here, far from the memory of what had just happened.

He drove me back down to my apartment and helped me up the stairs, sat me down on the couch, and let me cry it all out. He offered a few words of condolence and support where he could but he must have known that this all had to come from me – there was little that he could do that would make this better, because he hadn't been the one to hurt me in the first place. No, as always, that had been down to my family. And no doubt they were somewhere across town patting themselves on the back for a job well done. I hated the thought of it, Nate and my father together somewhere, chortling over the fact that they had finally gotten what they wanted out of me. The pain that they had left behind in their wake, they had hardly even thought about that. Otherwise, they wouldn't have come down to the office to humiliate me to my face over all of this.

"I'm going to find a way around this," Jon told me firmly, and he paused in front of me again, his hands on my knees. "Do you hear me, baby? I'm going to find a way to stop it."

I looked at him, and God, I wanted to believe that more than anything else in the world. It would have been bliss to be able to let go of what I had been clinging on to, to believe that everything was going to be alright, that he could stand up against my family and win. But I didn't believe him. I couldn't.

"You don't understand," I told him. "They're going to throw as much dirty shit at you as they can to try and get you to give in. And I don't want you to have to deal with that..."

"I don't care what they throw at me," He replied. "I'll take it. It's ridiculous that they're even trying to pull something as archaic as this, but we're going to stop them, mark my words."

I managed to smile at him. I was touched by how passionate he was about all of this. This was a man whose goals lined up so perfectly with my own, and I could hardly believe that soon enough all of this was going to be over. Because when they took the company from us...

"And if we can't?" I asked him softly. It was something that I had hardly considered for myself yet, but I needed him to be honest with me. I needed him to tell me that we could survive outside the company now, even if he didn't believe it. We had agreed to keep everything else strictly business, but surely he could see that whatever we had went deeper than that by now. I certainly felt it, deep down in my guts, that sureness that told me that whatever we had was real.

"That's not going to happen," he told me firmly, but I shook my head.

"But what if we can't?" I asked him, a sudden edge of desperation to my voice. "I want...I need you to tell me that we're not going to be over if you can't do this, Jon. I know that we said that it was about the company, but if we take that out of this, what do we have left?"

I gazed at him keenly, waiting for an answer, and his eyes widened as though that thought hadn't so much as crossed his mind.

"Do you want this to be over?" He asked quietly, standing there in front of me. He looked so young all of a sudden, not the man I had known all this time, but something more vulnerable than that.

"No," I told him at once. "I don't want that. But if we don't have this anymore..."

"Then we still have each other," he shot back fervently. He was suddenly on his knees in front of me, and he grasped my hands in his and pulled them to his mouth. Closing his eyes, he kissed over my knuckles, and I looked down at him, this man I knew I was falling for, and I realized that I was in love with him.

He reached up to cup my face in his hands, and I was so shocked by the sharpness of the revelation that had just hit me that I had to catch my breath for a moment. I wanted to say the words to him, but I had no idea if that was the right idea or not. I didn't want to freak him out, not after we had already been through so much today.

And then, of course, he said it.

"I love you, Stephanie," he announced, his eyes burning deep into mine as though he was trying to see into my soul. I felt a wash of relief course through me at once – he loved me. He loved me, and that was surely all that could matter, at the end of the day. Despite everything that had happened, I felt a smile spread across my face – a smile that I couldn't hold back, didn't want to. He moved towards me and kissed me, not waiting for a response, because he already knew the answer. He knew that I loved him back, and that I perhaps had from the moment he had walked into my life once more.

His kiss seemed to wipe clean the memories that I had been carrying from that meeting earlier today, and I gratefully let go of them, willing to bid them farewell. He moved from the floor up and towards me, pushing me back down on the couch, and I let the weight of him rest on top of me as I wound my arms tight around him and pulled him in close. How could I have ever wanted for anything else? How could I have ever found myself craving anyone but him? I had waited all this time for someone to come into my life who made me feel the way he did, and now he loved me and I loved him and I couldn't think of anything that felt more perfect than this.

It didn't take long until he had stripped me down, undressing me eagerly, swiftly, tossing the clothes aside so that he could get his hands all over me. And I was more than willing to have him touch me properly; if we were going to go down for something like this, then we might as well have a little fun in the process, right?

"You're so beautiful," he murmured, and he leaned forward and planted a kiss on my collarbone, just lightly, a glancing blow that made everything go a little blurry around the edges. I caught his head by his hair and kissed him again, deeply, my tongue in his mouth so that I could taste every part of him. It was new, somehow, even though we had done this so many times before. It was new, because now I knew that he loved me and I wanted to get lost in the sheer, blissful sweetness of knowing that I loved him too. Of knowing that the man I had saved it for all these years had been the right one.

He dipped his hand between my legs and brushed his fingers over my sex; I was already getting wet, the closeness drawing us together in a way I had never felt before. I didn't know the thought of love could turn me on, but it had. There was something so profound about being wanted in that way that I had never imagined there would be – I knew that it might have sounded a little crazy, but when he touched me, it seemed like he was drawing me even closer than before, the space between us boiled down to near-nothing. And I loved every moment of it.

"You're so wet," he breathed, and he brought his fingers to my mouth as though to prove his point to me; I parted my lips to taste him eagerly, and my muskiness on his skin was enough to have me helplessly grinding against him on the couch. He was still mostly dressed and I was so ready for him to be naked right about then, I had to strip him down, had to have him bared to me.

"Please," I pleaded with him, my voice taking on this keening,

234

desperate edge that I knew he must have liked, judging by the look on his face. He swiftly took the condom he seemed to always carry with him in his pocket into his hand, pulled down his pants, and sheathed himself. And then, at last, he pushed himself inside of me.

The feeling was more than it had ever been to me before. I thought I had known pleasure before then, but it was nothing compared to the way that he made me feel now, now that he loved me. *He loved me.* I couldn't stop thinking about that. I knew that I loved him right back, but I hadn't said the words yet and I wanted to make sure that it was clear to him. I wanted him to have no doubts about the way I felt for him, and if that meant showing him with everything else I had, I would do it.

I kissed him and slipped one hand down his hand, sinking my fingers into his ass so that I could push him deeper inside of me. I had never wanted to be so close to someone before. It was a strange intensity, the kind that I might have been a little scared of before him, but when it came to this connection with the man I loved, I knew there was noting that could stop me giving in to the feelings I had for him.

"You feel so good," he murmured to me, pulling back for a moment so that he could look me in the eyes; normally, his gaze would get a little unfocused at this point in our lovemaking, but this time, he seemed sharper than ever. As though he was seeing me for the first time. I knew how he felt, it was like I couldn't take my eyes off him. I didn't want to. Not for a moment, in case I lost this intensity that we had between us right now, in case I forgot it, somehow.

I pushed my hips back against him and he thrust deep inside of me, filling me all the way up to the hilt and making me groan with pleasure. Even though we were as close as two people could be in that moment, I still wanted to be closer to him. Was that crazy? I craved him even deeper than that. Maybe it was something more than physical, something more than just his touch; it was his love I wanted, every way I could get it, and I had no intention of hiding out from that any longer.

I could feel myself getting close, and he buried his face in my neck and drove himself into me harder than before, as though he could sense that I was near to the edge. I gasped and tipped my head back, one hand planted against the arm of the couch above me so that I could push back against him, and I came, hard, my body contracting around and against his like it had been waiting for this moment all day long.

"Fuck," he growled, and moments later I felt him tip into his own release, the rush of it coursing through me as I spiraled in my own pleasure for a long, blissful moment. I loved him. I loved him so much that my body couldn't contain it any longer.

As he held himself inside of me, I grasped his chin in my hand so that I could look him in the eye. And I said it, I said it at last.

"I love you too."

He laughed – it wasn't the reaction that I had been expecting, but I found myself laughing, too. And, as he pulled himself out of me and kissed me again, he murmured the words over and over again into my ear.

"I love you, Stephanie. I love you so fucking much."

And I knew, in that moment, that no matter what my family threw at us, we would be able to make it through. It was going to be hard, no doubt about it, but we could do it. Because that's what happened when you were in love. You did everything you could to stay that way, and to make each other happy. And I knew that as long as we had each other, we had a fighting chance.

Chapter Sixteen – Jon

"Holy fucking shit."

As soon as I saw the numbers in front of me, all of this started to fall into place.

Ever since the visit from Stephanie's father and her brother, I had been working overtime trying to find something, anything that would prove that they hardly had the best intentions for the company that they essentially wanted to steal from us.

Stephanie had been focused on running the day-to-day stuff, thank goodness, so I was able to let go and focus on everything that we needed to come up with before the meeting with the lawyers soon enough. She was doing a killer job keeping all the clients happy, making sure that the factory was on top of its game and producing everything that we needed it to. She should have been so proud of everything that she was achieving, but all she was focused on right about now was making sure that we didn't lose this company that we had both poured so much time and energy into.

I hated the thought of losing this place. It wasn't just because it was a secure promise for my future, but because it was something that Stephanie and I had built together. There was no way, if I could avoid it, that I was letting anyone else come in here and take that from us. I wanted this to be ours for as long as we could manage it, as long as we could hold it together. Maybe even pass it down to our kids someday...

Kids. Yeah, I had actually started thinking like that now, and I could hardly believe it, either. A few months before, if you had told me that I would fall from someone so hard I would think about having actual children with them, I would have brushed you off as crazy. But now...well, when I looked at her, I could see everything that we could have. If I could just fight hard enough to hang on to this company, which I had every intention of doing.

I had to figure out why they were so keen to get their hands on it. I knew that the family didn't think much of Stephanie as a businesswoman, but we had the numbers and the proof to prove without a doubt that she was the woman for this job. Getting rid of her was about something other than keeping this place going, for sure. She could run this joint, and anyone who thought otherwise just wasn't looking hard enough.

But maybe that was what they were counting on. That we weren't going to look hard enough. Well, they had another fucking thing coming, and I wanted them to be pretty damn clear on that. I wasn't going to roll over and let this get stolen from me without a fight. I had put too much time, too much effort, too much passion into this project to just toss my hands up and be done with it because they kicked up a fuss.

I just couldn't work out what Nate wanted with this place. He was the parents' favorite already, so it wasn't like he had a whole lot to gain from getting in here. Even if he did a bad job, they would still be patting him on the back and telling him that he was the most talented guy they had ever seen in their lives. It was ridiculous, really, but I knew how they could be. I had seen it, first-hand, the way they had treated Stephanie in comparison to her brother. It was the short of shit that I would have assumed was invented if I didn't know better.

So, I had started a deep-dive into Nate and everything that Nate might have been trying to keep to himself. I knew there had to be a few somethings out there that he didn't want anyone to know about. Everyone had skeletons in their closet, and someone who had been as wild as Nate in their youth? Yeah, I had no doubt that there were a few bodies under the floorboards that he wanted to keep hidden from his family. And it was my job to dig them up.

Before he'd met Patty, he had been dating pretty much anyone he could get his hands on – well, I say dating, I really mean hooking up with and then dumping at once because the thought of commitment seemed to be enough to make him come out in hives. He had the money, he had the looks, and he could pretty much get any girl that he wanted. But, he had always been smart enough to make sure that they stayed hidden from his parents. Back in the day, I had thought he was a little silly to put so much effort into keeping his dating life from his family – he was an adult, after all, and they didn't get to decide what was right and what was wrong for him – but now I could see that it was a carefully-cultivated ploy to make sure that he stayed top of the pile when it came to his relations.

Still. There had to be something in his past, or his present, that I could use to prove that he was doing this for the wrong reasons. I knew that I was going to need stone-cold evidence, that nothing else was going to work as far as his family were concerned. He was the golden boy, and the golden boy would have to fuck up in a pretty impressive fashion for anyone to accept it had happened at all.

And so, I had taken a deep-dive into everything I could find about him. I mean, I worked for the family business now, so I could use that to my advantage. When I told people what I was involved with, they all seemed to be uninterested in questioning whether or not I actually had the right to be digging up this information on him. Or maybe it was just because he had managed to piss off pretty much everyone he'd ever met before that they were so willing to spill whatever beans I needed them to when I asked.

He and Patty had gotten married a few years ago now, and since then, he had been a lot less careful about keeping his business to himself. They had jetted off all over the world together, posting pictures on social media of the exotic locations that they visited; she was usually dripping in some designer gear, as well as rings and necklaces and other shit that I knew couldn't have come cheap. And I knew that, while the family had money, they weren't exactly rolling in it. Patty had married into cash, after all, and she wasn't bringing a lot to the table...

How were they financing these trips? I reached out to the hotels they stayed at, to check if they had offered them sponsorships to promote them on their social media, but nothing of the sort had actually happened. And I added up the costs of these trips, and they soon tipped into the hundreds of thousands. There was no way that he could have managed all this by himself...

I went deep-diving into his finances. It wasn't like he had done a whole lot of work, really, mainly positions that he was clearly just put in to make him look as though he was actually doing something. While they paid more than they should have, it would have been nowhere near enough to finance everything that they had been doing. And, with a little pushing and pulling, I was able to get my hands on their tax returns for the last few years...

And it was as soon as I saw them that it clicked. This was what he was trying to get away from, somehow, this was what he was trying to cover up. Because they were in debt. A *whole* lot of debt.

I had the proof of it right there in my hands. I skimmed through everything that I had gotten with the tax returns, all the details, all the numbers, and I couldn't help but feel my jaw drop. I couldn't believe someone would be this...well, would be this stupid about money. I mean, yeah, he had grown up in a family that likely hadn't bothered to teach him the value of a dollar, but he must have seen his supplies dwindling, the cash that he actually had dribbling out of his account on another expensive gift for Patty or another ridiculous European vacation.

I could have taken this right to his family and proved that he was the last person who should have been taking control of the company. I could have, if I was feeling particularly vindictive, and don't get me wrong, the thought crossed my mind. How fun would it be to turn up to that meeting we had planned with them and throw down this on the table? Proof that he was nothing more than a waster who was in this for the money? I could practically see the horror and anger on his face, and the thought of it was fucking delicious...

But if I was going to be dating his sister, then I supposed that I owed him a little kindness. I knew that he sure as hell didn't deserve it, but if it would keep things cool between me and the rest of the family, then I would do it.

"Where are you going?" Stephanie asked me, as I stuffed the files into my bag and slung it over my shoulder. I leaned over the desk and kissed her.

"Out," I replied. "I'll be back soon. I promise."

She gave me a funny look, but smiled, as though she could tell that I had some good news in my back pocket for a change. She kissed me again and watched as I walked out the door. Hopefully, by the time that I got back, this would all be over, and we could get back to reality for a change.

Nate had an office in town; I wasn't even sure what he did with it apart from wasting everyone's time and money, but at least it gave me a place to head to so I could speak to him in person. I called up as soon as I got there, and I guessed that he probably thought he was about to get the chance to lord over on me again, because he allowed me in at once. As soon as I closed the office door behind him, I had to cool my heels a little, because if not, I would have grabbed him by the lapels, slammed him against the door, and demanded to know what this smug little asshole thought he was doing with the company.

"Good to see you, Jon," Nate remarked, his voice pointedly cold. Jesus fucking Christ. I hated this man. I really did. He walked about this city like he just so happened to own it, when I knew that he had debt coming out of his ass that he would probably never get rid of. He was the kind of rich bitch that everyone liked to hate on, and for good reason, too. It was hard to think of anyone who oozed such a distinct unlikeability. Yet another reason why he shouldn't be let anywhere near the company.

"You too," I lied, and he gestured for me to take a seat; I did as I was told, wanting this to be over sooner rather than later.

"So, what can I help you with?" He asked, sinking down into the padded leather seat and locking his fingers behind his head, the very picture of confidence. Jesus, what I wouldn't have given to feel that kind of confidence even when I knew there was so much that the world in general could hold against me. That had to be some kind of superpower. It would have been almost impressive, if I didn't hate him so much.

"I wanted to give you one more chance to stop coming after the company," I told him, coolly. He shook his head at me, gave me a condescending grin.

"I know you're very attached to that place now," he remarked. "But you have to understand, you're just not the right fit for it. I know that it would be better off with Patty and I, and-"

"And do the people who want you to run the place know about your debt?" I asked, cutting him off mid-sentence. Probably not the best form, but who gave a shit? I couldn't listen to this smug jerk pat himself on the back about his business acumen for another moment.

His face seemed to freeze solid for a split second, as though he was trying to process what I had just said to him... I narrowed my eyes and waited for him to say something back to me, but it didn't seem like there was anything coming. I pulled the papers out of my bag, and slapped them down on the desk in front of him.

"Your tax returns," I explained. "Not that hard to get hold of. I could have a copy emailed to everyone in your family if I wanted to. Do you understand me?"

He stared at the papers for a long moment, and his face seemed to turn a shade of sickly yellow. I felt a rush of triumph. Yes, I had done it. I had managed to get this guy to see that he was wrong for this-

"I don't see how that's relevant."

"What?" I demanded, thrown by the calmness with which he was addressing me. How could he be acting so casual, when I had all but thrown the mechanism of his downfall down in front of him?

"Our debt," he replied. "It's not business debt, it's personal. It has nothing to do with this place."

"But why do you want it?" I demanded. "That's what I don't understand. You hardly work as it is, and taking on this place on top of trying to pay off your debts, it's crazy, you must see that..."

I trailed off, because he was just looking at me with this grin on his face as though he couldn't believe that I was being so dense. I stared at him, waiting for him to explain exactly what it was that was running through his head, but he didn't seem too forthcoming. I didn't like this, didn't like this at all, and I wanted an explanation as to why he was looking at me like that.

"You really haven't figured it out?" He asked, and his voice was quiet and pointed and enough to make the hair on the back of my neck stand on end.

"What are you talking about?"

"I'm not going to keep the company," he replied. "I'm not going to run it. We're going to sell it."

My jaw dropped. What the fuck? I couldn't believe what I was hearing, I hated this. The words went ringing around and around my ears, over and over until I couldn't hear anything else.

"What the hell are you talking about?"

"That's how we're going to pay off the debts," he replied, with a shrug. "By making sure that we get rid of that dead end so it's not weighing down the family any longer."

"I can't believe you-"

"Come on, you can't really think that hanging on to it is a good idea, can you?" He asked, shaking his head at me. "Jon, come on. I took you for smarter than that."

I wanted to flip the table right over there and then, just to wipe that smug look off his face, but I knew it wouldn't do anything to change the truth of what he was saying to me.

"Does your father..."?"

"He doesn't know yet, but I know that he'll be glad to have that place behind him," he replied. "It's just a reminder of something he would rather leave behind him, trust me."

"But...it's your family," I pointed out, stunned. "Your history..."

"And I think we can all agree that this is about the time that we can let all of that go and move on," he replied bluntly. "Don't you understand? This is going to be a good thing for the family as a whole. I know that Amanda-"

"Amaya," I corrected him, voice low.

"I know that she might not have wanted it gone," he continued, ignoring my correction, like the asshole he was. "But sometimes you just have to move on, don't you?"

I didn't say a word.

"Well, I suppose that's all we have to say to each other for now," he replied cheerfully. "I think you should be going before my sister ends up hooking up with someone else, huh?"

I got to my feet. He did the same thing. My hands were clenched to fists at my sides.

"What did you just say?"

"I mean, after she started with you, you can't expect her to pretend like there aren't any other men in this city," he replied, as though it was obvious. There was that fucking smile on his face, the one that told me he loved goading me like this, nudging me towards blowing my top. This was a guy who had so much going for him that it had never crossed his mind that someone might get the nerve together to remind him that life wasn't always going to be this kind to him.

"I guess I'm just a little surprised that my baby sister turned out to be such a..." He began, and he looked me in the eye, clearly savoring the chance to say this to my face. I dared him to go on. Fucking dared him. Because if he said what I thought he was going to say...

"Such a slut."

And that was it. As soon as I heard that word come out of his mouth, any semblance of control that I might have had vanished. The red mist came down, and the clenched fist at my side tightened, and before I knew it, I was swinging for him.

Chapter Seventeen – Stephanie

"Oh my God," I muttered to myself, as I headed out of the office. I felt like I needed to shout it at the top of my lungs, but there was nobody around to hear it.

I had just gotten off the phone with Jon – well, he had just been told that his time on the phone was up, given that he was at the police station being held there against his will. He had been arrested. And now, he needed me to go down there and get him out.

My head was spinning; I didn't know what had happened, but when he had walked out of the office, he had looked so light, so happy, so sure that what he was doing was going to solve everything for us. And now – well, now, I supposed, it was quite fair to say that it hadn't.

I had never been inside a police station before. It was quieter than I imagined, and could have passed for a regular office, not the dingy old-West cells that I had pictured when I had gotten the call. The woman at the desk smiled up at me, and I walked towards her, in something of a daze.

"I'm here to see – uh, Jon? Jon Wallace? I have bail for him..."

"Okay, if you want to come through here we can get everything sorted for you," she replied, and she gestured for me to come through a door to my right. I did as I was told, still in something of a daze. This had to be some kind of bad dream, didn't it? There was no other explanation than that. I felt like I was going to bump my knee on a table and wake up, covered in a cold sweat, in my bed.

I paid the money and sat there in the room and waited for him to come out; moments later, he did, and I leapt to my feet as he entered the small room I was sitting in.

"Jon!" I exclaimed, and I looked him up and down, trying to get a handle on what the hell had happened here.

"Are you alright?" I asked. He didn't look like anything too awful had happened to him, but I just couldn't imagine what he had done to land him in here in the first place. Something had to have gone seriously wrong.

"I'm fine," he replied, and he slumped into the chair opposite mine, looking exhausted. "But I'm not so sure your brother is."

"What are you talking about?" I asked, a rush of panic overtaking me. Had something happened to Nate? I might have hated him right now, but he was still my brother...

"He's fine," he assured me quickly. "I just punched him. That's why I'm here."

My eyes widened so much I was surprised they didn't bug right on out of my head.

"You hit him?" I gasped. "Like...you punched him?"

"Yeah," he replied, and he squeezed one hand in the other and winced. "And it hurt more than I thought it would. I think he came off worse, though. He had a bloody nose by the time I left."

"You punched him," I repeated, unable to quite wrap my head around the fact that this had actually happened.

"He was talking shit," he replied simply, as though it was that simple; I looked up at him, searching for a little more context, but he didn't rush to give it to me. I supposed that it probably had something to do with me, if he was so reluctant to let me hear what it truly was.

"Why were you seeing my brother, anyway?" I asked, as she slumped down into the chair opposite me and ran his fingers over his slightly bruised knuckles. That must have been what he was marching out of the office looking so confident about. But I couldn't imagine anyone meeting with Nate and actually looking forward to it.

"I thought I had him," he replied. "I dug up some tax returns from him and Patty, and it turns out that the two of them owe a whole lot of money. A whole lot. A lot more than I thought anyone could spend in their lifetime, but it seems like I was wrong."

"And?" I asked, keenly, leaning forward with interest.

"And I thought that I could get him to give up coming after the company if I threatened to expose them," he replied. "But it turns out that he doesn't even care about that. He wants the company so that he can take it from us, and then sell it on so he can pay off his debts."

Those words hit me hard, like a speeding bus running over me in the street. I did my best to catch my breath, but it felt like the life was being choked out of me for a moment. I hadn't realized just how much this place had meant to me until that moment, until I found out that it was on the brink of being snatched right out from underneath me. And suddenly, I felt all this fight rise up inside of me – all this anger that I had been doing my best to hide.

"I can't believe this," I muttered. Everything about this was so surreal, I couldn't wrap my head around any of it. I wanted to get up and walk right on out of there and pretend that none of this had happened in the first place; to just leave, not look back, and go back to the life that I had been living before all of this had started. I had been foolish to think for a moment that I could have things go my way, not after so long of watching them fall apart around me, because of me. My family didn't want me to have a life of my own and they didn't care who knew it. And now, my brother, my bastard brother, he was going to take something that actually mattered to me, and he was going to find some way to twist it and tear it apart till nothing that I had made mattered for a moment longer...

I put my head in my hands. I wanted to turn back time. Because the pain of losing all of this was too much to bear. It was hear, in this place, that I had found an identity, a purpose, a confidence that I had never known I could conjure. And they were going to take that from me, and for what? So that my brother could pay off his fucking debts? I didn't even want to think how much he had accumulated over the years. Thousands. Hundreds of thousands. He had been giving everything by my family, and he had tossed it all away while I was scrabbling under the table for the barest hint of the crumbs that would around me to do what I wanted with my life.

"I'm so sorry," Jon told me, gently, and he reached out to take my hands. I looked down at his slightly bruised knuckles, and couldn't help but chuckle to myself when I saw the marks on them.

"You know, you're not the first guy who's ever wanted to punch my brother," I remarked. "But I think you might be one of the first to actually go through with it."

"You're not mad?"

"No," I replied. "He probably deserved it. Let me guess, he called the cops on you right afterwards?"

"His security team took me down here," he replied, and I rolled my eyes and shook my head.

"Color me shocked," I sighed. "He must need those guys around to make sure he doesn't get everything he deserves, seriously. If there was any justice in the world..."

I trailed off and shook my head again. I didn't want to think about him. I was still holding his hands tight, and I was glad that I had a man like this to stand up for me, a man who would come to my defense whenever he felt like I might have needed it. Not a lot of people could say that about the person they loved, but I could, and I was never going to for granted the fact that he adored me as much as he did. I could never have guessed, not in a million years, that he was going to make me so happy, that he was going to stand by me with the sureness that he did right now, but I couldn't have asked for anything more than him.

"I'm sorry there's not more that I could do," He remarked. I shook my head.

"You did more than I ever could have," I told him, and he smiled at me. There was a tinge of happiness to his face, even though I could tell he was in a lot of pain at the same time. I reached out, cupped his face in my hand.

"Thank you," I told him. "Really. I don't know what I would have done without you. And even if we lose the company..."

I took a deep breath, gathering myself, not even wanting to think about the reality of that but really having no other choice.

"And even if we lose the company, I want you to know that I still love you," I told him, with certainty. I did. I loved him. I loved him more than I had loved anyone before in my life. Even my family. Because my family would never have gone to the mat for me the way he had done, they would never have fought for what they thought was right like he did. He smiled at me, kissed my hand again.

"You promise?" He replied softly, and I nodded.

"I promise."

He paused for a moment, just letting the moment wash over him, and then he glanced around as though realizing where he was for the first time.

"Then let's get the hell out of here," he replied. "There must be something else we can do to stop this. I'm not finished yet."

"Agreed," I replied. "Guess neither of us know when to give up, do we?"

"Guess not," he agreed, and he flashed me a big smile. I swear, I felt myself swoon just a little bit when he grinned at me. Even after all this time, something as simple as that could be enough to set something in me on fire.

"Okay, let's get out of here," He repeated, and this time he got to his feet, his hand still wrapped around mine. And I knew that, in that moment, everything was going to be alright, as long as I stuck it out with him. The odds were against us, but that didn't mean that we didn't have a fighting chance. Despite everything, I felt a little twinge of hope.

Chapter Eighteen – Stephanie

"I can't believe you hung on to all of those," I laughed, as Jon dumped down the stack of pictures on the table.

"Yeah, well, I have a hard time getting rid of stuff," he admitted. "Call me a hoarder. I just don't like saying goodbye to anything, you know?"

"I get that," I agreed, and I reached out and began to thumb through the photographs that he had brought over this evening.

It was really just something that would serve to get our minds off the mess that was going on with the company right now, and frankly I was grateful for anything that would allow me to pretend that it wasn't happening. We had that meeting with the lawyers and the rest of the family at the end of the week, and we had pretty much come to terms with the fact, though we hadn't spoken about it yet, that we would be bidding farewell to this place once and for all. No matter how much I wanted to pretend that it wasn't the case, the little world we had made for ourselves was about to come crashing down around us, and damn, we deserved a chance to pretend that everything was alright a little longer, didn't we?

I had tried not to think about the inevitable as it had drawn closer and closer and we had still failed to come up with something that would be enough to save us. We had gone down every path, tried every route we could to discover something that would give us the ammo to show my brother and his wife up, but none of it mattered.

From what Jon had told me, it sounded like everyone just wanted the business out of the family for good. Which upset me no end; after all, it was Amaya's hard work that had gotten us a decent standing and a solid amount of money to begin with, and the thought of leaving all that behind just because it seemed a little too ethnic for their liking hurt me. I knew that the clothes might not have been the most fashionable in the world, but they were beautiful and delicate and truly some of the most striking fashion that I'd ever had the pleasure of laying eyes on, and the thought of just letting all that go to pretend that we had never been through any of that as a family, as a culture...no. I didn't like it. Not one bit.

But, soon enough, it looked like, I wouldn't be the one getting the say on what worked and what didn't. Once again, I was going to be relegated to the bottom tier of the family so that they could make sure that every little thing my brother wanted came true for him. And honestly, I wasn't bitter –

no, really. Well, maybe a little, but not enough to make a fuss about it, not anymore. I had come to terms with it. I didn't want to let go, but I wasn't going to let him win again by sitting there stewing in it for weeks on end and letting him control my life from afar.

Besides, I had Jon in the middle of all of this. I loved him more than words could say. And at least I was never going to have to worry about introducing him to the family; I doubted they would what anything to do with him anyway, given the circumstances in which that they had discovered we were together in the first place. I had received a few worried texts from my mother, clearly attempting to parse out the truth of our relationship and work out how much she had to worry about when it came to us, and I had been blunt and honest with her and told her that I was with him and that I didn't intend to change that any time soon. If they got what they wanted, then I decided that it was about time that I got what I wanted.

And, as a little treat for the two of us this evening, Jon had brought over a few pictures that he had been hanging on to from years back; nothing too fancy, just a few bits and pieces that he'd hung on to from when we had first known one another, when he had taken pictures all the time for his company website in the hopes of showing himself fraternizing with people who had actual money and power and influence.

"Okay, just promise me you're not going to laugh at my hair, alright?" I warned him, and he grinned at me and raised his eyebrows.

"You know that I'm legally obliged to laugh at it now that you've asked me not to," he pointed out. I slapped him playfully on the upper arm.

"I thought you were meant to tell me that you'd been in love with me from the moment you laid eyes on me," I pointed out, and he shook his head and put his arm around me on the couch.

"Not at all," he replied cheerfully. "You were a kid then. And besides, I don't believe in love at first sight. Far too easy."

"And you like it to be hard?" I joked back. He looked over at me for a moment, his eyes a little misty around the edges.

"I like to know that we're both working for this," He replied, simply. "That we're both working towards the same goal. That's all."

I smiled back at him. Hard not to when he seemed to know just what to say to make my heart sing with excitement. I turned my attention to the pictures, and starting going through them, looking for a few of me.

"Oh, look, I'm in this one!" I exclaimed, and I pointed to myself, a little dorky-looking, probably around seventeen and dressed in what I thought were *very* cool suspenders with a waistcoat that I had beat-up myself over the top of them.

"Oh my God," he laughed. "That's a hell of a look. You ever think about going for something like that now, or...?"

"Yeah, I really want to look like the lead singer of a pop-punk group while I'm trying to be taken seriously in meetings with my clients," I laughed, and I traced my fingers over myself. I was just in the background of the photos, mostly, because I had been way too shy to be anywhere near Jon or his camera when I had been that age. I couldn't help but feel a little sorry for that version of me. She had been so nervous and so self-conscious, I wanted to reach back in time and tell her that there was nothing for her to worry about, not really.

"Okay, and why did nobody tell me that the suit I was wearing looked so bad?" Jon groaned, laughing at an old picture of himself.

"I thought it looked nice!" I protested. "I remember you in that suit. I thought you looked hot!"

"Okay, but how many actual men had you seen in your life up until that point?" He replied. I shrugged. He had a point.

"Not many," I agreed, and I leafed through another couple of pictures. And then one in particular caught my eye, and I found myself stopping dead in my tracks.

"Stephanie?" Jon asked, a little confused. "What is it? Are you alright?"

I stared blankly at the picture in front of me for a long moment as I tried to wrap my head around what the hell I was seeing. If I hadn't been so intently looking in the background of these images, I likely would have flipped right by it and never seen it at all. I narrowed my eyes at the glossy image, certain that I must have been seeing something wrong. Twisting it back and forth, I got to my feet so I could stand closer to the light and get a look at this properly. I was sure that that was...

And then, it hit me. Like an optical illusion game that had just clicked in my head, I could see it. I could see them. Together.

"What is it?" Jon asked again, and he got to his feet and came over to join me. He was probably worried that I was looking so thrown, especially after the month that we had had.

"This is what I think it is, right?" I asked him, and I held out the image to him. He took it from me and narrowed his eyes at it, trying to work out what it was about this particular picture that had gotten me so excited. At a glance, it would just look like an image of my family together – my mother, my father, me. It was my awkward smile that had gotten me to stop on it in the first place, but now that I had taken a closer look, I could see there was something more to it than I had originally thought.

"What am I looking at?" He asked. I pointed to the background of the picture – through a doorway that had been left ajar, you could just make out a couple of figures. A couple of figures, I was sure, that both of us recognized at once.

"Is that...?"

"I think it is," I replied, and I was so happy it felt as though the words came bubbling up and over, out of my mouth. I couldn't believe it. My skin was prickling, and I kept on waiting for the penny to drop, for something to happen that would undermine what the hell I was seeing right now.

In the background of the picture, probably where they thought they were out of view, Patty and Nate were making out. And not the kind of making out that could have passed for chaste; the kind where she was clearly reaching to take off her shirt, and already had her hand down his pants. I mean, yes, it was totally gross seeing my own brother in a position like that, but I didn't care. Because it meant that we had them just where we wanted them.

"These means..."

"These means that we can prove that they were involved before they got married," I replied. "Which I know he told my parents they weren't. I always knew that they had been, but I don't think my parents would have believed it...well, unless they were to see a picture like this, that is."

"Are you saying what I think you're saying?" He replied, and I nodded and bit my lip.

"I think we can bring this to the meeting," I told him, my voice tiny for a moment as the realization washed through me. "And then..."

"And then we can expose them," he finished up. It was like we were on the same wavelength at last, the two of us filling things in for one another, answering each other's questions, reading each other's minds. This was how I liked him best – when the two of us were bouncing off each other as though we had been made for one another. I couldn't get enough of him then. I hoped one day that my parents would be able to see this, would be able to see how good we were for one another, but even if they couldn't, I could live with it. Because he was mine.

He scooped me up in his arms, and I laughed and grabbed on tight to him.

"Careful with the picture!" I cried out. "We have to keep it safe, remember?"

"We will, we will," he promised me. "I have a digital copy of it, anyway. Don't worry, it's not going anywhere."

He pulled back, and planted a big kiss on my lips. I kissed him back, hanging on to him for dear life. God, this man had kept me afloat through so much. I wasn't sure how I would have survived any of this without him. It had been him, after all, who had convinced me that I was worth all of this, that I was worth fighting for in the first place. All this time, my family had fed into this idea in my head that I wasn't worth going the extra mile for – that I wasn't worth fighting for. But now, with him at my side, I could see it was a lie. He loved me just as I was, didn't love me as a back-up to someone else, didn't treat me as second-best to my brother or my father or anyone else in his life. Jon loved me just as I was, and I was grateful above all else that I would be able to show him how much I loved him right back. I was going to be able to help him save the company.

"You know, I would never have noticed that myself," he remarked, as he pulled back from me. "I need someone like you around to notice the little things."

"Hey, I'm sure I can keep a handle on the big things, too," I replied. As soon as I said it, I realized how it could be easily twisted into an innuendo, and felt myself get a little red.

"Oh, yeah?" He answered, and he waggled his eyebrows at me playfully. I had to laugh. He always knew how to brighten my mood, even when I felt like everything was tumbling down around me. Though, in all honesty, in that moment, it felt like I was building everything up once more.

"If you're making a reference to your dick..."

"I might well be," he confessed. I laughed.

"You're lucky I love you so much," I told him. "Otherwise I might have dumped you right there and then."

"Guess I am," he replied, and he dipped me low and kissed me like we were at the climactic moment of some gorgeously sweeping romance. And that's honestly what it felt like in that moment – like he was the man I had been waiting for all this time, the prince that those cartoon women sang about and waited for. My heart bounced up in my chest – would this ever change? Would his romance towards me ever cease? I hoped not. I wanted to spend every day feeling like I was the luckiest woman on the planet. And I got the feeling that he wanted to make me feel that way every chance that he got, too.

He brushed his nose against mine, and said those words again, those words that were still such a brilliant novelty to me, even though I had already heard them so many times.

"I love you."

And the light in his eyes and the glint in his smile and the strength of his arms wrapped tight around me told me that he meant every word of it.

Chapter Nineteen – Jon

The look on her brother's face was almost enough to make every moment of this worth it. Almost. I eyed him from across the table as everyone looked at the picture that we had blown up and annotated so nobody could miss what was going on, and I could tell that this was the last thing that he had expected.

"What is this, Nathan?" His father asked him, voice strained. When they had walked into this meeting, I doubted that they had expected us to come in with something that they couldn't deny – I mean, yeah, they had to assume that we would have come out swinging, but this was harder than anything they could have planned for.

Stephanie looked over at me, and she was struggling to keep the smile off her face as she waited for all of this to sink in. I knew this had to be a dream come true for her. To finally win in the face of her brother, to prove to herself that she was the one who should have laid claim to this company. And to do it with the very same tools that he had tried to use to dismantle her. It was almost too perfect, and I couldn't wait till this was over and we could go over every detail until it had sunk in for good.

"This much be doctored," Nate blustered, trying to come up with something that would deflect the horror of what was really happening right now.

"Okay, and how did we manage to get the outfits that Mom and Dad were wearing that day right?" Stephanie pointed out. "You can confirm this, right, Dad? That you wore that, and Mom wore that?"

Her father stared at the picture in front of him, and it was clear that he wished he could come up with something, anything, that would render this wrong. Because whether or not he wanted to admit it, this wasn't about making sure that the company ended up in the right hands – this was about being certain that his son took the reins of it, and now he was faced with the truth that he couldn't just hope for that any longer. He had been caught out, once and for all, and it was beyond delicious to see the abject shock written all over his face as he tried to take it in.

"This is real," Her father muttered. "And this is...you were involved with Patty before you were married, Nathan?"

Nathan shifted in his seat. If there was one thing worse than talking about your sex life with your family, it was talking about your sex life when you knew it might land you stuck in a stack of debt that you had been counting on getting yourself all the way out of.

"Yes," he blurted out. It wasn't like he could deny it much with the facts that we had just tossed down in front of them.

"But so is Stephanie," he pointed out hopelessly. "I mean, she is involved with Jon right now..."

"And we never tried to hide that from anyone," I cut in. "Because there's nothing to be ashamed of about it. But the fact that you were dishonest..."

I let the words hang in the air, not needing to fill them in any further. The damage had already been done. Now, it was just about hearing the words coming out of her father's mouth, the ones that admitted that Stephanie and I were the ones to run this business and he knew it. I wanted that. I needed that. I craved it more than anything right now.

"And Amaya did choose Stephanie in her will," I continued. "So it's not like there isn't precedent for her holding on to the company. Not to mention how well we've done running it together..."

Her father looked too shocked to reply for a long moment, and I found myself holding my breath. I could tell that Stephanie was in just the same place right now, much as she was trying to keep it calm and casual. But finally, his shoulders sagged, and he shook his head.

"Fine," he agreed. "You know, I think you're right. We shouldn't have tried to take this from you, Steph. It's yours to keep."

"What?" Nate exclaimed, and Stephanie burst out laughing, her face lighting up in utter delight as she took in what she was being told.

"You can't give it to her, Dad," Nate protested stupidly. He sounded like such a petulant child, but then, I supposed, that was probably the most accurate representation of what he was right now. Relying on his daddy to get him out of the mess he had made for himself. He had only himself to blame and he must have known that, and I couldn't think of anything worse for him than realizing that this was all on his head. Well, maybe going back to Patty and admitting to her that he had managed to lose the company – yeah, that might come up there with some of the worst...

"I think I'd rather keep it with Stephanie given that she's the one who is honest with me," Her father replied. He couldn't even look at Nate. I knew that they were going to have a lot to figure out with this new information out in the open, but that wasn't my concern. I grabbed Stephanie's hand and squeezed it beneath the table. God, I loved this woman. If it hadn't been for her eagle eye, then we would never have seen that image of her brother and we would never have been able to catch him out like this.

"Not to mention that the company seems to be thriving with the two of them at the top of it," He admitted. I knew it must have taken a lot for a man like that to come out and say that he knew that his daughter was better for this job than his son, but I wasn't going to be giving him any pats on the back for it anytime soon. He had just finally done what he knew he should have in the first place. Maybe, as time passed, he would come to see that Stephanie had always been the obvious choice. I didn't much care. All I cared about was that she had won, and that I had that victory right along with her.

Nate bitched and moaned a little more, as we had expected, but soon enough the meeting was over, and Stephanie and I had made it back to our office in an excited mess.

"I can't believe that actually worked!" She exclaimed. "This is crazy. This is crazy! I never thought that they would ever take me seriously over Nate..."

"Yeah, well, I think Nate has a lot of explaining to do," I replied, and she grinned at me widely and nodded.

"I think he does," she agreed. "Oh my goodness, this is really happening, right? Like, I'm not going to wake up and it's all going to be over?"

"No, this is really happening," I promised her, and I closed the door behind us and kissed her once more, pulling her into my arms. We didn't have to worry so much about hiding this anymore. I could be honest about the fact that I loved her, the truth that I needed her more than anything in the world.

"You know," she teased lightly, as the two of us kissed. "None of this would have happened if you had just done the gentlemanly thing and married me when we had first met."

I eyed her for a moment. And a crazy thought passed through my head. So crazy that I was sure that I was going to have to dismiss it right away. But instead, I found it hooking in – I found it taking shape, making form inside my head. Because maybe...

I got down on one knee.

"Jon, what the hell are you doing?" She laughed, and I grabbed her hands.

"You're right," I replied. "I should have married you then. But I'm not going to make that mistake again, trust me."

"What are you talking about?" She asked, and I could see that she was practically breathless even as I spoke.

"I want to be with you, Stephanie," I told her. "I want to be with you more than anything. And I don't want to waste any more time waiting for that. Will you marry me?"

She stared down at me in silence for a long moment as though she could hardly believe that this was happening. I thought that she might say no, call me crazy, tell me to stand up and stop acting like such a madman. But instead, slowly, but surely, I saw the smile dawn over her face. She squeezed my hands tight in hers. And then she nodded.

"Okay," She replied.

"I think the usual answer is yes," I teased her.

"Then yes," she replied, and she shook her head, the huge smile on her face looking as though she could barely contain it. "Yes. Yes, I'll marry you."

"I love you so fucking much," I told her, and I rose to my feet once more and kissed her again; this woman who had just agreed to spend the rest of her life with me. I was so blessed to have her in my life, and I knew that I would continue to feel that way for as long as we were together. Lucky. More than lucky. As though the whole world had fallen in my favor and I should have thanked whatever Gods were up there for the helping hand.

"You're serious?" She asked me, once I had stopped kissing her. "You really mean this?"

"I really mean this," I promised her. "I'll get you the ring as soon as I can. But I mean this. I mean everything about it, alright?"

"Oh my God," she murmured, and she laughed again, her joyous giggle bubbling up from inside her to fill the whole room, as though she could barely manage to keep all that happiness in.

"This might be the best day of my life," she told me, and I wrapped my arms around her and kissed her once more. I didn't want to stop kissing her. I didn't know how to tell her everything that I wanted her to hear without my tongue speaking it into her mouth, bringing it to life with my touch...

I backed her towards the desk behind us, and hitched her off the ground so that I could place her down on top of it. She spread her legs at once and pulled me in close to her, her breath coming harder and faster than it had before. I wasn't sure this was exactly what you were meant to do right after you got engaged, but we had never much been the kind of people who did things by the rules.

She was wearing a skirt, thank God, so I was able to just reach up between her legs and pull down her panties. She kicked them off her legs and giggled delightedly as I tossed them to the ground. I had never seen her so happy in all her life, and God, there was something joyous about knowing that I had been the one to put her in such a mood. I was hardly thinking of anything but just how I could pleasure her, how I could make her happy. I supposed that was how you knew that it was love for sure – when there was nothing you wouldn't have done to make the other person feel good. That was how I knew it with her, and that was how I wanted her to know it with me.

She grabbed my hand and pulled it to her mouth, slipping my fingers past her lips so that she could taste me, sucking lightly for a moment before she pushed them back between my legs. I took her cue to slip them inside of her, and she shifted herself to the edge of the desk and let me push deep into her, guiding my fingers around and inside so that I could caress her G-spot just lightly. She shuddered with delight, and I felt myself stirring to an almost unbearable hardness between my legs. Just knowing that she was turned on, that was enough to get me off. Knowing that this woman wanted me the way I wanted her.

"Fuck me," she moaned in my ear, and that was all I needed to hear. I took myself into my hand, glancing over my shoulder to make sure that the door was shut before I started, and rolled her skirt a few inches further up her thighs. She wrapped her arms around me and shifted herself forward on the desk, arching her back so that she could tip her hips up towards me and I could have all the access I wanted to her delicious, perfect little pussy.

I pressed my head to her slit, rubbing it up and down a couple of times, letting her feel my warmth and how ready I was for her. She moaned again, and I figured that her torture was ready to be over, so I pushed myself inside of her, slowly, letting her feel every inch of me as I moved into her. For the first time as a couple who had actually committed themselves to one another. It was the strangest feeling, in the best possible way.

"Fuck," she gasped, and she hooked her ankles behind my back and pulled me in even deeper. It was hard to remember that this woman had been a virgin when we had first started sleeping together; she was so passionate, so powerfully sexy to me, that it just didn't seem to track any longer. I had imagined first-timers to be boring in bed, but she was anything but boring. And anything but in bed, at least in that moment.

She began to rock her hips back and forth against him, driving me even deeper inside of her with every motion, and I reached down to grab hold of her hip and keep her in place.

"You feel so good," I told her, my mouth pressed to her ear, as I put my arms around her and held her tight in place against me. I knew that this was dangerous, and that we could get caught at any time, but I actually loved that idea. The two of us, so hot for each other that we were willing to get into a whole lot of trouble in the process of consummating our engagement. I couldn't think of anything more perfect to prove that we had been made for one another.

"Mmm," she moaned back softly, and I felt the vibrations of her throat rush through my body. It was like everything was revolving around this moment, this feeling that she was giving me; our connection was deeper than it ever had been before in all the time I had known her, and I wanted her to feel it just the same way that I felt it, too. I wanted her to know it, deep down in her guts, that this was meant to be. That we had always been meant to be.

I slowed my thrusts inside of her, taking my time, letting myself feel every gorgeous inch of her pussy around me. This was the woman who I had just committed myself to for the rest of my life, and somehow, that thought didn't scare me the way it might have just a few months ago. I hadn't even known her that long, but I was certain of it. You knew love when it came to you, and I could see that now; all those other times I had tried to let myself fall, they had been the wrong person, the wrong time, the wrong place in my life. It had all been leading to her. To Stephanie. And I was never going to let either of us forget that.

"Ah," she gasped, as I slipped myself almost out of her, and then thrust deep back inside. I loved watching her face when I had her like this, when I could tell that she felt like she was going a little crazy for what I could give her. I needed to know that she felt just the same way about, that those feelings burned just as bright inside of her as they did in me. I could feel myself getting close, just looking at her, at the sight of her face as it grew a little slack with the pleasure that I was giving her.

"Come inside me," she pleaded softly, and it was in that moment that I realized I had forgotten to put on a condom. But she didn't seem to care, and I had to admit, neither did I. The thought of filling her up with my seed was enough to tip me over the edge right then and there, and I felt my knees shaking a little as I pushed deep inside her one last time and filled her up to the very brim.

"Fuck," I groaned, and I held myself there so that I could feel every inch of her around me as she took me in deep; it was only moments later that I felt her contract around me, the warmth of her muscles tightening against me over and over again, as she came, as the orgasm washed through her. She sank her fingers into my shoulders and leaned her head against my chest for a moment, not pulling away, not ready for this to be over. I knew just how she felt. This was far too good to be done with just yet.

But there was the office to think of, and the last thing we needed was to be caught in the middle of this. While we had won this round, I got the feeling that things wouldn't run so smoothly if they found out that we had been hooking up in here mere hours after we had actually managed to hang on to the company.

"Okay, that was amazing," she breathed, as though she could hardly believe just how good it had been. "Is it always that good when it's with you?"

"Well, I like to think so," I replied, and she grinned and laughed.

"So you're still totally cocky I see," She remarked.

"I just got the woman I love to agree to marry me," I pointed out. "I think I'm allowed to be a little cocky, aren't I?"

"I suppose I can let you away with it this time," she agreed, and she hopped down off the desk and nearly fell over at once, her legs still obviously shaky from what we had just done.

"Woah, careful, there," I laughed, and I caught her and kept her from crashing right to the ground. She hung on to me for dear life, and shook her head, clearly amused with herself.

"Okay," she remarked, patting my arm. "I think I have my legs under me now. But good to know that you're there to jump in whenever I don't."

"Isn't that what marriage is all about?" I replied.

"Save it for the vows," she teased, and she paused for a moment and just looked at me.

"What is it?" I asked, and she shook her head.

"I just can't believe this is really happening," she confessed. "I mean, I...I love you, so much, and you know I love this company, too. But I didn't think that I would get to have both at once. I didn't think it worked like that for me."

"Well, it does," I assured her. "It always will, as long as I'm around. And you deserve all of this. You know that, right?"

She let out a deep breath and then nodded.

"I think so," she agreed. "I think I do. I mean, it's going to take me a little time to figure all of this out and start believing that I've got a right to it, but I can get there. One day."

"Damn straight you will," I replied, and I took her hand and kissed the spot where I was going to put a ring as soon as I got the chance. "And you know that I'm going to do whatever it takes to convince you in the meantime."

"I know," she replied softly, and she smiled at me. And I knew that I had done the right thing in proposing to her. Because I loved her – I loved her, and I knew that. But it was about more than just love. It was about looking into the eyes of a woman that I knew I could grow with, who I knew complemented so much about me so perfectly. We could grow together, change each other for the better, just the way we had since we had started work at this company. And I was beyond grateful for the chance to get to show her how much I believed in her, and how that faith was never going to change. No matter what.

"Come on, get your panties on," I told her playfully. "I think this calls for us to go out and celebrate with a drink, right?"

"I think so," she agreed. "Can this be our engagement party? I can call up Terri and Marjorie, you can actually meet them finally..."

"I think that sounds perfect," I agreed, and I watched as she leaned on the desk and got herself back in presentable mode. Because I had every intention of making her as un-presentable as possible again, just as soon as I got the chance to.

Chapter Twenty – Stephanie

"So, when are you going to tell him?" Terri asked with excited interest, practically hopping back and forth as she helped me unload the new stack of clothes that we had laid out for the next collection the shop was going to sell.

"I honestly have no idea," I admitted. "Soon. Today, maybe."

"I think it should be today," Marjorie agreed. "I mean, I got lucky, the father of my baby found out the same time that I did. But it looks like you get to pull the surprise card."

"I don't know if I actually want to have to," I replied, pulling a face. "It's going to be so strange coming out and telling him all of that, don't you think?"

"Oh, Jon is going to jump right into it," Terri replied at once, waving a hand as though she was dismissing my concerns at once. "He's good like that."

"Bear in mind that I'm the one engaged to him," I teased her playfully. Ever since Terri and Marjorie had first met Jon, on our pseudo-engagement party a few weeks before, they hadn't been able to stop talking about him. Which I had to assume was a good thing, given that I always wanted the most important people in my life to get on as well as they possibly could.

I still couldn't quite believe that all of this was actually happening. It had been such a wild whirlwind of activity, and to call it intense would have been a wild understatement.

"I can't believe you're actually engaged!" Terri had shrieked to me as soon as we had come out and broken the news to them at the bar that we were going to get married. Marjorie just leaned over and gave me a giant hug, looking a little tearful; I supposed, she was the oldest one out of this group, and sometimes she did get a little emotional at the thought of Terri and I actually becoming grown-ass adults the way she was, too.

"Me neither," I agreed, and Jon returned with our drinks and put his arm around me.

"Still talking about the engagement?"

"Well, this is meant to be an engagement party," Terri pointed out. "It would be a little strange if we were talking about anything else, don't you think?"

"Point taken," he replied with a grin, and he handed out the drinks that he had purchased for everyone at the bar. I could already tell that the girls like him, but that didn't mean that I didn't want to sit around and let them tell me how great he was every time he headed to the bathroom or to the bar for another round of drinks.

And I knew they were totally right. He was amazing. He was the man who had my back no matter what, and I would be eternally and truly grateful for that. If it hadn't been for his belief in me, I would never have had the nerve to go out there and get the company back; I would have looked at the photograph of Nate and Patty together, and I would have found some way to convince myself that nobody would believe me in the first place. I loved him, but more to the point, he loved me, and he wanted to see me succeed in every single way that I could. I couldn't imagine anything more perfect to build a marriage on than that, and I had drunkenly told that to practically anyone who would listen at the bar where we celebrated that evening. I was quite sure that even the people slipping out for cigarette breaks knew by the time that we were out of there, but I didn't care. I wanted to shout it from the rooftops. He loved me, and he wanted to marry me. It didn't get much better than that.

Of course, the next day, I met with Marjorie and Terri and they gushed about how great he was. I knew that they just wouldn't have said a thing if they didn't like him, but they seemed hardly able to keep their total delight at his newfound presence in their lives to themselves.

"I mean, I know it doesn't really matter what we think of him," Marjorie remarked. "It's what you think of him that does."

"But since you ask," Terri cut in. "He's great. We both think he's amazing, don't we, Marjorie?"

"Yeah, we do," Marjorie replied with a grin. "And it's clear that he's totally nuts about you as well, which is about all that I can really ask for when it comes to the man who's going to marry you."

I smiled at Marjorie. She was the one out of the three of us who had settled down first, and it meant a lot to me to know that she approved of the choice of man that I had made to spend the rest of my life with. I knew if I had her approval, then I had to be doing something right.

When I told my family, I had expected something of a little pushback after everything that had happened, but to my surprise, they seemed totally on-board with the idea. I mean, Nate had a few snide comments to make here and there about what he thought of us together, but that wasn't a problem, since he was practically the black sheep of the family now. I didn't have to worry about him anymore, and I had no intention of doing that now that he wasn't going to be an issue.

"You're really getting married?" Mom had asked me, her eyes lighting up as she clasped her hands to her chest.

"Yes, really, Mom," I replied. I hadn't gotten the ring to show her yet; Jon was taking his time, making sure that he picked out the perfect creation that would go with everything in my wardrobe, but I was in no rush at all. Any pace that suited him was the one that worked for me, too, and I wanted to make sure that everything was just how he wanted it before we went a moment further.

"I think Jon is a good lad," Dad remarked, a little stiffly, but I could tell that he meant it. He might have had a hard time coming out with the emotional stuff – almost as hard a time as he had had accepting that I was the person who deserved to run Amaya's company – but he was getting there, and his support meant the world to me. If Jon was going to become part of this family, then I wanted to be damn sure that he fit in as well as he possibly could.

We travelled down to meet his family, too, and they were totally sweet with me as long as I was there. Jon took a few of them aside just to make sure that it wasn't politeness and that yes, they really did think I was the right woman for him, and he had it all confirmed, which was a major relief. After all the drama that we had had with my family, the last thing I wanted was anything more to come from his. We had worked too hard, committed too much time and energy into this, not to have it run as easy as it possibly could have now that we were here, ready to take the next step together.

One evening, Jon came home from work at the office, and I noticed a little glimmer in his eye.

"What is it?" I asked, but I already got the feeling that I knew what was going on.

"I found your ring," he told me, and I put down the book I was reading at once and gestured for him to come over and join me.

"Oh my God, you have no idea how much I've been looking forward to this," I told him, thrilled that the day was finally here.

He got down on his knee in front of me, just like he had back in the office, and held the little box that he pulled from his pocket out to me. I couldn't help but smile. He could just be the sweetest thing when he wanted to be. Though, often, that wasn't exactly what I craved from him...

"Will you marry me, Stephanie?" He asked, and with that, he popped the box open. In it, a beautiful ring, silver, imprinted with an emerald, glimmered back at me.

"Oh my God, "I gasped as soon as I laid eyes on it. "Jon, this is perfect..."

"You like it?" He asked, and he took it out of the box and took my hand and gently slipped it over my finger. I held my hand out for a moment so that I could admire my new accessory, and I bit my lip and shook my head, unable to take this all in.

"This is just perfect," I breathed. "Really. How did you know that this one would look so good?"

"I've been looking for so long," he admitted. "But none of them were really speaking to me. But then, I saw this one, and I thought...well, I just knew. I knew that this was the one that you needed in your life."

I closed my eyes and let the sweetness of his words pass through me. I could hardly believe that I had truly been gifted with someone so utterly and abjectly perfect in every single way. To say I was lucky...no, that didn't even come close to summing up how I felt about him. I had been gifted something, from far up above, something that I would never take for granted. I leaned over to him, and planted a gentle kiss on his lips, letting the hand with the ring on it rest gently on his face.

"It's perfect," I told him. "I love it. Thank you so much."

"Thank you for agreeing to marry me," he replied. "I was worried you might take one look at the ring and think better of it..."

"You really thought I might do that?" I laughed, and he shrugged.

"Well, I know how discerning you are with everything that you wear," he pointed out. "You can't blame me for being a little nervous that you weren't going to take to this so well."

"Well, you had nothing to worry about," I assured him. "It's perfect. Totally, utterly perfect. You should be pretty damn pleased with yourself."

"Oh, I always am," he replied, and he kissed me again, and suddenly, the ring was the last thing on my mind.

After that, the wedding planning began in earnest, and everything seemed to kick into high-gear. My family wanted to be involved with putting it all together, and I supposed there was some part of them that was hoping to make up for all the time and effort they had poured into my brother when they could see, now, that I was just as worthy of it. In all fairness, until I had met Jon, I hadn't been totally convinced of that myself, but now, it was obvious to see that I had as much worth as anyone else in my family.

Picking out the dress was a no-brainer. I knew that I wanted to wear when I went down the aisle, and it would only be right if it was one of Amaya's stunningly perfect designs. She might not have planned for them to be used like this, but I knew that she would love the twist that I had brought to her pieces by wearing them as wedding dresses. I used one of her perfect designs and got it made in red and gold, the traditional Indian wedding colors. It was modern and vintage all at the same time, and it was totally perfect for me. Not to mention the fact that it was utterly bespoke. That was my favorite thing about it, knowing that nobody else would ever be able to wear this very same piece down the aisle.

"Are you sure you don't want to produce at least a limited run of it?" Marjorie had asked, looking it over. "I mean, it's beyond gorgeous. I know you would sell a bunch if you did."

"Probably," I agreed. "But I like the idea of it being just for me, you know?"

"Hmm, I can get behind that," Marjorie replied. "Maybe I'm just a little jealous because I know I'll never get a chance to wear it."

"Maybe," I giggled. I liked the thought of my very own wedding dress being this lavishly covetable item, and I couldn't wait to wear it at the wedding six months from now.

And that was when, of course, I found out the news that brought everything grinding to a halt.

I had missed my period – not a big deal, sometimes they could come late or early depending on what was going on in my life. It wasn't something that I usually got overly distressed about, but I decided to pick up a pregnancy test anyway, just to make sure that there was nothing that I had to be worried about.

Which is the exact moment, of course, that I found out that there was something to be worried about.

I could remember vividly sitting there on the bathroom floor, staring at the positive test, wondering if this was some kind of sick joke at my expense. It had to be, didn't it? Because the alternative was...well, the alternative was far too horrible for me to even consider. There was no way that I could be pregnant, not really, not with so much else going on in my life. I had the wedding to plan, the company to run, too much to do to think about anything like this...

But the more time I gave it to sink in, the more I supposed I could actually handle this. I wanted to start a family with him anyway, didn't I? So, this had come a little quicker than I had expected. There was nothing wrong with that. I had waited for so long for my perfect man to come along, was I really going to duck and hide from him now that I had found him?

I went to Marjorie first, and Terri, since she was there too, and I came clean about the fact that I was with child and that I had no clue at all how I was meant to feel about it. Marjorie was the one who talked me through it, stopped me from going crazy.

"It's going to be fine," Marjorie promised me, and Terri squeezed my hand tight, letting me know that she was right here and that she always would be. I was so grateful for them. Sometimes, even when things felt like they would be too much for me to handle, I knew that I could rely on them.

"But you need to tell you," Marjorie told me gently. "You know? You need to let him be a part of this. It's important for the both of you, and I think you know that."

"I do," I sighed. "I'm just worried that this is going to be too quick for him."

"This is the guy who proposed to you with no ring on a hunch," Terri pointed out. "I don't think moving too quickly is something you're going to have to worry about when it comes to him."

"You make a fair point," I agreed, and I smiled at them both. "Thank you, by the way. You know I couldn't have done this without you."

"I think it's really him you couldn't have done it without," Terri joked, and I burst out laughing. She always knew just what to say to make me feel better, and to stop me from taking everything too seriously.

By the time that I was ready to tell him, a week had passed, and I had finally come to terms with what was going on inside of me. I was ready for him to be a part of it; in fact, I wanted that more than anything. We had shared so much together and now we were going to share this, too, and it thrilled me more than anything else in the world to think about everything that we were going to have together when this little kid came into our lives.

I sat him down one evening after dinner – I had all but moved into his apartment, though we had been making some noises about getting one of our own to have a fresh start in when the time came – and I supposed from the look in my eye he must have known that this was something serious.

"Something you want to tell me?" He asked, and I took a deep breath and nodded.

"I think there is."

"Please tell me you're not calling off the wedding..."

"I'm not calling off the wedding," I told him, with a slight laugh. "We've done too much planning for me to even think about that, don't worry."

"Good to know that's all that's standing between me and getting left at the altar..."

"You know what I mean," I replied, and I took his hands in mine and looked him dead in the eyes. Taking a deep breath, I took a run-up at the statement. I had to just come out and say it.

"Jon," I announced, trying not to let the words catch at the back of my throat. "Jon, I'm...I'm pregnant."

He stared at me for a long, silent second, and as that time ticked by, I thought that he hadn't heard me. I squeezed his hands again, hoping to elicit some kind of response.

"Jon?" I said his name again. "Jon, did you hear me alright?"

"I heard you," he replied quietly. My heart was pounding as I waited for him to say something else. Anything else. I needed the promise that he wasn't going anywhere, I needed to hear it from his mouth. I couldn't bear the thought of losing him, but I knew by now that this baby wasn't going anywhere, and if that meant-

"You really mean it?" He asked, and his voice was soft and so overflowing with delight that I wondered for a second how I had ever managed to doubt him.

"I mean it," I assured him, and a huge smile cracked across his face. He pulled me on to his lap and kissed me passionately, running his hands over my body as though he could barely believe the multitudes that I contained with just that one little statement.

"Oh my God," he murmured, and he planted a hand on my belly and shook his head. "I had no idea. I don't...I mean, you want to keep it, don't you?"

"Of course I do," I assured him. He leaned his head up against mine and closed his eyes.

"We're going to have a family," he told me, and I grinned. I knew that he was going to be an amazing father. And I knew that, no matter what, we were never going to be those parents who took sides or had preferences with our kids. We were never going to put them through what I had been through with my brother, and I would do anything to make totally sure of that.

"This is amazing," he murmured, and he cupped his face in my hand. "You're amazing, Stephanie. You know that, right?"

"You make it pretty difficult to forget," I confessed, a little bashfully, and he smiled and kissed me again, one hand still resting on my belly, where the beginnings of our beautiful baby were just starting to brew. And, in that moment, I knew there was nothing in the world that could have made me happier than knowing I was at the start of a future with the man I loved.

Epilogue – Stephanie

"Oh my God, you look incredible," Terri gasped, as soon as she saw me emerge in my dress. I spun around in front of her and smiled.

"You really think?"

"I really think," Terri replied. "Oh, it looks so cute over your bump!"

"Yeah, they managed to get the alterations just right," I agreed, and I smoothed down the beautiful crimson fabric so that it cascaded perfectly down over my bump. I loved the way it looked, I had to admit; I had even flown out to the workshops in India so that I could oversee the making of it, and it had been such a gift to see such amazing crafts-women at work putting this piece together. A few of them had had stories of Amaya, too, and I had been happy to lap them all up, taking them in, finally connecting with the history that my family often seemed like it was trying to pretend had never happened.

I had so much to thank Amaya for, even though I knew that I would never get a chance to do so. I wished there was some way I could go back in time and tell her that she had made such a different in my life – that everything she had done had not gone unnoticed, and that her clothes were turning up in stores all over the States and even across the world now. That her name would be known, and her beautiful clothes would be worn by so many people.

Because the business had taken off like crazy in the last few months. Some minor celebrity blogger had picked up one of the outfits that Marjorie had put together in her store, and from there, things had just blown way out of control; people were keen for this design or that one, and we had to hire new workers just to keep up with the demand. Oh, and we actually moved into an office all of our own, as opposed to a room in an office building where we would run into other people all the time. I was pretty sure that was my favorite part. And yes, Jon and I had christened both of our office spaces a few times over with each other, because it just seemed straight-up rude for us not to, you know?

I knew that my parents were proud of everything we had done with the business, and they surely had to accept by now that I was the better call to run it. It wasn't just about their bullshit rules on hooking up before a wedding, which I assumed they had long-since come to terms with given that I was going to be walking up the aisle heavily pregnant. But there had been a palpable shift recently, in the last few months especially, where they seemed to have accepted that there was nothing they could do to control the lives of me or my brother any longer. They had to accept that we were adults, and that we got to make our own rules and live by them, for better or for worse. I knew that my parents had just been fighting to do what they thought was right for us, but by now, at least, I hoped they could see how wrong they had been.

I had sworn to myself a million times over that I was never going to treat my own children in that way. I was going to let them make their own mistakes, to a certain point, and I wasn't going to spend my life hovering over them and trying to make sure they did everything the way I wanted them to. At some point, you just had to let go and allow them to be their own people, and I couldn't wait to see what our children would blossom into being when we gave them the chance.

And yes, we were already thinking about the children that we were going to have. Plural. I couldn't wait to raise a whole gaggle of kids with him; something about having a bun in the oven meant that I was constantly broody, constantly ready and waiting for the next kid. We still didn't know the gender of this one yet, but that was fine by me; I liked the idea of being surprised. Jon wasn't in total agreement with me on that one, until I pointed out that whatever we had, we could have another to make up the gender-set.

We had moved into that bigger apartment, room enough for a nursery with an office that I could already see being repurposed into a room from the little ones, and Jon had spent hours making sure that everything was just the way he wanted it for when his kid finally came into the world. Watching him put together his perfect nursery was a delight.

"You know, I think you missed your calling as an interior designer," I had teased him, and he had cocked an eyebrow at me and shook his head.

"I'm not sure about that," he replied, stepping back to take a look at the work he had been doing; this time around, he was painting the wall opposite the window yellow, so that when the sun caught it, it would practically glow in the light.

"It's going to look so beautiful in here when you're all done with it," I told him wistfully, already existed to know what that would look like. Even standing here now got me all emotional, I couldn't imagine how I would feel when it was finished.

But before I could think about that, we had the wedding to get through. Not get through – no, I was looking forward to being his wife, and we had planned the most perfect little ceremony in the whole world. A few magazines, much to my surprise, had asked for the photo rights since we were known in the fashion world now, but I turned them down. I wanted this to stay just between us, a perfect little love story that only involved the people who mattered most to us in the world.

And speaking of those people. Something had crossed my mind after I had gotten engaged; especially after I had gotten pregnant. I knew that I had a lot of reasons to be angry at my dear brother, but that didn't mean that I necessarily wanted to keep him and his wife at arm's length for the rest of my life. I could have sat around and stewed in anger a little longer, but there wasn't much point in that, not when we had a little one on the way who was going to make everything significantly more complicated and more exciting.

And so, with Jon's help and consent, I came up with a plan. It took a while to brew in my head, to make it perfect so that I knew it would work, but once I had clicked it into place in my mind, I knew that it was the perfect way to make everything right between us once more.

"Are you sure?" Jon had asked, as we waited for them to arrive. I planted a hand on my stomach, and nodded. I didn't want to go another day in this pregnancy without being honest about the way that I felt, until I had cleared the air in my family so that I never had to fear about it again.

"I'm sure," I replied firmly. And with that, the door opened, and Nate and Patty stepped inside of my office.

They looked a little worse-for-wear. I had heard through the family grapevine that the two of them had had something of a hard time since Nate's plan to take the company from us had fallen through. I couldn't say that I was surprised, but seeing them in person, it was a little bit of a shock. It wasn't that they were traipsing through the door in tattered rags or anything, but something about the way that they were carrying themselves just seemed heavier than it had before. As though even lifting their foot and putting it in front of the other was too much effort for them to handle.

"Thanks for coming in today," I told them both, and I gestured for my brother and my sister-in-law to sit. I had to say, I wasn't sure that their marriage was going to survive all the stress that the debt had clearly put on them – Jon was certain Patty was a gold-digger, after all – but maybe there was some real affection there. Maybe they were really in love. And, despite everything he had done to me, I couldn't help but feel a little happy for my brother.

"I don't know why you brought us down here," Nate told me, a little stubbornly; Jon had remarked that he came across like a petulant kid when he was like this, and now that he had mentioned it, it was hard to not see it. He had a point. My brother could act like such a child if he wasn't making the effort to be mature for a change.

"If it's just to gloat over us-"

"It's not," I told him. "Though God knows I'd be well within my rights to do that-"

I stopped myself before I went any further. This wasn't about making a point as to how much better my life was going than his. I was here to help. I wanted to help. I wanted to make their lives better and I wanted them to be able to move forward into this new start with us.

"We wanted to offer you an amnesty," I explained to him. "That's why you're here. We want to pay off the rest of your debt."

"What?" Patty gasped. Her face lit up, and it looked for a moment as though a weight that had been resting on her shoulders had finally begun to lift.

"We know that you're still struggling with a lot of debt," Jon explained, patting my leg under the table. "And the company is working well at the moment, we're making a lot of money to spare. We don't need all of it, even with the baby coming."

"What are you saying?" Nate murmured, suddenly looking like a kid again. I felt so sorry for him. He was still my brother, after all, and he had likely been just as fucked up by the upbringing my parents had given him as I had. He needed help, and I was blessed that I could give it to him.

"No debts," I replied. "All done. You come to the wedding, you promise to be a part of your niece and nephew's life – and you have to agree not to come after anything that's ours again."

Nate leaned forward, and he looked me dead in the eye.

"If you're kidding about this, sister-"

"I'm not," I told him. "I mean this. I want the slate wiped clean for all of us. Do you think you can work with me on that?"

Nate closed his eyes and leaned back in his seat for a moment, as though he was letting the relief wash over him. I glanced over at Jon; was this a good sign? I had to think so.

"Stephanie, you have no idea how much this means to us," Patty told me, and she leaned forward and took my hands. Her eyes were shining and I could tell that she was having a hard time restraining herself from bursting into tears right there and then.

"So, I'll take that as a yes?" I asked her, and she nodded.

"Yes," she agreed at once, and she looked over at Nate. "Right, Nathan? We need this."

"We need this," he agreed, even though there was a little pride to his voice. Patty smiled at me, and Nate put his arm around his wife.

"So, does this mean that we can come to the wedding now?" Patty asked, and I nodded. She clapped her hands together delightedly.

"Yay!" She exclaimed. "Oh, I love weddings. I can't wait to be there for your special day..."

And with that, the bridges were mended between my brother, his wife, and Jon and I. And I couldn't have been happier knowing that all the bad stuff between us was finally over.

"You know, you're much more generous than I would have been in your scenario," Jon had told me, and I shrugged.

"I just don't see anything to gain from holding all that against them," I pointed out. "I want to move on from all of it, and I'm not going to be able to do that if I had to avoid my brother every time that I go to visit my parents when the baby comes."

"Not that we're going to be letting them have any influence over the kid," he warned me. He had been stringently committed to the idea of a new style of parenting, one that didn't revolve around trying to define anything in our child's life. And, more to the point, not treating them any differently whether they were a boy or a girl.

"Not that we're going to let them," I agreed. I knew that parenting was going to present plenty of challenges, but I knew that I would be able to navigate them all as long as he was there to help me.

And now, I was going to be his wife. It was just...it was so much for me to take in. As I stood there, flanked by Marjorie and Terri, looking at myself in the beautiful vintage mirror of the hotel we had congregated at before the actual ceremony, it was almost hard for me to wrap my head around.

"I can't believe that you're going to be a Mrs.," Marjorie remarked, putting her arm around my waist and squeezing tight. "Barefoot and pregnant in the kitchen, right?"

"Yeah, good luck with that," Terri joked. "You're never out of heels, Stephanie."

"Fair point," I conceded, and I took a deep breath and put my hands on my bump. Even though I knew it was crazy and that it had no basis in reality, sometimes, I felt like I could communicate with the little person inside of me. Right now, I was sending them good vibes, telling them that I was about to seal their family into law and love so that when they came into the world, they would have a mommy and daddy who were already connected.

"Okay, I think I'm ready to get out there," I told them. Terri, in her beautiful blood-red pantsuit, linked an arm through mine, and Marjorie, with the red maxi-dress, took the other. They were the ones who were giving me away today. My dad had offered but it just seemed a little old-fashioned for me. I wanted to be given away into my new life by the people who had supported me through so much of my old one; Marjorie and Terri were already going to be such big parts of my baby's life, and I knew that. It felt right that they should be here for this part, too.

I heard the band strike up as I prepared to enter the hall where we were getting wed; it had taken ages to find the perfect venue, but I was confident that this was the one. When I came through the door, the light was pouring through the window above the altar, lighting up the space that I would get married in in a gorgeous ray of light.

And standing there, right in the middle of it, was the man that I was going to marry. And the music seemed to dim to nothing and the world slimmed down around me as I focused on nothing but him, him, him.

This had been the man I had fallen for such a long time ago. Before I even really understood what love was. Back when I had been a teenager, and I had seen him and thought, yes, that's him. That's the one.

It had taken me a while to trust myself completely, to believe that I was totally right in what I wanted. And he had known, he had known that first night we had spent together, before we had even so much as had sex. I knew that he might not admit it, because he wanted to think of himself as smart and logical and not the dude who jumped into anything too quickly, but it was true. He had gotten down on one knee out of nowhere, after all. He was impulsive. He was totally a romantic, and I thoroughly expected our first Valentine's Day together to be a totally swoon-worthy affair.

It was strange to think that we had barely spent a whole year together yet. We were just hitting it now; and so much had changed in that time, so much had shifted, the world moving out from under me in a way I hadn't been ready for but I had needed more than anything else.

I arrived in front of him, and Terri and Marjorie gave me a squeeze and retreated back to their spots in the wedding party. He reached out to take my hands, and he squeezed them tight.

"Hey," he greeted me, softly.

"Hey," I replied. It felt like such a small word, for something that encompassed so much, but I was smiling so hard that I could hardly come up with anything else to say to him.

"If you're ready," The registrar began. "Shall we begin?"

And I looked at him, at Jon, at the father of my child, the co-owner of my company, the love of my life. And, with a smile so big I could barely contain it on my face, I nodded.

"Yes," I replied. "Yes, I sure am."

THE END

Book 3: His Fake Fiancée

Chapter One – Terri

Okay. So I needed to forget about going out for the rest of the month. Maybe see if I could sell some of the clothes I had picked up last year at that fashion expo online to make a little cash. And then focus on getting as many hours at the store as I could manage, and then, hopefully, maybe...

I scribbled down all the numbers frantically on the paper in front of me as I tried to make sense of everything that was running through my mind. My mom had once told me that there was nothing worse in this world than having to worry about money, and the more time I spent doing just that, the more I realized she had a pretty good point.

But I could make it for this month. Just this month. That was something, right? I looked around the small studio apartment that I called home, and sighed. Nobody should have been bending over backwards to make rent on a place this tiny, this minute. But I was. Because of course I was. Because I hadn't actually learned how to be a fully-functioning adult in all the time that I had allegedly been one.

I sat back in my couch – second hand, snatched up from the street when I saw someone getting rid of it and knew that I could make something of it – and let out a long, irritated sigh. I wished there was something out there in the rest of the world that I could be pissed about, but the truth was, this was all my fault and I damn well knew it. I was the one who had never been able to crack the code of being responsible with money, and I was twenty-six years old and needed to start acting like it sooner or later.

Maybe it was just playing on my mind a little more than usual because Marjorie and Steph had both moved on into the big adult phases of their lives. I mean, not that both of them weren't mature before, but now it seemed like all they spent their time doing was talking about grown-up stuff that I could hardly even wrap my head around. Marjorie had her daughter, and Stephanie was pregnant, and the two of them were in long-term relationships that were soon going to turn into marriages. They had money, they had security, they had the ability to buy the bottle of wine that wasn't priced the cheapest in any given corner store that they stopped off at to pick up supplies for the night. Lucky for some.

But I knew it wasn't luck. You didn't just stumble into a life like that, you had to strike out and make it from yourself, much as I would have liked to pretend otherwise. They had worked their asses off doing what mattered most to them in the world, focusing on their futures and their lives and their families, while I had been...

Okay, I was going to stop that in its tracks. That was negative self-talk, and I had taken a course online last year that was meant to help me address that. I was going to treat myself better, I had decided, and that had meant no more talking myself down, acting like a kid, not taking care of myself. Oh, and of course spending money on everything I would need to solidify my self-care regime. Candles and books and new sheets and pillow spray. All of that. Because it was what I needed to change my life. Wasn't it?

I had managed to convince myself then that it was how my life was meant to be. Every time I found myself getting drawn into something new, I would convince myself that this was it, this was the change that I needed to make everything better. I was proud of myself for my commitment to it, talking about it to anyone who would listen, telling everyone in a ten-mile radius how this was going to change their lives just the same way that it had changed mine. Which made me look even sillier than normal when I flaked out on it and wound up getting pulled in by the next thing, no matter how objectively crazy it might how looked.

Short attention span. That had always been my problem. I was on to the next thing before I had a chance to wrap up what had come before, and I knew that it was a weakness that I needed to work on. I had identified it as such in that self-help course, though, obviously, that course hadn't been meant to actually treat that aspect of myself, and I started looking for the next thing that would fix that problem for me.

Maybe that was what I needed to change. The constant search for the next thing and the next thing and the next thing. Well, at least stopping spending money on all of that would probably have been a start, so that I could actually make rent for myself every month without having to do this frantic crunching of the numbers the week before my rent was due.

I needed to see Marjorie and beg for some extra hours at work; I knew that she would probably give them to me, since Stephanie was off running the company now, but she would ask why in that gentle tone of voice that let me know that she was worried about me and I would have to pretend that there was no reason, I was just feeling extra-productive this week and wanted to make the most of it, and why on Earth would she consider anything different?

Of course, though, Marjorie was well aware of all the trouble that I'd had with money over the years. She was the oldest of the three of us, and the one who was most likely to come in and offer to fix everything for you. She didn't like to see us struggling, and I knew that her helpfulness came from a place of profound care. But sometimes, I didn't feel like I even deserved it, given that I was the one who had gotten myself into all of this in the first place.

I got myself dressed and cleaned up to look at my most respectable for when I went to visit Marjorie at the store, and I took my time wandering down there. It was late in the year and it was cold outside, but in the nice way before it got too piercing to think about walking around without full winter battle-gear on. It was at times like this that I was reminded why I came to New York in the first place; I had grown up in a tiny little town, middle-of-nowhere-ville USA, and I had always dreamed of coming to the big city and just finding out what life was like without the weight of everyone knowing me hanging around my neck. I knew it was a cliché, but that was because the lure of New York, the siren call that it had to people like me, was insurmountable and impossible to deny.

I had never regretted coming here. Even though I hadn't gone through university, even though I had to scramble to make enough cash to survive, especially in those first couple of years, before I turned twenty and when I was still trying to figure out how to get by without the help of my mom's cooking. Those were tough, for sure, but in the back of my mind I was already relegating them to the first few pages of my memoir, a little struggle that I would have to overcome to get to that thing that had been made for me. That thing that was going to make my life utterly and completely perfect. I would take one look at it and go *yes, this, here, now*, and that would be it. I would be full.

But I had yet to work out what that thing was. And it wasn't for lack of trying. Sometimes, I was so jealous of Marjorie and Stephanie, because they seemed to have that on lock-down already. Marjorie had had the store, and even when she had been going through her divorce and everything, she'd focused so much time on that, all her passion poured into that place because she knew it meant that much to her. And Stephanie had always been passionate about fashion, to the point that when the perfect opportunity for her came along, she was able to take it at once and succeed at it totally. And the two of them had both been able to find partners who fit around and into their lives, who supported their passions – hell, Stephanie even ran the business with Jon, for goodness sake. I needed to find me a man like that. But first, I was going to need to figure out what the hell my *thing* was. And I had no clue where to start on figuring it out.

Not that I exactly had a whole bunch of men just battering down my door to try and take me out on a date, anyway. I spent most of my time at the store, and the time that I wasn't there I was usually caught up in whatever project that I had committed to recently, whatever course I was sending myself on that I was sure was going to change my life this time. Stephanie and Marjorie and I tried to make time for one another wherever we could, and in between keeping up with them and keeping up with the rest of my life, I didn't have all that much extra time to find a man of my own.

I wasn't even sure that I wanted one, not yet, anyway. I needed to get my life in order before I brought a man on into it. It just would have seemed wrong, inviting someone into my world when it was already such a mess. Besides, I was getting to that point in my life now when I was surrounded by people my own age who were looking to actually settle down. And apparently, for reasons that were totally beyond me, most of them didn't want to do it with a girl who couldn't even make rent without sweating over it every month.

But that was something I could work on, I promised myself, as I walked down the street and took the turn to the left that would bring me to the store. I could work on that. I had a lot to work on, but really, that was exciting, wasn't it? I could turn myself into a totally new person, and then I would...

And then, I would probably find myself back here again in the midst of all of this, trying to figure out who the hell I was and what the hell I was doing with my life. I sighed, watching my breath mingle with the cool air in front of me. I liked the way it looked, cold and crisp, and it made me smile, despite the mood I was in. I could always rely on this city to keep me happy, even when I felt like there was so much that I couldn't do, couldn't pull off, and couldn't make work.

The lights of the store were glowing in the early-evening darkness as I approached it, and I picked up my pace to get down there already. It was cold out, and I knew that talking to Marjorie about all of this would make me feel better. She was totally the responsible one, the Mom friend, the one who could help me no matter what. Stephanie was the sweetest, but she was caught up with this family that she was making and this company that she was bringing to life, and I didn't want to get in the way of that with my petty stuff. Or maybe I just didn't want to compare my life to hers right about then, all things considered, given that I doubted that I would come out of that comparison particularly well.

Plus if I could actually get someone else in to all of this, if I could let someone else know that I needed this help, maybe I would be more likely to stick to the accountability of what I needed to do to make the money tree give fruit again. Marjorie was always sensible when it came to this stuff, and I needed sensible in my life right now. Given that nobody in their right might would ever have described me in those terms.

I headed through the door and peeled off the coat that I had been wearing, tossing it behind the counter; the place was quiet, and not even Marjorie was behind the counter. I glanced around, trying to locate her, and figured she must have been in the back office.

As I got closer, I heard something, and I should have known then that it was my sign to step the fuck off and leave that place before I ran into something that I didn't want to see. But, instead, of course, me being me, I had to continue striding forward, wondering what those funny noises were, why it sounded like there were two people in the office and-

"Marjorie? Oh, shit!"

I exclaimed as soon as I was through the door. Marjorie leapt off the desk where she had been splayed, her skirt over her hips, and Blake, her boyfriend, turned his back to me as he swiftly tucked himself away. I wasn't sure whether I should apologize and run out of there or burst out laughing and start roasting the two of them. Marjorie might have liked to pretend that she was totally professional at all times, but totally professional at all times women didn't hook up with their partners at work when the shop was sitting unattended.

"Uh, Terri, could you-?" Marjorie asked, nodding to the door swiftly. I grinned and nodded, realizing that I was just standing there.

"Right away, ma'am," I giggled, and I slipped out of the room and left the two of them to get themselves back to decency. I knew that Marjorie

was going to be totally freaked over this, but honestly, it was just pretty funny to me. Sometimes, I needed the reminder that the women I looked up to as examples of everything responsible and sensible in life were capable of blowing off steam and having a little naughty fun, even when they should have been focused on serious business.

Blake nodded to me as he ducked out of the store, and I just about managed to keep a straight face as I nodded back. I had always liked Blake, but I got the feeling that he wasn't going to be the biggest fan of me after what I had just walked in on the two of them doing.

"Hello, yes, hey," Marjorie greeted me, emerging from the office and swiftly re-adjusting her skirt. She was totally blushing, but she was managing to play it off pretty cool. I decided to let her, even though I wanted nothing more than to lightly roast her for the fact that she had just been caught in the act right in the middle of work.

"Hey," I replied, and I grinned and leaned in the door. "Sorry for interrupting."

"I guess we just got a little...distracted," Marjorie remarked, and a small smile flicked up her face. It was cute to me to see how crazy she still was about Blake, even though they had been together for ages now – and back in high school before that. I hoped I would have something like that one day, though I had no clue what that would look like for me.

"Looks like it," I agreed. "Maybe put a sock on the door next time?"

"This is a clothes store," She pointed out. "I think people would just guess that there had been a slip-up with a delivery or something."

"Fair point," I laughed.

"So, what are you doing down here?" She asked, ever-blunt. Since she had become a mother, she'd had much less time for beating around the bush, and I supposed that it was for the best. Those customers who came into the store with anything but sweetness and light, though, I doubted that they would have felt the same way, because they got swiftly told-off if they were anything other than nice to all of us. I knew not many people could claim to have a boss like that, and I knew that I was lucky to be able to say that I did.

"I was wondering if you might be able to give me a few extra hours this week," I replied. "Maybe I could cover for you while you're in the process of trying to make another baby...?"

She shot me a look, but I could tell that she was amused by my little jibe. A smile spread across her face, and she shrugged.

"Sure thing," she replied. "You can start now, actually – we have a delivery coming in later this afternoon, and I need to pick up my baby from daycare. You think you could handle that?"

"Sure thing, boss," I replied, and I shot her a playful salute to let her know that she could trust me. She grinned back.

"And if you're okay to cover then I'll take off," she told me. "Thanks for this, it's a big help."

"Anytime, boss," I replied, and I headed behind the counter to flick through the fashion magazines that we kept under there and wait for the delivery guy to arrive. Marjorie gave me a quick hug before she left, and, within moments, I was in the store all by myself once more. And, as the quiet settled in around me, I promised myself that I was going to find some way to fix all those financial problems that I was having.

Because I wanted to have a real life, which revolved around more than just making the money I needed to survive. I wanted a real life that I could live freely and with ease and no matter what was going on in my bank account. I was twenty-six years old, and I was ready to switch things up. I just had to hope that the universe was willing to offer me the chance to do just that.

Chapter Two – Xander

"Can you handle the rest of this?" I asked Fred, raising my eyebrows at her pointedly. She nodded at once, knowing that I already had one foot out the door and didn't want to have to hang around to keep an eye on her any longer.

"Of course I can," she assured me. "You go, go pick up Mel. You know I've got this all covered."

"If you need anything, just call me, alright?" I told her, as I went to gather my stuff as quickly as I could. I was just going through the motions, really, knowing that the sooner I got out of this place, the better for me and my daughter.

"Yeah, I know," Fred replied, and she smiled at me and then pointed to the door. "Go on, get out of here. I know you don't have a lot of time."

"Thanks," I told her, and I pulled on my jacket and hurried over to the door and to the car outside, thanking God that I had thought to hire Fred as my second-in-command this time last year. She had replaced Rupert, who had been working at the company with me for years, and honestly, she was already doing a better job than he was. And she had always taken my relationship with Mel super-seriously, which I needed right now, given that everything about my daughter and our relationship was on the line and I needed to make sure that I was always there for her when I said I would be. No room for fuck-ups now; if I made even the slightest slip, then Talia was going to come sliding back in and make sure that I paid for it. And I didn't want my daughter stuck in the middle of that.

It pissed me off, though, if I was being honest – because part of the reason I had worked my ass off for so long in this place had been so I could secure a future for my baby girl. Philipson Industries wasn't just a passion project for me, though I was proud of how far we had taken it in the time that I had been running the joint. I had stepped in to this ailing white goods distribution company because I had seen a chance to make sure that everything that my daughter could possibly ever want or need, she would get. No questions. She would be provided for, no matter what, and if that meant working my ass off to do it, then I would.

But, of course, Talia had always found ways to hold that against me. She managed to do that with most everything that she had on me, actually, whether or not it was objectively positive. That had been true all the way through the divorce, and it was even more true now that she was making my life hell for daring to have a world that existed outside of her and what we'd used to have.

It had been three years since we had split up, and honestly, looking back, it had been the best decision of my life. I had been the one to push for it in the end, even though she had tried to use every trick in the book to guilt me into sticking around. It had worked for a while, especially when she had thrown my daughter at me, told me that I would ruin her young life if I left and split this family up. But it didn't take long for me to figure out that the last thing I wanted was to tell my baby girl that living a life that made you miserable was better than moving on and embracing something new, no matter how scary that might have been.

It was strange, looking back, to think that I had seen Talia as the woman I wanted to spend the rest of my life with. The two of us had met when we were both in college, but she had dropped out as soon as I had proposed and had started focusing on building our life together instead. Which would have been sweet, I supposed, if it hadn't been for the fact that she had basically tried to undo everything that I was working towards in the process. I wanted to go out and focus on my career, on getting my degree in business management and actually doing something with it. But she was in a constant rush to get married, have kids, and do everything that we were meant to do as a young couple. Sometimes, I wondered if she had been able to sense the fact that I was starting to check out, and if she had decided that this was the best way to make sure that I stuck around.

Of course, she hadn't counted on the fact that my career was actually going to take off. When she got pregnant – and I was still pretty sure that she had been lying to me about taking her birth control at the time, but I had no proof of that so I tried my best not to think about it – I threw myself into work, determined to make sure that we both had everything we could possibly want or need to raise our little boy or girl. Sure enough, it didn't take long until I had actually started to get somewhere.

"You know I totally support you in whatever you want to do," Talia told me, one evening, out of nowhere. I looked at her, an eyebrow raised, over the small space of the tiny apartment she had chosen for us after we had gotten married.

"I know that," I replied. I got the feeling that this was going to come with a *but*, and sure enough, a few seconds later, she followed it up with just that.

"But you can't spend all your time away from home and expect me to do all the work," she replied. I shook my head.

"You know I'm not going to do that," I assured her. It was the dozenth time we had had this conversation, as though it simply leaked out of her head when I had finished telling her all over again, but she was pregnant and I didn't want to push things.

Maybe I should have laid things down a little more plainly for her then. But honestly, I should have been able to see that, even back then, things just weren't going to work out the way that I wanted them to. I had carefully constructed everything about my job to make sure that I would be able to spend plenty of time with her and the baby by the time she came into the world, but Talia was constantly finding ways that it wasn't enough, that I was letting her down. She didn't intend to work, and I found myself getting frustrated with the fact that she seemed to want me to be both a stay-at-home-dad and the main breadwinner for the family. If I thought that was unreasonable, though, I should have waited to see what came next.

The first few years were tough, but they ran by in that fuzz that the initial years of childhood tend to; it's hard to think about anything else but raising your baby, and you don't really have time for anyone or anything but that. Including each other, in our case. Which I thought was for the best at the time, since she seemed to be so difficult all of a sudden. Nothing I did was good enough for her, none of the work I did was hard enough for her, every time I tried to take care of my daughter, it was lacking in some way in her eyes. And I knew that she was right to be protective, but it came to a point where I felt like nothing I did would even come close to being good enough for her. And it was hard not to let that drive me a little insane.

By the time that Melody turned four, I knew that I needed to get out of there. I adored my daughter, more than I knew I could love anything in the world, but my love for her had only thrown into sharper relief the fact that I didn't feel that way about Talia – not anymore, at least. And that I needed to find some way to move on before I got locked into this for life.

The business had started to seriously take off by then, and, as the money came in faster than before, she seemed to sink her talons into me even further than she had the first time around. Like she never wanted to let me go. And I knew that I should have put my foot down a little more firmly and made it a little clearer that I didn't want anything to do with her beyond raising our daughter together, but she wasn't ready to let go of me so soon.

Thus started the divorce that would basically consume my life for the next few years. It had been so intense and demanded so much of my time and energy that it had been nearly impossible to think about or focus on anything else. I had worked so much with the lawyer who was dealing with my case, Timothy, that he had actually become one of my best friends in the process. Everything had centered on Talia, and she had forced me to pay attention to her every which way she could make me.

When, of course, it should have been about our daughter. Sometimes, I was sure that she forgot that, or she just chose to detach herself from the reality of it. She claimed to love Melody, and she at least had the decency to treat her as though she did, but sometimes I felt like she was using our daughter as a pawn to get me to do whatever she wanted me to do. To dance to her beat. I hated it.

But I did it because it was what I needed to do to make sure that I kept my daughter in my life. Getting custody as the father, let alone a father who worked and was committed to a business, was hard enough, without Talia trying to trip me up at every turn and make me look like a fool. Eventually, we came to the agreement that I would get to split custody with my ex, seeing my daughter every weekend so that we could get some quality time together. It wasn't as much as I would have liked, but if it was all I could get, I would take it.

But she had started pushing right up against what she could get away with these last few months. Talia was dating some new guy, who she had introduced to our daughter, and since he had come into her life, it had been like something had shifted. Like she knew that there was more at stake now, more on the table. I had been part of her old life, and she wanted a new one now, one that had nothing to do with me. And I got the feeling that she was going to do anything she could to make that happen.

Which was why I was certain that she would be at the school right now, counting down the minutes till I was meant to arrive there and hoping against hope that I failed to do so. I had never given her the satisfaction of actually winning this part of our game, and I never intended to, either, but that didn't stop her pushing and pushing to try and convince me that my life would just be easier if I let Mel go to her and her alone.

And, to be honest, she was probably right. My life would be easier if I just allowed that to happen. Would it be better, though? Hell, no. She was my daughter and there wasn't a thing in this world that was going to keep me from her. I loved her. Adored her. Needed to be around her every second that I could. And I wasn't going to let anyone get in the way of that, not her mother, not anyone. It wasn't their choice to make, it was mine, and I intended to make sure that I made the right choice for the both of us, for me and my daughter.

Which was why I hoofed it down to the school and made it there just before the bell rang, rolling out of the front seat and heading to the gate just as the sound of the chime cut through the air to let all the parents know that school was finally out. I grinned – I had made it. And that meant that I got to spend the weekend with my daughter.

Talia liked to pull this shit where she would snatch up Mel as soon as she was out of school if I wasn't there five minutes early, and argue that she wasn't going to leave her daughter standing around and waiting to be taken home. Which would have been fine and dandy if she hadn't known that I was on my way, or sending someone down to pick her up the first chance I got. Talia could be totally sneaky about this, and I hated that I had to match her attitude or risk missing out on the chance to spend time with my daughter.

Then I saw her – my little girl, coming out of the bright red door that led to her classroom. She was talking animatedly to a couple of her friends; I tried to remember their names, but it was so difficult when she had so many. I had been worried that the divorce might get in the way of some of her socializing, but if it had, I hadn't noticed it. She was constantly surrounded by friends, and always telling me about what was going on with this one or that one as I keenly tried to keep up. In a few years' time, she would be old enough to have her own social calendar, and I knew that I wasn't going to see much of her once that happened, but for now, at least, I got her to myself.

She waved at me enthusiastically as soon as she saw me on the other side of the gate, and I waved back; I knew that Talia would be watching somewhere, probably irritated no end that I had actually bothered to turn out today. Not that I was going to give her any thought, and certainly not that I was going to allow her any attention.

I crouched down to give my daughter a huge hug, and she practically threw herself into my arms and nestled herself against me. Her hair was long and blonde and she refused to let anyone cut it – it was the same color mine had been when I was a kid, before mine had darkened to the dull brown speckled with grey that it was now. She was so tiny that sometimes it shocked me a little to feel how small she was in my arms, but she was strong, too, constantly running around and swinging from monkey bars and climbing trees every chance she got. She always had a ravenous appetite, and would have eaten most everything in the house that she could get her hands on if we let her.

"Hey, baby," I greeted her, planting a kiss on the top of her head. It was hard to believe she was eight whole years old now; it felt like she had been part of my life for so long that it must have been longer than that, but at the same time, it had gone so quickly that I wanted to back in time and live it all out again. I already missed those days when I could carry her around in my arms like it was easy, when I could toss her up into the air and make her giggle with delight when she came back down and landed in my arms. I missed those keenly, but I knew that I couldn't get hung up on what had been before; I had to look forward, to what I could bring her now that she was growing up, and I was never going to forget that.

"Hey, daddy," she replied, and she grabbed my hand and started marching me towards the car. I grinned. She was always the one in charge. Sometimes, the adults around her might have wanted to believe it was them, but they couldn't have been more wrong about that.

"So, tell me about your week," I told her, as I pulled open the car door and helped her hop in to the front seat. She could manage it totally fine by herself these days, but call me a sucker, I liked helping her where I could. Made me feel needed.

"It was amazing!" She exclaimed, and she buckled herself in and waited for me to join her in the front of the car before she went on. "I won this tournament at soccer, and then we went to a farm..."

I pulled the car away from the school as I listened to her chat away, and I felt myself begin to relax. It was just easy being around her like this. I knew that it was meant to be, but the way some of my co-workers talked, it sounded like they were having a hard time connecting with their kids, especially if they were girls. I had no such problem. I loved being around her, no matter what she was talking about, no matter what was on her mind that day.

We made it home, and I had really fully intended on cooking her something healthy that night. But, if I was being honest, the way she looked at me as soon as we were through the door told me that we weren't going to be doing anything healthy tonight.

"Pizza?" She suggested hopefully. I planted my hands on my sides and looked down at her, eyebrows raised.

"You promise not to tell your mom?"

"Promise," she agreed. Talia was on some weird health kick and didn't want Mel eating anything other than the most purely organic and perfect and superfood out there. I didn't think it was healthy to stick a child so young on a diet so restrictive, and I tried to listen to her when she told me what she wanted to it. Most of the time, she would regulate it pretty well herself, asking for healthy food and fruit for dessert, but an indulgence once in a while was healthy, wasn't it?

So we curled up on the couch together and ordered pizza and picked out a silly blockbuster movie that had just come on available for streaming. And, as I looked over at my little girl, nibbling on the edge of a crust and yawning sleepily, I knew that I would have done anything to make sure that I didn't lose this. I knew that Talia wanted to make it hard for me to be around her, but I would have turned the world around to make sure that I could be with her as much as I wanted to. She was everything to me, it was that simple – that marriage to her mother might have taken a lot from me, but when it came to Mel, it all seemed worthwhile.

I put my arm around her, and she snuggled against me, closing her eyes and letting her head rest comfortably against my shoulder. I kissed the top of her head again.

"Love you," I murmured to her, and she wrapped her arms around me and gave me a hug back.

"Love you, too," she replied, tiredly. And with that, I closed my eyes, and let the warmth of her small body against mine soothe me to sleep.

Chapter Three – Terri

Okay. I could do this. I had known Marjorie for years. I could ask her about this if I needed to. She was my friend, not just my boss, and...

I stared at myself in the mirror as I tried to get myself hyped up to get out of the house, and then my shoulders sagged and I sighed. I wasn't good at this. I hated having to admit that I hadn't been able to keep up with what mattered most, let alone to someone like Marjorie, who had her life so utterly together.

This was my own fault, for forgetting that I had to pay up my phone bill; I always forgot to factor it in to the payments I had to make for the month, and if I skipped out on it, I would get a charge on my account, and that was the last thing I needed right now. If I had to come up with any more money next month, I was pretty sure I was going to have to start breakdancing in the street for donations or something.

And to avoid that, I was going to have to go to Marjorie to ask for my paycheck a little early. I had done it a couple of times before, but she would probably put the pieces together when she took into consideration the fact that I had been asking for extra shifts too. I didn't want her to worry about me, but that was the issue with having a friend responsible for your cashflow at the end of every month.

I had a shift today anyway, so at least it wouldn't just be me turning up to the store to come scrape around for cash. I could phrase it really casually – *oh, yeah, since I'm here, could I get my paycheck a little early? Just having some cashflow issues, nothing serious...*

Even as I spoke the words in my head, I felt like I couldn't pull it off. Marjorie knew me too well for that. She had heard me talking excitedly about this plan that I had gotten involved in, about this group that I wanted to join, about this book that I had purchased because I had heard it would totally change my life. She knew where my money was going. Maybe I needed to stop being so gushing about every new thing that came into my life – or maybe I just needed to stop tossing my cash at stuff like that all the time. That would have solved both issues.

I dressed in my sharpest work outfit – the bootcut jeans and the white shirt that made me feel like I could have been Audrey Hepburn if you squinted a little and pretended that I wasn't five inches taller than her – and headed out to see Marjorie. I could do this, right? I didn't really have much choice. I had that churning dread in the pit of my stomach, the one that would stay there until I had this sorted. Money trouble was the fucking worst. And it seemed like it was a totally unavoidable part of living, at least for me.

The streets were oddly quiet as I headed down to the store; something that seemed to reflect the state of mind that I was in right about now. There was only one thing on my mind, instead of the usual crowd of thoughts that constantly demanded my attention at all times. Sometimes, I felt like I couldn't switch it off, my brain running at a hundred miles an hour even when I wanted to lie in bed and get some sleep of an evening. But, I supposed, I could live with it if the solution was having to think about this chaotic money problems instead.

When I got there, Marjorie was in the front of the store, arranging these beautiful loose pants on the mannequin; I recognized the colors at once as the ones that Stephanie was using in her new collection, and I grinned when I saw how gorgeous they looked. She really knew what she was doing, and I was so proud to be able to say that one of my best friends was making such stunning clothes. A few weeks ago, I had been out and spotted a woman wearing one of her shirts; I had run up to her to gush over her outfit, and the woman looked as though she wanted to vanish into a manhole rather than be the focus on my enthusiastic appreciation of what she was wearing. I had insisted on taking a picture to send to Stephanie, and I knew that she was totally tickled by seeing her clothes out and about in public.

I headed into the store, and Marjorie glanced over, wobbling slightly dangerously on the stool that she was standing on. I hurried over and steadied it for her, and she smiled at me in thanks.

"Cheers," she thanked me, and she quickly finished tidying up the shirt and stepped back on to the ground.

"No problem," I replied. "You can't get hurt, then you're going to have an excuse not to pay me."

"Hmm, yeah, couldn't possibly lift my hand to write you a check if I was in casts," she joked, and she dusted her hands off and smiled at the two customers who wandered in off the street. I dived back behind the counter to cover the cash desk, wanting to show Marjorie just how good I was at this. How worthy I was of getting my money a little early.

Marjorie chatted to the two women who had just come in with ease, talking to them about what they were looking for, the designers they liked, and pointing them in the direction of a few pieces that fit their specifications. I listened to her intently, taking it all in, promising myself that I would be able to cover the store if I could just absorb as much of her knowledge as I possibly could.

By the time that the women had left, they had purchased a couple of hundred dollars worth of clothes between them, and I rang them up and packed their new garments up carefully in boxes before they headed out the door. Marjorie bid them goodbye, and, with her hands on her hips, turned her attention back to me.

"Well, I think that went pretty well," She remarked, and I nodded, grabbing the broom so that I would have something to do with my hands while I had this conversation with her. Better to get it over with quicker rather than dragging it out for a while longer than it had to.

"It really did," I agreed, and I took a deep breath. Marjorie, seeming to sense what was going through my mind, turned to me and raised her eyebrows.

"Something on your mind?" She asked, and I nodded. I had planned it out in my head, but suddenly, it was all gone and I just had to blurt out whatever passed through my head.

"I think I need my paycheck early," I replied. "I'm sorry, I don't want to be an asshole or feel like I'm taking advantage of you, and if the answer's no, if you can't do it or if you don't want to, then..."

"Hey, hey," she stopped me in my tracks gently. "It's fine, really. We're doing well this month. You figure out how much I owe you and I can get it written up and with you by the end of the week, okay?"

"Thank you," I replied, and a weight lifted from my shoulders. A weight that lifted at the end of every month, once I knew had I had everything paid up, and then lowered back on as soon as the calendar ticked over to the new one once again.

"Are you alright?" She asked, and I slumped my shoulders down and leaned the broom up against a rack of clothes. I shook my head.

"I don't think so," I admitted. "I've been having a hard time with money stuff lately, to be honest."

"Yeah, I noticed," She replied gently. "You coming in here looking for extra shifts doesn't normally happen unless you're dealing with something heavy."

I glanced up at her and offered her a wry smile.

"Yeah, well, you got me," I agreed. "I haven't been able to relax for a long time, it feels like. I get one month behind me and the other one just...starts. No breaks. No rests. No nothing."

"Yeah, that is how it tends to work," she replied. I giggled. I felt a little tearful, actually, but there was no way I was going to stand here and start crying in the middle of the store. What if someone walked in? I would have to try and pretend that I was just totally overwhelmed by how beautiful the clothes were or something. Yeah, that would do it.

"I don't know how I'm meant to get ahead of it," I explained. "I just want to...I don't know, I want a break."

"Well, I don't think I'm going to be able to give you enough hours every month for that," Marjorie replied. "You know I'd love to pay you to be around here all the time, but..."

"But you can't justify it in terms of pay," I finished up for her. "I get it, I do. I'm not expecting you to fix this for me."

"Right," she agreed. "But there must be something else you can do, right?"

"I guess so," I admitted. "But I don't know what it is. I haven't thought of it yet."

"Hmm, well, it's not like there aren't a bunch of part-time jobs going round here..."

"Yeah, but I don't know if I'm the kind of person people would want to do them," I pointed out. "You know how I can come across..."

She cocked an eyebrow, then shook her head and laughed. She knew just what I was talking about, even if she wanted to pretend that she didn't.

"Yeah, I guess I do," She conceded. "You're...a lot. And people don't always want that."

"I think I could just about manage dog walking, but I'll need to build up a clientele and everything, and there's so much competition in this city as it is..."

"You could always go for the bitch angle," she teased me. "That could be a good selling point, right?"

"What, tell them that I'm a bitch so they can totally trust me to read their dogs' minds or something?" I laughed. "You're lucky I love you so much, Marjorie, otherwise I'd totally have messed up that mannequin for that."

"Okay, and I'd have fired you on the spot," she shot back, and she leaned up on the desk and eyed me for a moment, like there was something she was considering.

"I just need a kick up the ass," I remarked. "Someone to hang over my shoulder at all times and remind me not to spend money on stupid shit and that I need to save it for rent."

"Well, okay," she replied. "How about this – I'll give you your paycheck early, but only if you can guarantee that you'll have some more work by this time next month."

"Oh?" I replied, a little taken-aback. To be honest, I hadn't been totally expecting to have something as blunt and blatant as that laid on the table. I mean, I liked the idea of having someone to keep me accountable, but it also scared the shit out of me. What if I just couldn't do it, and let them down as well as myself?

"Yeah," she told me, hands on her hips, surveying me like I was this new business prospect that she was considering. "Just for the month. It doesn't have to be much, but it has to be something. I'll be there to kick you in the ass about it a little, you know I'm good at nagging, that's my mom special skill."

"So what you're saying is that you're paying me so that you'll have even more right to be on my ass about stuff?" I joked. She nodded, rubbing her hands together as though she could hardly wait.

"And when you put it like that, it's even more tempting," she replied. "You up for it? If it makes your life easier, I can do it, no problem."

"You know, much as I want to continue living like a carefree idiot," I admitted. "I think this actually does sound like a good idea. You really don't mind? I know you've got a lot on your plate what with the kid and Blake and the store and everything..."

"Exactly, so one more thing isn't going to make a difference," she replied with certainty. "I wouldn't be offering if I couldn't do this, babe. You know that."

I smiled at her.

"Thanks, Marj," I told her. "You're - you really know how to help me out."

"Hey, okay, wait till I've actually managed to help you first," she replied, and I laughed.

"Yeah, credit where credit is due, I guess," I replied. "You haven't actually done anything yet."

"And maybe I'm just out to sabotage you for my own twisted sense of fun," she teased.

"Guess I'll have to wait and see," I answered her, and I picked up the broom again, suddenly filled with a renewed sense of energy. I had no idea where I was going to start looking for the jobs that were going to drag my hopeless ass out of the hole that I had managed to get stuck in, but now that I had a glimmer of hope on the horizon, suddenly it felt a hell of a lot easier to deal with.

I spent the rest of that shift running around and making sure that every little detail in this place was taken care of. I wanted to show Marjorie that she hadn't made the wrong choice, putting her faith in me. I had no clue how I was going to get started with all of this; I hadn't looked for a new job in a long time, not since I had started working here. But maybe if I approached it like another one of my projects, I could find a way to make it work. This was important, this could change my life, and I had always been a sucker for anything that promised something as tantalizing and new as that.

"Alright, I think we're all done for the day," Marjorie told me, as six in the evening rolled around and I had finished cashing out and laying out the displays for the next day.

"Sure there's nothing else I can do?" I asked keenly. She smiled and shook her head.

"Just hang around a little longer so I can get you that check," she replied, and she vanished into the back office to get my cash sorted. And, standing there, leaning on the desk, I felt a rush of resolve. I could do this. I could do anything that was thrown my way. It was going to be hard, but I wanted to prove that I could take it on. Goodbye money troubles, hello the new version of me who never had to think twice about buying a coffee on the way to work in the mornings. I was starting fresh, and nothing had ever felt so good to me in all my life.

Chapter Four – Xander

"Hey, buddy, how's it going?"

"Hey, Timothy," I replied, leaning back in my seat at my desk, glad to hear the voice of my best friend down the line; it had been a while since we had spoken, and I had been meaning to catch up with him properly sooner rather than later. Between work and the weekend visits with Mel, I didn't have a hell of a lot of extra time on my hands.

"Not too bad," I continued. "How about you? Nothing but good news on your end, I hope?"

There was a moment of silence, and I got the bad feeling that this wasn't strictly a business call. I winced.

"What's going on?" I asked. "Do I need to come down to the office?"

"As soon as you can, yeah," he replied. "Sorry to spring this on you at work, but it's about Melody and Talia."

"Jesus," I muttered, and I glanced at my watch. "I have a meeting in an hour, can I come down after that?"

"Sure," he replied. "I'll clear my schedule for the rest of the day. We're going to figure this out, alright?"

"Alright," I replied, and we bid our farewells and I focused on getting through the rest of this Monday without losing my mind. Mondays were never good days for me, since I always had to drop my little girl off with her mom on a Sunday night and come home all by myself, and I would find myself missing her company by midday, already counting down the minutes to Friday when I got the chance to see her again.

I might as well have called off that meeting and driven straight down to see Timothy; I was so distracted all the way through it, trying to work out what might be going on, that I could hardly focus on anything the investor was saying. He was one of our foreign partners, the ones who worked distributing our refrigerators across Europe, and he was talking about switching things up and bringing in some more of our products. It could have been a seriously lucrative deal, when I actually had the time to think about brokering it instead of wondering what the hell my nightmare ex wanted out of me next.

By the time I got down there, it was starting to get dark, and Timothy was waiting outside the office to hustle me inside. He was smoking a cigarette by the time I got there, which I knew wasn't a good sign; he only had those when he was seriously stressed, keeping a cheap packet in his expensive suit pocket for when things got too hot to handle. And I had to imagine that this was about Talia, because I hadn't seen anyone who could push his buttons as consistently and accurately as she could. He had told me it was just because he cared so much about me and didn't want to see me get fucked over by her, but sometimes I was sure it was just because he wanted to make sure that he won their little battle of wills, and that my involvement or otherwise was totally secondary.

He stubbed out his cig on the wall beside him and greeted me with a firm handshake; he wasn't a guy for hugs, especially not when there was business to attend to, but I was grateful for it today. I just wanted to cut to the chase.

"Alright, buddy, I'm going to be real with you," he told me, a slightly regretful tone in his voice as he led me through the door.

"Things aren't looking good," He explained, taking me into his office, right past the secretary who always gave me what she thought were probably sexy-eyes but that always made her look constipated. Normally, I found it funny, but today, I was too distracted.

"What's she doing now?" I asked, my heart already heavy with how much I wanted to avoid this. I thought that we had dealt with this already. With the divorce, I felt like I had already hit my limit for how much I could take from her, and now, she was coming at me with it again?

"She's married that guy," He replied, and my jaw dropped.

"I'm sorry, she did what?"

"She got married to him," he replied, with a grimace this time to underline just how distasteful he found this entire thing. "Seems like they've been planning it for a while, and they did it over the weekend while you had Mel."

"Shit," I muttered. "And what does this change for us?"

"It shouldn't change anything," He replied. "But she's applying for full custody now."

"Of Mel?" I replied, stupidly. I just couldn't believe that I was hearing this. After all we had been through, after all the back and forth, she was really trying to drag this out once more?

"Yeah, she's claiming that this whole set-up you have going now is actually disruptive," he explained, his voice heavy, his brow furrowed.

"How is that more disruptive than her cutting her off from my daughter entirely?" I shot back, furious. My blood was boiling. If she had been right there in front of me, I would have torn a chunk out of her right there and then. She knew what she was doing; this wasn't about what was best for Mel, this was about what was best for her, and what was best for her right now was pretending that I had never existed because she had a new husband now.

"Look, I don't know how her mind works," He admitted. "If I did, I probably would be out there making money off being able to read minds and get anything I wanted. But she's pushing for this as hard as she can, and you know what a hard time you had holding on to your daughter in the first place..."

"So what are you saying?" I asked, more than a little nervous.

"I'm saying you might need to think about switching up your tactics," He replied with a sigh. "I know that it's not what you want to hear, especially after everything you've already been through with her, but just hear me out, okay?"

"You know I'll do anything if it means I get to hang on to her," I told him, and I meant it. There wasn't a thing in the world I could think of that I would allow to keep me from my little girl. My ex might have been sharp around the edges, but she didn't know that I was hiding out razor blades that I would whip out if I thought for a second that she would win this fight.

"I think the most important thing for you right now is selling the idea of a stable family unit for your daughter," he explained to me. "Which means, you know, actually getting a family."

"Oh, sure, I'll just call up the family delivery system and get them to drop one off to me later today," I replied, a little incredulous. "How do you mean?"

"I can't tell you to do anything that isn't within the bounds of the law," he replied carefully. "But if you can just convince them that you're as stable as she is-"

"Not that it should be hard."

"Not that it should be hard," he agreed. "If you can convince them of that, then you're in the clear, and that's what really matters here, isn't it?"

I rubbed my hand over my face. Just when I felt like I was starting to put my life together after the divorce, and then something like this comes along to fuck everything up. My fucking ex-wife, she knew what she was doing, and she knew that she had no damn right to do any of it. Which was why she was playing with such dirty rules. That was the only chance in hell she had of actually winning. I wondered what her new man made of this, if he was disgusted by it or on board with it or – hell, maybe he had been the one to come up with it in the first place, right? Maybe this was what he thought would make her happy, and he would have done anything to make sure that happened. I knew what it felt like to be bending over backwards to try and get that woman what she wanted. It wasn't a good feeling, and some part of me, some small part of me, actually felt a little sorry for this asshole.

Not that sorry, though. Not if he thought for a second that he could get in the way of me and my daughter. I levelled my gaze at my best friend, and promised myself in that moment that there wasn't a thing that anyone could do that could keep me from what mattered most here – my little girl.

"Off the record," I suggested. "Can you tell me what you're thinking? Tell me what I need to do?"

"Find someone who's willing to help you," he continued, still being carefully evasive – not letting anything that he said come out too obvious, just in case someone called him on it later. It could be frustrating sometimes, when we met in his office, to have to do this dance with him, but at least I knew that he had my best interests at heart. Unlike some people out there in the world.

"And what will they look like?"

"Someone who can help you form that family unit," he went on. "She's married now, so maybe..."

"Maybe I need to get married again too?" I replied, and he shrugged.

"Well, you at least need to project the *idea* that you're married," he told me, and he raised his eyebrows in my direction. It took me a second to click in to what he was saying, and as soon as it fell into place, my jaw dropped.

"You think I should...?"

"I don't think you should do anything in particular," he replied. "But you can handle all of this any way you see fit. And if that involves getting someone on your side to help you put forth the image you're going to need to in order to keep Mel around, then what of it?"

"You're crazy," I replied, and I couldn't help but laugh at the mere thought of what he was putting forward.

I hadn't been with a woman in a long time. I hadn't wanted to be with one. What was it they said – once bitten, twice shy? Yeah, I felt like Talia had nearly chewed my leg off, and I was a little more than twice shy to the trigger again. The thought of dating someone after everything we had been through together was hellish. I didn't have time in my life for something like that, or someone else. You didn't just fall out of a marriage like that, and then want to jump back into dating again. I had no idea how she had managed to do something like that. Maybe the fact that she needed someone to treat like shit to make sure that they knew their place kept her out on the market. Some poor man had to be under her spell for her to feel like she had a claim to her normal life once more. Like I said, I felt sorry for the guy who was with her now – at least a little. Sometimes, you just didn't know better.

Not to mention the fact that dating as a man who had a kid and a divorce behind him wasn't exactly easy. Even if I had been looking, I had heard enough horror stories about guys diving into a new marriage way too quickly, and ending up getting another divorce a few years later after a miserable time trying to make it work. Or you just didn't get anyone who looked at you twice, because divorce was such a heavy thing to be heaving around and nobody wanted to have to take it on.

"You should give it some thought," he told me. "It doesn't have to be a long-term thing. Just something to consider for now. I'm sure you could find someone who would be happy to help you out like this."

"If you find someone, let me know," I remarked, and I shook my head. "I don't think anyone's beating down my door to date me, so no danger..."

"Hey, come on, look at you," He replied jovially. "You have a lot going for you. Lots of women I can think of would want to get a piece of you..."

"Like I said, point them in my direction if you find them," I shot back. He sighed, smiled, and sat back in his seat.

"Okay, put it this way," he continued, approaching it from a new tack. He knew that I could be stubborn, but that he probably knew how this worked better than I did. He had dealt with a dozen divorces this year alone, probably, and I knew he was fiercely on my side when it came to stuff like this.

"Find someone who's just going to make it work for you for a few months," He suggested. "Think of it as a job prospect, right? Not a romance."

"That's a strange way to look at it."

"Yeah, but I don't think you're going to take it any other way," he remarked. I shrugged. He had a point.

"You need to stop being such a stubborn dick about this," he told me, in his usual bluntly cheerful way. "This is the right thing for you and your daughter, alright? Unless you can think of something better for the two of you."

"Yeah, I know," I replied. "Thanks for the advice, really. And thanks for the heads-up that this was going on at all. Glad I didn't have to hear about it from Talia."

"Yeah, fuck that, man, you know I've always got your back," he promised me. "You have nothing to worry about as long as I'm here, okay?"

"Yeah, and thank Christ for that," I agreed. "You want to go out for a drink? I could use something to take the edge off for a while."

"Yeah, me too," he replied. "Bannerman's? It's not far from here, and they do cheap booze..."

"It feels like a cheap booze kind of night," I replied with a nod, and I meant it. Just because you could afford the good stuff didn't mean that you didn't sometimes crave the cheap stuff, the memories it came with of drowning your sorrows when times were tough.

"I'm on board with that," he replied. "Hey, that woman who works with you – what's her name again?"

"You're going to have to be a little more specific than that," I replied, and he grinned and slapped me on the shoulder.

"Well, let's go through all of them while we're getting that drink, huh?" He suggested. "That way you can be sure that you've got the right one."

"Alright, alright," I laughed. "Let's not get me into any more trouble with the women in my life than I need, huh?"

"What's to say that I'm going to get you in more trouble?" He protested, playing at wounded. "Surely you'd be happy for any woman you know to get a chance to date your best friend."

"You'd think that," I teased. "And yet, here we are."

He rolled his eyes at me and shook his head.

"You need to loosen up a little," he remarked. "You're the reason I keep going out and not meeting anyone to hook up with, you know. You just give off that vibe."

"Or maybe it's the fact that I have a daughter and an ex-wife who regularly likes to come into my life and make a mess of shit," I pointed out. He waved his hand.

"Either or," he conceded. "Whatever it is, you're going to be my wingman tonight, okay?"

"And what about the honor of that random girl from my office you were asking about?" I fired back, pretended to play at affronted over his apparent faithlessness. He shrugged.

"She'll always be in my heart," He replied. "But I wouldn't want to settle down until I've had a chance to play the field now, would I?"

"You're a total asshole," I told him, as he pulled on his coat and reached to make sure that his wallet was waiting for him. He always had impeccably-tailored clothes, which always made him look as though he had just rolled off the front pages of some lifestyle magazine. He had offered to let me know who his tailor was so that I could get set up with a wardrobe that would do my bank balance justice, but I had never much had the time or the inclination to bother with what I looked like any more than I already did.

"Yeah, well, you're the one going out with a total asshole," he pointed out. He had a decent argument there. I supposed that was why he was a lawyer.

"So that means that I'm getting the first round, then?" I replied, and he nodded.

"You read my mind," he agreed, and with that, the two of us headed out of the office and back into the street. He still smelled of that stress-cigarette he had been working on when I'd arrived, but at least now I knew what he had been stressing about.

Chapter Five – Terri

Ugh.

I had forgotten how awful job-searching could be.

Was there anything grimmer than traipsing through every job posting that you could find in the newspaper and online, and finding nothing that matched your skillset? I hoped that I would be able to come up with something that I could at least throw an application in the direction of, but there was still nothing that had cropped up that came close to what I was actually looking for.

Dog-walkers – yeah, I could manage one or two, but in order to make any money with the time you poured into it, you had to bend over backwards and fit as many dogs in as you could, and I wasn't sure I had the strength to handle that many at once. Or the responsibility not to mix them up and accidentally send back the wrong dog to the wrong home, knowing how confused I could be sometimes. And I didn't think that the kind of people who could pay for dog-walkers would be too happy with the level of service that I could provide to them and their pooches.

Babysitting – many of the same problems, really, except higher stakes because there were actual people involved and not random pups. Though, knowing the way some people could be around here, the dogs would probably take precedence for a lot of them. There were other shop assistant jobs here and there, but they would have certainly overlapped with the time I already spent working for Marjorie, and honestly the last thing I needed was to put that work in danger. It was the most important thing that I had going for me right now, and taking on something that could have gotten in the way of that would have just been spectacularly dumb.

Not to mention the fact that I didn't want to let Marjorie down. She had been so sweet to me in helping me get my wages early, and in making sure I had a few extra hours so that I could make some more money. I didn't want to have to go back on that and tell her that actually, no, I couldn't do that after all, and that she was going to have to sit back and let me tell her what hours I could work instead of the other way around. I knew that she would have supported me through it no matter what, but it would have felt far too much like taking advantage of a friend for my liking.

And so, I continued to look. And look. And look. Either they were offering too many hours, or too few, or not enough at the right time for me to think about taking it on. I spent a good hour looking through the postings every day and felt like I was coming back with a stone-cold nothing. And yes, it was really starting to get to me. I felt like I was going crazy. I knew that I was qualified for a whole lot of stuff, and yet, doing this, I felt like I had never so much as thought about working in my life before, like I had been spending the last few years of my life lounging around on some giant princess pillow pretending like the rules didn't apply to me or something.

But then, I spotted it. The only job advert that had remotely jumped out to me amongst the stacks and stacks of posts that were asking for babysitters or dog-walkers or someone who could do both in one without getting overwhelmed.

I drew little stars in bright red pen all around the ad as I read through it for the first time, surrounding it with a small galaxy of scarlet by the time that I was done. It was asking for a female applicant, someone who knew how to work social functions and who wouldn't mind an intensive but totally flexible few months working alongside a male client.

And yes, that sort of thing made my mind jump instantly to the sort of man who would go through the job section looking for sex. But they had an area for personals and stuff, and this wasn't part of that, so I had to assume that it was legit. The pay was off the charts – though I was sure that came with some disclaimers, it was enough to attract my attention. I looked at the number at the bottom and chewed my lip. If something seemed too good to be true, then chances are it was exactly that. But maybe, just maybe, I could get lucky for once, and find something that was just good enough not to turn out to be fiction.

I had never much liked making phone calls, but I figured that this was the only chance I had of proving that I was actually serious about this. I dialed the number, left a message, and listened to the man's voice on the answering machine. He didn't sound like the kind of dude who was going to try and kidnap or sell me to some foreign prince or something, but I guessed you couldn't parse that stuff from someone's voice alone. I would have to hope that my instincts were on-point for a change, if I really did go through with meeting him.

I tried to keep myself distracted the next few days, continuing my daily job applications and trawling of the adverts that I could get my hands on, but in truth, there was something at the back of my mind that told me to hold out for this one. It had stuck in my head, like the line of a song I couldn't shake, maybe just because it was so totally out there and I hadn't seen anything like it since.

"It sounds like an escort job if you ask me," Stephanie had remarked, when I had told her and Marjorie how the job search was going.

"I don't think it's anything like that," I replied. "I don't think they'd be allowed to put a job like that in the paper..."

"I'm sorry, it's just that...well, anything that specifies your gender has to be something to do with that, doesn't it?" Stephanie remarked, pulling a face. She had grown a lot more wary since she had started the business with her man, and I supposed that came as part and parcel of dealing with the world of fashion. She had to be a little harder around the edges, and maybe that was something that I needed in my life these days. Maybe I let things roll over me a little easier than I should have.

"I'm going to be safe," I promised her. "I know that it sounds like a lot, but..."

"But you're totally going to Pretty Woman all over this city," Marjorie cut in, as she emerged from the back room of the store where she had been sorting clothes. I didn't even realize that she had been listening to the conversation.

"Just make sure that you bring him in here when you do that part where you spend all of his money, right?" She ordered me, and I rolled my eyes.

"It's not going to be like that," I protested, and Marjorie and Stephanie exchanged glances.

"What's that look supposed to mean?" I exclaimed, only half-joking. Marjorie shook her head.

"Nothing..."

"Good, because I haven't even heard from him yet," I replied. "I don't think I even will, they probably got a hundred messages from other girls already."

"Probably," Stephanie agreed. "But you just make sure to look after yourself, okay? I can't have anything happening to you."

"I will," I promised her. "It's going to be fine, really, it's not a big deal."

"I'll make sure to remind you of that when Julia Roberts plays you in the movie adaptation," Marjorie teased me. I rolled my eyes at her.

"It's not going to be like that," I protested, but I knew that it was a lost cause when it came to them. They had clearly made their minds up on what this was going to be like for me, and nothing that I could possibly say was going to change that for them.

And anyway, like I told them, I hadn't heard a word from him anyway, and I was starting to let go of the belief that I actually would. I knew that it was better to pretend that I had never put in that application at all than hang on a call I didn't know was coming. Applying for new jobs was just like dating – you couldn't wait around on one person, when you knew that putting yourself out there was going to get you more attention and potentially more long-term success.

And by the end of that week, I had pretty much let go of any belief that I was going to hear from that job at all. I guessed that my curiosity about what the position came with was going to go unsatisfied, and I was just going to have to live with that. Some lucky girl was out there, getting the answers to the questions that I'd had as soon as I had laid eyes on that advert, and yeah, okay, I would have been lying if I'd said that I wasn't a little jealous. It wasn't even about the paycheck at this point, but more about knowing that it was another job that had turned me down, another position that I hadn't been right for. If even something like that was work that I could get beat out to, what chance did I have of finding something that could get me through?

Of course, it was at the moment that I stopped thinking about it that my phone rang with an unknown number – and I picked it up to find someone from that job calling me back. I was pretty sure that I recognized the voice off the answering machine, though I couldn't be sure.

"Hello?"

"Hello, Terri Chambers?" The voice asked me. I nodded, forgetting for a moment that he couldn't see me.

"Yes, uh, hello, this is Terri Chambers," I finally blurted out, after a moment of silence. Already off to a resoundingly good start, there, obviously.

"You reached out to me about the job I posted," He continued. He had a crisp, to-the-point tone, and I could imagine the kind of man who might have laid claim to that; a good bit older than me, the kind of person who was totally sure and secure in himself. He sounded cool, sexy, charming, and I could already imagine exactly how let-down he was going to be when he came across me.

"Yes, that's right," I replied, trying to settle the waver in my tone and hoping that he didn't notice it. I got to my feet and started pacing back and forth over the apartment, trying to burn off the excess energy that was pulsing through my system in that moment. Finally, this was going somewhere – I was getting somewhere. It was the first call back I'd had since I had started applying for jobs, and I promised myself in that moment that there was no way in hell that I was going to blow it.

"I'd like to meet with you," he told me. "For a quick meeting, to explain a little more about what this job will entail. Are you free this weekend?"

"Uh, yes, sure," I replied at once. I grabbed a pen and paper and bit off the lid of the pen, spitting it aside and hoping he hadn't heard my distinctly unglamorous actions at the other end of the line.

"Great," he responded. "You know the Fire Brasserie?"

"I think so," I replied, and I scribbled down the words he had just said to me and circled them three times, and then drew a giant question mark over the top of it. I had never heard of that place in my life. But I didn't want him to know that, in case it blew up my chances. As far as he was concerned, I was *au fait* with every eatery in the city, just in case that was what he needed from me in order to get this job.

"I have a table booked there for Saturday morning at ten," he told me. "I'll book under your name, alright?"

"Alright," I agreed, too breathless to think about why that might have been or if I should have been a little thrown by it. I was just so glad to have heard from him, I couldn't focus on anything else at all.

"Excellent," He responded. "I look forward to seeing you then."

And with that, he hung up – and I punched the air. I was going to an actual interview. Well, a working brunch, but that was as close as made no odds, right?

Marjorie was a little nervous when I told her what was going on.

"You have nothing to worry about," I tried to assure her, but she shook her head.

"I don't know," she replied. "I might be on the other side of the road with a pair of binoculars just to make sure he's not looking for anything too crazy."

"It's going to be fine..."

"You just text me when you're there, alright?" She told me, fussing lightly. "And when you leave. And I'll make sure I know where this place is, so I can come by and bail you out if you need it."

"But only if I need it," I warned her. "Which I probably won't. I've looked at this place online, it seems like it's pretty fancy. I don't think anyone who's looking to throw me into the back of a van and make off with me would pick somewhere that's so busy on a Saturday."

"Still, just for my peace of mind," Marjorie implored me. I nodded.

"Okay," I promised her. "If that's what you need to be sure that I'm safe, then I'll text you all of that, okay?"

"Thank you..."

"And a picture of me with today's paper," I teased her. She laughed.

"Okay, maybe I'm being a little over-protective," she conceded. "But I'm your friend, it's my job to be over-protective, you know?"

"I get it," I replied. "And I'm glad you're looking out for me, really."

"Yeah, because sometimes it feels like you can't do that for yourself," She shot back. I grinned. She had a point. I could be a little reckless, and I doubted that anyone else I knew would have jumped into this interview quite so quickly.

By the time that Saturday morning came around, my nerves had gotten so intense that I could hardly keep myself together. I tried to dress myself up for what I thought this meeting was going to be, but honestly, I had no clue what to expect and it was totally throwing me off. Did I go strictly professional? Did I allow a little flirtation into my outfit? That job had indicated anything about sex, but everyone that I had spoken to about it had acted like it was blindingly obvious that the man who had posted it was looking for something very specific from me. Maybe I was the only one who couldn't see it.

I picked out a skirt, a blouse, and some heels, and then changed the skirt for a pair of pants and the heels for some flats and settled on the outfit that I was comfortable with. I let my hair down, and then pulled it back into a ponytail, and hoped that it would be good enough for him. My make-up was an afterthought, and it was only as I was rolling out the door that I thought to put on a little mascara and some lipgloss. I caught sight of myself in the reflection of my face in the subway window, and quickly fixed the smudge of mascara that had migrated to just below my eyebrow. By the time I got there, a little flustered, I was sure at least that I looked alright.

This place really was fancy. Really fancy. So much so that when I stepped inside the restaurant for the first time, I could practically feel the disbelieving eyes pinning themselves to me. I knew I looked out-of-place, compared to the perfectly-coiffed women sitting opposite their no-doubt wealthy dates, but I straightened my back and tried to gather my confidence as I strode up to the host and gave her my name. She, at least, was sweet, smiling politely and leading me to a small table at the back of the room, far from the door and away from other people. The kind of table that only someone who was in good standing with the people who ran this place might have been able to get. My heart was pounding hard in my chest as I approached my very first job interview since I had started work at the store. I could do this, couldn't I? I could do this, no matter what, I could do this...

"Terri?"

I heard a voice say my name, and I blinked and looked up and there he was. The man I was here to meet. The man whose voice had been on the other end of the line, the man who had made everything in me feel like it was swooning helplessly when I had heard him talk. And let me tell you – seeing him in person, he didn't disappoint. Not one bit.

He was dressed in an impeccable suit, one that looked as though it probably cost as much as a single month's rent at my shitty little apartment. His hair was dark, a little overgrown as though he hadn't had a chance to get it cut in a while, but it suited him like that. Took off the edge of looking so pulled-together and adult, made me remember that other people could forget to get their hair cut when they should have, too. He was just...he was just gorgeous. And when I put together the man in front of me with the voice that I had heard over the phone, well, that did something to me that I wasn't sure I was prepared for.

"Come on, sit down," He suggested with a warm smile. "I think we have a lot to talk about, don't we?"

"I think we do," I agreed, and I joined him at the table, trying to prepare myself for whatever might come next. This had already been crazy – seeing that strange ad in the paper, calling up to show my interest, and then actually hearing back from them – but seeing him sitting before me now, I knew that the crazy was only really just starting.

Chapter Six – Xander

As she settled into the seat opposite mine, I couldn't help but notice how much younger she looked than I had imagined. I hadn't set an age limit on the ad that I had posted, of course, but in my head people who were that much younger than me didn't even really exist. Let alone one confident enough to just roll up to this meeting like she had every right to be here, even though the ad I'd posted had looked totally shady to pretty much everyone else.

"It's good to meet you," she offered me, and I could hear a little shyness in her voice – she might have had the nerve to come down here, but that didn't mean that she wasn't a little nervous about how this was going to go. I supposed, as far as she knew, this was just like any other job interview. I had to keep reminding myself, actually, that it really was just like any other job interview – it might have been for a position that nobody had taken on for me before, but that didn't mean that it wasn't the same as all the other times that I had met with someone to parse their suitability for a new position.

"You too," I replied. "I'm honestly a little surprised that you turned up. I thought I was going to have a much harder time finding someone to meet with me about this."

Yes, that was the perfect way to act – letting her know that there wasn't any competition for this position. I knew better than that. I tried to gather myself, but there was something about the way she was looking at me that had me a little...well, on edge wasn't the right term, but I felt as though I was ready to get up and run out of there at any moment. Everything about this was profoundly weird, and I just had to find a way to get through that without losing my mind and making a fool of myself. I could do this, couldn't I? I could do this. I just had to push through the next hour, find out if she was up for what I was throwing out there, and then we could both move on with our lives.

Thankfully, she found my little confession pretty funny. She giggled with delight, and shook her head.

"Yeah, I couldn't imagine that you got too many responses to that one," She agreed. "I mean, it really read like you were looking for someone to do evil torture experiments on or something."

"And yet, you still put in an application," I pointed out. She shrugged.

"Hey, this is New York," she pointed out. "If it's got good hours, evil torture experiments still ranks higher than working at a bodega when it's late on a Saturday."

I laughed. She had a bright, sparky sense of humor, that much was clear, and I liked how it made me feel when she talked to me like that. As though there was no shit in the world that she would have taken, not from anyone. We were off to a good start, that much I could say for sure.

"That's a fair point," I agreed, and I waved the waiter over so that I could get myself a coffee. I had decided to forgo the booze today, given that I had to pick up Mel from the friend's house she was staying at while I was out on this – well, I supposed it was somewhere between a date and a job interview, I just had to find a way to make sure that I didn't get the two mixed up in my own head. Not until, at least, I'd had a chance to tell her what this was all about.

"So, I'm still not totally clear on what this job is," she admitted, once the waiter had backed off and left us alone. "And you didn't say it wasn't evil torture experiments, so..."

"Okay, well, consider this my firm and public denial that it's nothing to do with that," I assured her. "I don't want to throw you in the back of a van and make off with you or anything like that."

"Well, that's good to hear," she agreed. "Though I can't imagine you'd say anything else, really."

I grinned. She smiled back. We had good chemistry, I could feel that already, and I wondered if she could sense it, too. Shit, I hadn't even asked if this woman had a boyfriend or a husband or anything like that – if she did, I doubted that she would be down for the situation that I was proposing to her. Or the proposal I was proposing, I supposed. I realized that I had been sitting there without saying a word for a long moment, and that she was eyeing me with some concern as she waited for me to say something back to her.

"So, you lived in New York long?" I asked her. I didn't want to dive straight in to the full-blown "so, I need you to pose as a member of my family to make sure that I can lock down my ex on a custody arrangement she's trying to undercut right in front of me". Partly because I knew it would sound crazy diving into it right off the bat, and partly because I was enjoying her company and didn't want this to be over quite so soon.

"All my adult life," she replied. "Which is why I'm totally broke right now. I thought that you came here and things just worked out, but that only happens when you're the star of a sitcom, it seems like."

"Yeah, seems that way," I agreed. I had never much had to worry about money, but I heard concerns that mirrored hers from people I worked with all the time. This city could be ruthless, and if you weren't willing to throw down and fight for your place here, it would chew you up and spit you out before you had a chance to catch your breath. The fact that she was still here after all this time, even despite her struggles, told me that she was tough – that was a good start.

"But I came from a tiny little town and I didn't like the idea of spending the rest of my life there," she remarked. "That's why I stuck it out here."

"And do you work?"

"Yeah, I have a job at my friend's clothing store," she replied. "But it's not an issue for me to get time off when I need to come help out with whatever...well, whatever you're proposing."

"Right," I agreed, and the waiter returned with my coffee. He held out two menus to us, his eyebrows raised, as though asking if we wanted them for ourselves. She glanced over at me, letting me take the lead, and I nodded.

"Yes, we'll take menus," I told the waiter, and he laid the leather-bound books in front of us and backed off to leave us in peace. She smiled at me.

"Thank God," she told me. "I thought that you were going to make me sit around here and watch all these people with their amazing food and then not let me eat."

"Maybe that's the evil torture that you were talking about," I remarked, and she laughed. She had a bright, easy laugh, the kind that seemed to escape her mouth like it had just been waiting to burst out of her. I liked the way it sounded. In fact, so far, I liked everything about her.

As she looked over her menu, I took a moment just to check her out. Sure, she was a good bit younger than me, but it was clear that she had a sharp wit and a good attitude. She was pretty, too, not that I was going to let that play into my decision too much; long hair, bright grey-green eyes, and a beautiful mouth with soft, full lips that looked as though they had been made for make-out sessions. I knew that I shouldn't hire anyone based on their looks alone, but if I was going to get someone to act as my fake-fiancée in order to get back at my ex-wife, then I felt like I was allowed to go for someone pretty, wasn't I?

She picked out her food and the waiter returned to take her order, and she turned her attention back to me. This time, I knew I wasn't getting out of giving her the answer to the question she had been chasing me with.

"So I have to ask," she remarked, running her fingers through her hair and eyeing me with interest. "What is this job actually about?"

I couldn't get away with no answer any longer. The more I tried to avoid the question, the more she was probably going to think that I was just wasting her time or looking for something sleazy from her here, and that was the last thing on my mind right now. I wanted to be honest with her, but I just had no clue had to do that – how to go about breaking the news to her about what I wanted.

I figured it was best to start at the beginning with all of this, peel it all the way back so that I could make clear everything that was driving this choice. If she understood every detail of it the way I needed her to, then it was going to be clear why I had to go about finding a solution to my problem in such a strange way.

"Okay, so I have a daughter," I began, and she nodded, furrowing her brow.

"And I share custody of her with my ex-wife," I went on. "Well, at least, I did. I used to. I found out recently that she is getting remarried – that she is already, actually – and that she wants to get full custody of my little girl."

"Oh my God, that's awful," Terri replied, and she shook her head as though she could hardly believe what she was hearing. I wasn't sure if she was just playing to me to be polite or if she actually thought this was some serious affront, but I couldn't consider how she really felt right now. I had to give her the outline of this job, not the sob story of my life so far. That wasn't what she was here for.

"Which means that I'm going to have to find some way to counter that," I explained. "I spoke to my lawyer about the best course of action moving forward, and, well, we've been back and forth on it a lot, but we think that we've come up with the best thing for it."

"Which is?"

I took a deep breath. It was now or never – I had to come out and be honest with her about what I was actually looking for from this.

"I need someone to pose as my partner so that I can project the same image of family stability that she's banking on using against me when she goes for full custody," I explained.

For a long moment, Terri just stared at me as though I was totally insane. I supposed, to her, that was exactly what it must have sounded like. I had come out with a lot of wild shit over the years, the pitches for the business, arguing my case for staying in Mel's life, but this had to be up there with the craziest. I wouldn't have been surprised at all if she'd just gotten to her feet and walked out of there, marched off and made it clear that she never wanted to hear from me again as long as she lived. I don't think anyone would have held that against her. In fact, it was probably the most sensible option.

But, after a long pause, she was still there. Which either meant that she hadn't understood what I had just said to her, or she wasn't totally averse to the thought of what I was putting forward.

"So, you're saying that..."

"I'm saying that you would be the one who played my partner," I explained. "And yes, I know it doesn't exactly make any sense, but it's the only chance I have to counter what my ex is putting out there right now. This is the best I could come up with, and I don't want to lose my daughter, Terri, you have to understand that."

"Okay, now that advert makes a little more sense," she remarked, mostly to herself, it seemed. I was still sure that she was going to stand up and walk out of there at any moment, but she was still in front of me, still considering the deal that I had laid out in front of her, even though it must have sounded so abjectly fucking ridiculous to her. To anyone.

"And this is something that goes on for how long?" She asked. "Am I ever allowed to have my own life again, or do I just...?"

"Just a few months," I replied. "Six, at the most. We'll stage a break-up after that to make sure that there are no ties between us any longer, and that'll be us, over with. You never have to see me again after that. As soon as my daughter is back in my care, I'll have everything under control."

"I see," she muttered, and the waiter arrived with our food. I had been so focused on her I had all but forgotten we were at the brasserie at all in the first place. Other people just seemed extraneous to requirements right now. I needed this from her and nobody else, and I had no clue if this was going to be a massive disaster or something that was actually going to get me what I wanted.

"And the payment is more than generous," I continued. "All expenses will be covered, of course, anything that you need to come out and join me wherever I am."

"I can't believe you're actually suggesting this," she told me bluntly, finally showing a little disbelief – she glanced up and into my eyes, and I could tell that she was waiting for the penny to drop, for something to happen that would reveal all of this as nothing more than a crazy joke with her at the butt of it. But there was nothing to reveal – this was all true, and I needed to have her on board for it. She was the only person who had reached out to us who hadn't been an obvious troll or spammer or scammer, and I didn't want her to walk out of here without the two of us having nailed something useful down together.

"Do you think you can do it?" I asked her, honestly. I needed to know. If the answer was no, then I could go back to looking again. I knew that time was running short, and if she was going to shoot me down, then I had to know sooner rather than later. This was a matter of me seeing my daughter again or not – there was no room for time-wasters. I stared at her, waiting for her to tell me what I needed to hear, or to laugh me out of the joint and tell me never to get in touch with her again.

But instead, she nodded. Slowly, surely, she nodded, as though she could hardly believe that she was agreeing to this herself. A moment later, she burst out laughing, and then clapped her hand over her mouth like she was trying to contain all the sheer shock and excitement that was coming off her right now.

"Sure," she replied. "Sure, I'll do it. Do you have...I mean, this is all going to be above-board, right? No... Physical relationship or anything like that..."

"No, no, nothing like that," I promised her. "We'll have to put on a show for a few people here and there, but nothing more than holding hands and maybe a kiss once in a while."

"I think I can handle that," she agreed. Her face was shining with a bright, irrepressible excitement, and I could hardly focus anymore. I was sure that this had to be some kind of joke. There was no way that someone would actually have agreed to this so willingly, was there?

"So, is there some sort of contract you want to put in place for this, or..."

"Yes, a contract," I agreed at once. I was in such total shock that it was taking me more than a moment to catch up with the fact that she had really just agreed to this. It seemed insane, but there it was – she had come out and taken it in and decided that yes, this was something that she could handle. So that was sorted, just like that. I didn't have to worry about finding anyone else, not when the woman who had already stepped up to the plate was right there opposite me.

"Obviously, it's going to be something that we keep totally secret," I told her, and she nodded at once, tapping the side of her nose like she had just heard an enormous state secret.

"Of course, chief," she replied. "Your wish is my command."

"And I have to work with my lawyer to put together the NDA and everything," I went on. "I'll need your name, address, all of that..."

"I'll pass it on to you the first chance I get," she assured me. She eyed me for a moment across the table, and then lowered her voice and leaned towards me.

"I'm sorry, are you alright?" She asked. "You look a little...shocked."

"Yes, well, I didn't expect you to actually agree to this," I confessed. "I thought that I was going to have to be looking for a while before I found someone who was actually on board with everything."

"Good thing I turned up then, right?" She replied, flipping her hair playfully like she was posing for a camera. I nodded.

"Good thing," I echoed. She reached across the table and patted my hand.

"Hey, I'm in for this," she told me. "I know it sounds crazy, but – shit, I've done crazier things than this, I promise. This isn't that out-there."

"You're sure?" I asked her. I needed to know that she wasn't going to back out the first chance she got. She might have been able to play bravado right now, but when it came down to it, I needed to know that she was going to stick it out instead of panicking and backing out when she realized what this was going to entail. She nodded.

"I'm sure," she promised me. I let out a long breath I didn't know that I had been holding. Until I had her signature on the pages of the documents that I would need to have her promise that she wasn't going anywhere, I knew that I wouldn't be able to relax, not totally, not fully. But for now, this would do. I had a woman who had agreed to take on this role for me. And a woman who, as she smiled at me from across the table, I couldn't help but find myself looking forward to getting to know even further.

Chapter Seven – Terri

"Are you ready?" Xander asked me, as we stood outside the main room where all the people he knew were waiting for him to enter. I was practically dancing back and forth from foot to foot with nerves, fearful that I was about to step over that threshold and make an unendingly stupid fool of myself.

"I think so," I agreed. I was lying. I had no idea how I was going to survive this without making a total fool of myself, and I was starting to have some serious doubts about agreeing to this all in the first place.

When Xander had first told me what he was looking for me to do for him, I thought it was some kind of immensely silly joke. Because there was no way in hell that a man like him could be looking for a woman, right? Let alone a woman like me. He was rich and handsome and successful and he had everything that he could possibly ever want or need, and someone like me was just surplus to requirements in a way that seemed utterly crazy.

I had gone and looked him up when I had gotten home after that first meeting we'd had together. Because I was sure there was no way that he could actually be offering me the kind of money he said he was. We got into the nitty-gritty details over brunch together, and when he told me how much he was willing to pay me, I swear I nearly swooned to the ground right there and then – we were talking thousands, more than enough for me to live on for the next year even if I quit work at the store and spent most of my time sipping daiquiris on rooftop bars.

Really, if I had been sensible about it, I should have taken some time to sit back and work out if this was really what I wanted. After all, he was asking for a whole lot of commitment from me, a whole lot of commitment that I had no idea if I could really deliver on; I wanted to think that I would be able to sell myself as someone's other half, but I had never been in a relationship beyond six months before and I had no idea what it would look like to really fall for someone like that. How was I meant to play that role? What did it look like? How did it feel? I needed a crash-course in method acting, but, by the time that this first event had come around, I had barely had time to read through the contracts before I was hustled out of the apartment and down to a family gathering.

It had all gone so quickly. I knew that the contracts were legit – I'd gotten Marjorie and Stephanie to look over them for me, to confirm that I wasn't about to get screwed over in some profound way once I had signed up – and even despite their misgivings, they had to admit that there was nothing there that looked even a little shady. Apart from the fact, of course, that this guy was asking me to be his stand-in other half for as long as it took to get his daughter back.

"You know it sounds crazy, right?" Marjorie pointed out to me, and I nodded.

"I know, I know..."

"Like, totally insane," Stephanie jumped in to add on to her protests. "He thinks that this is going to get him his daughter back?"

"Not back," I corrected her. "He has joint custody of her now. He wants to prove that he's as secure as his ex."

"And he's doing that by getting someone to stand in as his fiancée," Marjorie added on. I could hear the total disbelief in her voice, and, well, when she put it like that, of course it was going to sound a little out-there, wasn't it?

"He says it's hard for the dads to get taken seriously by the courts," I replied. "I don't know much about it, but he seems like a good guy..."

"I don't know about this," Stephanie sighed, shaking her head. "It all seems...I don't know. Like you're going to get hurt or something."

"You have nothing to worry about," I tried to soothe her, but she shook her head.

"Oh, I think there's a lot to worry about here," she replied grimly. "I just haven't had a chance to figure it all out yet."

"Such a pessimist," I teased her, trying to lighten the mood. "Can't you just be happy for me for a change? Maybe this is all going to go well and I'm going to get everything I ever wanted from him, did you think about that?"

"Let us know if that happens," Marjorie cut in. "Because if you do, I think I owe us all a drink."

"See, that's the spirit," I agreed happily. "This could work out. You just need to look a little more on the bright side for a change, yeah?"

"Right," Marjorie agreed, but she didn't sound sold on this whole thing. Honestly, neither was I – but I needed the money, and I had to admit, there was part of me that thought that it would make a good story in ten years' time when this was all behind me. Oh, I haven't told you about the time I posed as a billionaire's fiancée to help him keep custody of his daughter? Wait until I get into this one, you're going to be blown away by it.

And yes, he really was a billionaire. I could hardly believe it when I got a look at his net worth. It had to be some kind of mistake, right? An extra zero or two tossed on there by someone who didn't know any better? But then I went and checked it at a few different sources, and sure enough, he actually did have that amount of money to his name. Which was why he could afford to pay me such an absurd amount for my help in his little heist.

What surprised me, to be honest, was the fact that he didn't have a woman in his life already. I mean, he was insanely rich, gorgeous, seemed like a pretty decent guy to spend time with from the hour or two that I had passed with him over brunch. He had a daughter, sure, but he seemed like a dedicated, protective father, not the guy who was going to throw you into the deep end and make you a co-parent before you'd had a chance to catch your breath. Women should have been beating down his door to get a date with him, and yet, it seemed like he was totally single and had no interest in anything but a relationship where he got to make the rules.

Maybe it was something to do with this ex of his, the one that he was currently battling for custody of his daughter. The fact that he had dived so instantly into a scheme as harebrained as this one told me that he had good reason to doubt her and her ability to actually work with him on raising their daughter together. He had gone straight to battle stations, for better or for worse, and it seemed like I was his main general on the front line right now.

He had decked me out pretty quickly with everything that I was going to need to sell myself to the people around him. The ring had come first – it was a beautiful silver band with a diamond pressed into the center, simple but stunning, and I got the feeling that he hadn't skimped out on getting a real gem for me. After that, he had nudged me in the direction of the clothes that I would need to look the part; I had an allowance to buy up everything that I wanted, and yes, of course, I spent a lot of it at Marjorie's store, because that was just what friends did, right?

And all of that had been fun, but now I was faced with the fact that I actually had to go through with this. I had the ring on my finger, I had the clothes on my back, and now, I had the man on my arm who I had to convince people that I hadn't totally met just two weeks before and signed a contract with to pretend to be his life partner.

Nobody in his world knew about this, except for his lawyer. Which put all the more pressure on me to make sure that I actually pulled this off. I was still sure that I was going to walk into that party, surrounded by people who knew him, and be laughed out at once; if this whole thing didn't turn out to be a set-up for an elaborate hidden camera prank show, of course, which was a possibility I still hadn't ruled out entirely. I stood there with him, outside, trying to gather myself, trying to absorb the last few moments when I wasn't going to be his fiancée.

It was too late to back out now. Everything had been agreed upon. We were ready to kick into action. I had to go through with this. I looked at the ring on my finger, and tried to remind myself of the money that was coming with it – this was a job, like any other, right?

"Okay, yes, I'm ready," I told him finally. "Let's do this. I want this out of the way and then I can..."

I wanted to say that I could skip forward to the part where this night was over and I didn't have to worry about my dramatic introduction to everyone in his life, but that wasn't what he wanted to hear, I would have imagined. This man was paying me to be here as his fake-partner. And fake-partners, good ones, at least, knew better than to be looking forward to whenever this event was going to be over.

"Then you can relax," He finished up for me. Reaching down, he took my hand and held on to it tight. It felt a little strange to be holding hands with this man that I had only really just met – especially given the circumstances of our meeting – but at the same time, there was something soothing and comforting about his touch. I took a deep breath, let it out, and then nodded.

"Okay, I'm ready for this," I told him. "Let's do it."

And with that, the night had begun.

The event was a yearly gathering for his business partners – he had decided to start there with my introduction because it was a little more low-stakes than just bringing me out to the family right away, who might have had an easier time seeing through this whole scheme if I wasn't totally comfortable with him. Still, I felt like it must have been obvious to everyone that I must have been standing there with a great big *I am not meant to be here, ask me how,* sticker on the middle of the beautiful dress that he had helped me pick out for the occasion.

As soon as we stepped over the threshold, a million eyes turned to face us all at once – that's what it felt like, anyway. I had to catch my breath to keep from going crazy with panic. And I clung to him a little tighter for the support that I knew I needed right now. Which was probably what any girlfriend would have done, right? So I was already pulling this off. I just had to be needy and nervous and hang off his every word, and then people would believe that it was real.

"Xander!" A man announced, as he strode up to us and extended his hand to the man by my side. "I didn't realize you were coming with a plus-one this year."

Xander took a deep breath, and tightened his grip on my hand.

"This is Terri," He introduced me to the man in front of us. "My fiancée."

There was a beat of silence, as the man just stared at me as though he must have heard that announcement wrong. I offered him a smile, hoping that it would be enough to convince him that I was really who I said I was. I mean, what was a fiancée, honestly? Just someone who had promised to get married? It wasn't like I had to do or say anything to sell this, just look happy to be there with my alleged man and keep a smile on my face so as not to piss off any of the other business partners here.

Finally, the man responded, though I could tell that he was being achingly careful not to come out with anything that would seem too sharp or focused on me.

"Well, I suppose you really do get a lot done in a year," he remarked, and he turned his attention to me. "Nice to meet you, Terri. I'm Bolton."

"Nice to meet you too," I replied, noticing that my voice had taken on a slightly squeaky tone to it. But maybe that was just how I sounded when I was in a room surrounded by people who probably could have brought and sold me if they wanted to.

I kept off the booze for the time being, sticking to seltzer water and making sure that I didn't get tipsy enough to say anything that might have exposed our little con. He did most of the talking, thank goodness, inventing this backstory where we'd met because I was a disgruntled customer and we had just fallen in love since then. I had to admit, it was pretty cute, as though it was something that he had considered before. Maybe he actually was a romantic, after all, even though the fact that he had paid me to be here with him seemed to go totally against that idea.

The rest of the night was interesting, to say the least. Being surrounded by all these people was a trial I had never had to go through before, and I was totally out of my depth for a while, listening to them talking about their business deals and their business plans and their business, business, business. I just had to nod along and act like I had a damn clue what they were talking about. I supposed it was a good thing that they seemed so self-involved because it meant that I didn't have to come up with too much to talk about myself. In fact, once people had discovered that I was his bride-to-be, they pretty much stopped paying attention to me there. As though me being off the table just made me basically invisible from there on out. Which was insulting when I thought about it, but in practice, it was a total relief not to have to engage too deeply.

Especially since Xander was being so freaking distracting the whole night through.

I knew that we had to sell this, given that it was our first official appearance together as husband and wife-to-be, but the way he was playing it, it was almost as though he actually believed it himself. He held my hand most of the night through, and when he wasn't, he had his hand lightly placed on the small of my back, the heat of his fingers even through the fabric of the dress so intense that it made it hard to think straight. He even planted a couple of kisses on my cheek, even when we weren't directly in front of anyone else, and I wondered and wondered and wondered if he knew what he was doing to me...

Of course, that didn't matter. It was just a little physical contact. The fact that he happened to smell so good and feel so sweet standing so close to me was just a coincidence that I was going to have to get over sooner rather than later. It had been a long time since I'd had any kind of man in my life, and I supposed that I needed some time to get over this hump of thinking that physical contact meant actual romance. Because it didn't. It was just part of the deal, nothing more, and I needed to remember that above all else in the world right now.

By the time that the event was winding down to a close, Xander had called me a cab and was waiting outside for it to arrive; he was going to get in it with me to make sure that people saw us leaving together, but then we were going to split up and head to our respective homes. I waited till I was actually inside the car before I turned to him to hit him with the question that I had been holding back on all night long.

"Did I do a good job?" I asked him, and he paused for a moment and leaned forward to roll up the partition between us and the driver. Couldn't risk even someone like that catching wind of what was going on, I supposed. I felt like an international spy, but for the most low-stakes mission ever.

"You did a great job," he assured me at once. "I think they all brought it. I didn't think that we were going to be able to sell it so well, but I suppose they actually don't look that hard at my relationships – or maybe they're just more interested in the business side of things."

"Yeah, I don't think that any of them could have come close to guessing the truth," I replied excitedly. He leaned over and patted my knee – it felt natural, given the fact that he had had his hands all over me tonight, but something about being touched like that when the two of us were all alone made the hairs on the back of my neck stand up.

"Next time we take on the family, right?" He remarked, with a grin. I didn't have the ability to talk, so I just nodded back instead.

We chatted a little on the way home, and I teased him about coming up with a story that was so romantic right off the bat.

"Hey, I spend all my time at work or with my daughter," he pointed out. "They weren't going to believe me if I'd said that I'd met you through anything that wasn't one of those two things."

"Good point," I laughed, and the car pulled to a halt outside my house. Even though I knew it was crazy, I had the urge to lean forward and kiss him goodnight. There was a beat of silence between us, and I wondered if he was feeling the same thing.

"I'll see you soon," I promised him instead, and swung my legs out of the car quickly before I could allow my brain to go any further down those dangerous routes.

"See you soon," he replied, and I closed the door behind me and with that the night was over. I should have been relieved, but instead, I found that I was already craving him again.

I headed upstairs and rolled myself into a shower as soon as I got the chance. I needed to scrub this night off of me before it got any further stuck into my head. I needed to wash clean the memory of his touch as soon as I could, because I could already feel it taking root inside of me and I knew, I knew more than anything that it was a dangerous thing to allow to take hold...

And even as the hot water rushed over me, I felt myself beginning to warm from the inside out. He had touched me with such ease, and it had been such a long time since I had ever allowed anyone to touch me like that. He made the rules, and there was something kind of exciting about the very thought of it. I could argue and protest and lay down my own laws, of course, but he was the one in charge. And I was pretty sure that I liked the way that made me feel.

I skimmed my hand down my body, brushing it over the bush on my mound, and then down between my legs. I was just overstimulated, that was all, and as soon as I got this out of my system I would be able to move on and remember the reality of this once more. I closed my eyes and let the hot water rush over me as I imagined him in there with me.

I knew that it was dangerous to allow those thoughts into my head, but maybe the only way out was through, right? That was totally a thing. I focused on the feeling of my hand between my legs, and imagined his hand cupped over it, guiding me, letting me know just how I was to touch myself as long as I was in his presence – I felt my skin start to prickle as though all the tension that had been building the whole day through was starting to take control, and I knew that I couldn't control it anymore.

His voice was deep and strong and I could almost hear it echoing in my ears, just like it had the very first time that I had heard him over the phone. I loved this. I needed this. I felt my body arch towards my hand, my fingers moving harder against my clit, as I focused on the thought of him wrapped around me, his warm body cradling mine in the shower and pulling me close so that I couldn't get away. Not that I would want to. His mouth on my neck, the warmth of his kiss blurring with the water until there was no way that I could tell the difference between the two of them at all and they would just become one, glorious, beautiful touch...

"Mmm," I groaned, the sound drawing me out of my head, as I felt the orgasm ripple through me. It wasn't so much pleasure as it was about the release that I had so keenly needed since I had walked back through the door. I withdrew my hand from between my thighs and caught my breath, my knees a little shaky as I came back down to Earth.

Had I really just masturbated to the thought of the guy who was basically my boss? I grabbed the shampoo and started scrubbing it into my hair, as though that would be enough to get the memory of what I had just done out of my head. I needed to get myself together, that was for damn sure. I couldn't believe that I had really just...that I had really just...

Nope. I wasn't even going to allow myself to think about what it might have meant. It was just me relieving some of the tension that had built up, especially since I hadn't been with anyone properly in such a long time. It didn't mean anything. And, as I finished cleaning off my hair and taking off the last remnants of my now-running make-up, I promised myself that it never would.

Chapter Eight – Xander

"Yes," I muttered to myself as soon as I saw the headline on the online news site that I had been trawling since I had come in to the office.

There were no pictures yet, but that didn't bother me - the paper was reporting that I had been seen out with a woman I had introduced around as my fiancée, and that was all that mattered. Any inch of legitimacy I could get to add to this would make things easier for me to handle, easier for me to sell this lie when the time came for it.

Not that I thought that we had exactly done a bad job at that so far. That gathering of all my business partners had gone better than it had had any right to. I had never expected things to run so smoothly; I had really thought that I was going to be bending over backwards to try and make sure that everyone believed what I was selling them, but swiftly found out that, for the most part, people didn't really care about my personal life one way or the other. I had been totally convinced that people would be inspecting it with a magnifying glass to try and expose any cracks in the foundation, but most of them, it seemed, really couldn't care less about what I got up to outside of work as long as I made sure that I was delivering on everything that we had agreed on.

Terri had been totally sweet, too, though I had been able to tell that she had been seriously nervous about this whole thing. And who could blame her? These people were intense, a lot of them so focused on themselves that maintaining conversation about anything remotely outside of that was a big ask in and of itself. But she had done well, and I could tell that everyone who had come across her had liked her well enough not to look any further into what was happening between us.

It had been a good test-run, too, for when I would have to bring her in front of my family. I had no intention of introducing her to Mel, obviously, since she wasn't going to be part of my life for long enough for me to justify inviting my daughter into her life, but everyone else would have to buy and believe it when I told them that she was really the woman for me. And honestly, I didn't think it was going to be too hard to pull off.

Because there was something about her, something that sparked a little smile to life deep inside my head. I knew that it was probably crazy, all things considered, given that we had already signed a contract to make sure that things would stay strictly platonic between us and that she was in this totally for the money, but I couldn't deny the fact that there was something there between us. I had no idea if she felt it or not, and honestly, I didn't think it really mattered one way or another – I was going to have this little crush no matter what, and whether or not she felt anything back was irrelevant. Not that I hoped that she was, obviously, because that would have made things way more complicated than they had ever needed to be. I could have sworn that she snuggled closer to me a few times through the night, as though she craved my closeness and my touch, but that could have just been nerves on her part. No point reading much into it, if I was being honest with myself.

And now the papers were reporting on it like it was fact. This was perfect. It was already going better than I could have imagined it would, and we were just getting started. Was this all it had taken? I just needed to go out there into the world and tell people that I had settled down with someone and everyone would just believe it without a second thought? If I had known that it was this easy all along, I would have done this a long time ago, back when the custody agreement was first getting threshed out and I could have used every inch of help that I could get.

I tried to focus on work for the rest of the day, but I would have been lying if I'd said that she hadn't crossed my mind a few more times than was strictly professional. Terri, that was. It was odd, it had been such a long time since I had allowed myself to be with anyone that I supposed there was a part of me that craved her. Craved her touch, craved her attention, and craved everything about her in a way that I didn't know I had been lacking all this time. When she held my hand, when she pushed herself into my side, I felt needed and wanted and desired in a way that I hadn't in a hell of a long time. There was something to be said for that, for being wanted in that way, even if it was only an act. It was enough to get a man a little puffed-up around the chest, that was for sure, and I could already feel my ego threatening to take on whole new dimensions if I wasn't careful with it.

I managed to keep my head in the game long enough to get everything that I needed to finished for the day – and just as I was about to head out of the office, my phone rang. I picked it up at once, not thinking for a moment that it might be bad news on the other end – hell, maybe it could even have been one of the papers calling about what had been reported earlier this weekend, on the fact that I actually had a woman on my arm and finally another person who would be the co-owner of my fortune. That had to be worth something to the gossip tabloids, didn't it?

"Hello?"

"Xander," A familiar voice came snapping down the line. I groaned internally. She was the last person that I wanted to hear from right now, but I supposed that I needed to talk to her about this one time or another.

"Talia," I replied, trying to keep the grimace out of my voice. She was going to be scrutinizing every single one of our actions, and the last thing I needed was for her to catch on to the fact that I was holding a lot against her right about now.

"So I was just checking the alert I have for your name," She began, but I had to stop her in her tracks before she could go any further.

"I'm sorry, you have an alert set up for my name...?"

"I need to know what's going on with you, Xander, and God knows you're not exactly forthcoming about it when it comes to me," she replied briskly, voice barbed with a harsh edge that made me wince. I had heard that so many times before, and it had never meant anything good.

"And I saw that you were seen out with a fiancée," she told me, and she sounded genuinely shocked by the revelation. I couldn't help but smirk. She liked to think that she was always totally and utterly caught-up with everything that was going on in our social circle, and when something came along that threw that reality off its axis, it never sat right with her.

"Yes, that's right," I replied coolly. She snorted with anger at the other end of the line.

"And how long have you know her for?" She demanded.

"About a year," I replied smoothly. I had been prepared for this conversation, even if I hadn't intended to have it quite so soon into proceedings.

"And you didn't think to tell me about her?"

"I didn't think that you cared much about my dating life, Talia," I replied. "Besides, you were hardly forthcoming about the fact that you were going to run off and get married, were you?"

She fell silent. She knew I had a point there, much as she would have liked to deny it. She had gotten married on a whim, and now she was having to deal with the backlash to that. I wondered, in some cruel part in my brain, if the man she had chosen had already started to see through her.

Not that it mattered – all that mattered was proving to her that she couldn't take my daughter away from me just because I didn't fit with her vision of a perfect life any longer.

"Fine," She snapped back, and I could tell that she was getting seriously pissed with all of this. Good. I wanted her rattled. Now I had the upper hand.

"But you can't expect me to just sign off on this woman I've never met," she remarked. I felt a rush of panic. No way in fucking hell I was ready for her to meet Terri face-to-face yet. Not just because I didn't think Terri was ready for it – but for some reason, because the thought of them coming together just seemed like it didn't belong. Like it couldn't possibly fit.

"What do you mean?"

"I asked Mel about her and she doesn't seem to know a thing about her existence," she replied. I winced. Last thing I wanted was for Mel to get pulled into this so soon. I knew that she was going to have to be a part of this eventually, but I had hoped that I could keep her at arm's length for as long as possible so I didn't have to worry about her getting attached to someone who wasn't going to be around for all that long. I needed to keep this as stable as possible for her, she was the priority in all of this.

"Well, I haven't spoken to Mel too much about her, given that I didn't know-"

"If you're going to be marrying this woman, I think it's important that she gets to know your daughter," Talia shot back, and I could hear that edge of testing to her voice - like she was trying to figure out what the hell was going on in my head, how this had all happened without her catching on to a bit of it. I wanted to tell her that she was crazy, to butt out of my business, and that I would deal with introducing my little girl to this woman when the time was right, but she had a point. I couldn't sell this idea of inviting Terri to spend the rest of her life with me if I had just gone ahead and pretended that I wasn't going to introduce her to my daughter.

"I'll let you have her this weekend if you promise that you'll introduce her to this girl," she told me. I pulled a face on the other end of the line. That was the last thing I wanted, really, but I didn't see much functional way that I could get out of it. I needed to convince that Terri was an actual, important part of my life, and that was only going to happen if I introduced her to Mel.

"Fine," I replied. "I'll pick her up as usual. But I don't want to see you there ready to swoop down on her if I don't get there twenty minutes early, okay?"

"Okay," she answered, though I could hear the irritation in her voice. "I just want what's best for our daughter, Xander, you know that, don't you?"

I sighed and pinched the bridge of my nose. I wanted to point out that what was best for our daughter was me actually being a part of her life and not my ex trying to shift me out of any connection with her at all, but I knew that it wasn't going to fly right now.

"I know that," I muttered back. "I'll be there to pick her up on Friday and I'll make sure that she gets to meet Terri after school."

"Terri," Talia repeated after me, as though she was testing out the way the name felt on her tongue. I winced. Wished I could tell her not to say it like that. I didn't know why, but her having Terri's name in her mouth made something feel unsettled inside of me.

"That's her name," I replied swiftly. "So you don't have to worry about keeping that alert on your phone anymore, alright?"

"Alright-"

But before she could say another word, I hung up, and let out a long sigh. I didn't want to have to listen to her for another moment. I knew that she was trying to be a good mother, even if she was able to use my own parenting skills as a stick to beat me with in the process. I needed to remember that. She might not have been the person I wanted to raise a kid with, but Mel had turned out okay so far and I at least had a little of her to thank for that.

But I didn't want to introduce Terri to my daughter so soon. Not when I still really didn't know this woman. I liked Terri, sure, but I couldn't be certain that it wasn't some other factor that was leading me to have such a fondness for her already. I knew that I should have known better, should have been able to keep my head in the game and focused on what mattered, but it was difficult when Terri was just so...present.

I had no clue had Terri would react to this, and I just had to hope that she understood that my hand had been forced here. That I wouldn't have been asking for such a big step out of her if I thought that there was any way I could avoid it. But I needed this if I was going to convince the people who mattered to this case that I was actually settling down, that there was going to be a woman in my life once and for all. I hated that I even had to think that way, hated that people needed me to have a chick around just to convince themselves that I was a worthwhile father, but still – I would have time to buck against the system later. For now, I needed to work in it to get my daughter and make sure that nobody could take her away from me.

Chapter Nine – Terri

"You!" Marjorie called to me as soon as I came through the door. "You're actually here!"

"I'm actually here?" I replied, a little nervous that she seemed so happy to see me given that I had been out of the store for a couple of weeks now. With everything that had been going on with Xander, I just hadn't had enough time to take on my usual shifts, and she had been totally understanding of that – well, at least, I thought she had, right up until the moment I walked through the door and she called out to me like she could hardly believe I would dare to show my face around here again.

"What's going on?" I asked, raising my eyebrows at her as I tried to wrap my head around what I could have done to piss her off. In fact, though, she didn't look pissed off – she had a big grin on her face, as though there was something that she couldn't wait to talk to me about.

"I saw those stories about the two of you out together," she remarked, as Stephanie emerged from the back room, her face lighting up as soon as she laid eyes on me.

"About who?" I asked, furrowing my brow. I had been hiding out the last few days, totally happy to just spend my time lazing around the house and getting back to reality after what I had been through with Xander. I knew it had gone well, but I would have been lying if I'd said that there wasn't a part of me that was still a little worried that I had somehow managed to fuck all of this up, that he was going to call me in a few days' time and tell me that he appreciated my interest but that this just wasn't going to work out between us and thanks for my time anyway.

"About you and Xander!" Stephanie exclaimed. I shook my head.

"Okay, sorry, I still don't know what you're talking about..."

"Are you being serious right now?" She exclaimed. "Come on, you must have seen them. If it was me I would have been looking them up as soon as I was out of the party in the first place..."

Marjorie waved me over, and a moment later she had pulled up a story on her phone to show to me – I gaped at it in total shock as I read what was right in front of me. I couldn't believe it. It was a story about Xander and I, some commentary on the fact that he had finally turned out with an actual date for a change, and that he was claiming that the two of us were engaged. It was the last thing I had expected to see. I didn't realize, until that moment, exactly how serious this was with him – that my name was going to be tied up with his for the foreseeable future, and that I would just have to find a way to be alright with that.

"You said you were signing a contract with this guy, but you didn't say anything about this," Marjorie pointed out.

"I told you what he wanted from me-"

"Yeah, and if we'd known that it had meant going along to swanky parties I think we'd have been a little more supportive," Stephanie teased lightly. Marjorie shook her head, and I could see the furrow in her brow.

"I'm not sure about this," she remarked.

"What do you mean?" I replied. I knew that Marjorie was the one I could turn to, the one who would always have my best interests at heart and the actual sensibility to make sure that they came first.

"Your name is in this story," she pointed out. "You know that, right? So if anyone goes ahead and looks you up..."

"Then they're going to see that I was engaged to one of the richest men in the city and therefore they should feel lucky that they even get to know me," I shot back. Marjorie laughed, but shook her head.

"I know you don't take anything seriously," she told me, as gently as she could. "But I'm just asking you to think about this a little more, that's all. This is going to be around forever, and I don't want you feeling like you made a mistake getting involved in this in the first place."

"I know that I'm never going to feel that way," I replied cheerfully, trying to keep the edge of doubt out of my voice. I didn't want her to know that she might just have had a point there. I hadn't considered that there would be so very much interest in what I was getting up to with this guy, and the fact that there was threw me a little off-guard. This wasn't what I had expected. It wasn't what I had signed up for. And I was pretty sure, if I was being honest with myself, that this wasn't what I wanted people to remember me for, either.

"Are you sure?" Marjorie asked, and I shrugged.

"Well, I have to think that," I pointed out. "Too late to change any of it now, right?"

"I guess so," Marjorie conceded, as Stephanie took the phone and started scrolling through the story in front of her. "But you could always ask for a little more time...I don't know, maybe see if you could get a fake name out there so nobody would know that it was actually you?"

"I like that idea," I agreed. "But I don't want people to get any more suspicious. If I have a fake name that's different from the one that's already out there, I'm sure people are going to start asking more questions."

"I think this whole thing is kind of cute," Stephanie remarked, looking up from the phone and diving in to our conversation all at once. "I can't believe that you're actually going through with this, Terri. I would never have had the nerve."

"Well, someone's got to be the bold one out of the three of us," I teased them both, and Marjorie smiled at me again. I knew she only wanted the best for me, but she didn't know the kind of dire straits I was in with my finances. I couldn't afford to slip out of this job now, no matter how strange it might have been getting.

"I suppose so," She conceded, and Stephanie handed her back her phone and she tucked it away.

"You know, he's pretty hot," Stephanie remarked. It had been so sweet to see the way that she had come into this confidence around men since she had started dating Jon; before, she had never been the one who was first to offer her opinion on the people we were dating, but these days, it was clear that she saw no reason to hold back.

"Perks of the job," I replied with a shrug. I felt a little heat rush up my neck as I thought back to the steamy shower that I'd taken after he had dropped me off. Yeah, I might have been an oversharer, but I had my limits and that was certainly one of them. Nobody else needed to know about that.

"Just make sure you don't...you don't let him take you for a ride, okay?" Marjorie told me. I nodded.

"I'll let you look over the contracts if you want," I offered her, but she shook her head.

"No, I trust you," she promised me. "It's just...it's just I don't want to see you get hurt in all of this. It can be confusing, work and dating stuff all getting on top of each other, especially if you haven't been with anyone for a while..."

"Hey, I'll thank you to leave my nonexistent dating life out of this," I scolded her playfully.

"Very existent all of a sudden these days," Stephanie pointed out with a laugh.

"Well, that's what we want people to think," I replied, tapping the side of my nose. "All in a days' work for an undercover agent, right?"

"Just make sure not to get too lost in the role," Marjorie warned me. "I still want you at the end of this when it's all over, alright?"

"Of course," I promised her. "You know you're never getting rid of me."

"Damn," Marjorie joked, snapping her fingers as though she had been foiled in the midst of a plan. "Just when I thought I might be getting out from under you."

"No, now she's getting out under Xander," Stephanie remarked, and I pinched her lightly on the arm, making her squirm.

"Nobody's getting under anyone," I told her. "It's just business. That's it."

"Yeah, that's what I told myself with Jon," she pointed out. "And look what a mess that ended up dumping me in."

"Yeah, you're a total mess," I joked. "Getting married to the man you love and running that amazing business together."

"I just like to hear you say it out loud," she replied, a little giddily. I put an arm around her and squeezed her close.

"You know he's totally lucky to have you, right?"

"Oh, I know," she replied. "But thanks, I'll make sure to remind him of that tonight, make sure I get a few extra brownie points."

"Only what you deserve," I replied. With that, I turned to Marjorie, content that the conversation was done with for now. "So, what do you need me to do today?"

Working at the store was a good distraction from the slight chaos going on in my head at that moment – it was strange to think that other people actually knew about Xander and me, and that we were already something of a talking point around the city at large. People were writing articles on us, for goodness sake – I couldn't think of anything stranger than that. It had been a long time since anyone had shown any actual interest in my life, and now, this fake one that I was helping build with this guy was turning out to be the one that people cared about. A strange notion, for sure, but not an entirely unwelcome one. If I was going to be in the public eye, even vaguely, then I wanted to do it as a whole other personality – so that I could slip back into my real life when it was all done without a second thought.

I made it through the rest of the day and felt a little brighter by the time that I walked out and headed back to my place. It was always good to know that these women had my back, even if I knew that I could take care of myself. Marjorie was like a big sister to me, and she would always look out for me and make sure that I wasn't getting screwed over in any way. Not that I needed it. That's what I kept telling myself, anyway.

I hadn't heard from Xander since the day of the party we had been to together, and to be honest, I was starting to miss the sound of his voice. Which was getting a little too close to actually admitting that I missed him, which would have been ridiculous given that we really hardly knew one another. I knew that he didn't want me to start developing these feelings for him, and I had no intention of doing anything that might have put this job at risk. And that's what it was to me, a job that was it, nothing more. And you didn't fall in love with the people you worked with unless you were looking for a serious dose of trouble.

I took a shower, made some pasta for dinner, and ate it in front of the few videos I had missed while I had been out at work; I was proud of myself for budgeting today, even managing to walk to the store and back so that I didn't spend anything extra on transport. Maybe this could become my new obsession, low-cost living. Except I would have to make sure that I didn't get drawn into buying any crazy programs to try and make it work this time...

I was just getting ready for bed by the time that I heard my phone ring; I picked it up at once, lifting it to my ear as I put my toothbrush away and pinning it between my shoulder and my ear. I looked at myself in the mirror and pulled a goofy face – it helped take the edge off the anxiety that came with being on the phone, not to mention the fact that it always made me giggle.

"Hello?" I greeted the caller on the other end of the line.

"Hey, Terri?" A familiar voice met mine. And, as soon as it clicked who was calling me, I saw my face light up in the mirror at once.

"Hey, Xander," I replied, and I turned away from my reflection in the mirror so I didn't have to look at the huge smile that had crossed my face as soon as I heard his voice.

"Have you seen those articles about us?" I asked him excitedly. Us – there was a word that made my head spin. I couldn't believe that I could actually refer to us as that. We were an us now, a unit, the two of us together as one for a change.

"Yeah, pretty funny," he remarked, chuckling to himself. He had a nice laugh, the kind of full, open sound that seemed to come from deep inside of him.

"Yeah, I feel a little bad for them," I joked. "I feel like we should come clean before they make a fool of themselves."

"I don't think the contract allows for that," he replied, though I could hear the smile in his voice.

"You don't have to worry, I'm not going to throw you to the wolves," I replied. "Well, not until I get paid, anyway."

"Good to know where your priorities are," he shot back, and I laughed. I liked talking to him. It felt like we had this comfortable, easy chemistry, even now. Maybe it was just because we had had to jump right over the part where we got to know one another and into the serious part of the relationship, but it was as though we had known each other for years.

"So, I was hoping that you might be able to come over to my place this weekend," he explained. "I have an event that I need you here for."

"Yeah, of course," I replied. "What is it? How do you want me?"

I paused for a moment, realizing just how suggestive those words must have sounded; I bit my lip, hoped he would have the decency to just breeze on by them. Luckily for me, he did just that.

"Just come casual," he told me. "Nothing serious. It's not anything big, there aren't going to be many people there."

"Good," I replied with a sigh of relief. "I'm not sure I could handle being around all those people again."

"Well, you're in luck there," he assured me. "Just a few of us. But you think you can handle it?"

"That's what you hired me for, right?" I replied.

"Sure did," he agreed. "I'll text you the details of when and wear as soon as I get the chance."

"Sounds good," I replied, and even though I knew there was no reason for me to stay on the phone, I wanted to keep talking to him. I wasn't ready to say goodbye yet, and I didn't want to be the one to hang up first.

"So, I'll see you over the weekend," he finished up.

"Catch you then," I agreed, and with that, he hung up. And I was left standing there, just outside my bathroom, his voice ringing in my ears – and the promise of another date coming up over this weekend running around and around my head. I couldn't help but smile. This was already shaping up to be the most fun job I'd ever had in my life – and I had only just gotten started.

Chapter Ten – Xander

"Wait, I'm going to meet your daughter?"

As soon as I had told Terri what my actual plan was for her for this weekend together, her jaw dropped, and she sounded totally gob smacked. I felt a little bad for not telling her that this was the plan beforehand, but I wasn't sure if she would find it a little too much to handle.

We were at my house, and Mel was due to arrive there at any moment – Terri had arrived a half-hour before, in a maroon sweater and a pair of blue jeans, and she looked every bit the brilliant stepmom that I knew she could totally make everyone believe that she could be.

"Yeah, I'm sorry I couldn't tell you sooner," I replied. "It was...yeah, it was kind of sprung on me. Do you think you'll be able to handle it?"

"I think so," she replied. "I'm not great with kids, though, fair warning."

"How bad are we talking here?" I asked her. "Do I have something to worry about?"

"No, no," She assured me, shaking her head. "It's just...well, I was the youngest in my family, I was never really around younger kids than me, I don't have that mothering thing all built-in, I guess."

"It's going to be fine," I promised her. "I have a lot planned for us today, I'm not going to give you a lot of time to fill with her, I promise."

"Fuck," she muttered, and then she clapped her hand over her mouth. "Wait, no, I can't curse, can I?"

"I think I would prefer it if you didn't," I replied, and I couldn't help but chuckle. She sounded so panicked, but I knew that she had this in hand. I knew lots of people who claimed they were no good with kids, only to find themselves totally taken with Mel as soon as they met her. I just had to hope that this was going to apply here – and that she wasn't understating her difficulty with kids.

"Okay, I'll bear that in mind," she answered, and she patted her hair nervously. "This is...quick, that's all. I didn't think I'd ever get to this point with you, let alone so quickly."

"Honestly, me neither," I admitted. "I didn't think I really wanted to bring you and her together at all, if I could avoid it."

"Because you thought I'd be too bad an influence on your daughter?"

She replied, and I shook my head, grinning.

"No, because I don't want to get her involved with someone who's not going to be around for that long," I pointed out. She nodded.

"I get it," She agreed. "And I promise I'm going to be a total nightmare so she hopes that you dump me."

"Perfect," I replied, and I heard a car crunching up the driveway towards the house.

"My ex is going to be here, but I'll deal with her, don't worry," I promised her.

"I don't mind talking with her-"

"Yeah, but trust me, I mind her talking with you," I replied. "You haven't done anything in your life to deserve being stuck with her."

"That bad, huh?"

"That bad," I agreed. "Go on, go inside, I'll come get you in a couple of minutes..."

Talia and I did the handover of Mel, and she pressed with some questions about Terri that I did my best to avoid. She didn't need to hear anything about her, not yet, not until Mel had had a chance to get to know her.

"You have a good weekend, baby," Talia told our daughter, giving her a tight hug before she hustled her off into my arms. I scooped her up off the ground, and she hung on to me, laughing as I carried her into the house. I knew that she was going to have the most perfect weekend she'd ever had with me. I had put every detail in place to make sure of that.

"Okay, baby, are you ready to meet my friend Terri?" I asked her, as I planted Mel back on the ground, and she nodded. I felt nervous, actually nervous. Because kids could be a lot more insightful than people gave them credit for, and the last thing I needed was for my girl to take one look at what was going on here and see all the way through it.

"Yes!" She exclaimed, and I could tell that she was nervous, too. She always got really hyper when she was nervous. Something she had gotten from me – I had been just the same way when I was younger, and it had taken me a long time to get over that urge to fill a nervous silence with noise even when I would have done better to leave off.

I led her through to the living room, where I had stashed Terri while we were making the handover, and I took a deep breath and smiled at her as I stepped inside.

"Terri, this is Mel," I introduced her. "My daughter."

"Nice to meet you, Mel," Terri said to my little girl, and Mel smiled and hung back a little bit, still clearly not quite sure how she was meant to carry herself in the face of all of this.

"Hey, is that a soccer ball?" Terri asked, gesturing to the little charm that Mel had hanging off one of the loops of the jeans she was wearing. Mel looked down, as though she had almost forgotten that she was wearing it, but then pinched the little charm between her fingers and nodded.

"Do you play?" Terri pressed, and Mel nodded again.

"That's awesome," she replied. "I used to play when I was in school, too. What position do you like?"

"Striker," Mel answered her, her voice getting a little bit fuller and more confident.

"I used to be in defense," Terri replied, pulling a playful little face for a moment. "I never had the nerve to actually go up there and score all the goals."

"I could show you!" Mel suggested, and she sounded genuinely excited now, not just trying to cover up her nerves from before. Terri glanced to me, as though checking in that she was doing a good job. I nodded at once, telling her to go on.

"That would be nice," Terri agreed, and she straightened up again. "So, what are we up to today, Xan?"

That little nickname for me, for some reason, made me smile. It had been a long time since anyone had called me that, and it felt nice to remember that I actually had this other side to me, too, the one that was capable of a little casual every now and then. Even if this did technically count as a work meeting, I supposed.

I bundled them both into the car as I explained what I had planned for the day, and drove us down to the science museum – one of Mel's favorite places in the city, the kind of venue I could just let her loose in and trust that she would have a good time with. Exactly what I needed for this day with Terri. I had promised Terri that she wasn't going to need to worry much about entertaining Mel, and I planned to stick to that. As soon as my daughter got one look at those little neutron glass ball things that had the

346

lightning on the inside, she would be set for the rest of the day.

As soon as we arrived, though, Mel basically dragged Terri into the museum and started showing off all the little details that she loved here so much. I stayed close behind them, making sure that nothing was coming out that I didn't want to, but to my surprise, Terri seemed just as engaged with all of it as Mel did.

"It's been such a long time since I'd actually been to a museum," she remarked to me, as Mel went to check out one of the displays that required her to step inside this great big egg-shaped thing and vanish for a little while.

"You seem like you're enjoying yourself," I replied, and she grinned and nodded.

"This is exactly the kind of stuff I liked to do when I was a kid," she explained. "I lived in a small town, so I didn't get much of a chance to actually visit all these places, but every chance I got, I took it. I always loved anything that I got to learn from."

"You sound like a total nerd," I teased, and she parted her lips in faux-surprise. I couldn't help but notice how sweet her mouth looked in that moment, even though I knew that I shouldn't even have been thinking about that. She had full, soft lips, the color of a fresh strawberry, and I had to fight the urge to lean forward and sink my teeth into them just to see how she would react.

"Well, if I'm a nerd then you're raising one," she pointed out playfully, and I grinned back at her. I liked hanging out with her like this. I didn't have a whole lot of friends, and most of the ones I did have had come through work, not making for the most laid-back days out if I did go anywhere with them. Not to mention the fact that there was something really fun about sharing my daughter with someone else for the day. I knew that sounded a little silly, but I was so proud of Mel and I really thought she was the best kid in the whole world; seeing Terri interact with her only confirmed that for me, and it was something that made me happier than I could ever have imagined it would.

"I think we've seen everything in here by now, honey," I told Mel as we came to the final exhibit. I could see that she would have gone around again if I had let her, so I swiftly suggested that we go get ice-cream at this little stall that was nearby; if there was anything Mel liked more than the museum, it was frozen desserts, and she agreed at once.

"What do you think is the best ice-cream at this place, then?" Terri asked Mel with interest as we approached the stall.

"I like the strawberry," she replied with certainty. "It has pieces of real strawberry in it, and they put a vanilla cream through it, too!"

"Oh, that sounds perfect," Terri replied, and she looked to me with a smile on her face. "Can I get that one?"

"Whatever you want," I promised her, and I found my hand reaching for hers even though I knew that there was no good reason for me to touch her in that moment. I should have been able to restrain myself, but before I knew it, our fingers were linked and it would have looked way too suspicious if we had let go just as suddenly.

As soon as we got to the stall, we ordered our cones and headed down to a park not far away so we could sit and eat them and talk a little more. Terri and Mel were chatting away happily about soccer, and it was clear that the two of them already had so much in common, so much more than I had expected. I knew that Terri was the right woman for the job now for certain – though, as this day went on, I couldn't help but wonder if this was starting to tip out of job territory for her and into something else entirely. On the cold metal bench we chose to sit on, I draped my arm over the back and she shifted a little closer to me, closing the distance between us. As though it just came to her on instinct.

By the time we'd finished our ice-cream it was starting to get a little cold out, and I figured that it was prime time to head home and warm up and maybe order a pizza; Terri and Mel sat in the back seat on the way home, and I listened to them chat away to one another. What a gift it was to be able to hear her interacting with someone else like that, with the same enthusiasm she went about the rest of her life with; Mel was such a wonderful little girl, and I knew that, by the end of the day, Terri was going to see it too.

"I don't know about pizza," Terri remarked, once we had made it home and I had pitched my idea of food to the two of them. "How about something a bit spicier?"

"Yeah, something more spicy!" Mel echoed after her, as she hopped up on to the breakfast bar stool and leaned up on it. I was surprised – normally, Mel liked to eat a very specific selection of very specific stuff, but clearly that wasn't the case now that Terri was in the picture. She wanted to impress her. Which was about the sweetest thing I had ever seen in my life.

So we ordered in Chinese food, which had to be one of the first times Mel had ever had it, and the three of us watched some kid's movie that Mel had already seen before but had wanted to show me. I was always happy to enjoy this sort of thing with her; because it meant that when she had seen it the first time, she had been thinking of me, and sometimes I needed reminding that I was still part of her life even when I wasn't around.

The film was funny, and the three of us laughed along with it as we picked at our food. By the time that it was done, Mel was starting to get a little droopy around the edges, and I knew she would have to be in bed soon or else she would be a moody grump for the whole day tomorrow.

"Come on, honey, you need some sleep," I told her gently, as I scooped her up into my arms.

"Can I say goodnight to Terri first?" She asked, and I put her down again at once, surprised at how easily she seemed to be taking to all of this Terri stuff.

"Of course," I replied. And I watched as she gave Terri a quick hug, and then came back to me.

"Okay, now I'm ready," she told me firmly, and Terri beamed at her and waved her goodnight as I took her up the stairs.

Today had gone better than it had any right to. So well, in fact, that I had almost started to forget that the contract was in place at all.

I put Mel to bed, and when I came back downstairs again, Terri was clearing up the plates that we had left out from when we had been eating together.

"You don't need to do that," I told her, but she smiled and shook her head.

"I really don't mind," she assured me cheerfully. I was surprised that she still had so much energy given how much we had been doing that day. I was ready to crawl into bed and get some sleep – or I might have been, had it not been for the little look that she snuck me that told me something else was on her mind entirely.

"What is it?" I asked, and she cocked her head towards my wine cabinet.

"I couldn't help but notice," She remarked. "You have some really nice bottles in there."

"Oh, you know wine?" I asked, perking up and ready to chat to her about vintages and growth rates. She shook her head.

"No," she admitted. "But since they're in your house, I assumed they had to be nice bottles, right?"

I grinned.

"Yeah, they are," I replied. "Would you like to try one?"

"I thought you'd never ask," she replied, and she stepped away from the sink where she was finishing up the last of the washing up and let me pick out a bottle for her to try. I didn't know whether she preferred red or white, so I took a shot and picked out the red.

"Perfect," she told me. "Where do you keep your glasses?"

"Up on the top shelf, over the stove," I replied, and she stood on her tiptoes to reach up and grab what she could. She wobbled a little, balancing on the tiny tips of her toes, and I darted over to her and put my hands on her waist before she keeled over right in front of me.

"Oh, thanks," she laughed, once she noticed that I was holding her up. "I promise I didn't get into them while you were out of the room, I know it might seem like I did."

"I believe you," I murmured, and I realized my hands were still on her waist. I didn't want to move them, not yet. I was too happy to have her close. I could feel her small, soft body against mine, and, as she grabbed the glasses, I noticed that she seemed in no great rush to get away from me. I could smell her perfume, the bite of it at the back of my throat, like I could just about reach out and swallow her whole if the urge took me. Not that I was going to let myself go there, not for a moment...

Slowly, I pulled back from her, and she turned to face me – she was standing so close to me that she had to tip her head back so that she could look into my eyes, and I could have sworn that there was a little flush to her cheeks that hadn't been there before. Did she feel it, too? Did she feel that rush?

"The wine," she reminded me, with a little smile on her face, and I blinked and came back to reality and remembered what I was meant to be doing here in the first place. Of course, the wine, just like she had suggested in the first place.

"Right, right," I agreed, and I swiftly opened up the bottle and poured us both a glass; she hopped up on the stool at the counter, and hooked her ankles around each other like she was trying to contain something she knew that she shouldn't have let out. And I would have been lying if I'd said that I wasn't more than a little intrigued to know what it was.

"So, you collect that stuff?" She asked, nodding to the wine.

"Yeah, but I'm going to have to do a better job hiding it by the time that she gets old enough to know what it is," I remarked, flipping my gaze upstairs to gesture to my daughter. "I'll need to put a lock on that door to make sure that she doesn't get into it."

"You should tint the windows, too," she replied with authority. "If she can see it, then she's going to want it."

"Sounds like you're speaking from experience..."

"I might be," Terri replied, waggling her eyebrows. I took a sip of the wine, but the truth was, I didn't need it to get me feeling a little tipsy around the edges right now. I was just a little lighter when I was around her, something that I hadn't felt in a long time. Something that I knew was totally and utterly dangerous, but something that I didn't mind one little bit at the same time.

"So, how do you think it went today?" She asked me, clearly a little nervous as she got the truth of how this day had gone out of me. I nodded.

"You know, I actually think it went really well," I replied. "I didn't know how you were going to be with her, that's why I put together so much stuff for us to do, but you guys got on better than I thought you would."

"Because of my likeable and sparkling personality, right?" She teased, and I laughed.

"Yeah, something like that," I agreed. "She doesn't hug many people out of choice. I think that she must have been really taken with you to actually come to you for a hug."

Terri put a hand on her chest, her gaze softening.

"Oh, that's so sweet to hear," she remarked. "I thought I was going to make a total fool of myself, I really did."

"To be fair, though, kids tend to like it when you make a total fool of yourself," I pointed out to her, and she giggled and nodded, tucking a loose strand of hair back behind her ear. When her fingers grazed her skin, it was hard not to think about how much better it would have felt if I could have been the one touching her, instead.

"That's a good point," she agreed. "But I just feel a little strange, knowing that I'm going to be out of her life soon enough, you know what I mean?"

"Yeah, it's not ideal," I replied with a sigh. "But we can make the most of it while you're here, right?"

"And what does making the most of it look like to you?" She fired back, playfully. I knew that she was just having a little fun with me, but the look in her eyes hinted to something more.

"I could show you, if you like," I joked, but I knew in my heart of hearts that it wasn't a joke at all and then there was something short and sweet and a little savage that was taking control of me. I wanted to tell her just how I felt, wanted to slide my hand over her thigh beneath the table and show her. But I knew that would have been wrong. It wasn't in the contract – but then, neither was her hanging around after hours and drinking wine with me when she could have been headed home already. All of this was new territory for us, and I would have been lying if I'd said that I didn't want to do a little more to explore it while we had the chance.

"Then show me," she shot back. And she put down her glass of wine. As though she was getting ready for something, getting ready for me to lay hands on her or something. And not that I didn't want to, but my daughter was upstairs and we had signed a contract and there was so much that was going against me leaning over and making the choice that I knew I wanted to make but wasn't sure that I could.

"Or I could show you?" She remarked. And, just like that, she had gotten to her feet, and slipped down on to my lap. Her arms wound around my neck and I felt the weight of her small, soft body against mine.

"Terri," I murmured, not moving her, not making any motion to. "What are you doing?"

"Making the most of it," she replied, and she sank her nails into my back. "Just like you said-"

But before she could say another word, I pinched her chin between my thumb and my forefinger, and I drew her gaze down to mine, and I kissed her.

Fuck. It had been so long since I had kissed someone, really kissed someone that I had almost forgotten what it felt like to do it for the very first time. The intensity of it, the way it made your skin feel like it was burning, and the way everything seemed to slow down around you until there was only this left in the world. I put an arm around her waist and pulled her even closer to me, tucking my hand behind her head to hold her in place. She was smiling into the kiss, like this was what she had been waiting for all day long. Had she? Had she, just the same way I had? I wanted to stop and ask, but at the same time, there was no part of me that was willing to break this embrace now that we had started.

She caught her breath for a moment, and brushed her nose against mine.

"I just want to check," I murmured to her. "This isn't you getting really into the act, is it?"

She giggled and shook her head.

"Nope," she replied. "This is as real as they come."

"Perks of the job, I guess," I murmured, and with that, I kissed her again. Harder. My tongue in her mouth. So that her breath seemed to be knocked from her lungs and so she had to cling on to me for dear life. I was hungry for her now, starving, and I had waited all day to have her like this. I wasn't going to miss out on the chance to do more now that she was where I wanted her to be.

I slipped my hand down her back and sank my fingers into her ass. God, she had the most perfect body. Small and supple but strong, perfectly curvy. I could have scooped her up in my arms and carried her to my bedroom if I had been so inclined, but to be honest, there was something way too fun about just making out like a pair of horny teenagers in the kitchen.

She wiggled in my lap a little, once she could feel me getting hard, and I pushed myself up against her and let her feel what she was doing to me. She reached down and skimmed her fingers over my length, and let out the softest little moan against my mouth.

"Mmm," she sighed, and she pulled back for a moment so she could look at me. "You want me, Xander?"

The playful tone to her voice was offset by the keen need in her eyes, and I nodded and kissed her again, unable to think of anything else to say to her that could convey the depth of my want for her in that moment.

Before I knew it, the two of us were stripping down, as fast as we could, as though we knew that a moment's hesitation would only serve to slow us down and get us to rethink what we were doing. And damn, that was the last thing we needed right now. I just wanted her, wanted her more than I could put into words, and there was nothing else in my head but feeling her around me. It was the strangest thing; for such a long time, I had been able to put my sexuality to the back of my mind, but now it was here and back with a vengeance and I was ready to explore it any way she would let me.

I pulled her back on to my lap once she had kicked off her jeans and her panties, and I unzipped my fly so that I could take my cock into her hand. Her breath was coming hard, and I got the feeling that it had been a long time since she had been taken, too – long enough that even the thought of what we were going to do together thrilled her. I slid my hand between her legs, felt her wetness, and watched her eyes glaze with need as I touched her for the first time. She let out this needy mewl, and I took that as all the invitation I needed to push myself inside her for the very first time.

I grasped her hips and pulled her down on top of me, and I focused all my attention on her face so I could take in the way she reacted to being penetrated. Her eyes seemed to soften, her jaw slackening, and her whole body shivered like someone had just struck a match off her very skin. I wrapped one arm around her waist to keep her steady and she planted a hand on my bare chest, her nails digging in ruthlessly to my skin. Like she wanted me to know that she owned me now.

Thrusting up, I held her tight as I felt her flex around me. She was tight and warm and wet and welcoming, and she clenched her thighs around me as she felt me push deeper and deeper into her. I couldn't stop staring at her face; I knew that I was meant to be obsessing over her body, but there was something so erotic about seeing the way that she reacted to me that I could hardly think about anything else but that.

I had to keep reminding myself that this was real, that it was really happening. It was so easy to forget that she was mine, at least for these moments; that this was real, even if everything that had happened today had been part of the game we were building together. I didn't even know if I could tell the difference any longer, didn't even know if I wanted to. Where were the lines between reality and fiction now that we had done this? I didn't know, and I had to admit, I didn't much care either.

Her eyes drifted shut for a moment, and I slipped my hand down her spine to bring her back to me.

"Look at me," I ordered her, and her eyes sprang open at once, taking a moment to focus their gaze on me once more. And, it was with that, with the look on her face and the fact that she obeyed me without a second thought that I came inside of her.

I groaned with pleasure as I felt the release tingle all the way up my shaft and into her – Terri's body seemed to crumple in reaction, her back arching as she moved against me and then tumbling forward towards me as I felt her pussy clench around my dick. She didn't make a noise but I could feel her orgasm, and that was all that mattered.

I held her close and tight, not ready for this to be over yet. Not ready, really, for what would happen when we had to accept that it was. She didn't seem any more ready for it than I was, as she kissed across my shoulder, her mouth eager and sweet as she traced the shape of my body with her tongue. My hands had fallen to her hips again, just the same way they had been placed when I had been keeping her from falling while she was getting the wine earlier, and I couldn't help but smile at the synchronicity of it.

"Yeah, you should for sure keep that wine cabinet hidden away in future," she giggled, as she slowly lifted herself off of me.

"After this? Yeah, no chance," I replied, and she went to start collecting her clothes – and, as I watched her, I wondered what exactly happened next. We had broken one of the major rules of our contract. And both of us, it seemed, had enjoyed every second of it. It really did seem like some rules were way better broken.

Chapter Eleven – Terri

I woke up early the next morning, and it took me a second to remember where the hell in the world that I was.

I blinked, glanced around, stretched a little – I was lying in a huge bed, with crisp grey covers and puffy pillows, opposite a huge window that glowed in light from the morning sun outside. Far removed from my tiny little place with the window that needed cleaning before it would let in anything other than flies and a bad smell.

And then, after I heard a slight groan from beside me, I looked over and remembered. *Xander.* I had spent the night with Xander. I peeled back the covers a few inches from his sleeping form, and saw that he was still naked under there. So, last night really had happened the way I remembered it, huh?

I couldn't believe that I had really let myself do that. It was crazy, I could see that now, but when it had been happening, it seemed crazier for me not to do it. He had been looking at me with that edge to his gaze, speaking to me in that tone of voice, and I had known what was on his mind and had been unable to pretend that it wasn't on mine for another moment. Playing at being a couple all day, it seemed, made it hard to just switch off when you weren't mean to do it any longer.

I slipped out of bed and reached for the clothes that we had strewn on the floor the night before. I had gotten dressed after our encounter in the kitchen, but then he had dragged me upstairs and we had gone at it again. I thanked goodness that I was on birth control, so I didn't have to worry about getting the morning-after pill. I had to hope that he was clean, but we could have that conversation later...

If he ever wanted to talk to me again, of course. I still couldn't believe that I had actually let that happen.

I was pretty sure that this was outside the bounds of the contract that we had agreed on. Pretty damn certain, actually. I couldn't fight the feeling that I had fucked things up beyond all repair. I had promised myself, and promised Marjorie and Stephanie that I was going to keep my feelings out of it. But as soon as I had kissed him for the first time, that had been lost. I had to have him. Just to get it out of my system.

Keeping half an eye on Xander, I got dressed as quietly as I could and hoped that Mel was still in bed and asleep so that I wouldn't have to deal with explaining what I was still doing at the house. And why I was sneaking out this early without so much as waking her dad.

In some ways, this was going to make things easier to sell. Sleeping over at his house, spending a steamy evening with him – yeah, that was just what couples did when they first got engaged. Not that we had been performing for anyone. I had made that very clear to him. That was just about wanting him, and I was sure that he had just wanted me in the same way.

Slipping out of the door and down the stairs, I tiptoed as silently as I could to the door, my shoes in my hand so that they wouldn't tap on the polished wood below me. The door was locked when I got down there, of course, and I panicked for a split second until I remembered a side door with an inside lock that I had seen leading out of the kitchen. I hurried around there, keeping an eye out for Mel as I went, and finally, made it out into the cool morning air.

Planting a hand on the wall beside me, I slipped my shoes on and straightened back up. Okay. I had made it out and now I was going to get out of there without getting tripped up. Mel didn't need to see me in there – hell, I felt a little guilty that I had even let things go that far. She seemed to like me so much, but I was pretty sure that would change if she had seen me sneaking out of her house first thing in the morning. I had no idea what the circumstances of her parents' divorce was, but I doubted that I doing that would have done much to soothe her on that basis.

I made my way to the driveway, and headed out on to the street, pausing for a moment to look around and trying to remember exactly where I was right now. I was sure that we had come down from the center of the city, and taken the side street out of the – or had it been the other way? I couldn't recall. I rubbed one hand over my head and furrowed my brow, casting my gaze around to place myself somewhere.

And that's when I saw it. A car, sitting on the other side of the road. Silver. It was the only one on the street that had someone in it, not surprising, really given how early it was in the morning. Everyone else was still likely in bed.

I didn't recognize the woman, but there was something about her that made the hair on the back of my neck stand up. Like my instincts were telling me to watch the fuck out because there was something wrong with her. Her eyes were trained on me, and I moved a little to see if her gaze would follow me. Sure enough, it did. I winced. I didn't like this, not one bit.

I tried to calm myself down. She was probably just looking at me because she was bored and I was the first person to emerge from the houses all morning, the first person to offer the slightest bit of excitement to her life. I offered her a brief smile, but she didn't return it. In fact, as soon as she saw me acknowledge her presence, she looked away, as though pretending that she had never been looking at me in the first place.

Be that way, then, I thought to myself. I was probably just paranoid from being on high alert coming out of the house. I didn't want to be caught by anyone, and then I stepped outside and this woman was there looking at me? Yeah, no wonder I hardly had the best reaction to it.

I managed to find a bus that would take me back into the center of the city, and I made my way straight to my apartment so that I could have some time to think about what the hell had just happened to me. No, I couldn't think of it like that. It hadn't happened *to* me, it had happened because I had made it happen. I had wanted him, and I had made the first move, and I had taken everything that I wanted from him. This was on me. For better or for worse.

How strange that the wedding vows popped into my head to explain how I was feeling right now. Given that, as far as everyone else was concerned, we were meant to be getting married for real. Did everyone else actually believe that, or were they all just playing along because the thought of calling us out was too painfully awkward for them to consider in any real way?

I took a shower, reluctantly, because it meant that I would get the scent of it off of me and that was the last thing I wanted. It would be admitting that things were really done between us, at least for now, and I didn't want to have to accept that. I wanted to stay near him, which I knew was rich coming from someone who had just walked out of his house while he was still asleep because I couldn't do the morning-after thing quite yet.

In fact, it had been so long since I had done the morning-after thing that I had almost forgotten how it worked. One-night-stands had never been a big part of my life – I had had my fair share when I had first arrived in the city, but had swiftly discovered that they weren't for me. I liked dating people, or at least getting to know them a little better than a tipsy fumble after a night at the bar would allow.

I didn't even know what I would call what we had done. Way more than a fumble. It had been incredible; our connection was intense, as though both of us had been waiting for this as long as we had known one another, and I was already craving more. But I couldn't go after it, right? I couldn't go after him.

It was strange, because in some ways, I already had him. To the rest of the world, at least, we were already together. We were going to get married, and no woman in her right mind would have tried to put the moves on him while I was in the picture. I was so close to having him for real, and so far, at the same time. A confusing mix, to say the least, and one that I wasn't sure that I liked, not really.

After the shower, I crawled into my bed and pulled the covers up over my head. I had slept like a log when I had been next to him, but suddenly, I was hit by a groundswell of exhaustion all over again, and I needed to sleep it off before I dropped to unconsciousness on my feet.

Probably all that work I had done with Mel the day before. Mel – God, what a sweetie she was. I thought I would be terrible with her, given that I had such little experience with kids, but she was the most adorable little thing and it was impossible not to fall a little in love with her. She had so much in common with me, and she reminded me so much of myself when I had been that age. And she had gone out of her way to give me a big hug before she'd gone to bed, something that Xander had made pretty clear was a big deal for her. She liked me, she really liked me. And yet...

And yet, I was going to be out of her life in just a few months. My heart twisted at the thought. It felt dishonest, in some way, to involve this little girl in all of this given that she hardly got a choice as to what she could check out of or otherwise. She couldn't just wrap her head around what was happening. She had taken my arrival in her life at face value, and seemed to be looking forward to the idea of having me spend even more time with her. Maybe I could pull back a little? But wouldn't being cold with her be just as bad as being kind? I had no idea what I should do. I hadn't signed up for so much this soon into the game.

I let my head flop back into my pillow, and stared at the ceiling above me. And I found myself wishing that I was back with Xander, instead. That I hadn't left, that we had woken up next to one another, that he had rolled over and sleepily hugged me close as we dozed.

That would have been the perfect way to start the day. But it would have been a start to the day that wasn't honest. Because, for every moment that I spent in his bed, I knew that I shouldn't have been letting myself get caught up in what was going on between us, or what wasn't. I would have been allowing myself to sleep in a lie, which felt a little dramatic, but at the same time, the only way that I could describe it.

My eyes started to drift shut. My brain had never been good at processing all this shit at once. There was a reason I didn't get involved in overcomplicated situations like this, and that was because I had no idea how to handle them. I was already getting tired just thinking about it. And I decided that the best course of action for the time being was just to get some rest, and I could deal with it when I woke up. For certain. Well, at least, maybe.

Chapter Twelve – Xander

I hugged Mel at the door, squeezing her tight. This was always the worst part, the part that I hated the most. I never wanted to say goodbye to her, but it wasn't like I had much of a choice.

"I'll see you again soon, baby, okay?" I promised her, and she wound her little arms around me one last time and squeezed me tight.

"See you soon, daddy," she replied, and with that, the door opened, and Talia appeared in front of us.

"Mel," She exclaimed, reaching for her daughter, and Mel stepped over the threshold to join her. I straightened up again, trying to hide the hurt that I was feeling right now. I didn't want Mel to see it, and think that it was her fault that I was struggling in this moment. Because it wasn't. It had everything to do with the choices I had made the night before, and I was still trying to wrap my head around what they meant.

As soon as I got back in the car, I let out a long sigh of what might have been relief and what might have been just sheer panic. Because I had no clue what I was supposed to do now.

When I had woken up this morning and seen Terri missing from the bed beside me, I had known that I'd made a mistake, for sure. Because if I had done something right, then she would have been there waiting for me. We could have talked it out, figured out the details, and then moved on the way that worked best for the both of us. But she had rolled out before I had even woken up, sneaking out under cover of what had to be super early morning, just to avoid that. Not a great sign.

And then, I was having a hard time putting together how I felt about it, too. Because I wanted to do it again, God only knew how much I wanted that, but I wasn't sure how I was meant to go about getting that from her – or if that was even something that she would agree to. It had been in our contract, no mandatory physical contact, and now...and now, we had overstepped those marks by about as far as I could possibly imagine, and I didn't know how we were meant to move forward from there.

She had been an amazing lay. More than amazing. Maybe because I had gone so long without hooking up with anyone, but I felt like she was maybe the best I'd ever had. The chemistry between us, the spontaneity of it, the knowing that this probably went against everything that both of us knew to be a good idea – all of it was building, building, building to make that one of the most intense encounters of my life, and I was already craving her over and over again.

I had to speak to her. There was only one way to thresh this out, and that was talking about it like adults. I might not have been great at this side of things, but Terri could talk for her country and I had to hope that it extended to the way she dealt with this, too. Though, given her fleeing the scene early this morning, I had my doubts.

I knew where she lived, and I figured that dropping by wouldn't be the worst idea. I just had to see her again, clear the air, and make sure that everything was still in place for us. Because if she had changed her mind and wanted out, then I was totally and utterly fucked and didn't know what I would do to fix things. If she backed out now, then I would have to come up with a decent explanation as to why my one-time fiancée was no longer interested in me, and where exactly she had taken off to after we had seemed so happy together.

Heading to her apartment, I hesitated before I buzzed the buzzer that would lead me to her place. She had her surname scrawled on a white strip of paper next to it, along with a little smiley face with a halo over it. I took a deep breath and buzzed. I had to see her. Had to speak to her. This wasn't up for debate.

A few moments later, her voice came crackling down the line.

"Hello?"

"Hey, it's me," I greeted her. "Xander. Can we talk?"

She paused for a moment, and in the silence, I was expecting her to hang up and tell me to go. But instead, thank God, the door clicked open.

"Come on up," she replied, and I headed upstairs to her place, wishing that I had brought something so that I would have been able to do something with my hands.

When I got to her door, she was already waiting there for me, leaning in it and watching me come up the stairs. She had a slightly nervous smile on her face. Better than her greeting me with a face like thunder, I supposed.

"Hey," she greeted me, and she stepped aside and gestured for me to come in. "Sorry the place is a mess, I wasn't really expecting guests."

"Not a problem," I assured her, and I slipped inside her apartment. It was so small that, for a moment, I was sure I must have been missing some of it. It couldn't have been more than a hundred square feet, and it seemed crammed full of everything that she had ever owned or thought about owning; books were stacked high on the counters, paintings were propped up against the walls, and clothes were strewn about at random, some of them on hangers but for the most part just hanging out randomly across the room.

"Like I said, I wasn't expecting guests," she told me, a little sharply, as she noticed me looking around the room and taking in all the mess.

"Sorry, right," I replied, shaking my head. "And I'm sorry to just drop in on you like this. I think we need to...talk."

She let out a sigh, and perched down on the edge of her bed – it seemed to be the only place that there was actually available to sit in this apartment, and so I joined her on the edge of it, distinctly aware of how dangerous it seemed to be this close to her on an actual bed once more.

"I think we need to talk, too," she agreed. "I'm sorry I left without telling you this morning. I just didn't know what to do, and I figured it would be easier for you if I was gone. Especially with Mel still in the house and everything."

"Yeah, I don't know if she would have been able to wrap her head around that," I agreed. "But next time, leave a note, huh?"

"Next time?" She giggled. "That's a little forward, don't you think?"

"I mean, I enjoyed myself," I replied, deciding to roll with it even though that I hadn't intended to make my interest in a repeat performance so clear. "Didn't you?"

"Oh, yeah, I totally did," She agreed, and I noticed that little flush on her neck again – fuck, she could be so cute when she was playing coy. It totally suited her. I liked seeing this other side of her, the one that wasn't quite so confident and ballsy, the one that I got the feeling not everyone in her life got a chance to see.

"Okay, so..." I began, and I had no idea where I was going with the rest of that sentence. I wanted to come out with something definitive, but I had no idea where to begin. I wanted to tell her that I couldn't stop thinking about kissing her again, but I knew that wasn't what I was here for, and I had to keep my head in the game otherwise I was going to lose my mind.

"So, I was thinking about it," she went on. "And I was wondering...well, you know how we're meant to be a couple?"

"I think I recall," I replied, and she grinned at me.

"Yeah, well, I think that we could just...make this a part of the act, you know?"

"What, like take video and post it online?" I asked, surprised. She laughed and shook her head at once.

"No, no, nothing like that," She promised me. "But if we're going to be together, and if we want people to think we're together, then this is only going to make that more authentic, don't you think?"

"A little more authentic?"

"Like, we're not going to be tripping over ourselves to make sure that people don't guess that it's fake if at least some part of it is real," She pointed out. "I know it sounds a little silly, and I know that the contract didn't have that as a term, but I thought that it might...well, I thought that it might make things run a little smoother, you know?"

"Perks of the job, I guess," I conceded, as though this was really taking me any time at all to agree to. I wanted that. I wanted that badly. Worse than I had thought I actually could. I needed to feel her again, needed to fuck her again, needed to take her again just like I had done before, and nothing was going to satisfy me until she did. And there wasn't much anything in the world that I wanted more than to hear her say that she wanted just the same thing.

"Perks of the job," she echoed, and she bit her lip and just looked at me for a long moment. I knew what she was thinking. I knew, because it was just the same thing that was running through my mind, too, and I could see it written all over her pretty little face.

"Just until you get the custody agreement in place," she added. "Like we agreed. The contract, when that expires..."

I kissed her, then, because there was nothing else to do but kiss her. She smiled into the kiss, letting me take the lead this time, happily, as though this was what she wanted more than anything in the world, and as soon as our lips met I knew that this was all that either of us had needed. My tongue slipped past her lips, and I pushed her down on to the bed, rolling on top of her so that I could feel her body beneath mine, her skin against mine. It felt like it had been an age since we had last been together like this, even though it had barely been twelve hours. How could I miss someone's body so much, when I had only just gotten to know it? It didn't make sense to me. But, at the same time, I knew that this craving was something that already ran deep inside of me and that I wasn't going to be able to stop myself wanting more, taking more.

Moving my hands down her body, I easily slipped off the loose pajama pants that she had been wearing when I had walked through the door; she kicked them to the ground, to get lost in the other clothes that were kicking about down there, and I slipped my fingers between her legs to feel her wetness once more. There was something unarguably sexy about knowing that she was so hot and ready for me, and I was already addicted to the sweetness of her slickness beneath my fingers.

"Go down on me?" She breathed in my ear, phrased as a question – as though there was going to be any other answer for her than *yes, any time you fucking want.* I planted one last kiss on her lips and began to work my way down, over her breasts, rolling up her shirt so that I could kiss her belly and along the line of her panties. They were black and edged with pink and looked so gorgeous against the paleness of her skin; I couldn't take my eyes off of them. But that just seemed to be the effect she had on me no matter what she was wearing. I was always drawn back for more.

I slowly eased her panties off her hips and brushed my mouth over the bareness of her mound. She smelled so good, her wetness coming off her in waves, and I was already craving that lusty sensation of having her deep in my mouth – it had been so long since I had gone down on someone that I couldn't help but worry a little that I was going to do something wrong, but she placed her hand on the back of my head and guided me towards her and I knew that she didn't care what I did wrong or right. She just needed me to give her the relief that she wanted so badly, and who was I to deny her that?

Slowly, I lowered my tongue to her pussy, swirling it around the engorged nub of her clit and guiding it into my mouth for the first time. I could feel her whole body trembling and shaking as I tasted her like this – she was musky and sweet and so tempting that I could hardly handle it, so tasty that I didn't have any self-control as I moved to eat her out for the very first time.

I slipped my hands beneath her ass and tugged her towards me, so that I could fill my mouth greedily with her all at once. She groaned loudly and her fingers dug into the back of my scalp, and I began to eat her like I was a man starved.

She tasted so fucking good. That was what I couldn't get over. I had gone down on women before, of course I had, but there was something about Terri that was different – something about the way she reacted and the way she moved and the way she pressed her hips up to meet my face that made it even more intense. I felt like nothing existed outside of this. And to think, I had doubted the thought that she might want to do this again – looking back, it seemed crazy that either of us would pass up this chance once more.

"Fuck, that feels good," she moaned, as I trailed my tongue down to her slit and gently pushed it inside of her before I moved back up to swirl it around her clit once more. She seemed to respond best to the lightest pressure, and I watched her and took in her reactions as best I could so that I could give her everything that she seemed to need in that moment.

I moaned softly against her pussy and she shuddered like the sound of it had travelled all the way up and through her entire system. That was what I wanted from her – I wanted her to show me how much she wanted me. I needed to know that this wasn't just one-sided. I had to take in the truth that she desired this as badly as I did, and that neither of us could have stopped even if we wanted to.

She was soon grinding herself back against me, hopelessly out of control, as I went down on her. I could tell that she was getting close, and I wanted to feel her come, wanted to feel it with my mouth so I knew that it was real. She didn't strike me as the kind of woman who would have felt compelled to fake it out of politeness, so I knew that if I got this out of her, it would be because she meant it. I heard a rush of noise from above me, felt her muscles clench around my head, and then, moments later, and felt her reach her release at last.

When she cried out in pleasure, it was so loud that I was sure her neighbors would come running up to make sure what the trouble was all about. I held on to her tight, her whole body practically vibrating with energy as the orgasm rushed through her, and she continued to move against me like she was squeezing the last vestiges of pleasure out of this while she still could. As though I wouldn't have stayed there all day long if she had asked me to.

Slowly, I peeled my head back and looked back up at her; she moved down towards me at once and planted a kiss on my lips, the taste of her and her pussy and everything else mingling on my mouth for a moment, impossibly erotic, impossibly her.

"That was amazing," she murmured to me, and I noticed that she was still shaking helplessly above me. I grinned. I must have done a damn good job to have her still reacting the way that she was.

"If you need a second," I remarked to her, and she shook her head.

"You're not getting away with it that easily, mister," She replied, and she kissed me again – and I knew that we had made the right choice. This was only going to make things more authentic, like she said. And that could only be a good thing. Right?

Chapter Thirteen – Terri

"Hey, Mel!" I called to the little girl, who was out in the garden kicking a ball around, even though it was getting icy-cold outside. She looked up and beamed when she saw me, and I couldn't help but smile right back. There was something about knowing that a little kid was so looking forward to seeing you that made everything a little better. And seeing Mel was always one of the highlights of my week.

I had fallen into a comfortable routine, lately, since Xander and I had updated the terms of our agreement. I would come to his place every weekend, sleep over, and spend time with him and Mel; it was a strange set-up, but it worked, and it meant that I got some guaranteed Xander-time every single week.

It was funny, actually, because if we hadn't met the way that we had, he had made it pretty clear that he would have never had time to date me in the first place.

"What with work and everything," he had pointed out. "I just don't have the space in my schedule for something like this. I might have liked you a lot, but I haven't been with anyone in such a long time, and it would have just seemed like too much of a leap for me to get into it out of nowhere like that."

"Good thing you hired me to date you instead," I teased him, as I lay propped up on his chest in our bed – no, his bed, I had to remind myself of that. Sometimes, it was all too easy to forget that this space still belonged to him and his daughter, because I spent so much time around them that I found myself slotting into it far too easily for my liking.

"Good thing," he replied, and he leaned down to plant a kiss on the top of my head. I closed my eyes and snuggled closer to him, and tried not to think about what would happen when the contract was over and done with.

I supposed the good thing about it was that there was no specific end point in mind. It would be in place as long as it took him to get the custody agreement, and then it would be dissolved pretty much right away and we could both move on. Not that I was in any great rush for that, of course, but I didn't want to think about that much of the future right now. The present was far too much fun for my liking, and I didn't want anything to get in the way of that.

"Are you sure that you're giving yourself the time away from him you need?" Marjorie had asked, once she had noticed the spring in my step and had deduced that it had come from the back that I was getting good dick for once in my life.

"Of course I am," I replied at once. "We only see each other on the weekends, so we hardly spend any time together, not in the grand scheme of things."

"But when you're not together," she went on. "You're giving yourself space, right? You're not thinking about him all the time. Or what you're going to do when the two of you get together again."

"Of course not," I lied swiftly, and I put down the top that I had been thinking of buying for when I saw him again that weekend. I didn't like that Marjorie seemed to be able to read my mind like that sometimes, and I would had much preferred it if she could just keep to being amused by the whole thing instead of so damn concerned about it.

Maybe because her concern was striking a little too close to home for my liking. Maybe because I knew she had something like a point. It wasn't just the physical time that we were spending in each other's company that mattered, it was all the time that I was dedicating to him outside of that. Texting him, flirting with him, sneaking off at the store so I could snap a sexy selfie that I could send to him just to keep him all excited for what was to come that weekend. He was constantly on my mind, filling my brain, and I knew that it probably wasn't a good thing. In the long-term, at least.

But that had always been my problem, hadn't it? I would get caught up in the here and now, in what I thought could make my life better right in that instant, and then it would turn around and blow up on me when I least expected it somewhere down the line. Most of the time, it was just that investing my money in a scheme wouldn't work out, but this time...this time, I was investing more than money. I was investing my time, my energy, my emotion. And I knew that was going to be a hell of a lot harder to get back when the time came for me to take it away.

Not that I was in any great rush to do that. Because this was the most grounded and comfortable I had ever felt in a relationship before in my life. Maybe because everything that we had agreed on together was so blatant and easy for me to look back on. There would be no second-guessing because we had left no room for it at all; we had been honest and open and we had gotten this clearness back in return. Maybe every relationship should have started that way. Would have made things a lot more obvious...

But then, there was a good reason that people didn't do this. Because it turned romance and love into something that could be quantified, and I understood why so few people actually wanted that to be their lives. It was a little unsettling, thinking that everything that we had together was tied up in a few pieces of paper that could end things at any time if we reached the terms of our agreement.

Still. At least I was going to be able to get a payout from this break-up. That was something, wasn't it? Not many people got to say that. When things went wrong, for the most part, the best you would get would be a pat on the head and an apology and then all your emotions to deal with in the aftermath. I would get enough money to live on for at least a year, and I was still looking forward to that part of it coming through.

But I was going to miss them. And it wasn't like I could stay in their lives. When people saw the break-up that we were going to stage, which was going to have to be dramatic and over-the-top to sell it to anyone who had been paying attention to us, they would never believe that we could ever be part of each other's lives again.

Which meant no Mel. It meant to weekends at Xander's place, waking up in his bed next to him. No more breakfasts that he would cook for me, so that when I came downstairs there was already something there waiting for me to eat. No Xander. No Xander – that was going to be the hardest part of all of this, I could tell...

But I couldn't think about that. I had always been the girl who was focused on the time being, and that would serve me well right now. I needed to forget about my problems for a while and just enjoy what I had right in front of me for as long as it lasted. I didn't know how long that would be, how many months or days or weeks or hours, but that didn't mean that I couldn't invest myself in it now.

This particular day, I had a gift for Mel. The two of us had bonded over playing soccer, and we loved watching the highlight programs on a Sunday morning together. She really knew her stuff, and I could already imagine her playing it professionally; the look she got in her eyes when she was watching these men play, it was determination, as though she was out to prove that she could do it just as well as any of them ever could.

We kicked a ball around occasionally, thought my skills were more than a little rusty by now; she was always patient with me, even though she would score so many goals against me and make me look like a total fool.

The gift for Mel was a shirt that I had spotted in a thrift store when I had been trawling for some new clothes to spice up my wardrobe. The bright red of it caught my eye, and I turned back around to see what it was. A strip, a soccer strip, for Manchester United, one of her favorite teams. She would always keenly point them out to me when they were playing on the screen, and even though I didn't know a huge amount about the players or the team set-up, I knew that this would be a perfect present for her. It was huge, but I didn't think that mattered – the fact that it was an actual strip from a team she actually liked would make up for it, right?

And so, I stood there in the doorway to the kitchen, the one that I had snuck out of that very first morning. It was strange to think that there had been a time when I had wanted to get away from this place when, now, I couldn't imagine wanting to leave at all. When I had to go back to my real life when the weekends were over, I would find myself wishing the week away so I could come back.

Mel came up to me, panting slightly, cheeks pink from the cold and the exertion, and I reached into my bag and pulled out the gift for her. I couldn't wait any longer.

"I got this for you," I told her, a little nervously. I hoped she didn't think this was an overstep or anything. Hoped she actually liked the gift that I had brought her. But as soon as she saw what I was holding out in her direction, her face lit up, and she dropped the ball and sent it scattering away as she dived towards me to grab the shirt from me.

"Oh my goodness!" She exclaimed, and she hugged it close to her for a moment, closing her eyes as though she was just taking it in. "Is this a real strip?"

"I think so," I replied, and she flipped it over in her hands to check the back.

"And it's for Rashford!" She went on, so excited that it seemed as though she could hardly contain herself. Rashford – that was a name I recognized. She liked him, I was sure of it. I hadn't even though to check that.

Inside, Xander was cooking dinner for the three of us, but before he could grab the spices down from the rack, Mel had come racing in to show him what she had just been given.

"Look, Dad!" She called to him, and she held up the strip that was so comically big compared to her I wouldn't be surprised if she used it as a nightshirt.

"Oh, wow," Xander remarked, as he turned his attention to the shirt and then glanced to me. I hadn't told him that I was bringing this for her, and I hoped he didn't mind. But, a moment later, his face broke out into this huge smile, and I knew that he didn't have an inch of a problem with it.

"I'm going to go put it on right now!" Mel exclaimed, and with that, she bolted out of the room to put on her strip for the first time. I watched her for a moment, a smile on my face, and he raised his eyebrows at me.

"You know you didn't have to get her anything," He remarked, and I nodded.

"I know," I replied. "But I saw that and it just seemed too perfect a gift for me to pass up, you know?"

"Something for her to remember you by," he added, and my heart sank. He was right. This would be all that remained of me in her life when I was gone. It was a strange, discomforting though, but something that I supposed that I was going to have to come to terms with at some time or another. I was going to be out of her life, and all she would have of me would be a few months of memories and that damn shirt.

She returned a moment later, and I couldn't help but burst out laughing when I set eyes on her. She was wearing the shirt, and it was so big that it looked like it was trying to engulf her whole, almost down to her knees as she stood there proudly in front of us.

"Do you like it?" I asked her, and she nodded delightedly.

"I love it," she exclaimed, and she twirled around in front of us, the shirt spreading out around her like it was the hem of a ball gown. I glanced over at Xander, and noticed that he had this big smile on his face, a slightly dreamy look in his eyes, as though he was imagining what it might have been like to do this day in and day out.

The rest of the weekend was seriously busy; Mel had a soccer tournament on, and Xander insisted that I come along to them with it, telling me that Mel would be looking for me in the crowd and that she would have been so down if she hadn't been able to see me there.

"You know you're just guilt-tripping me, right?" I remarked to him, and he held his hands up and shrugged.

"Hey, you're the one who's going to be letting her down if you don't turn up," he replied, and I smacked his arm playfully. He knew that I couldn't say no to that little girl. As far as I was concerned, she was about the most precious thing in the world, and I was going to do anything that I could to make sure that she knew that I felt that way about her.

Mel's team came in second place, and we took her out for ice-cream to celebrate her almost-victory. She was wearing the shirt that I gave her as we munched down on our cones, and I tried not to let the big, goofy grin that wanted to overtake me too obvious on my face.

Xander and I slept next to each other that evening, but he didn't try anything – as though he was more than happy just being close to me like this. I snuggled against him, his arms wrapped tight around me, and thanked whoever was up there watching over me that I had been given the best job in the history of the world.

When I woke up the next day, Mel got me outside to play some soccer with her first thing in the morning, while Xander cooked us up some breakfast; I was ravenous by the time that I came in to eat, and Xander was more than happy to serve us up a generous helping of toast and eggs and beans.

"You girls earned it," he told us, and he dropped a kiss on Mel's head, and then on mine – something about the little gesture of sweetness made my heart feel like it was going to come swelling and bursting out of my chest, and I tilted my head to plant a proper kiss on his lips. He gave me one at once, and Mel squealed in faux-disgust as soon as our lips touched.

Before long, though, it was the end of Sunday, and I had to go back home to the real world and to my real life, even though I wanted nothing more than to stay with them a little longer. Xander kissed me goodbye at the door, and I lingered a little longer than I had to, wishing that he would invite me to stay another night.

"I'll see you next weekend, alright?" I told him, and he nodded.

"Next weekend," he echoed, and for a moment, it looked like his brain had gone the same place that mind had – that he was thinking about asking me to stay a little longer. But instead, he smiled once more, and nudged me in the direction of my car so I could get home without hitting the bad stack of traffic.

And with that, it was over. Another weekend gone. Another step closer to the end of this thing for good. I knew that I shouldn't have been thinking of it in those terms, but still – hard not to. Every time I left them, it was a reminder that sooner rather than later, I was going to have to do it for real. And something in me rejected the very notion of that, right down to its bones, and that was when I realized that I had started to fall for him.

For Xander. God, as I sat there in the car and tried to wrap my head around it, I felt a little stupid. How could I think that playing house with a man like him would have ended in anything other than disaster? He was everything that I could have wanted from someone I was dating – smart, funny, charming, clever, accomplished, compassionate...the list just went on and on, and I had only started putting the pieces together. Sleeping with him, letting him be physically close to me, it was just asking for a while heap more trouble than I had been ready to take on.

But it was more than just him. More than just the way he kissed me on the top of my head when he was passing as though it was normal for him to do that, more than the way he held me close when we slept next to one another. It was her, too – it was Mel. Spending time with her had made it clearer than ever to me that I could handle being a part of a family, no matter how much I might have liked to convince myself that I didn't have it in me before. I looked at Marjorie and Steph and told myself that what they had, I would never be suitable for, but the more time that passed, the more attached I got to that little girl, the more I found myself wondering – well, just maybe, maybe I could actually do it.

But Xander had me sign that contract. He had me on lockdown that I wasn't going to go looking for anything more than he had offered me. Hell, when he had come around to my place after we'd first hooked up, we had agreed on it then, too. That this was just a ploy to make the contract stick a little faster. And I had really been stupid enough to believe that I could make that work.

Jesus. By the time that I got back to my place, I had so squarely beaten myself up inside my head that I could hardly think straight. I had really just let this happen. I had really believed that I could walk out of this without anything to show for it but some more cash in my pocket than I'd had to start with. I should have been able to see it before then, before it got to this point – should have been able to stop myself before I had fallen so fast and so hard and so hopelessly for this man.

This man who would rather have me sign a contract than actually get involved with anyone for real. Xander wasn't the kind to let people into his life so easily; hell, he would never have met me in the first place if it hadn't been for the chaos with his custody agreement and his ex-wife. That was the kind of man I was dealing with here, that was the kind of man that I had fallen for.

I couldn't help but think back to what Marjorie had told me when I had first gotten started on all of this. She had been able to see that it was clearly a bad idea, that I was obviously walking into a bear trap that was about to snap shut around my ankles and leave me stuck there on the spot. But I had been too cocky to listen to her, and now I was paying the price, paying every cent of it because I couldn't stop thinking about him, or thinking about the life that we might have had together. I wanted it all. I wanted it now...

And yet, I had managed to back myself into a corner where all of that would be nigh-on impossible.

When I slumped on to my couch that evening, I looked up at the ceiling and promised that I wasn't going to let this go any further. I had the contract to fulfil, sure, but that was where it ended. Nothing more, nothing less. I had to keep myself safe, first and foremost – and the way I was feeling about Xander right then and there was anything but safe for me right now.

Chapter Fourteen – Xander

Tap. Tap. Tap.

The sound of my pen on the desk in front of me was driving me crazy. I knew that I could have just stopped, but I felt like I was going to start shooting steam out of my ears if I did that, all the excess energy pulsing through me threatening to set off the fire alarm above me.

It was Wednesday now, and I had been feeling the same way since Monday morning – it seemed as though as soon as I hit that twelve-hour mark without Terri, every bone in my body starting craving her presence once again.

It had been hard to focus on my work since I had seen her off at the door on Sunday evening. It had been a particularly good weekend that we had spent together, and I was sure she noticed it too – saying goodbye to her was harder than normal, and the house felt empty and quiet that evening without her in it.

"Maybe she could stay longer next time?" Mel had suggested, apparently noticing how down-and-out I was doing after she had left.

"Maybe," I agreed, but I knew that I was walking a fine line as it was; we were already spending a lot of time together, and at any moment the custody agreement could come through in my favor and then she would have filled out her side of the contract. And, as soon as she had done that, I got the feeling that she would be on the move again. Terri had never much struck me as the girl who let herself get tied down too much, let alone a guy with a job and a house and a kid to think about. She was out there living her life, and we just happened to be a part of it for the time being. Soon enough, she would get tired of keeping us around, if she hadn't already gotten there by now, and would be counting down the days until she could make her exit from whatever it was that we had going on.

Still. I missed her. A lot. More than I should have. Maybe it was a natural reaction to not having someone by my side for such a long time – I had had to deal with all of this alone for so long, that having Terri around to take some of the weight off made things easier, and I had likely just become attached to that aspect of the easiness. That's what I could keep telling myself, at least. Maybe I would even start to believe it one of these days.

Fuck it. I had missed her enough this week, and I wanted to do something about it. I told my secretary that I was going on, hopped in the car, and hoped that I hadn't forgotten about any big meetings the rest of the day. Because I had something that I needed to do, and I wasn't going to be able to focus on reality again until I had taken care of it.

I arrived at her apartment building, remembering all at once that she actually had another job that she could well have been at right now. But, thank God, as soon as I buzzed on her door, her voice came crackling down the line.

"Hello?"

"Hey, Terri?" I greeted her. "Can I come up? I want to see you."

"Of course," she replied, and she sounded a little surprised; moments later, the door clicked open, and I headed up the stairs to see her once more. I felt like I could sense the blood whooshing around my body with every step. By the time that I got there, she was already waiting with the door open, looking a little surprised; she was dressed in a light pair of pajamas, tiny shorts and a wife beater, her long, slender legs on show for the world to see. My eyes traced up and down her body, taking every inch of her in.

"Is everything okay?" She asked, but I could tell that she knew just what I was there for before I so much as opened my mouth. I moved towards her, and slipped an arm around her waist, pulling her towards me like I was a man starved of touch. She giggled and planted her hands on my chest, and gazed up at me.

"I'll take that as a yes," she replied, just moments before I sealed my mouth over hers and kissed her for the first time in what felt like way too long.

She sank against me as though this was what she had been waiting for from the moment she had heard my voice, and I managed to convince myself that she had missed me as much as I had missed her. Maybe I was just deluding myself, but it was a pleasant delusion, that was for sure. She traced her fingers over my neck and my collarbone, the stiff fabric of my shirt.

"Let's get this off, huh?" She murmured to me, as I kicked the door shut behind us and kissed her properly, deeply, letting my tongue traverse every inch of her mouth like I couldn't get enough. It was the strangest thing, wanting her this badly, feeling as though I was out of control with that need; it had been a long time since I had allowed my instincts to rule me in this way, but when it came to her, it was like I had no choice. I was totally hypnotized by her, couldn't get enough of her, even when I knew there were better things that I should have been doing with my time.

Moments later, the two of us had toppled back on to her bed, and she had rolled on top of me and started undoing the buttons of my shirt. I slid my hands over her bare legs, sinking my fingers into her thighs, looking at the way goose pimples erupted on her skin wherever I touched her.

"Mmm," she moaned softly, squirming a little on top of me, knowing full well that she was grinding right against my cock. "I've been thinking about this all week."

"Me too," I replied, and, once she had pulled my shirt off, I sat up and kissed her again. I couldn't get enough. She wound her arms around me, letting her nails dig into my bare skin, and kissed me right back.

"We need to make the most of the weekends," She murmured against my ear. "So I don't have to drag you out of work for this..."

"I consider this my priority right now," I replied, and I flipped her over on to her back. She squealed with delight as I moved down her body, pressing kisses to her soft belly, her hips, pushing up her shirt to expose her pert breasts. As I whipped off her panties and her shorts, I took each one of her nipples into my mouth in turn, baring my teeth to feel them swell under my touch.

Soon enough, I had her naked – at least as naked as I was going to need her for what came next. She rolled over to grab a condom and pressed it into my hand, and I pulled down my pants just far enough to sheath myself. She wrapped her legs behind my back and pulled me towards her eagerly, and soon enough, I was pushing inside her for the first time.

And fuck, did it feel like a relief. I could hardly hold myself back. It felt like I had been waiting for this for so long that I couldn't believe it was actually happening right now. All week, I had been fizzing with need for her, overflowing with the desires that pulsed through my head and demanded every inch of my attention. But now that I had her...*fuck*.

"You feel so big right now," she gasped, as she tipped her hips back to allow me to plunge into her a little deeper, a little harder.

I could only kiss her in return; I didn't have the clarity of words right now, just the passion of what was physically happening between us in that moment. Did she know what she was doing to me? Did she know how good it felt to be inside her? Did she know how much I had missed her, body and soul, every inch? I wished there was some way for to convey that all at once, but words failed me, so I kissed her and kissed her and kissed her and hoped that it would be enough.

She arched her back and hung on to me for dear life, her nails raking marks in my back that I knew would glow red even through the fabric of my shirt. I didn't care. I wanted everyone to know that we had been together like this. No, more than that, I needed everyone to know – I needed them to see that this woman wanted me as badly as I wanted her, the reminder that there were parts of this, at least, that were as real as they had even been. My head against her shoulder, my face against the crook of her neck, I took her hard and fast and passionately, filling her up with every thrust.

"Oh my God, yes," she groaned, and I could tell that she was getting close. Just the way I wanted her. I slowed down a little, teasing her, pushing her to that point where I knew she wouldn't be able to take any more. She was grinding against me helplessly, rolling her hips back against mine so that she could take me as deep as she could, greedy for me, for the pleasure that I could give her.

"You close?" I asked her, finally finding my ability to speak again. She nodded, her face creased with the nearness, with how close she was to going over the edge. I picked up the pace again, and sure enough, I watched as she flooded with the relief that she had been craving for so long, her body shivering and trembling in mine as she came. The sight of her going over the edge was all that I needed to get me there, too, and soon enough I was filling the condom with my seed, unable to stop the release getting the better of me.

I held her tight as we both came back down to the real world, and by the time that I drew out of her, she had a huge smile on her face.

"You need to skip out of work and see me more often," she told me, that smile spreading till it looked like it was going to reach her ears.

"Tempting," I replied, as I went to dispose of the condom. "But I wouldn't want to get in the way of your busy schedule."

"Yeah, you can tell that I am wall-to-wall stacked right now," she replied, gesturing around her quit apartment. Now that we were finished, it was so peaceful and calm in there that I could have just flopped down next to her and gone to sleep. Well, if I hadn't known that they were expecting me back at the office sooner rather than later.

"Sorry to bother you in the middle of the week," I apologized, and she shook her head.

"No, not at all," she assured me. "It was...it was fun. I've been thinking a lot about you, and then you just turn up out of nowhere, and it felt right, you know?"

"I think I do," I replied, and I zipped up my pants and sat on the edge of the bed. She reached up for me, lazily tracing her hand over my bare back, and I closed my eyes and enjoyed the warmth of her touch. She was so gentle with me. It had been a long time since someone had been truly gentle with me, and God only knew how much I needed it.

"I've been thinking about you a lot, too," I admitted, and I glanced over to look at her, to read her reaction to what I was saying.

"Really?" She replied, and she seemed more than a little surprised by the revelation. I nodded.

"I know that I shouldn't be," I confessed. I hadn't even thought these words through before they had started falling from my mouth, but I knew that she had to hear them – I knew I had to speak them into being, or else they were going to get caught up inside me and then I was going to have to try to move on without her, and I wasn't sure that I could cope with that.

"But I miss you when you're not here," I went on. "And I miss the way you are with Mel. I know she misses you when you're not there, too, though I don't think she would ever want to admit it. And I know we agreed on this, I know we agreed that we wouldn't take things any further, but I..."

I trailed off. I didn't know what I was saying. I did know, however, that she was just sitting there in complete and utter silence, frozen to the spot, as though if she moved then it might shatter the moment around her and bring all of this crashing down on her head.

"Terri?" I asked her, and I took her hand and squeezed it lightly. "Terri, do you hear me right now?"

"I hear you," she finally replied, though it seemed to take all the effort she had in her to get those words out to me. She looked up at me, and her eyes were burning with confusion.

"I think I'm falling for you, Terri," I confessed. I meant it. Surprised myself with how much I meant it, actually. When I had been around Mel, too, I had been able to convince myself that it was just the family time that I was craving. But when I was around Terri, there was no denying the truth. It was her. It had always been her. There had been a reason I had pulled that ad as soon as I had met her, and that was because I knew that nobody would even come close to giving me what I needed, not the way that she could. It might have seemed crazy, but I could tell, even then, that there was some part of her meant for me, some part of me meant for her.

Her eyes were fixed on mine, like she was waiting for me to take it all back and tell her that I was joking. But I didn't. I couldn't. Because I wasn't. I meant every single word of it. I would have said it all over again if she didn't believe me, but I knew that she did. She had known me long enough now to be able to tell when I was making things up and when I was telling her the truth, and this was the truth, loud and clear, every single word of it.

"I think..." She finally breathed, the words catching in her throat as she struggled to get them out. "I think you should leave."

"What?" I asked, and she got to her feet, pulling the blankets around her protectively.

"I think you should leave," she repeated, and this time there was less room in her voice for a debate. I couldn't believe what I was hearing. Was she really going to kick me out when I had just spilled my guts to her? I thought about protesting, but no – that was only going to serve to make things worse, I was sure of that. I was going to have to respect what she asked for. And hope that she came to her senses soon enough, and was able to give me an answer.

"Of course," I replied, and I reached for my shirt and turned my back to her while I buttoned it up. I could hear her breathing hard behind me, and I felt a little guilty for putting her in the position where she had to come up with an answer for me so quickly. I had really come out of the blue with this, and she deserved a little more time to put the pieces together, I was sure of that.

By the time that I had buttoned my shirt, I was feeling a little more grounded, a little more back in my body.

"I'll see you this weekend?" I asked her, managing to keep my voice somewhat steady as I stood there in front of her and waited for a response. Her gaze lifted to meet mine, and, finally, it seemed as though she had acknowledged that I was right there in the room with her.

"Hmm?" She murmured, sounding a little surprised, as though I was the last person she expected me to be talking to.

"This weekend," I repeated to her. "We're still on, aren't we?"

"Yes, yes, we're still on," She promised me. For a moment, I forgot about her silence, forgot that she hadn't given me an answer yet. I wanted to go back to her and just lie with her again, let the two of us just enjoy each other's company once more and forget that there was so much unspoken between us right now.

"Good," I replied, bringing myself back to reality. Because that had happened. And she had asked me to go. And I was sure as hell going to respect that, because I didn't want anything to get in the way of her accepting my spontaneous expression of – well, whatever it was I had expressed.

I went for the door, pausing for one last split-second to give her the chance to change her mind and tell me how she felt, but she didn't move a muscle and I wasn't going to go pushing for something that I knew I wasn't going to get. First rule of business was to know and accept when you were out of the game, and right now, I needed to cut my losses and leave.

I headed down to the street outside, and, as soon as the cool air hit me, I wondered what the hell I had been thinking with all of that. I had really just spewed all my feelings to her, out of nowhere. No wonder she had been so silent in response to what I had told her. If someone had just dumped that on me – shit, I wasn't sure that I ever would have been able to speak again. But there was something about the way she had looked at me, something about the way she had welcomed me as though she had been waiting for this as long as she could remember, something that drew those words out of me helplessly. I couldn't stop spilling my feelings to her. I adored her. I was falling for her. She was beautiful and intelligent and she made me happy in ways that I honestly didn't know were possible after my marriage had bitten the dust. I had thought that I would be settling for just myself, at least until Mel was all grown up, but she had shown me that I could have a dating life, have my daughter, have it all – even if this was all built on a lie.

That was a heavy thought. All of this, built on that contract – all of this, built from the knowledge that we were exchanging goods and services for what we both needed. She was playing the role so well that I had started to believe that I really did love her, and yet she hadn't been able to say it back to me. It was clear that she didn't feel the same way – or at least that she didn't have the confidence in those feelings to tell me if she did or if she didn't.

I came to a halt right outside her apartment building, needing a second to catch my breath and work out what the hell was going on in my head right now. Why had I dumped all that on her without thinking twice? I should have thought it through, at least a little, worked out how to make it sound more genuine than a post-fuck revelation. She would probably think that it was just about the sex, when I knew it was far more than that.

Suddenly, I felt a pair of eyes on me – I glanced around, wondering if Terri had come to check that I had actually left her apartment building instead of hanging around outside like I was currently doing, but she wasn't anywhere to be seen.

Instead, I tracked the sensation from a car across the road – I couldn't make out who was inside, but it was the only one parked on the block, and it seemed out-of-place on a street like this. And I was certain that whoever was watching me was on the inside of that car. I squinted to see if I could get a better look at whoever was observing me, but nope, no luck. The windows were catching the light in such a way as to obscure whoever might have been in there. I gave up and looked away. Maybe someone had heard that I had managed to fuck up this thing beyond all repair, and had come to look at the train wreck that I had left behind me. That would have made more sense.

I trudged away from the house and tried not to think about what I had just managed to fuck up. I could make this better, couldn't I? I still hadn't heard an answer from her, after all, so that meant that all was not lost. For now, at least, that was what I was going to keep telling myself. Because it was the only thing that was going to keep me sane.

Chapter Fifteen – Terri

"Honey, what's wrong?"

As soon as I heard Marjorie asking for me, I disintegrated. I couldn't keep it in any longer. I felt like I had been fighting too hard for too long, and now everything was falling apart around me and there was nothing I could do to stop it. I managed to get through the door of the store and close it behind me, but as soon as I heard it swing shut, the tears started to fall.

"Oh my God," Stephanie hurried towards me, putting an arm around me as though she half-expected me to just collapse on to the ground right there and then. Honestly, it wouldn't have surprised me. I felt like my feet were going to slide through the ground and into the Earth below, that I was going to be swallowed up whole by all of this.

It had been the same ever since I had asked him to leave my apartment. I couldn't believe that all of this was happening. He had confessed real feelings for me, and I had just kicked him out because – well, because the thought of sharing mine back was too terrifying to think about. And I knew that I had blown it now, that any chance I might have had to put these pieces back together was over and done with and that I was going to have to live with the pieces of this mess that I had made.

I loved him. God, I loved him, and there was nothing I could do to deny that any longer. So why hadn't I been able to say it back to him? If I had truly loved him the way that I thought I did, then I would have been able to look him in the eye and tell him the truth of my feelings for him. But I had doubted myself too much, hidden from what was really going on in my head, and now it was all ruined.

"What happened?" Marjorie asked me, as I leaned up against the counter for support. I could hear the concern coming off her in waves and felt great guilt for making them worry about me like this, but I couldn't help it. I couldn't keep it in. I needed to talk to someone about this.

"I think I'm in love with Xander," I confessed. Stephanie actually gasped beside me.

"You think you're in love with him?" She repeated, and I finally managed to look up at the two of them and talk to them properly. I had come rolling in here, all drama, the least they deserved was an actual explanation.

"I...I think so," I admitted, wiping away some of the tears that had started to fall over my face. "I just can't stop thinking about him. And I was spending the weekend with him and his daughter, and then when I had to leave, it just...hit me. I think I love him. I think I want to be with him properly."

"Oh my God," Marjorie muttered. She had told me that something bad was going to come of this and she had been right; I just had to hope that she was still willing to help me out even though I had been such an idiot about all of it. So convinced that I could handle this and that I wasn't going to be the girl who fell for the guy who was paying her to stick around.

"And then, yesterday, he came to my apartment," I went on. "And we...we had sex and he told me that he had real feelings for me. And I..."

They both sat there in silence, waiting for me to deliver the death blow.

"And I told him to leave," I finished up, and I felt a flood of tears come once more.

"Oh, Terri," Marjorie sighed, and she wrapped her arms around me tight, always the mom-friend who was willing to do anything to make it better.

"Wait, what?" Stephanie cut in. "You told him to leave? Why?"

"I don't know," I confessed. "I just didn't...I didn't feel like I could believe him, I guess. I mean, I wanted to, I still want to, but he was paying me to be there in the first place. It's all messed up and tied up with that and I don't think I'm ever going to be able to let go of it."

"So you didn't even give it a chance?" Stephanie replied, incredulous. I looked up at her and shook my head.

"I don't think I can," I admitted. "It's not just him I'm taking on if I get with him, remember. It's his daughter. And his ex. And...And, shit, all that stuff that comes with them. I don't think I'm ready to handle all of that yet, you know?"

"You made the right choice," Marjorie soothed me gently. "You can't just jump in to something like that, you need time to think. And of course it's going to be a lot to take in, you've only just found out that he feels the same way."

"I just don't know what I'm going to do," I admitted. "I need the money, still, but if I take it then I'm going to have to accept that this is just a job for us."

"Shit, that's tough," Stephanie remarked, and Marjorie let go of me so that I could grab a tissue from the box on the counter, the ones that were usually kept for dusting off the displays when they had been sitting out for a while. I blew my nose, dabbed at my eyes, and tried to gather myself. I didn't normally do big displays of emotion, and there was a good reason for that – I always felt like I was overstating things, making a fool of myself in some way that I would never be able to make right again. But these guys were my best friends, and if anyone was going to be able to help me through this without losing my mind, then it would be them.

"What do I do?" I asked them both, despairingly. I knew that they couldn't just give me a straight answer, but I needed some advice, something that would help me take the edge off the rush of questions that were pulsing around my brain and had been since he had left my apartment the day before.

"You know we can't just tell you what you should do," Marjorie reminded me gently. "You need to figure that out on your own terms."

"I know, I know," I replied, and I managed a smile. "But you know how I am. I'm not always the most sensible. I could use...I don't know, I could use a little good sense up in here, you know?"

"I think we can manage a little of that," Stephanie agreed, and she squeezed my hand gently. "What do you need from us right now, Terri?"

"Should I go after something with him?" I asked her, and I glanced over at Marjorie, too. These were the women I respected above all else, truly and honestly. Whatever they told me to do, I would have taken it as gospel, and I was quite sure that they both knew that. So they stayed quiet for a long time, as they thought through the answer to my question.

"How do you feel about him right now?" Marjorie asked, and I shrugged and shook my head.

"I know that I miss him," I confessed. "I miss being around him. We've only spent a few weekends together, but we get on so well, and I really like being around his daughter, too – I feel like I've really gotten to know the both of them..."

"But you've only done a few weekends with them?" Stephanie cut in. I nodded.

"So I guess I really don't," I admitted. "And I know that I should wait and see, but the contract could be over any day now, and when that happens there's going to be no reason for him to keep me in my life."

"But he said he had real feelings for you," Marjorie pointed out. I shook my head.

"But it was right after we had just hooked up," I reminded her. "I'm not sure it didn't just come from that. And he's been single for such a long time, I guess he's just slipping back into the old routines that he had when he was last dating someone..."

"And then you've got the little girl to think of," Marjorie added. As a momma-bear herself, I knew that this would have particular power over her, and I respected her opinion on it above anything else.

"Exactly," I confessed. "And I don't want to make her life more complicated. This was all about making things more secure and stable for her in the long run, and me getting actually involved with her dad after lying about it is just going to throw a wrench into things all over again."

"Fuck," Marjorie remarked, and she slumped back against the table and took a deep breath. "I'm not even dealing with this, and I feel exhausted by it already."

"Tell me about it," Stephanie agreed, and I managed to laugh. It was a little thin, but it was something other than the tears I had been holding back all day.

"Just think about how I'm doing right now," I protested playfully. "I actually have to make a choice here. And hope to God it's the right one."

"The contract is still in place right now, isn't it?" Marjorie asked, and I nodded.

"As far as I know, yes."

"Then I think you should stick to what you agreed originally," she told me. "I know it's going to be hard, since both of you have actual feelings now, but you don't know what's going to happen with this guy or his daughter or anything else surrounding this, to be honest. But what you *do* know is that the money is going to make your life much easier, and you can rely on that."

"Yeah, dollar's not going to let you down," Stephanie added. "Men might, though."

"Especially since you guys don't even know if you can work things out outside of this contract," Marjorie continued. "It might sound harsh, but when you factor that little girl into it, too – she's already been through so much with her mother and the divorce and the custody stuff as it is. Throwing more confusion in there for her is really not fair."

I took a deep breath. I hated to admit it. But they were right. I had that slow-burning dread at the bottom of my stomach, the one I got when I knew that I had made the wrong choice yet again and that I was going to have to deal with the nightmare of picking up the pieces. When I threw my money at another project I was sure would make things better. And, this time, now that I had tossed my feelings at someone I knew I could never really get involved with. If not for my sake, then for the sake of his daughter – for Mel. When I thought of her, all I wanted was the best, and I knew that wrapping myself up in her life when I had no idea if I could handle being part of a family for real wasn't going to bring that for her.

And besides – I needed that money. I still needed it, even now. And I had no idea if things were going to work out with Xander or not. If they didn't, then I was going to have to forgo the cash to prove that I was serious about this relationship, and the thought of that – no. I wasn't going to go back to where I had been before. To counting every cent and crunching every number to try and make the pieces fit together. I couldn't live like that again, I refused to, I had better things to do with my life than try to twist and turn it to fit near-poverty once more. Even if it meant giving up Xander.

Even if it meant giving up Xander.

The very thought of that made something seize with panic in my guts. But I had promised myself when all of this had started that I was going to be the more sensible version of myself from here on out. That I wasn't going to let my emotions and my impulses rule me. I had to think about my future, and if that meant leaving Xander behind – so be it.

"I think you're right," I finally managed to speak once more. "I think I need to break it off with him. I can't...I can't do it. Not when I don't know how it's going to turn out."

"You're a stronger woman than I am, honey," Marjorie told me, and she put her arm around me again. "But you're making the right choice. I'm sure of that. Right, Steph?"

"Right," Stephanie agreed, and she smiled at me. "Like you said, it could be over any day now, and then you can move on, can't you?"

"Yeah," I replied, though my voice was shaking so much it came out as several different syllables. I needed to get myself together. If I was going to survive this, I had to accept that this was the logical choice – that for once, I wasn't going to let my emotions rule me, and that I was more than capable of making the decision that I needed to here. I would do what he had asked of me, and then I would get out of his life and move on. It was the best thing for both of us. We couldn't guarantee that what we had would work going forward, and I wasn't going to inflict that kind of doubt on him or his daughter, not when I knew I had no practice doing the family thing, doing the relationship thing, doing the motherhood thing.

"You're going to be able to get through this," Marjorie told me, and she planted a kiss on my forehead and hugged me tight. I knew that I was going to need them both more than ever now, now that I had managed to walk myself backwards into this mess. But they were here for me, and that was all that mattered, and with them by my side, I could survive it. With them reminding me what my future would look like, I could make it through. No matter how painful it was to think of a life without Xander, I would come out the other side stronger for it.

At least, I better damn well come out stronger. Because otherwise, all this pain was for nothing. And I didn't know if I could handle that.

Chapter Sixteen – Xander

"Xander!"

As soon as I heard her voice, a wash of dread passed through me. It was amazing that, after all this time, she could still have that kind of impact. I lifted my eyes from my computer screen, and sure enough, there she was – the woman of my nightmares, standing there in the door of my office like she had crawled out of hell itself just to catch up with me.

"Talia, can you at least book an appointment before you come busting in here?" I asked her, irritated. "I have a life, you know, and I don't-"

"I knew that if you had any idea what I wanted to talk to you about you wouldn't let me get close," she replied, and she crossed her arms over her chest in triumph. I had no idea what it was that she had to feel so happy about, but I got the feeling that it was going to be bad news for me. Beyond the door, I could see a few people peering in, trying to see what was going on; I gestured for her to close it behind her.

"Do you mind? You're distracting my staff right now," I warned her, and she glanced over her shoulder as though she had almost forgotten that she was in an office in the middle of the day.

"Oh, sorry," she replied, sickly-sweet. "You don't want everyone you work with to know that you've been faking a relationship with this girl you claim you're engaged to?"

My heart dropped. Through the floor, through all the floors of this building, until it felt like it had embedded itself in the ground below, swallowed up by the dirt, never to be seen again. I sprang to my feet and slammed the door behind her, praying that nobody had heard what she had just said to me.

"What the fuck did you just say?" I demanded, and she crossed her arms over her chest and grinned. She knew that she had caught me off my guard, and she seemed to enjoy that.

"You heard me," she replied. "I know there's something off about you and that girl you claim you're seeing. And judging by this reaction, I'm not wrong."

I ran my hand over my face. What the fuck? How did she know? How had she found out? I should have played it a little cooler, but the shock was so strong and impossible to deny that I couldn't do anything but feed into what she already thought that she knew. This had to be some kind of joke, didn't it? Maybe she had just come here as a last-ditch attempt to unsettle me and throw me off my game, with no proof, maybe I could get rid of her without this escalating any further than it already had...

"I don't know what you're talking about," I replied, with as much coolness and calmness as I could muster. She shook her head, and reached for her purse.

"Oh, really?" She replied, and she reached in and tossed out a handful of printed-out pictures on to the desk in front of me. It took me a moment to figure out what they were, but soon enough, it clicked – it was Terri and I, at various stages of the last few weeks. None of them posed, all of them looking as though they had been snapped without our knowledge or consent.

"What the fuck are these, Talia?" I demanded, and she shrugged and smiled at me.

"I knew there was something wrong with the way you were going about things with that girl," she remarked. "Knew you wouldn't have gotten engaged to someone so quickly. And I'm sure that your lawyer gave me the same advice that mine did – that the more stable and family-values you can look, the better your chances of getting your daughter back, right?"

I couldn't say anything. I felt so violated. Staring at these pictures, at these moments when I had thought that I had been alone with my thoughts, and knowing that they had been invaded by whoever she'd asked to follow me around, it was enough to make me feel physically sick.

"What the fuck is wrong with you?" I snarled to her, the disgust swiftly morphing in to anger. How dare she? How fucking dare she come into my life like this and act like she had even the remotest right to have me followed around like this? She should be ashamed of herself, but instead she was sitting there in front of me with a big grin on her face like the cat who had gotten the damn cream.

"This was a woman who was going to be part of my daughter's life, Xander," she reminded me. "I wasn't just going to let you bring anyone in, now, was I?"

"So you had us followed?"

"Yes," she replied, as though it was as simple and as obvious as that. "And I found out – well, I soon started noticing that you were leaving each other's places at strange times. First thing in the morning, for example..."

She pointed to an image of Terri walking away from my house – judging by the clothes she was wearing, it must have been after the first time that we had slept together.

"And then in the middle of the day, looking like you would rather have stayed," she went on, pointing to another image, this one of me, leaving Terri's apartment after our most recent meeting. Shit – the car that I had seen, the one that looked so obviously and totally out of place. It had been. But I had been too distracted to give it any more thought than that.

"And I couldn't help but think, that seems like a strange thing for an engaged couple to do," She continued. "Seems like the kind of thing you might do if you were just trying to put on the front of making people think that you were involved, doesn't it?"

"Talia," I murmured, but I could already feel the defeat rising up inside of me. I had already been carrying the weight of it around for so long, after Terri had asked me to leave her place. I hadn't heard from her since, and it was Friday morning, the same day that we were meant to meet for our weekly get-together.

"And judging by the way you just freaked out when I said that to you," she went on. "I would say that I'm on to something. Am I right?"

I stared at her. She must have known there was something off about this from the start, but she had bided her time, made sure that she had everything in place before she came out with the declaration. Which was more than I had been able to do with Terri. I couldn't believe that I had let things get so far out of my control, and I promised myself, right there and then, that I was never going to let something like this happen again.

For now, though, the best I could hope for was honesty. Talia knew me well enough to see through my lies, and maybe she would understand – shit, it was a long shot, but I had to give it a try.

"You made this up, didn't you?" Talia pressed me. "I don't know what sort of woman would be willing to go through with something like this, but-"

"Yes," I told her, suddenly. It was a way to shut down her smug preening over this whole thing, at least, and she fell silent on the spot, her eyes wide for a moment as she tried to take in what I was telling her.

"Is that what you want to hear?" I asked her. "Yes. Yes, that's what the lawyer told me to do. Yes, I thought it would be enough to keep Mel."

"You faked it?" She pressed again. "Because if you're trying to double-cross me or something, I have these pictures, I can expose you to anyone who asks-"

"You don't have to do that," I told her, quickly. Honesty might get her on my side again. Might give her the win that she must have been craving to have come round here in the first place. Plus, lying further was only going to give her more ammo in the custody battle against me. And it didn't seem like Terri was going to be part of my life any longer anyway, so better to pull that band aid off and get it over with, once and for all.

"So you're admitting that you made it all up?" She replied. I took a deep breath, and nodded.

"I can't fucking believe you," she snarled at me, her upper lip curling in disgust. "I thought you wanted what was best for our daughter, but instead, you just get some random woman into your life to try and prove that you're a good father? You really doubted your own skills that much?"

I clenched my fists under the table. She knew that she had been the one to push me so hard in this direction, to the point where I couldn't do anything but pull out something big to try and counter this. She was coming at it from the point of view of a woman, someone who would never have to worry the same way I did about being perceived as a bad parent, as a failure to my daughter. But I had to keep my cool, at least for now. I needed her to hear me out. If she took this to the lawyers now, then there was going to be no chance in hell that I could spin this in my favor.

"Talia, I know that I made a rash decision," I tried to agree with her. "And if I could go back and undo it, you know that I would. But I was scared about losing Mel, and you were pushing for full custody, and I just didn't see what else I could do to protect myself."

"I should have expected something like this from you," she replied, shaking her head at me. "You were always the one who thought you could just negotiate your way out of any problem that came your way. It's exactly why Mel belongs with me. You don't have the emotional depth to deal with being a parent to her, and you know it."

Honestly, in that moment, it took everything that I had not to tip the table over, get to my feet, and yell in her face. She knew that I was a good father to my daughter. And she knew that she had backed me into a corner where this was the only choice I had left – where all I could do was pull out a hail-mary in the hopes of keeping Mel as part of my life. And yet, she had the temerity to sit there in front of me and act like all of this had just been me acting crazy, not reacting to years of her torment, of her treating me like I had never been good enough to be a part of her life.

"You can get rid of that girl for good now," she continued, grabbing the pictures and tucking them away in her bag once more, as though she was collecting crime-scene evidence. Shit, if I thought I could have gotten away with pressing charges against her for what she had pulled with all of this, I would have.

"Because I think that the custody team needs to hear about this," she finished up. "Wouldn't you agree? And then they can make their decision once and for all. With all the facts on the table, for a change."

I looked up at her. It was like she had landed a harsh punch to my gut, and now I was reeling to try and get back on my feet after she had thrown me off-guard. The breath was knocked from my body and it felt like I couldn't inhale, my lungs filled with too much panic to take in oxygen. She simply gazed down at me, waiting for a response, a response that she knew she wasn't going to get.

"I have a meeting booked with them tomorrow," she announced. "And I'll expect you to be there. I'm glad that you were finally able to be honest with me, because now I don't have to drag this all out in front of them, do we? We can just jump straight to the part where you tell them the truth about this crazy little game that you were trying to play with me."

"Tomorrow?" I muttered. That was too soon. I could feel the walls crushing in around me. I couldn't catch a breath, and the corners of my vision were starting to blur. Tomorrow. I would have to come up with an explanation for all of this by tomorrow. What the hell was I going to say to them? They would write me off at once. And just like that, after all this time, Talia would have won. She would finally have gotten what she wanted out of me, and there would be nothing I could do to stop her. Nothing at all.

"I'll see you then," she told me, and she turned on her heel and walked to the door and left me sitting there alone in my office, trying to work out what the hell had just happened to me. The whole world had tipped on its axis, out from underneath me, threatening to spill everything beyond my control for good.

I had to do something. And fast. The door clicked behind Talia, and my mind started racing. Time was already running short, and I could practically feel the hours on the clock starting to slip away. Every minute that passed was a minute closer to my ex getting hold of my daughter for good, and there was no way in hell that I was going to let that happen, not for a damn moment. I didn't know how I was going to stop it, but I would find a way. Because the alternative was unthinkable. And I still had a little fight left in me yet.

Chapter Seventeen – Terri

As I wrote the check, I stared at the number in front of me and wondered if it had really been worth it.

I wanted to tell myself that it had, of course it had – it had been worth it because the thought of letting go and giving in to the big-ass mess I had made of my finances before this was so utterly and completely unthinkable that it made my head physically hurt. But the money that I had received for this, had it been worth the pain that I was carrying in my chest right now?

I missed him. Good God, I already missed him *so* much. I had known that when the contract came to an end, that it was going to be hard for me to move on, but this was something else entirely. It had happened with such a suddenness that I hadn't had time to say goodbye, the contract dissolved just a few days before and leaving me spiraling helplessly out of control as I tried to work out what the hell I was meant to do next.

I didn't know what had happened, either. That was the hardest part. Had all of this been for nothing, at the end of the day? I could only hope and pray that it wasn't the case. I couldn't stop thinking about Mel, hoping against hope that she got to stay with her beloved father, even if I wasn't there to help with her any longer. But I hadn't heard a whisper from Xander or anyone else, which said to me that whatever the outcome had been, it was none of my damn business and I should accept that and move on.

At least my rent was paid. For six months, no less – I was putting together the check right now, so that I could pop it in the post to my landlord and make sure that I had nothing to worry about for the foreseeable future. By the time that the six months were up, I would have brought in enough money from the store that I wouldn't have to scramble for cash again any time soon. Which was a relief, or it would have been, had it not been for the fact that I had lost so much to get this at last.

I had thought that it would be easy. But I hadn't counted on Xander stealing my heart the way he had and making it impossible for me to think about moving on without him. Without his daughter. Without the life we could have had together.

But then, he clearly didn't feel the same way. He had confessed feelings for me, but they must have been spur-of-the-moment, given that he hadn't bothered his ass to follow up on them even for an instant. Not that I was salty – well, not that I was going to let anyone *know* that I was salty, at least. I hadn't had a chance to talk to Stephanie or Marjorie about it yet, and frankly, I knew that as soon as I did, I would be admitting that it was real. And I wasn't sure that I was ready for that yet.

Had he been thinking about me? No, no, I couldn't let that get stuck in my head. I had better things to do, more important things to think about than him. My future. Remember? This had all been about building for my future, and turning around to gaze back into the past wasn't going to serve the purpose it needed to right now. When I had first signed the contract, I'd had so many plans for what I would do when I got my hands on this money, but now...now, all of them seemed to have leaked straight out of my head, and there was nothing I could do to get them back where they belonged.

There was a knock at the door, and I glanced up at once – I wasn't expecting anyone, and unexpected visitors always made me anxious. But this was the new, post-money me, the one who was going to swan around the city making sure that everyone knew her name, probably wearing faux-fur and a bunch of diamonds or something. She was confident. She was calm. She was collected. And she could totally answer her door even if she hadn't been expecting a call at that time in the afternoon.

"Hello?" I spoke into the intercom, and, a moment later, a voice came through the speaker.

"Hey, Terri, it's me," Xander replied. My stomach dropped. Oh my God, I couldn't believe that he was here. What was going on right now? I couldn't wrap my head around it.

"I'm buzzing you up," I replied, and I clicked the button next to the intercom and stood there, staring at the door, until I heard his footsteps get close to me. I opened the door, not quite believing, still, that it could really be him. But there he was. In the flesh.

"Hi," I breathed, and he glanced inside the apartment.

"You mind if I come in?" He asked me, and I shook my head and stepped aside.

"Be my guest..."

"Thanks," he replied, and he brushed past me. He seemed agitated, as though there was something on his mind. I would have been lying if I said I wasn't curious as to what it was. What had brought him here again, when he had been so happy to just end the contract like that?

"What are you doing here?" I blurted out finally, as I closed the door behind him. Shutting us both in together. I wasn't sure how I felt about that. Some part of me wanted an escape route, even though I knew that that attitude wasn't going to get me anywhere. I needed to look him in the eye and hear this out, no matter how hard it might have been for me to take.

"Terri," he murmured my name, and as soon as he said it out loud, I felt something give inside of me. My defenses had already been weak, but in that moment, they fell away entirely. I couldn't have protected myself from him if I'd wanted to more than anything on Earth. I didn't get to. I loved him too much for that, and when he said my name, I could be convinced that he loved me just the same way, too.

"Xander?" I breathed, and he turned to me and look me in the eye. And then, all at once, he fell to one knee in front of me. Reaching into his pocket, he pulled out a small blue box, which he popped open and proffered up to me to reveal the delicate blue emerald against the silver wedding band inside.

"Will you marry me, Terri?" He asked. And for a long-ass second, I just stood there, trying to work out what the hell was happening.

"What are you talking about?" I finally blurted out, feeling stupid as all hell. But he had – we had already been engaged, even if the two of us had known that it wasn't for real. So why was he – why would he-

"I want to marry you, Terri," He explained, and a huge smile spread out over his face as though he could hardly believe that he was actually getting to say this to me in person.

"I want to marry you for real," He finished up, voice soft and laced with such love for me that it made my heart ache. I closed my eyes for a moment, and realized that my knees were shaking slightly.

"I don't understand," I whispered. It was the most I could manage through the fugue of shock that was settling in around me. And amongst it all, somewhere, there was that distant hope that somehow this could be real. I knew it was more than I could hope for, but maybe, just maybe, there was something real in this...

"That's why I ended the contract," He went on. "I don't want to play games anymore. I don't want us to lie about how we feel. I'm not ready to lie about it anymore, at least, and that's why I'm here. I'm just hoping you feel the same way, because if not, I'm going to feel like a grade-A idiot..."

He was smiling at me as he spoke, but I could see that his eyes were scanning mine for some kind of reaction. I was still sure, some part of me, at least, that this had to be a joke. No way this was reality, no way that this was happening.

"Will you marry me, Terri?" He asked again. I couldn't say anything. Jesus fucking Christ, what was I meant to say? I needed to come out with something, I couldn't just keep standing here staring at him like the idiot that I was.

"You mean it," I whispered. "For real. You want to get married...for real."

"Terri, I know this isn't what either of us expected from this," he told me gently. "But the way you are when you're part of our family, there's nothing that comes to close to that feeling for me. I know I'm not going to be able to move on without you, no matter what. I just want to know if you feel the same way. And if you don't, nothing changes, I want you to know that – you're still going to get everything that I promised you were going to get in the first place. But if you do..."

"I do," I breathed back, before I could stop myself, before I could think better of it. "I do."

I looked down at the ring, glistening in the box in front of me. A future. That was what he was promising me right now. A future. I loved the thought of that. A whole history that was still to come between us, memories that we had yet to make, there was nothing that made my heart happier than the mere thought of it. I wanted that. I needed it. And so, when I reached down to the box, and took the ring from the plush velvet in which is sat, and slid it over my finger. He gazed up at me as I moved, as though he could hardly believe that this was happening. *You and me both, buddy.*

"I do," I repeated again, and suddenly, he sprang to his feet and pulled me into his arms.

"Oh my God, Terri," He breathed in my ear, as he hung on to me tight as though he could never imagine letting me go. "You have no idea...you have no idea what that means to me."

"I think I might," I laughed, but I didn't care that he had contradicted me already; I was too happy to think about anything but how much I wanted him, how hopelessly I loved him. When I pulled back to look him in the eyes, they were shining with such love and such hope that I was certain I had never seen it before in my life.

"I thought that you were done with me," I confessed to him. "When I got the money through, when it said that it was over, I thought that I would never see you again."

"I had to put that behind us so that you would know that I was serious when I came to you with this," he pointed out. "I didn't want you to think this was part of some play."

"I think I'm sure now," I admitted. "I wasn't...I thought that maybe you thought you had made a mistake before, when you told me how you felt. But now..."

"Now you know it's real," He finished up for me, and he grabbed my hand and looked down at the ring that was shining up at him from my finger, newly anointed.

"You really mean this," I repeated again, waiting for the penny the drop, for him to reveal that this had all been a twisted joke at my expense and that he didn't intend to deliver on any of it. But he was just gazing at me, utterly happy, as though he couldn't believe that this was happening and that he wanted nothing more than for it to go on.

"I really mean," he told me, and he kissed me this time – and I felt something give inside of me, something slithering down, those defenses that I had put up around him vanishing all at once. I was ready to be with him now, ready to be with him for good. And, as he wrapped his arms around me tight, I knew that he felt just the same way.

Before I knew it, we were toppling back on to my bed together. In the early-morning light, I could see my ring catching the sun, glinting off around us to fill the space. This was real. *Real.* As real as they came. He kissed my neck and I grabbed his shoulders and felt this joyous bubble of laughter rise up in me, impossible to contain, irrepressible and so happy it felt like it came from someone else entirely.

"I love you," he breathed in my ear, and somehow the sound of those words served to turn me on. I didn't know what it was about the intimacy of them, but they drove me a little crazy. I had never allowed myself to be wanted like this before, but now, here, with him, with this – I was ready.

"I love you, too," I replied, and I kissed him again, and just like that, our clothes started to go flying off the bed. We had no need for them anymore. The sun was cool, the air a little cold, but his warm body against mine was all that I needed right now to keep me hot.

The weight of him on top of me as he grabbed my hands and pushed them above my head – I could hardly take it. I needed more. I arched my hips from the bed to push them against him, to tell him with my body that I was ready for more, more, more.

"You want me to fuck you?" He asked me, his voice tinged with that playful taunt that I knew was specifically constructed to make me go even crazier than I already had. I nodded.

"Tell me," he ordered me, and his voice left no room for argument. I squirmed, trying to remember how to speak again.

"I want you to fuck me," I admitted, finally, and with that, he gave me what I needed.

Taking his cock in his hand, and using the other to keep my wrists pinned above my head, he guided himself inside of me for the first time since he had proposed. There was something almost painfully intimate and raw about looking him in the eyes when he took me like that. But I wanted it. Craved it. Finally, and after all this time, I wasn't trying to hide from my feelings; I was ready to face up to them, once and for all, and they came wrapped in the perfect package of Xander and he had finally given me the chance to be honest with myself about them.

He held me down and fucked me like it was all that he had been able to think about since he had walked into my apartment, and I craned my neck up so that I could kiss him again. His mouth was warm, his tongue slipping past my lips as his cock spread me open, and the mesh of sensations all at once made my belly flame with want for him. Did he have any idea what he was doing to me? When he pulled back, and looked me in the eyes again, that slightly cocky sheen to his gaze, I got the feeling that he did. And he loved every moment of it.

Before I knew it, I could feel myself getting close, and I could tell that he was nearly there, too – there was something about being apart and then coming together like this that made it easier to, well, come together. I was grinding back against him, rolling my hips this way and that, trying to get every last ounce of pleasure that I could from this moment. And finally, it came over me, like a rush, like an explosion I couldn't hold back.

"Ah!" I cried out, the sound filling the small space of my apartment around me, as I felt myself clench around him, my muscles spasming with the release that I had been craving for so long. It didn't take long before I felt him get there, too, and I watched his face tense as he reached his own release inside of me, filling me up with his seed. For the briefest moment, I wondered what it would have been like to feel that knowing that I wasn't on birth control – knowing that we could have been building the start to a family between us right here. But that could wait. For now, it was just the two of us, and I was quite sure that that was the way I wanted it.

"Fuck," he groaned, and he slowly eased himself out of me and slid down on to the bed beside me. I could only lay there, trying to catch my breath, staring at the ceiling. He reached for my hand, the one with the ring on it, and brought it to his lips, pressing a kiss against the point of skin that held my promise to him. I turned my head to look at him, and couldn't help but smile when I saw the way he cradled my hand like it was something precious, utterly precious to him.

"We're really doing this, huh?" I asked him, and he nodded.

"We're really doing this," He replied. And, with that, I felt a weight lift from my shoulders. Because as long as he was sure, then I could be sure right along with him.

Chapter Eighteen – Xander

"Are you sure that this is going to work?" Terri fretted, as we sat there in the car, counting down the minutes till we would have to go in there and face down the custody agreement. I shook my head.

"I have no idea," I confessed. "But we have to try."

"We have to try," she echoed after me, and she managed to give me a smile. "For Mel, right?"

"For all of us," I replied, and she squeezed my hand tight. She was wearing that ring that I had given her. Which was normal, obviously, given that we had just gotten engaged, but there was some part of me that was still dazzled at the fact that she had said yes.

I knew that no matter what came out of this custody hearing, I was going to have Terri by my side. And that was something. More than something, actually, that might have just been enough to help me survive the thought of not having my daughter close to me where she belonged. But it wasn't over yet. We still had one last grasp at keeping her in my life, and I was going to do everything I could to make sure that I got what I wanted.

"We should go in," Terri remarked, checking the time on her phone, as she had been doing compulsively since we arrived. "If we get there late..."

"Yeah, you're right," I agreed. I had been putting off getting out of the car, because the thought of going out there and coming up against a *no* was more than I could take, but I was guaranteed that answer if I didn't try my luck.

"Let's do this," I murmured, mostly to myself, and Terri smiled at me and nodded and with that, we had no excuses to hide from this any longer.

I knew that Talia was going to try everything to undermine me here. She wouldn't be counting on the engagement being real now, of course, but it was – that might be enough to throw her off her game, but still. My heart was pounding as I walked into the office, signed in at reception, and was guided through to a small room at the end of a long hall where we would wait for Talia and the lawyers to arrive.

"Jesus, I can't believe this is actually happening," Terri muttered to herself, and she looked down at her hands as though she was trying to ground herself in this moment, in this reality. I knew how she felt. There was something scary about all of this. The thought that we might not get the future that we wanted, it made me feel ill. I knew that we were the family that my little girl needed, and that she would be lacking so much in her life if Talia got her way and earned the right to keep her from me. But I had also seen how these cases went before, and it was rarely in favor of the man in the picture.

Talia swept into the room exactly one minute early, and took her seat as far from us as she could in the small room that we had been assigned. She glanced over at Terri, and I could see the beginnings of a sneer on her face, but she thought better than to say anything as the adjudicator entered the room.

"Good morning," He greeted us, with a slightly droning voice that seemed to announce that he was already bored with the very thought of this. "Are you ready to begin?"

"Yes, I think so," Talia told him, and she tossed her hair with confidence over her shoulder. She hadn't bothered to bring her new husband with her – that had to count for something in my favor. Maybe she didn't think he would present too well in front of the judge like this. But I knew that Terri was the picture of the perfect parent, and that anyone who couldn't see it would have to be damn well blind.

"Good," He replied, and he took his seat opposite us. "Is there any new information either of you would like to put forward before we begin?"

"Yes, there is," I told him quickly, and I grabbed Terri's hand and lifted it to show the ring that I had given her. She caught her breath, as though she could hardly believe that it was real any more than I could.

"We're going to get married," I explained to him, as swiftly as I could, before Talia could dive in and fuck things up for us. She opened her mouth, but I went on.

"Terri has spent a lot of time with Mel, and the two of them have bonded," I continued. "I really hope that you'll take this into consideration with regards to the custody agreement. I understand that leaving her with me alone might seem...difficult, but we have a fully-fledged family ready for her. I want her to be able to be a part of that."

"I can't believe that you're really still trying to pull this shit," Talia sneered at me. The man before us turned his attention to her with some interest.

"Is there something you would like to add to this, Talia?" he asked, and she nodded.

"I was speaking to Xander only a few days ago," She explained, stabbing her finger in my direction angrily, as though she could hardly believe that she was being made to talk this out like an actual adult.

"And he admitted that this whole thing with Terri is a complete fake," She went on. I furrowed my brow, shook my head.

"I don't know what you're talking about," I replied. It didn't feel great, lying like that, but there was too much on the line for me now to think about being honest and I was willing to play as dirty as she had to bring us here in the first place.

"When I showed you the pictures, you caved right away," she continued. "I have them here, don't you think that I wasn't going to bring them with me — I knew you were going to try and play me like this, but I'm not going to let you get away with it, you hear?"

"What pictures?" I asked, furrowing my brow and shaking my head. "I'm sorry, Talia, I don't know what you're talking about..."

"You know the ones," she snapped back impatiently, and she stuck her hand into her purse and shuffled around in there for a moment. My heart was pounding faster than ever. Those pictures — if the man before us took them the same way that she had, then we were fucked. I had told Terri about them, but seeing them in person wouldn't be fair on her. I could still remember the abject fucking horror of seeing them for the first time myself, and I wouldn't have wished that on anyone, let alone the woman I actually happened to love.

"Here," Talia went on, and she pulled out the pictures and sent them flying over the desk, all of them splayed out in front of us. Terri sucked in a sharp breath, and I knew she had to be fighting the urge to come out and say something about them, but she managed to bite it back, thank goodness. I knew that Terri had a tongue on her, and I could imagine her tearing chunks out of my ex the way she deserved for this bullshit. But that would hardly go along with the family-friendly image that we were trying to portray, now, would it?

"What are these?" The man asked, and he seemed as thrown as I had been by the images.

"I knew that there was something up with that relationship," Talia explained triumphantly. "And here, you can see that they're sneaking around, out of each other's places in the middle of the night or first thing in the morning..."

"You had them followed?" The man asked her, and his voice was carefully opinion-free, as though he was attempting to encourage her to fall into the pit that she had made for himself.

"Of course I did," She snapped back, angrily. She was worked-up, that was for sure, and she was starting to lose her cool. She had likely thought that this was going to be easy, and now that I had put up even the barest hint of a fight, she was digging her heels in and making a fool of herself.

"I wasn't going to let just anyone around my daughter," she went on. "I needed to know why he'd just turned up with some girl after all this time single..."

"Because we fell in love," Terri told her. Her voice was shaking slightly, as though she was still trying to come to terms with the images that she had just seen laid out in front of her, but she was in control and that was what mattered – it might have been hard for her, but she knew that this was the most important meeting that the two of us were ever going to have about our future, that every word counted, every second mattered.

"So what were you doing sneaking around like this?" She snapped back, and she jabbed her finger at the pictures once more. There was a dead silence in the room, and it was clear, even though she couldn't see it, that everyone else could make this out for the pure insanity that it was.

"I'm sure you're aware of the laws regarding illegal image capture in this state," The man told Talia, sharply, as though he could barely believe that he was being forced into having this conversation. She barely looked at him, eyes still stuck on me.

"What about them?"

"That capturing images of people without their consent for your own personal gain could result in serious damage to your custody case," He replied. And, with that, for the first time since all of this had started, I saw her face drop. Her eyes widened, and she slowly turned her face to look at the man in front of her again.

"What did you just say?"

"We're going to need to re-evaluate the case in light of the new material," he remarked, and he gathered up the pictures and started leafing through them. "Are these the sum of all the images, Talia?"

She stuttered out a few words, but they didn't come to much. I couldn't have cared less. I wanted to punch the air in relief. We finally had a win, and God only knew how much I had needed one of them for a long time. She had been taking pictures of us without our knowledge, and if that wasn't the direct opposite of someone who would have been a stable and secure home for our daughter, then I didn't know what was.

"Thank you for your attendance, Xander," The man told me. "We will be in touch to re-establish a new date once we've had time to analyze the new evidence and information."

"Of course," I replied at once. "Anytime you need me."

"Anytime you need us," Terri cut in, and I put an arm around her happily, squeezing her in close.

"Anytime you need us," I corrected myself. Talia was still sitting there, seething across the room, but I didn't care one little bit. I couldn't care. Not when it looked like things were finally starting to swing in my direction. I had waited so long for this, and now, it was finally happening. And I was going to enjoy every single moment of it while I still could.

Talia stormed out before anything else could be said to her, and we spoke a little more with the man before we left – making sure to underline how violating it was to be followed around like that, exactly how angry we were about it, all the questions it raised about her appropriateness as a parent. And, by the time we left, I knew that we had done everything we could.

"I think we actually pulled that off," Terri gushed as soon as we were outside once more. It was bright and sunshiny by the time we left the office, as though the weather was trying to match our energy.

"I think we did," I agreed, and I swept her into my arms and planted a dramatic kiss on her lips. She giggled and gazed at me for a moment.

"What's that in aid of?"

"Celebrating," I replied, kissing her on the cheek again before I unwound my arms from her. I noticed a few people looking in our direction. Before, I would have been totally averse to the very thought of anyone else observing my most intimate moments with my other half, but with her, it was different. I wanted everyone to see us together. I wanted people to know that I loved this woman, and that there wasn't anything I wouldn't have done to get her everything in the world that she might have wanted.

"We haven't won yet," she warned me, and I shook my head and shrugged.

"Not yet," I agreed. "But we're closer than we've ever been. You have no idea how good it feels, Terri. We're going to have the whole family together..."

She paused for a moment, her feet coming to a standstill as we headed back to the car, and she closed her eyes.

"What is it?" I asked, and she shook her head.

"I'm just...happy," she admitted. "The thought of us being all together as a family like that. It's a lot. It's more than I thought I would ever get out of this, really."

"Tell me about it," I agreed, and she opened her eyes and looked at me and smiled widely.

"Hey, you want to go out for dinner somewhere? Celebrate all of this?" She suggested.

"I think we would be pretty dumb not to take the chance," I agreed, and I wound my fingers around hers and squeezed her hand tight.

"Let's go celebrate," I replied, and I pulled her towards the car. I didn't know where we were going to go together, but that didn't matter. Because as long as I had her by my side, then I was going to be able to make it through whatever the world threw at me next.

Chapter Nineteen – Terri

"Oh my God, I can't believe that we're going to know by the end of the day," I murmured to myself, as I paced back and forth in the kitchen and tried my best to keep my cool. It wasn't working very well. I had been in a complete state since I had gotten up that morning, and things had only gotten harder the more than I had thought about the weight of everything that we were about to take on.

Today was the day, the day that we would find out one way or another what was happening with Mel and the custody agreement, and it felt like my brain was going to come leaking out of my ears after all the stress that had led to this moment. I still had no idea which way it was going to go, really, even though I thought we had a better chance than we ever had before.

It had been a tense couple of weeks, to say the least, since we had gone into that last custody meeting and they had taken everything into account and put the pieces together once and for all. Talia was a complete bitch, I was confident in saying that now, even though I had been taught never to describe another woman in those terms. But when it was the only thing that came close to capturing the sheer, intense dis-likability of her, I didn't see what else would do.

The pictures had been the final nail in the coffin for her, and I was sure that she knew it, too. She might have wanted to deny herself that, deny that she had been the one to fuck this up for herself, but we all knew it was true. And yes, I was fucking mad as hell at her for daring to invade my privacy like that, but in some ways, I was grateful, too. Because if she hadn't, then there might have been a harder fight ahead of us to make sure Mel stayed where she needed to – with her father, with me. With the lift that we were going to put together for her the first chance we got, just as soon as we had secured her custody once and for all.

The call was coming in at some point today, that was all we knew. They had offered to make the announcement in person, but we had turned them down. I didn't want to be in the room with Talia if won. I wasn't sure that I would be able to restrain myself, after all the bullshit she had pulled in our direction over the past few months.

Of course, she had been right about some of it – I had to remember that, because it felt like it was so far in the past now that I couldn't recall what it had been like not to love Xander, not to love the thought of the family that we were building together. She might have seen through us then, but there was nothing to see through now. We were solid, one moving part, opaque, and we were never going to let someone like her even think about getting close to us ever again, not as long as we lived.

"It's going to be alright," Xander soothed me, trying to calm me down as I worked the same ten feet of the kitchen over and over again. I wanted to believe him, but I knew that I couldn't, not until I had heard one way or another.

I didn't know how I was going to survive if the answer was no. It was that simple. I couldn't do it. I couldn't do it without Mel, couldn't do it without all of us together, and somewhere, deep down, Xander must have known that. I knew he loved that girl more than he had loved anything before in his life, and that nothing was going to draw him away from loving her until the day he died. Living life without her would have been a cruel and unusual torture. And today was the day that we were going to find out whether or not he was going to be subjected to that for the rest of his days.

Suddenly, the phone rang – his phone, planted on the kitchen counter in front of us. I practically jumped out of my skin, and he grabbed it at once. Looking at me, he took a deep breath, and then answered the call.

"Hello?" He spoke into the receiver. His voice had an edge of fear to it, but he was managing to keep the shake out of it, somehow. I didn't know how he was managing that. If that had been me on the line, my voice would have been trembling so much I would have had a hard time getting the words out.

He got to his feet, starting pacing, and in the meantime, I felt like I had been glued to the ground below me. I couldn't do this. I couldn't handle the answer if the answer wasn't yes. I watched his face for a reaction, trying to make out the words on the other end of the line, but I couldn't come up with anything that made sense. His eyes were darting back and forth, as though he was just trying to make sense of what he was being told. Was it because it was good news, or because it was worse than he had been prepared for? I held my breath and begged, begged, begged the universe that it would give us what we wanted, what we knew we deserved so badly.

When he finally hung up the phone, he didn't say a word. He turned his gaze to meet mine, and, at last, a huge smile broke out over his face.

"They want to give us full custody," he announced. And, with that, I felt my knees tremble, and I had to grab hold of the counter to keep myself from keeling over on the spot.

"What did you just say?" I gasped, certain that I must have misheard this man.

"They don't want her involved in Mel's life at all," he went on, and the way he was speaking, it was almost as though he couldn't believe what he was saying. "Not mandated, anyway – we can play it by ear if we want to involve her, but other than that..."

"It's just us," I finished up for him, and he nodded.

"Just us," he repeated after me, and I clapped my hand over my mouth to hold in the delighted explosion of laughter that threatened to burst on out of me.

"Oh my God," I gasped. "Oh my God. Us? Just us? They want us to have her?"

"They want us to have her," he repeated, and he moved towards me and kissed me, kissed me like he loved me, kissed me like he wanted me to raise his daughter with him. Kissed me like he could already see our future together, all laid out for the two of us. And I kissed him back, because I could see it, too, and because I was more than ready to take that on with him.

What happened next was an utter blur; Mel was ours now, and it didn't take us too long to move her into the house once and for all. She had her own room there already, and the stuff that she had left with her mom was surprisingly thin on the ground, as though she'd always had one foot out the door like this, ready to go, ready to get out the first chance she got. We ran back and forth with the boxes from Xander's car, and I noticed that, on top of one of them, I could see a glimpse of the bright red shirt that I had picked up for her. Like she had been wearing it so much that she had only just thought to pack it at all.

I had no idea how Talia was going to react to all of this. Xander had told me that she hadn't so much as been at the house when he had been packing up his daughter's stuff. Like she had already taken off in a fit of anger at the realization that she hadn't managed to get what she wanted. As long as she was far away from us, I didn't care where she went. She had already proved that she was willing to invade our privacy, to make life stupidly hard for us, and frankly, I had no interest in keeping her a part of any of this going forward. But that would be up to Xander to decide on, one way or the other, when the time came.

All of this was so damn *adult*. That was the thing that struck me more than anything else. As I helped Xander move his daughter into his home once more, I couldn't shake this feeling that there was something inherently grown-up about everything that was going on. I was part of a family now – I was a mother figure to a little girl. I was a fiancée, soon to be wife, no doubt. I lived with my other half, and I got to call him my other half and mean it. I was finally catching up with everyone around me, and it felt pretty damn good.

It was strange to think that, only a few months before, I had been panicking over the thought of making enough money to live on for the next year. All of that seemed so far behind me now, so far removed from what I was, from who I was. I had changed for the better, I was sure of that. It might have come fast, and, as far as some people were concerned, out of nowhere, but for me, it had been exactly as it needed to. I couldn't have jumped into this if I had known just where it was going to take me. I had needed this slow build of intensity, so that when I came to this point, I could handle it without a second thought.

"What do you want to do tonight?" I asked Mel, once her dad had finished unloading the car and bringing all her stuff up to her new room. I had been keeping an eye on her all day, making sure that she wasn't too thrown by all of this, but I was quite sure that she was taking it in stride; in fact, she seemed a little relieved, as though this was what she had been hoping for from all of this. I wondered how much of this she had been aware of, really, but I couldn't focus on that too long – all that mattered was that she was here, with us, and that we were finally and truly and legally and in all sense of the word a family. For good. The way we belonged.

"I just want to hang out with you and dad," she replied, and I pretended like I was waving a fairy wand.

"Your wish is my command," I promised her. "Hey, do you think we could get Chinese food tonight, too? I know if you ask, your dad's going to say yes straight away..."

"Of course we can," she replied, and she giggled happily. She seemed a little lighter than she had before, as though she had shed some of the excess weight that she had been carrying around on her shoulders. I hated the thought of her having had to haul it so far as it was, but at least now, it seemed to have lifted. And I knew that I would do anything to make sure that I could shoulder the load as much as she would let me. That was what family did. And I was family now, once and for all.

We ordered in and watched a movie that she had been obsessed with for years – I had never seen it, and she insisted on showing it to me, and I was pretty certain that Xander would have let her remake the damn thing shot-for-shot if it meant that he got to be around her right now. He put his arm around me and pulled me close, and I let my eyes drift shut and leaned my head on his shoulder. It had been a hell of a day, more emotion than I had been prepared for, but it had gone right, at least. The judges had made the right call, and now we were family, and nothing could change that.

By the time that the movie was done, her eyes were starting to droop, and Xander carried her to bed like he must have done when she was a little girl; she held on to him for dear life, nestled against his chest, and I couldn't help but smile as I watched the two of them together. They were meant to be, soulmates in a way I had never seen any two people before, and he seemed truly whole with her back in his life.

He came back down the stairs a few minutes later, once he had put her to bed, when I was standing at the sink and working on the washing up. Even though I had paid up rent at my old place, I had all but moved in here, and I planned to let the lease run out and make this my home for real as soon as I could. He wound his arms around me from behind and hooked his head over my shoulder, planting a warm kiss on my neck.

"Thank you for today," he murmured to me. I smiled.

"You have nothing to thank me for," I pointed out to him. "This was all you."

"And I know that I wouldn't have been able to get all of this without you," he replied. "I wasn't enough for them. But you...you were. You're the reason I have my daughter with me right now, and I'm not going to forget it. Not ever."

"Hmm, sounds like I can hold that over your head," I teased him lightly. "You don't want me to have leverage, now, do you?"

"Depends what you plan to do with it," He shot back, and I nestled back against him happily.

"I haven't decided yet," I replied. "But I promise I won't us my powers for evil, you have my word on that."

"That's a relief," he murmured back, and he kissed my neck again. I moaned softly.

"Careful, or I'm going to get distracted from doing these dishes," I warned him.

"Maybe that's what I want from you," He replied, and I giggled, dried my hands, and turned around.

"And what exactly do you plan to do with me now that you have me good and distracted?" I asked, winding my arms around his shoulders and pressing myself against him properly.

"Hmm, I think it's better to show, not tell," he replied softly, and with that, he lowered his mouth to mine — and everything that I had been waiting for today finally came to a head.

Epilogue – Xander

"Do you have everything you need for practice today?" I asked Mel, a little distracted as I tried to make sure that I had eaten breakfast before I had taken off to work in the morning.

"I think so," Mel replied. "Did you pack the Manchester United shirt, Mom?"

"Yes, I did," Terri replied, and she dropped a kiss on the little girl's head as she rushed past her to grab her purse before she headed off to work for the rest of the day.

"Then I think I'm good," Mel replied, and I nodded with relief.

"Then I can drive you up to school whenever you want," I told her, and I checked my watch. "Sooner rather than later, actually. Are you ready?"

"I'm ready," She replied, and she stuffed the last bite of toast into her mouth and got to her feet. "Let's go."

I hustled her to the car and we high-tailed it to school so that I would have time to get to the office before my first meeting that morning – Terri was getting a lift with her friend Stephanie to go into the store that day, and I knew she was looking forward to getting a chance to catch up with her properly. Since she had moved out to the suburbs with Mel and me, she didn't get to see so much of her friends in the city, and I always encouraged her to meet up with them every chance that she got. Life could be so chaotic with a full-time kid, and I didn't want her to ever feel like she had made the wrong choice in choosing to be with us once and for all.

That said, I didn't think we were in any danger of that these days. Ever since the custody agreement had come through for good, I knew that Terri had totally fallen in love with the life that came with raising a kid. Mel had started calling her *Mom* within weeks, which had totally shocked Terri, but she had gone along with it. In fact, she had confessed, she had been hoping that Mel might get there one day, but hadn't expected that day to come swerving along quite so soon, that was all.

But it wasn't exactly a surprise, really, given that her own mother had checked out of things so quickly after the agreement had been made. I had been willing to work with her on letting her see her little girl, knowing the pure horror of not being able to see your kid when all you wanted was to hold them in your arms, but she had already taken off across the world with her new man. Which I shouldn't have been surprised by, but still – she had fought so hard, I had let myself believe that she actually meant it. But the more time the past, the more distance that she put between us and her new life, it was clear that all of that had just been about getting one over on me. Proving that she had moved on, and taking the one last connection that we had to each other away from me so she could cut ties with me for good. Her new man was welcome to her; if he could deal with a mother who would use her own kid as a pawn in her games as easily as she did, then he was a stronger man than I was. Or maybe just a more naïve one.

I was determined to make sure that Mel never felt like she was lacking anything, though, that she never thought for even a second that she had been the reason that her mother had left. She was getting to that age now where she could make connections about her own involvement in situations and how they had turned out, and I would be damned if I would let her believe for an instant that she hadn't been enough for Talia. If anything, she had been too much, and that was why she was gone – because she couldn't face up to knowing that her dear daughter was going to outshine her, that she was going to be greater than anything that Talia herself had ever achieved.

Honestly, I was glad she was gone. It meant that we didn't have to look over our shoulders to make sure we weren't being followed, meant that we could just relax and enjoy this small, perfect little life that we had made together. It had only been five months or so since she had left, but she was so far from my brain that it was as though she had moved to another planet decades ago. And she was welcome to stay there for as long as she wanted. I had a life without her, finally, and that was just the way I wanted it to stay.

It was strange, in some ways, I supposed, that I was so looking forward to being married again. Terri and I had decided on a low-key ceremony, with just our closest friends and family in attendance, and I could hardly wait to look her in the eyes and call her my wife once and for all. Her best friends would be bridesmaids, and the planning process had meant that I'd gotten to know them a lot better – they were amazing women, just like her, and Mel was lucky to have a cabal of such strong girls propping her up from every angle. All of them adored my little girl, and it made me so happy to see her basking in their attention every chance that she got. She deserved it. She was blossoming in her new role, as step-daughter, as full-time child, and I was so proud of her that sometimes it hurt a little.

The day sped by quickly, thank goodness, which was something of a surprise since it was a Monday and those days had a habit of dragging on for what felt like years at a time. I was due to pick up Mel after her soccer practice, and Terri was going to cook us a meal that we could enjoy together that evening before Mel rolled out to a tournament later in the evening. It was going to be a busy night, but those were the kind I liked the most; the ones that I had to work double-time at, just to make sure everything got done. Because all of this was work for my family, for the people I loved most. And that was the best kind of work in the world.

"Okay, what have you conjured up for us this time?" I called to Terri, as Mel and I made our way into the house – it was filled with a delicious savory scent, and my mouth started watering at once.

"Why do you always talk about my cooking like it's some witch's potion?" She demanded, laughing. She greeted me with a kiss as I came into the kitchen, and Mel gave her a hug and stood on tiptoes to see what she was putting together on the stove.

"It's meant to be a curry," Terri remarked. "But I'm not sure how well it's come out..."

"I'm sure it'll be tasty," Mel told her confidently, and Terri smiled at her then shot a raised-eyebrow looked at me.

"You see?" She pointed out. "It's not hard to just be supportive, is it?"

"You're making me look bad," I teased Mel lightly, but she had already headed out of the kitchen to go practice against the back wall of the house. I planted a kiss on Terri's cheek, and looked down at the food she was making for us.

"I think it looks good," I remarked, and she shook her head.

"You're sweet to say it, but I know when you're lying," she replied. I shrugged.

"I'll need to taste it before I make any bold statements either way," I told her, and I went off to change out of my work clothes so that I could be more casual for dinner. I liked kicking back with my girls – nothing like getting to the end of a long day and knowing that I had the two of them to come back to.

Dinner was better than I had expected it to be; Terri hadn't been the best cook a few months ago, but she had been putting in the effort lately and wanted to become a good chef for me and Mel. The curry was a little too spicy, but we all munched down on it anyway, glad for something to warm us up on such a cold night.

I drove Mel out to her soccer game and left Terri to clear up – usually, I would come back and find her humming to herself as she danced around the kitchen, but instead, this time, she was in the living room, sitting on the couch and waiting for me. She smiled, a little nervously, as I came in.

"What's up?" I asked her, furrowing my brow and cocking my head to the side with interest. She took a deep breath, and patted the spot next to her.

"I think you need to hear this now," She told me, and I felt my heart skip a beat.

"Is everything alright?" I asked hurriedly. She nodded, and I came to join her.

"I think it is," she confessed. "I just wasn't sure how to tell you this. But I wanted to do it when it was just the two of us, and now seems as good a time as any..."

She sounded like she was dancing around the point, and I stared at her, waiting for her to hit me with what I needed to hear. I had no clue what it was going to be – was she leaving me? Was Talia back in town? But she seemed too happy for it to be anything as bad as all that...

And then, she planted her hand on her stomach, and it hit me. Just a moment before she came out and said it, the rush of it flooded through me.

"I'm pregnant," she told me, and I felt the world narrow down to this moment, to the look in her eyes right now. She was scanning my face for a reaction, and honestly, I was struggling to come up with one that would adequately capture everything that I was feeling right now.

"Xander?" She prompted me, sounding a little worried. "Xander, it would really help if you could say something right now..."

"Oh my God," I murmured, and I leaned down and planted a kiss on her belly. "This is..."

She held her breath. I tried to find the words.

"This is perfect," I finally finished up, and a huge smile spread over her face.

"You mean it?" She asked. "I was worried you'd be angry or something, I didn't plan it, but now that we have Mel and everything it just feels right..."

"It feels perfect," I told her again, and I clasped her hand in my face and leaned in close to kiss her. My woman. My other half. She would be my wife soon enough, and she was already the mother of one of my children – soon, she would be the mother to a whole new one. I could hardly believe how happy she could make me. I had never known love like this before, but now that I had learned that it existed, I knew I would never forget it.

"God, I love you so much," I breathed to her, and she smiled and leaned her head against mine.

"I love you, too," she replied. And, after everything we had been through, the future was finally starting to open up in front of us. And I knew that I was ready for anything that it threw at me. With her by my side, I could take anything.

THE END

Dear reader,

thank you so much for reading my book, it really means the world to me! If you liked it and want to do me a little favor, please leave a short review on Amazon – that would be too wonderful!

XOXO
Mia

Milton Keynes UK
Ingram Content Group UK Ltd.
UKHW041123040923
428016UK00001B/26

9 781638 216421